THAT JAZZ!

Books by Ethan Mordden

BETTER FOOT FORWARD: THE HISTORY OF AMERICAN MUSICAL THEATRE
OPERA IN THE TWENTIETH CENTURY: SACRED, PROFANE, GODOT
THAT JAZZ!: AN IDIOSYNCRATIC SOCIAL HISTORY OF THE AMERICAN TWENTIES

THAT JAZZ!

AN IDIOSYNCRATIC SOCIAL HISTORY OF THE AMERICAN TWENTIES

ETHAN MORDDEN

G.P. PUTNAM'S SONS

New York

The author wishes to acknowledge the crucial assistance and criticisms of the tireless Hugh Howard and the inveterate Dorothy Pittman, two invisible front-runners on the literary track. Also, an amazed salute to Mary Solak, keen of query and correction, superb.

Copyright © 1978 by Ethan Mordden

SBN 399-12159-5

Library of Congress Cataloging in Publication Data

Mordden, Ethan
That Jazz!: an idiosyncratic social history of the American twenties

Bibliography
Includes index
1.   United States—History—1919-1933.   2. Mass media—United States—History.   3. Lindbergh, Charles Augustus, 1902-   I. Title.
E784.M66   1978   973.91   77-26759

Passages from "mehitabel has an adventure" in *archy and mehitabel* by Don Marquis. Copyright 1927 by Doubleday and Company, Inc. Reprinted by permission of the publisher.

Lines from "Bohemia" from *The Portable Dorothy Parker*. Copyright 1928, © 1956 by Dorothy Parker. Reprinted by permission of The Viking Press.

Printed in the United States of America

To my fair, faithless friends on the beach:
" 'Tis new to thee"

Table of Contents

Americans found themselves in the twenties: the Ku Klux Klan, fads, the businessman-God of *The Man Nobody Knows,* the movies, tabloid journalism.

reaction and progression. The myth of isolationism. The Scopes Trial: old-time Bryan versus new-wave Darrow. Charles Evans Hughes and the State Department.

Introduction

Only by risking cliché will a writer tax the incantatory potential of his Preface with reasons why—why another book on America's postwar era, why now? But cliché, often enough, is truth, and worth risking; the truth of the matter is that periodic reappraisals of the past help us comprehend the present and, one hopes, offer a perspective to apply to coping with the future.

Indeed, on the face of it we Americans of the 1970s have much in common with those of the 1920s. Ours, too, is a postwar era, burdened as the twenties were with the problems of a huge presidential scandal, a clumsy national Prohibition (of liquor; of marijuana) that is everywhere ridiculed and violated, a convulsion of the younger generation, a siege of political terrorism, an upsurge of intrusive and/or repressive hyper-religious movements, a primacy of sleazy tabloid journalism, a reaction against excessive policies of social engineering, and a crisis in national identity.

More profoundly, we of the seventies may peer back at the twenties to mark the seedtime of what was to become of us over the course of fifty very, very fast years. The ostensive parallels cited above have a newsy sort of appeal in a picturesquely coincidental way, but the point is not how much the twenties and the seventies have in common, but how much more thoroughly the angles of shared experience influence the straight line of our lives today. Things have been getting progressively bigger since the days when poets were read and movies were silent, when the federal government was run like a business, on a limited charter and payroll, when the automobile and the toaster were, to much of the population, a curious entailment on the rules of Creation. The world is smaller now, they say; no, the world is bigger. The new model has more parts, runs on machine energy, touches every aspect of our lives, and what was influential in the twenties is, today, positively sovereign.

What happened in the twenties, that brought us to this pass in the seventies?—a climacteric of history happened, a turn of the great wheel. The twenties marked both the last decade of the old America and the first decade of the new. A technoartistic revolution reintegrated the culture in the space of a few years, replacing, transforming, undoing, and refixing virtually all of the America that was—and charting the route that drove us ineluctably, as if on automatic pilot, to the present, to what they—lucky stiffs, innocents!—could still call the future. As the new America, the twenties gave us the media, an alignment of radio blitz, public-relations hype, and news salesmanship, all aimed at a pragmatic, one-size-fits-all "presentation" that developed a majority trendex while shaving the individualistic edges off the national character. As the old America, the twenties gave us our last hero— Charles Lindbergh, a real national character—the last man to win the admiration and affection of the public in toto. Lindbergh's flight, the great solo voyage in *The Spirit of St. Louis* from Long Island to Paris in May of 1927, was, from planning through victory to celebration, a free act, not automated, not sold; it was a human feat, one of the last such in a time when the direct and personal address of American leadership was beginning to collaborate with the canny machinery of the media store. We shared in that feat, we as Americans, as free men—but that was the final such act, perhaps, and all that we are offered in its place now are the productions of an oppressive communications industry; and we buy, and are sold.

The Jazz Age, they call those days, pointing to certain reverberations in the work of F. Scott Fitzgerald, George Gershwin, and Al Capone, to the staccato burstlets of Gertrude Stein, the shirty bravura of Bessie Smith, and the racket of Texas Guinan. But if jazz was the tune of the times, it was more than song and dance, more than sass and parties and hooch. As will be seen, jazz was very much an anthem for the decade, the tempo in the tempora's mores, but jazz was no mere overlay: in its feverish nihilism, its libidinous money-take, its rotten, egoistic energy, jazz essentialized the falseness of the new electronic America, the irresponsibility of freedom without ambition. It was an age of celebrities and fads, but not of heroism or belief. Except where Lindbergh in his brief heyday broke through the jive with the perfect individualism of that flight in that plane—for it is less the deed than the man, always— jazz was the urge of the era, and the era, in sum, was jazz.

The twenties are still with us, not only because technical innovations made in those years proved bigger than we were and transformed us into the golden-mean audience, but as well in the little afterpieces that strut before us so long after the final curtain fell. What a finale: the stock-market crash, a production number in the grand style, with imposing decor, a star-studded cast, special effects from the stock ticker, and phenomenal cost! But melodies do linger on.

One such echo of those years was the recent ruling by a judge in Indiana that a ninth-grade biology textbook that denied the theory of evolution was unconstitutional, thus overturning the decision of the famous Scopes Trial of 1925. Movies do their part to keep the period in view, albeit sometimes in heavy "interpretations"—as in Ken Russell's abysmal *Valentino*, which portrayed the dissolute Italian hustler as an innocent lamb manipulated by American greed. Lindbergh, too, was in the air again in 1977 in little observances here and there of the fiftieth anniversary of his flight; that year also marked the half-century for the execution of Sacco and Vanzetti for robbery and murder after a controversial trial and no little protest from the liberal community. In 1977, the Sacco-Vanzetti affair seemed to happen, in little, all over again. Editorials railed anew, new books on the subject were published and graffiti raised, and the governor of Massachusetts proclaimed August 23 Sacco and Vanzetti Memorial Day for the state—yet the governor assured his constituency, in a giddy gasblow of that fulsome realpolitik known as Making a National Noise

No Matter How Louche, that he wished to remove the "stigma and disgrace" from the two men's names without taking any stand on their guilt or innocence.

But if the pair were guilty after all, why memorialize them, except in infamy? And if they were innocent, and thus deserving of regretful memorial, why not come out and vindicate them? The titles of two books published in 1977, *Justice Crucified* and *The Never-Ending Wrong*, also testify to the current craze for willful memorializing, often by those closed to an unbiased examination of the record. Why another book on America's post-World War I era? Because, among other reasons, some of us are recalling it wrong.

It has been fifty years, and the jazz plays yet, louder than ever; we could do worse than learn how it started. They of the twenties inhabited a spiritual vacuum without caring why or wondering how long the license could last, but we of today seem aware of our shortcomings and eager to remedy them. This we may do by reaffirming a moral context for American individuality and leadership—and *that* we may do by rejecting the corrupt hype of newsy, telegenic celebrity. Think of the old ideals, that offhand bravura of action and expression, a role for greatness on the world stage. We cannot resist the inevitable, but we need not mistake fame for merit, nor the follies of an era for historical drift. In the twenties, Americans willed resistance yet succumbed to change, in both cases without thinking things through. Let us know better, to accept and even exploit the future, to tame the machine—yet to hold the electronic image at a distance with suspicion. We can stop our ears to jazz.

ONE

"The Bolsheviks'll Get You Ef You Don't Watch Out!"

The jazz will come: just wait. Rotgut jazz, falsehooded jazz, jazz of the flesh, the jazz of bunk and debunk. Any old way we chose it, let there be jazz. First, however, there was war—a world war, but not World War I; it was just the war, without a number, because there wasn't going to be another—and by the time it had ended and we had spent our nineteen months bailing Europe out of its Gothic scrape, we were feeling imposed upon, exasperated, crucified, and downright quick to quarrel.

"One might as well expect a high sense of tragedy in an undertaker, as heroism in the generation that follows a war," wrote Lewis Mumford, with a historian's probity. The poetess Amy Lowell phrased it more resonantly, in the language of bohemia, cigar clamped between her teeth and outrage bared for education so the Babbitts could catch up with her: "A pattern called a war. Christ! What are patterns for?" Patterns were for the arrangement of flowers, the sewing up of samplers, the building of a meetinghouse, the serrying of families around a neighborly table for a picnic supper—not for upheaval and destruction.

When the fighting began over there, the prospect of American intervention was largely unpopular, so much so that it was thought that the slogan, "He kept us out of war," got Woodrow Wilson a second term as President in 1916 (a *very* close election, however) even after the tactics of German submarine warfare drove many pacifists to change their minds. Few were they who noticed, and fewer they who cared, that the Germans had bent over backward to define their war zones around the British Isles and to warn neutrals to stay out of them. The U.S. government had announced a disinterest in the war, but under the guise of asserting the freedom of the seas, the U.S. merchant marine showed itself quite willing to wander interestedly in and out of it. Clearly, U.S. "neutrality" was a euphemism, but most Americans saw only the horror of submarine sinkings, not the horror of baiting them. Folks were far more entranced by the story about a bag of ears, apparently Belgian, that a tourist claimed to have spotted in the hand of a smirking German soldier—and, more reasonably, by the "Zimmerman note" promoting entente between Germany and Mexico. (Intercepted and decoded, this message, too, fired popular militancy with Germany's promise of "generous financial support" to Mexico in the matter of her recon-quering Texas, New Mexico, and Arizona. Fat chance.)

By the time Wilson delivered a war message to Congress on April 2 of 19.7, both houses were ready with a standing ovation. Only the old Progressive reformers hung back, they of the basically agrarian regions west of the Mississippi. Senator George Norris of Nebraska, who tied with Christ and Nietzsche for granitic, icon-busting truth-speak, exposed this so-called fight for democracy as a payoff for "munitions manufacturers, stockbrokers, and bond dealers," and his Progressive fellow traveler, Robert La Follette, spit that Senate silly with four hours of invective arraigning the undemocracy of Britain and its "hereditary monarchy," while praising the "high ideals" of Germany. If the United States were to dare a popular referendum on the war issue, La Follette promised, shaking with the fury of hopeless utopianism—would no one listen?—the vote must defeat it "more than ten to one."

This was an exaggeration, but doubtless a national referendum would have found for peace, especially since the Western states had already enfranchised wives and mothers. There was, however, no such vote, and war was declared on April 6 (on Germany alone at first, with Austria-Hungary added on December 7). Then, suddenly, as if donning the painted grins of comedy masks, everyone was shouting hooray for war. Wilson himself, the titular leader who . . . uh, kept us out of war . . . foresaw a terrible dissolution of the free American style in the coalition of a national war effort. "Once lead this people into war," he had said a year earlier, "and they'll forget there ever was such a thing as tolerance. To fight you must be brutal and ruthless, and the spirit of ruthless brutality will enter into the very fibre of our national life, infecting Congress, the courts, the policeman on the beat, the man in the street."

They did forget. The United States was born of dissent, built and nurtured on it, and even, in the distant past, fought wars with a home front blistered by it. But the consolidation of federal discipline had gradually clamped down on faction. Thought was still free, but speech less so, and no one in his right mind was going to raise a complaint now that *this* war was on. The zeitgeist demanded a solid front: sauerkraut was renamed "liberty cabbage," dachshunds were stoned, opera companies suppressed Wagnerian Valhalla, a German surname was taken as a priori advertisement of fifth column intrigue, and oh, the trouble at the office if you didn't buy a Liberty Bond.

Perhaps this long and various continent of local heresies, lefties, and third parties was never meant to be a country; they should have kept it as states and invested heavily in fences. The song "Over There" is our last surviving memento of what turned out after all to be only the first of the world wars, and its line, "The Yanks are coming," sounds like every man jack of us marching forward in a body, but remember that the song is by that superstar author and actor-manager George M. Cohan, the smart aleck, the lone wolf, the arrogant Man Who Owned Broadway—the dissenter—and as such is only to be taken as a concession to wartime bravado. Far more characteristically American were the humorous war cries, less pugnacious than satiric—"Oh, How I Hate to Get Up in the Morning," "I Didn't Raise My Boy to Be a Soldier" (English title, however:

"I'm Glad My Boy Grew Up to Be a Soldier"), "How Ya Gonna Keep 'Em Down on the Farm?" and a mother's proud report, "They Were All Out of Step but Jim": songs for dissenters.

Well, we did keep our sense of humor, anyway. But the ruthless brutality that Wilson dreaded as an escort of making the world safe for democracy washed some of the glow out of this particular democracy—"buy Bonds, buster!"—and we weren't ever going to feel quite whole again. But then we weren't all that together before the war in the first place. In fact, we were two nations, one the far-flung hinterland, with its earthy wisdom, settlers' grandsons, and serene continuity, and the other the tight-packed city, with its sassy comebacks, half-breed assimilations, and hell-bent convulsion. Until the 1920 census, population demographics preferred the country to the town, but as of 1920 the majority of Americans dwelled in cities, and to the farmers, laborers, and little merchants of the land, it looked as if the majority were going to rule.

The flaming issues of the eras, both pre- and postwar, testify to the ruckus going on between the rurals and the urbans. Here the country moved against the town: scandalized by the corner saloon, country drys in the West and South called for a ban on liquor, and in 1915 the Ku Klux Klan was revived in Georgia to wage war on Catholics, uppity blacks, immigrants, internationalism, arty decadence, and scientific skulduggery, all of them by-products of the urban parade. But here the town blasted back at the country: the cities spawned millionaire businessmen to crush the farmer, restructured the world with technology, and generally acted like disciples of the anti-Christ. Even as Wilson changed his mind about staying out of the European cataclysm and began to urge preparedness on us, we were already prepared: we'd been fighting each other for years.

The fighting was to continue throughout the 1920s, year after year, country versus town. We could, finally, arrange a cease-fire with the Axis powers, but not, in peacetime, within the awesome cornucopia of local needs and antagonisms in a nation that was simply too big to move in unity. Year after year . . . in 1924, the rurals met the urbans at the siege of Madison Square Garden, otherwise known as the Democratic Convention, where a California–New York deadlock on both platform and candidate decimated Democratic hopes and, very nearly, the Democratic party. In 1925, the battle took the form of a vaudeville tragicomedy entitled "The Monkey Trial," in which the Fundamentalism of William Jennings Bryan wrestled and joked with but somehow failed to upstage the Darwinism of Clarence Darrow. In 1926, President Calvin Coolidge's Secretary of the Treasury, Andrew Mellon, made a sortie for the money powers of the urban Northeast, lowering the ceiling on top-bracket corporate and personal income taxes. In 1927, Coolidge vetoed the McNary-Haugen Bill, a pearl beyond price for the beleaguered farmer. In 1928, he vetoed it again, for good. And so on, before and after, year after year, town versus country.

On the other hand, this rural-urban war isn't that simple a matter. In the area of to drink or not to drink, for example, there were plenty of wets in the outposts where there wasn't even a crossroads at which to erect a corner saloon, and the cities were filled with agitating teetotalers. Moreover, the profile of the regions is a wildly complex one, as witness the disparity in tone and tempo between an agrarian reformer such as Bryan, who devoted his energies to the extinct notions of the last century, and an agrarian reformer such as Senator Robert La Follette, a populist of the Space Age. And note the bizarre division of the cities: Boston yields the courtly Henry Cabot Lodge, for Boston is courtly, but Lodge was no ally of New York's superannuated urchin, Al Smith. Other than natal soil, they had almost nothing in common, any of them.

They all did share one experience, though—surviving a world war, then a ghastly pandemic of what was known as Spanish influenza, and then the obnoxious quicksand of inflation . . . *one* experience, for the three plagues were viewed as a single disaster. Returning soldiers had brought the flu home with them from overseas, and rising prices were blamed on the upward spiral of the war industries. All of it, all!—the loss of sons and fathers, the regimentation of meatless and heatless days, lightless nights, gasless Sundays, the prohibition on liquor "for the duration," the federal price-fixing and regulation of industry, the harassment of any private citizen who committed some lapse in this full-time, paranoid national unity . . . then the flu attack in the fall of

1918, with business and pleasure at a standstill, people picking their way through city streets wearing ghostly gauze masks, one-quarter of the population stricken and nearly five hundred thousand deaths—and these mostly among the healthy young adults, not infants or the aged—then more despair as postwar prices shot up to about double what they had been in 1913, as veterans tried to squeeze back into the job pool and unemployment figures rose.

One other pest occupied all Americans in the postwar years, radicalism—and this, for many, was the bitterest trial of all. After the common yoke of the war effort was thrown off and Americans slipped back into their distinct niches—the comedy ended and the masks dropped—this last unity yet bound them all: the fear, hatred, and misapprehension of the several varieties of left-wing extremists. Here, at least, was one way for us all to keep in touch, by despising the Socialists, anarchists, syndicalists, Marxists, Wobblies, and nonpolitical labor leaders who were lumped together, for easy identification, as Bolsheviks—Bolos for short.

Later on, a more sophisticated reaction against the Left would take on the protective coloring of anti-intellectualism, and as such would identify—correctly—an alignment of nice subversions connecting the universities, the news media of the Northeast, and most sociopolitical movements, but back at the turn of the century and through the Red scare of 1919–20, the Left was taken not as antidemocratic but anti-Christian. Bolshevism was Godless; that was all they knew on America's fat green earth and all they needed to know, drawing, to fund their fire, on the evangelical ash that still sparks the heartland. Of totalitarianism they understood nothing—indeed, some of them understood nothing of freedom, either, which is one reason why we endured Prohibition. But they recognized the devil's minions when they saw them, especially when said minions wore heavy beards and spoke with impenetrable accents.

Radicalism, everyone was aware, meant foreigners; here was more disquiet from Europe, and not just as speeches and strikes but as bomb throwing as well. The radical Left in America had been slowly building up to its psychopathic stage, and now it had the encouragement of the Russian Revolution to inspire it. "I have seen the future," observed Lincoln Steffens in 1919, returning from a secret diplomatic mission to Moscow, "and it works"—but never were nonconformist ideologies more intolerable in America than during the postwar years of unemployment and "the high cost of living." Steffens' avant-garde coterie of liberals and intellectuals could experience frisson at his words all they liked, but for ninety-nine percent of the nation pronouncements about anything Russian, especially a future, only added to the tension. Who could say what radicals weren't capable of doing? When the bombs began to fly—literally— President Wilson turned the other cheek, obsessed with the ratification of the Versailles Treaty and its built-in League of Nations. He pleaded with his Attorney General, A. Mitchell Palmer, not to "let the country see Red," but something had to be done about terrorism, and Wilson obviously wasn't up to it. Palmer, however, was, and 1919, the peak year of the radical onslaught, brought mass arrests and high-handed roundups of, in a few places, everyone in sight as well as hordes of radicals and suspected radicals.

Times were hard, but not to the point that people might be convinced that anything new would be an improvement. One train of thought has it that America is a nation that hates its past, wasting tradition as new gods shatter the old, ever movin' on, traveling light and branding history as superstition. But it may be that this is, on the contrary, the most willfully traditional country in the West, and in more than a fondness for monuments. For despite the amazing changes that have bought us tomorrow as early as fifty years ago (changes not always invented, but usually marketed, by American know-how), only science and art have sold their souls in hell—the folk, as it were, regard innovation as an assault on uprightness. Foreign visitors have often remarked our delight in the useful beauty of simple things that grow old along with us and never change, our old wives' trust in the revealed religion of old ways. Then, too, on a less primitive level, we have our grandly traditional Constitution, intended as a compact between imperfect man and perfect freedom. What past-hating people could get so het up over what is and what is not "constitutional" in their daily disputes? What wasters of tradition have feared revolution so sturdily as we?

Certainly, the great mass of Americans in the postwar years had no intention even of debating the ins and outs of any new order with the Left. Action of any kind by presumed seditionists was met by vigilantes acting in due process or, before the mill of justice could be got to grinding, in spontaneous and bloody concert. On the eve of Armistice Day, 1919, the House of Representatives arranged for the seemly unseating of the Socialist Victor L. Berger of Milwaukee by a vote of 309 to 1; the next afternoon American Legionnaires in Centralia, Washington, stormed the local headquarters of the Industrial Workers of the World (Wobblies), lost three of their number to Wobbly bullets; and, when a fourth died of gunshot wounds, tortured and lynched one of the culprits, Wesley Everest, a veteran himself.

There had been talk of a Bolshevik plot to take America by force, some of it even among Bolsheviks—and sure enough, somebody out there wasn't kidding. April of 1919 saw the mailing, in authentic Gimbel Brothers wrapping, of thirty-six dynamite bombs addressed to such as J. P. Morgan (the younger; Dad had passed on), Supreme Court Justice Oliver Wendell Holmes, and Secretary of Labor William B. Wilson. One of the parcels arrived at the home of Seattle's Mayor Ole Hanson, who had just resisted a general strike, and a second one got to the Atlanta residence of Senator Thomas R. Hardwick; this one, when opened, blew off the hands of that Machiavellian capitalist tycoon, the Hardwicks' black maid. (A streak of ground-zero stupidity informed this bestial stunt: did anyone really believe that millionaires and Senators open their own mail?) By chance, a New York post-office worker named Charles Caplan read the story in the newspaper on his way home to Harlem. Recognizing the description of the package, he raced back downtown to work where he had stored sixteen similar boxes to be returned for insufficient postage and checked them against the description. They were identical.

A communal shudder from the populace and the press demanded that steps be taken, but none was at first. None could be taken, for the authorities were baffled: the Left had discovered anonymous terrorism before government agencies had discovered the cure for it, much less the prevention. Ah, this isn't quite the story one was expecting, was it? Roaring twenties? Sheiks and flappers, speakeasies, Garbo movies, and Gershwin musicals? Yes, the whole passacaglia is on its way, but so is an ostinato of much-less-well-remembered violence, of resistance and counterresistance. The terrorist fades out of the decade early on, but others will carry on for him, such as the Ku Klux Klan, founded more or less to be the hard-liners in the war between tradition and upheaval. That war was not won, for the upheaval that came proved not social but technoartistic, and no one had the weapons with which to contain it—we still don't today, in fact, when upheaval is not technoartistic but social.

Back then, in 1919, attempting to isolate the bad apples in the barrel of survival, Americans mistook the grievances of the labor population for the beefs of a radical cohort, and associated all labor troubles with Red riot. Not only misunderstood by the public, but also misrepresented by the Establishment, labor's aims were simply reasonable hours, a decent wage, and the right to organize; the violence that erupted at strike sites (as opposed to the violence of terrorism) was the modern worker's version of the self-defensive anarchy of the old frontier, only now the bad guys were strikebreakers or management thugs. Throughout the twenties, as before, management refused to recognize the unions that doggedly continued to assemble themselves like bad toys coming to life in the shop at midnight, and the press kept the country in the dark as to the unbearably primitive working conditions, hours, and wages. Sociopolitical suspicion ran so hot that in 1913, when Henry Ford upped his workers' minimum wage from two to five dollars a day, he was denounced as a crypto-socialist by, among others, *The New York Times*. (The real Socialists, on the other hand, knew who their comrades were, and, disdaining this sabotage of their class war, found no friend in Ford.)

Labor violence, like the Klan, the Prohibition debate, and the criticism and defense of free immigration, represented yet another aspect of the division between the rurals and the urbans. Though two of the most disgruntled labor pools, in coal and steel, inhabited industrial towns of the hinterland, they were isolated from pastoral acculturation by virtue of their caste as well as their labor camp existence. "I owe my soul to the company store," runs the song, and to a great extent the mine and factory worker, overseen, herded in packs, and virtually stuffed into containers when not engaged in useful activity (like a twelve-hour day), were suffering the faceless inevitability of Urbantown even out in the hills of Pennsylvania and West Virginia and the flats of Indiana. Then, too, the workers were largely immigrants; anything they did was greeted with suspicion. When the time came for them to demand fair treatment via the strike, small-town America looked upon them not as distressed neighbors but as mongrel intruders fired up by Bolshevik organizers with a bad case of the city smarts and terminal atheism.

The time, of course, did come; it had been coming on and off for years, in good times and bad. But 1919 was the all-time badland of desperate and notorious strikes. It was also one of the worst years in American history, in part because of the heartless complacency of business leaders, in part because of the honest ignorance of the populace, but worst of all because of the new breed of social agitator, the terrorist.

Terrorism in the United States officially dates back to the Molly Maguires and German anarchist troupes of the 1870s, but now, in the twenties, everything was getting grander and violence as sociopolitical art was no longer the personal property of coal-raped Pennsylvania or of Chicago, where the anarchists played. Cheered by the Soviet takeover in Russia, the radicals of the Left spread their dour freemasonry over the land, and wherever they went they trashed law and order with leaflets and explosives. At their meetings, they invoked the "propaganda of the deed," and were just as happy to murder a passerby as a politician.

The race was on. Six weeks after the Hardwick bomb, the trail of terrorism led, in Washington, D.C., right up to the house of the "Fighting Quaker," Wilson's Attorney General, A. Mitchell Palmer, at whose front door an anonymous donor deposited, synchronously with collaborators at the houses of mayors and judges from Boston to Cleveland, a salute in dynamite. Palmer's visitor took the worst of the explosion himself, and the police were hard-pressed to identify the parts of him that peppered the street, including, or so it seemed, two left legs. Franklin and Eleanor Roosevelt lived just opposite the Palmers, and that delectable Boswell of D.C., Alice Roosevelt Longworth, rushed over to R Street to visit her cousins and, incidentally, check out the scene.

With eyes alert to strafe the ignoble, understanding all but forgiving nothing, she was used to roaming the town at all hours, from Georgetown to the Hill, a model of the woman who needs no emancipation, having been born free. What a reporter she would have made! What a reporter she was: "A leg lay in the path to the house next to theirs," she wrote of her call on the Roosevelts after the bombing, "another leg farther up the street. A head was on the roof of yet another house. As we walked across it was difficult to avoid stepping on bloody hunks of human being. The man had been torn apart, fairly blown to butcher's meat." Spread about the scene were copies of a radical flyer headed *Plain Words,* tendering evidence as to who was responsible for the explosion and, perhaps, the "Gimbel's Bombs" as well. Signed "The Anarchist Fighters," the flyer proclaimed that the class war had been inaugurated "under cover of the powerful institutions you call order, in the darkness of your laws, behind the guns of your boneheaded slaves."

We had what might be called The Red Blues. Alerted to the omnipresent threat of propagandists infiltrating the labor unions, the country looked upon every strike as a subversion of democracy, though in fact most workers resisted the interference of Bolo organizers with loathing. The real cause of all those strikes—long hours and low wages—was something anybody should have understood: income cuts closer than ideology. Why, even while lobbying for the dismissal of eight thousand "disloyal" teachers, the *American Legion Weekly* devoted its greatest editorial zeal to the reentry of veterans into the working population. On the eve of the 1920 election, the journal's cover featured a man sitting disconsolately in front of a humming factory, one wall of which had No Help Wanted tacked in front of a faded Liberty Bond drive poster. God, first that stupid war, then the influenza, and now Bolshevik ambush and unemployment! Wasn't there anyone who could pull us out of this?

Not, it seemed, at first, for the trouble kept coming. The most

sinister of 1919's labor disputes was Seattle's shipbuilders' walkout, which erupted in a peaceful but extremely scary general strike of the city's workers, but the most unpopular of them all was the Boston's policemen's strike in September, brought on by an onerous workload and low salaries, and resulting in a garish two-day siege of carnival license. (The episode was badly mishandled by Boston's mayor Andrew Peters, by his police commissioner Edwin Curtis, and by the governor of Massachusetts, Calvin Coolidge, Peters through incompetence, Curtis through arrogant overlordism, and Coolidge by the simple maneuver of turning his rock-ribbed back on the whole business, waiting to see.) Striking laborers were heinous enough, but the forces of law and order weren't thought of as occupying jobs any more than the statues in the courthouse square were; such a defection was less a strike than an invitation to anarchism, a bid promptly picked up by rowdy proles who went on a spree of vandalism, thievery, and, at moments, rape.

Peters called out the state militia and helped himself to a volunteer brigade made up of do-gooders, ne'er-do-wells, and Harvard students, given a paternal blessing and the promise of academic credit for time lost by president Abbott Lawrence Lowell. After two days an uneasy order was implemented, mostly because the mobs simply dispersed, but eight people had been killed, national morale given another kick in the head, and not only did the policemen have to return to work at prestrike conditions, but the seventy percent of the force who had actually struck their jobs were summarily dismissed, and their uniforms immediately filled by new men, veterans especially welcome. Samuel Gompers, president of the American Federation of Labor, appealed to Peters and Coolidge to reinstate the broken policemen and submit the case to arbitration, and at this point the unknown governor of Massachusetts unveiled himself as an imperious presbyter of temperance, order, and evil-whuppin' horse sense. In a telegram to Gompers, Coolidge upheld the dismissal and fired off the theorem that made him a popular hero (and that would send him, up the back stairs, into the White House): "There is no right to strike against the public safety by anybody, anywhere, anytime."

A few weeks later striking steelworkers met the same opposition.

To the public, men like E. H. Gary, U.S. Steel's chairman of the board, who refused even to deal with a union, were men of sagacity and backbone. When their obstinacy had the ring of Coolidge's "anybody, anywhere, anytime," they sounded like heroes, though seen through the persecuted workers' eyes, the true heroes were their own organizers, later to be idealized in best-sellers during the thunderblast of social literature in the thirties. Gary and Coolidge spoke from the pulpits of position; they set the status quo. It was the union spokesmen who had to make the dark voyage, who braved the mythic initiations, and their vaulting flight often ended in some back alley, cut down by vigilantes or hired goons while the press jeered and the public, uncomprehending, raged.

Only one major strike of the year earned public sympathy—that of the actors, who evacuated theaters with the assurance of their show biz glamour to make personal appearances on thespian picket lines where declamation, portamento, and hit tunes put the labor message across—and only the actors of the major strikers actually won their battle. On the other hand, the vox populi waxed garrulous with the boycott, if not the right to organize, in a buyers' strike, a rather high-spirited one aimed mostly at luxuries like new clothing. A changeover from men's wool suits to cotton overalls made some headway, and women did their best to pretend that last year's styles were the consummation of vogue (betraying themselves, nonetheless, with some heavy, wistful window shopping). This was the respectable "strike": the dressy William G. McAdoo, Wilson's son-in-law, paraded the streets looking like a ragman's lost weekend, and shiny trousers were held up as proof of public spirit in the boardrooms of Wall Street.

It was a hot summer, toasted by violent racial outbreaks, mainly in the North, where escalating migrations of blacks tested whites' belief in equality. The worst aspect of 1919's disturbances was that they were enervating a country cut off from its titular leader by a massive difference of opinion. Wilson had insisted on going to Paris to lead the peace talks (and what's worse, muttered some, insisted on returning); now he was flourishing his handiwork, the League of Nations, his remedy for war, his gift of peace, and as far as the mutterers were concerned he was wearing a bit too much of the

Moses about him. Someone should have told the man—apparently some tried to, for suddenly he was cutting off such trusted old friends as his advisers Colonel Edward House and Joseph Tumulty without a word of explanation—that the country had revised its estimate of his qualities. No one on these shores had any intention of assisting victims of future territorial aggression, as posited in Article X of the League covenant. What peace was this that made provisions for more fighting? Ship more Americans over to die for Europeans? Over Bob La Follette's dead body! And yet, even as his dream of global harmony got the baleful eye, Wilson was actually considering running for a third term. Distressed by Congressional resistance to his treaty, he determined to appeal to the folk and embarked, against doctor's orders and flying blind—blind with mission—on a tour of the land to defend his League, just then being bitten into bits by the Senate.

From Washington, D.C., on September 3 in his private car, the *Mayflower*, Wilson set out to discover a new world populated by democratic reformers, pioneers to help him settle a frontier of incipient world leadership. To the West he went, speaking in cities, towns, and at cow crossings on a pilgrimage to doom in a frail, world-beaten body. He would stand at the rear of his car as often as ten times a day, shaking with rage and telling them what they had to do. This is what it had come to: he was killing himself, giving himself up to an almost ritual sacrifice, as the king must die in a rite of spring come late in a stupid fall. He refused to admit that the quest was hopeless, though it took no politician to read the dissent on those faces, refused to learn that the pioneers of the world frontier whom he sought were not available. There were visible Presidents in those days, and everywhere he went they thronged to see him, and they heard him out. But all they could see was a pattern called a war. "Sometimes people call me an idealist," he said at Sioux Falls. "Well, that is the way I know I am an American. America is the only idealistic nation in the world."

Was. America was the only idealistic nation. "Mr. Wilson's war" saw to that. Our sense of altruism had been pushed too far, and now even convinced Wilsonians and Bull Moosers had come around to seeing reform governments and moral sacrifices as being too high a price to pay for national, let alone a global, righteousness. Constituencies that had formerly worshiped their Progressive nuncios to Congress began to fall back in uncertainty, and suddenly everyone was remembering how close Wilson's second presidential victory had been. Why, Charles Evans Hughes had come *that* near to the White House—"a few thousand votes in California," they told each other. "That's what put Wilson over."

As the *Mayflower* plowed a zigzag course through the strenuously isolationist West like a cruiser fleeing enemy radar, submarines in the persons of Senators William E. Borah, Hiram Johnson, and James Reed harried his mission with rival speeches against the League, and the people themselves were busily realizing projects of their own, as retrograde and disruptive as Wilson's plan was ameliorative and unifying. In Chicago, which Wilson carefully avoided, they had just staged a race riot with a death toll of thirty-eight and arson to beat the band; in Seattle the President ran head-on into a grim demonstration of workers who had not forgotten the repression of those who spoke out against the war in 1917 and who glared silently at him as he passed, their hatbands, in the quiet, seeming to scream rather than read RELEASE POLITICAL PRISONERS! Westward it was, then to the south through California and bending about homeward—the plains, the mountains, the rivers, the rurals and the urbans . . . the whole damn thing was saying no. "Vade retro," it might have added, "Satanas."

By September 24 the Senate's first vote on the peace covenant and the League, a close one, went against Wilson, and the next day he sagged at Pueblo, Colorado, overcome by the wracking pains of incipient arteriosclerosis. He was rushed back to Washington, but there in his court the king was stricken again, badly, and carried out of sight. From that time until the inauguration of the next President seventeen months later, no one was running the country as far as anyone outside of federal circles could tell—and this at the country's peak of spendthrift contention. Strikes, unemployment, radicalism . . . on all sides, or so it seemed, the smooth face of American life—raw marble, but so resilient, we had thought—was under the chisel of disorder, and now here was this League of Nations, volunteering troops for the next war, and the next. Small wonder that, except for the Dixiecrat South, the electorate was beginning to feel like one giant registered Republican.

Strangely, having brought his party to a low ebb of esteem, Wilson had been acting like a popular hero before his collapse. The leader who Kept Us Out of War had attempted to renew himself as the leader who won the war; he should have quit while he was behind. Still, to his credit, his heroism was of the true sort, a moral exploit rather than the swashbuckling trip that careers across wasteland crying democratic updatings of "A Roland! An Oliver!", but like any hero who assumes a moral context, he had to take on the mob. This Wilson had never feared to do. Indeed, he would soon offend whole blocs of voters by favoring the amendment for women's suffrage and by vetoing the National Prohibition Act. And in 1919, he was preaching the international supercountry at a time when the United States was at its severest isolationist rage; this recently universal scholar, college administrator, state governor, Democratic Progressive, and twice President made of himself an item for ridicule and disgust.

A smart man, they say, knows how to compromise, and legend has it that anyone who gets to be President must be as compromised as a Ruritanian treaty. But giants don't compromise—thus their immensity. Wilson was convinced that his was the only plan for lasting peace, and, stiff-necked in his top hat, he demanded that the nation go along with him absolutely—the nation and the world as well. "Mr. Wilson bores me with his fourteen points," quoth France's foreign minister, Georges Clemenceau. "Even God Almighty has only ten!"

American disenchantment was more rigorously phrased. The voters had put a Republican majority into both houses of Congress in 1918, over Wilson's specific requisition for Democrats to support his peace, and no less an authority than Wilson's intimate, Colonel House, now reckoned that the President was acting like "God on the mountain." To Theodore Roosevelt, smashing his fist against desk and tabletops at Sagamore Hill, Wilson had always been "an apothecary's clerk," and would never be anything else—especially not a leader of men— while redoubtable Alice Roosevelt Longworth spoke not only for her father but for much of the nation by laying the evil eye and a medieval curse upon Wilson when he returned from the Versailles talks. Wilson had figured to come home like a crusader with the Holy Grail, but if American crowds will always gather to ogle the famous, they may not be moved sufficiently to contribute to that fame; besides, what's so holy about a grail that has to be shared with foreigners?

So they let him work himself into apoplexy defending himself—and the future—cross-country, and after he was brought back from Pueblo, little more was heard from the White House (which suddenly was seen to be sporting iron bars on the windows, like a madhouse; actually Roosevelt had had them put up years before). Wilson's doctor, Cary T. Grayson, and Mrs. Wilson were in charge of the invalid President, who, though unseen, was in fact still reasonably active. The invalid country was in less dainty hands, those of "the Fighting Quaker," Attorney General A. Mitchell Palmer.

As early as August 1919, with Wilson in spotty health but at least on his feet, Palmer had founded a General Intelligence Division within the Bureau of Investigation, to be headed by the young J. Edgar Hoover. This was just after the accidental assassination of Palmer's front door on R Street, and the head of the Department of Justice thus got the unique chance to protect himself and the public at the same time by disposing of all those perfervid aliens who were, despite the high profile of Wasp Bolos such as Big Bill Haywood and John Reed, thought to account for ninety percent of the radical population. Urged on by the public and most of the press, Palmer sifted through the laws looking for a statute that would empower him to imprison or deport every radical in the country.

Section Six of the criminal code, a Civil War relic, didn't pan out, so he turned to the Immigration Act of 1917, an amendment of which expressly ordered the deportation of alien anarchists and advocators of violence. Popular opinion, defined by the Reverend Billy Sunday, held that shooting was a good, cheap way to quiet radicalism, but Palmer was no hysterical Red-baiter, just a man who honestly felt that anarchism was just around the corner—as, incidentally, was the 1920 Democratic Convention, a footnote that vastly inspired Palmer's critics.

Whatever his true motivation, moral or political, Palmer was duty-bound to clean out the saboteurs' nests, but rather than launch a snowball, he sought a Quaker "clearness" and did not move until the Department of Justice was assaulted by demands from chambers of commerce, state legislatures, private individuals, and, at last, the U.S. Senate, for surcease from terrorism. On November 7 the counteraction commenced. Palmer and Hoover made a few practice swoops for a prelude that yielded star anarchists Alexander Berkman and Emma Goldman, both of them flagrant, would-be murderers to whom the worst that a Quaker could do is frankly too good, but when the tempo picked up and the raiding really took off, on January 2—into the 1920s proper now—the pitch turned shrill, and more than a few innocent bystanders were bagged in a callous blitz during which habeas corpus, search warrants, and human rights went off a-maying. Any alien was likely to be picked up, and even native Americans were hustled off to some nowhere if they happened to be around at the time. The innocent were, for the most part, immediately sorted out, not least by the American Civil Liberties Union, founded for the occasion. But in Hartford, Connecticut, people were held for five months without even a hearing. An efficient roundup of subversives was clearly called for, but not in such wholesale terms as these, and indignation, among many unquestionably loyal Americans, was rife.

Strangely enough, the press, which had been egging on coal and steel managements against their employees as if in a holy war, began to bleed at the heart, and some newspapers joined the outspoken in criticizing Palmer's and Hoover's methods. Perhaps a few individuals noted the self-serving aspect of the radiant publicity that Hoover's operatives had won for the Bureau of Investigation—the roundups were brilliantly executed where they didn't resort to shanghaiing everyone in sight—or perhaps they noted instead the built-in paradox of governmental action when that government is supposed to take its tone from the people and the popular tone is, however justified, hysterical. It's a problem that must bother us again in the 1970s, for terrorists are abroad again, and something, again, must be done to get rid of them. In any case, no one in 1919 was sorry to see the backs of Berkman, Goldman, and 247 others of their ilk when the U.S. ship *Buford* deported them to Russia via Finland on December 22.

After the New Year's roundups, and the accompanying disquiet expressed by, among others, twelve Harvard lawyers of national profile, the Palmer raids ceased to be news and then, not necessarily consequentially, ceased to be at all. It seems that that little era was over, for no swirl of renewed terror and calls for action followed a mysterious explosion in Manhattan at the intersection of Broad and Wall streets during a weekday lunch hour on September 16 in 1920. Thirty-eight were killed, fifty-seven hospitalized, the hair of thousands literally singed off their heads, and the police helpless, but Palmer's suggestion that an international conspiracy to subvert the country was still at it made no impression this year, and the same newspapers who had called for strenuous retaliation in 1919 almost shrugged off the Wall Street disaster. The *Cleveland Plain Dealer,* which had cried "the beast comes into the open," in honor of the general strike in Seattle, dismissed this new episode with the words, "Capitalism is untouched . . . the public is merely shocked, not terrorized, much less converted to the merits of anarchism. Business and life as usual."

Wrong. Business was, but life was not, usual—not even the life of rural continuity on the plains and prairies between the jiving cities of the Northeast and the promising land of the Far West. As America's literary spokesmen saw it, life had never been less usual. Psychosis, despair, transformation, and repression were read into the chronicles. Literature, it seems, had learned revolt. As early as 1915, when folks were shaking heads at the frivolous nature of European peacekeeping, Edgar Lee Masters invaded the countryside to unburden an Illinois graveyard of its accumulated anguish and bitterness in his *Spoon River Anthology.* If it is true, as has been suggested, that Masters' epitaphs originated, like Don Marquis' *archy and mehitabel,* as a spoof of the free verse craze, it is a clue to the frivolous nature of Illinois' public relations that everybody took Masters' dour plaints seriously. This was solemn poetry: "Wedded to him not through union but through separation," says Masters' Ann Rutledge of Abraham Lincoln . . . or says the South of the North. Either way, Spoon River's plangent wraiths sure took the ginger out of the profile of country life.

Similarly, Sherwood Anderson's *Winesburg, Ohio* stories in 1919 unlocked the awful privacies of an unassuming small town, and then came Sinclair Lewis's *Main Street* to outdo them both. A best-seller of late 1920, *Main Street* treated Minnesota not as a closetful of skeletons but as a wilderness lacking even the imagination—the "pulpy quick," as Masters put it—to cook up a few squalid secrets. Masters and Anderson revealed individuals in their idiosyncrasies; Lewis took on the whole pack in their masque as clubmen, icebergs showing public spirit above a bulk of atavistic nastiness. *Main Street* arrived simultaneously with the reemergence of the Ku Klux Klan, and though Lewis drew no parallels, the indictment of small-town repression is hard to miss.

The most popular book of 1920 was Zane Grey's *Man of the Desert,* and *Main Street* didn't even come close in sales, but it made a stir, especially in cosmopolitan circles. Spawn of the Midwest, Lewis wrote books for the East, as did his compatriot F. Scott Fitzgerald, and it was in the East that the recognitions of satirists and critics would deliver most tellingly. Radio had yet to create its national rapport; not till the close of the decade would the country be in any way connected to itself, though the press was making its first oracular stabs at long-distance rapport. We couldn't have gotten along on McGuffey's *Readers* forever: the world was changing, and Middletown, too, must change, squealing in pain, bellowing at Benedict Arnolds like Lewis, and the twenties now would bleed Middletown of its residue of nineteenth-century placidity. "In our day," wrote Anderson—in *Winesburg, Ohio,* to be exact—"a farmer standing by the stove in the store in his village has his mind filled to overflowing with the words of other men. The newspapers and the magazines have pumped him full. Much of the old brutal ignorance that had in it also a kind of beautiful childlike innocence is gone forever. The farmer by the stove is brother to the men of the cities, and if you listen you will find him talking as glibly and as senselessly as the best city man of us all."

Anderson got a little bit ahead of the times there, at least in relation to what was to come, but a few years of the twenties would prove him right. Still, a few years remain before the prehensile ganglia of the media would plug the corners of the nation into the central socket, and now we see the last golden days of regional discretion, a time when the Union acted as a family only in wartime and for certain presidential elections.

And this is going to be some election, now that 1920 is here. Wanted: someone to put a lid on the noise, to demolish the evil European constructions of Wilson and be *us* again. Surely the Republicans would take it—but which Republican had yet to be decided. And thus Warren Gamaliel Harding was produced . . . or, rather, the facade of Harding was, for the full-figure Harding, newspaperman, good guy, and Senator, was already there, presidential material in all but intelligence, ability, and vision.

Picking a winner isn't a simple business when the victory is certain, and the 1920 Republican Convention in Chicago was a deadlock. General Leonard Wood and Illinois' governor Frank Lowden, a former Rough Rider and self-made lawyer turned reformer, were the favorites in a tie too close to break. Finally that old horse trader, Harry Daugherty, called for the smoke-filled room—he is credited with minting the phrase, the rooms being 404, 405, and 406 of the Blackstone Hotel—and Daugherty rammed Harding home to cop the nomination.

Or so the legend goes. In actuality, no small-time manipulator such as Daugherty could stampede a convention single-handedly. He was, indeed, the major force behind Harding, but before the Chicago balloting would turn about for anyone, the party shoguns had to give the okay. General Wood could have had it, had he been willing to make a deal and agree to cede the powers that were three Cabinet posts. But the general wouldn't touch it, not that way. "Shady business, gentlemen," he is reported to have said, "and I'll have nothing to do with it."

He could have had it, and simply by doing what most politicians do every week of their lives. But Wood was a soldier, and a just man, so he faded away, as we are told old soldiers will, while the big guns decided to go with Harding. Harry Daugherty wasn't in the real smoke-filled room; that sanctum was reserved for the likes of Senators Henry Cabot Lodge, James Wadsworth, and Frank Brandegee, the influential press lord, George Harvey (who had squired Wilson to the top office and had two reasons to regret it, the War and the Peace), and Will Hays, chairman of the Republican National Committee, and destined for greater glory as the censorship tsar of Hollywood.

No one knows precisely what Daugherty had said about the Room, for each reporter who quoted him got it down differently, but basically it was something about a stalemate being broken by "fifteen men in a smoke-filled room at 2:11 in the morning." The portentously intimate lowdown of the exact moment made lightning of the phrase, even if it was pure pretension on Daugherty's part. He did get the time right, however, for it was close to 2:00 A.M. when Harding was summoned to stand before Harvey in the Room, fetid with tobacco, liquor, and barter. Said Harvey, "We think you may be nominated tomorrow; before acting finally, we think you should tell us, on your conscience before God, whether there is anything that might be brought up against you that would embarrass the party, any impediment that might disqualify you or make you inexpedient either as a candidate or as President." Harding thought it over for a bit, announced that all systems were expedient, and that was that: Harding, candidate, President.

The kicker in all this is that Teddy Roosevelt would have been the choice nomination, Teddy who had promised he wouldn't run again after his one elected term and the three years he spent covering for the assassinated William McKinley—but who did run, unsuccessfully, on the Bull Moose ticket in 1912—Teddy the St. George of Progressivism. Always a pain in the neck to party dragons, T.R. would have swept the country in 1920, Republicans, reformers, Democrats, and all, and the succeeding course of these here *soi-disant* united States would have been . . . well, who knows?—different, without question; better, almost certainly; glorious, perhaps. Teddy was everything that Harding was not, a doer, charging up the memory of San Juan Hill at every state boss, Chief Justice, and apothecary's clerk that got in his way. But Teddy had died in January of 1919, and with the once and future party leader gone, it was anybody's ball game.

It nearly was Herbert Hoover's. Returning from European relief work in 1919 as the much-admired humanitarian and efficiency expert who had kept nations from starvation, revived their rail and coal industries, and reorganized their communications technology, Hoover's abilities, plus his domestic fame, added up to those of a man of the hour. If he was too shy and undynamic to act up to the heroism of his qualifications, nobody knew that yet, and both parties made inquiries into the man's political affiliations. Hoover would have made an ideal vice-presidential candidate, vote-catching but harmless—and who knows what deal might not have been made for the top office, given Hoover's extraordinary popularity and the Lowden-Wood deadlock? But when Hoover declared for the Republicans, he described himself as an "independent progressive," uttered statements that came right out and mentioned the League of Nations—bad party style—and, worse style yet, called for a "forward-looking, liberal, constructive platform on the treaty and on our economic issues." Even if he hadn't lost the California Republican primary to a favorite son, Hiram Johnson (and, daftly, even though he had earlier won *Democratic* primaries in New Hampshire and Michigan), Hoover was out, for the time being.

God, what a tiny arena separates the heroes from the nobodies around here! With no popular war hero to parade before the polls, with Wood too chaste for compromise and Roosevelt dead, the Republicans had no god to run, and the Democrats, trying to squeeze out from under Wilson's malarial legacy, were in even worse shape. Whom did they have to lead, to reunite the land? —Bryan, the Fundamentalist hydropot? Pure imperialist ruralism. —Smith, the savvy East Side kid? Distrusted Anti-Federalist urbanism. There were others, but there was nobody: the well-knowns were too well-known for one failing or another, wet or dry, rural or urban, isolationist or Wilsonian, and the few men of striking abilities, such as Montana's Senator Thomas J. Walsh, a severe, self-made lawyer of relentless probity, had not yet burst upon the scene via happenstance, arrangement, or, Coolidge-style, telegram.

The Republicans did have one champion of note left them, Robert La Follette, the one-man flying wedge of Progressivism, leader of that "little group of willful men" who had opposed American entrance into the war right through the Senate's vote on the declaration. But La Follette was another of those who struck bargains with no one mortal, and with God, God knows, seldom enough. The party's last ace, La Follette—but with him in your hand four kings wouldn't save you, not outside of Wisconsin. He was as stubborn as Wilson, as clean as General Wood, and much more the gadfly than Roosevelt had been, and if he wasn't quite as unpredictable as his brother Progressive, Senator Borah of Idaho, he was still anathema to party machinery, and clung to what was left of Progressivism even after Roosevelt took the movement with him into the tomb, even unto running for President on a third-party ticket in 1924 and copping nearly five million votes.

All right, then, take notice of this hero business from now on—for a business it truly will be as the twenties get into gear—but see already the American attitude toward heroism, subclass political linchpins of the early 1900s. Roosevelt, Bryan, Smith, Wilson, La Follette . . . of them all, only Roosevelt and Wilson were grand enough to get elected President, to attract at least a functioning majority. The other three were hopelessly regional, devoted to tribal totems and therefore out of the running, though they ran nonetheless. But this was where Harding came in. A devout mediocrity, he left his sense of righteousness back in Marion, Ohio, and the editorial office of his newspaper, the *Star*, when he entered national politics, taking along only his gift for alliterative sententia and inadvertent neologism. And he it was who diagnosed the national case: not heroics, he prescribed, but healing. The Republicans' failure to place General Wood on the ballot in Chicago testifies to the general apathy toward heroism: "Give us Barabbas!"

When the Republican nomination was announced to the world, eyebrows rose and men said, "Who?" though it had been clear that this was to be a dark horse convention. Calvin Coolidge was named as the vice-presidential candidate, and that made sense; the man credited with squashing the Boston police strike was notably short on magnetism, but at least people knew who he was. But Harding? Well, as wily old Senator Brandegee put it when the Smoke cleared from the Room, "There ain't any first-raters this year."

To blame the system for not realizing that it had the first Watergate (or, alternatively, and more analogously, the second Crédit Mobilier, of President Grant's Administration) on its hands in the nomination of Harding is a worthless act of hindsight, but one guest at the convention had the gift of prophecy. Edna Ferber, covering the jamboree with William Allen White and the cartoonist Ding Darling for UPI, later recalled that her fellow correspondent William Slavens McNutt shouted, "There goes Harding!"—not when Harding took the top of the ticket, but when Coolidge was named as his running mate.

"What do you mean?" Ferber asked him.

"Harding'll never serve his term out," McNutt told her. "He'll die, and Coolidge will be President ... you'll see. Coolidge luck—he's shot with it."

One knows about the Warren Harding doll: you wind it up and it looks great and does nothing for four years ... well, three years, actually, for a doll can die. For the record, Harding didn't do anywhere nearly as much nothing as, say, New York's odious bon vivant mayor Jimmy Walker, and what he did do includes the unexpectedly progressive coup of pardoning the Socialist leader Eugene V. Debs, who was serving a ten-year sentence for denouncing Establishment hypocrisy in June of 1918 ("The master class has always declared the wars; the subject class has always fought the battles"—not historically accurate but certainly applicable to World War I), talk of this sort having been forbidden under the Espionage Act. Moreover, the Conference on the Limitation of Armaments, which restricted the navies of the United States, Britain, Japan, France and Italy (Russia wasn't invited), though not Harding's idea, was a bright moment in his regime. Ultimately, Harding is not much recalled for either of the foregoing, but for the corruption of his henchmen, including several Cabinet members, exposed piecemeal throughout the decade as a webbing of such evil, complacent arrogation that it constituted the worst federal scandal until Watergate. But Harding sure looked like the goods when he was elected.

To the voters of 1920, Harding was—no other word will do—"normalcy." He not only coined the term but personified the concept, tall, broad, and leonine as he was, solid but accessible, the successful businessman with his feet stacked up on the desk of a lazy afternoon, "bloviating," as Ohioans used to put it, the irresistibly genial poker crony, the small-town Republican, the Middletowner: the norm. Even his profession was a relief; he was the editor and owner of the *Marion Star,* one of Ohio's medium-sized journals, neither muckraker nor machine. Surely no one looked more like a President. (Harding's looks are one of the more tiresome clichés of our history, yet to see the photos is to surrender to cliché. His bearing bespeaks the lingua franca of well-tailored diplomacy rather than Ohio, but his size, his texture, his color are nothing but American prime.) They thought him a neo-Roman; they saw him cleansing the forum of jangling internationalists, easing off the sweeping federal centrism invoked by our entry into the war, a man to save the country from Reds, strikes, race riots, and the high cost of living not by being in charge, but by being. His fiat was no crusades.

Princess Alice of D.C. thought him a slob, but most voters hadn't her scruples, and they *had* had it up to there with Democrats in top hats who kept us out of war only until they were reelected. A fellow newspaperman from Ohio challenged Harding for the Presidency on the Democratic side, but Governor James Cox had inherited Wilson's League of Nations and Cox didn't stand a blue chance. There was but one clear issue in the 1920 campaign—the League, Wilson's League. Rebuffed by both houses of Congress, the best-known man in the world, international Wilson called the 1920 election "a great and solemn referendum." Cox seconded the motion. He scoured the countryside with pep talks on international peacekeeping while Harding equivocated in the last successful front-porch campaign in our history. With no national media to hustle, Harding could vary his flocculent stand on the League according to who was around at the moment. Advised by telegrams from more Republicans than he'd thought existed, he ran a calculated gamut from the vaguely unenthusiastic to the enthusiastically vague. In one of his final statements to soothe Wilsonian Republicans, Harding opted for a world congress founded on "justice" in place of force, one of American history's great examples of semantic scratch, immediately dubbed the "false-teeth proposal" by pro-Leaguers.

The reporters, whose business was skepticism, liked him. He'd wander across the lawn to their camp in a neighbor's backyard, bite off a chew, and say, "Shoot!" And they'd ask and he'd answer, in the natty camaraderie of newsmen who know all the games. What they would do was, they'd bloviate. And, when the time came, that's just what the voters figured they'd get to do under Harding—bloviate. Cox's running mate on the Democratic side was Franklin Delano Roosevelt—"a well-meaning, nice young fellow, but light," according to the sardonically papal Senator Henry Cabot Lodge—and Roosevelt saw, with a sinking heart, how narrow the bundle of campaign issues had become. "While I waited for the returns," he said, "I felt that if one could be beaten on such an issue, there was something rotten about the world."

At the back of the Democrats' minds must have been the perception that this continent of Spoon Rivers, Middletowns, and Brooklyn was on the verge of assuming the leadership of the mercantile West, but the Republicans of 1920 believed in walls as tangible as ever a city-state's were in the Middle Ages. Besides, Harding was meant to be a paternal, not an intrepid, figure, not a doer; he didn't even have the connections with party satraps such as prove so useful in the launching of New Ideas. He could count a few friends from his spell in the Senate and that was it. A dark horse at the Republican Convention to begin with, he was just what he looked like, a splendid, rural nobody, earnest but suggestible, a disinfectant sprayed on the odor of upheaval. It didn't matter who Harding was, anyway, though, nor who Cox was, for the electorate of 1920 were really voting against Wilson, against the Democratic party and its war. They would have voted for almost any Republican in 1920; they did.

On November 2, 1920, the electorate handed over to Harding the mandate for normalcy ("not heroics, but healing; not nostrums, but normalcy"—the misnomer, a chance misreading of "normality," virtually replaced the correct word in American English). So secure was the outcome of the election that fifty-one percent of the eligible voters didn't even bother to get to the polls, and the Democrats carried only eleven states, all of them Southern (and therefore Dixiecrat rather than Wilsonian), ending up with 9 million votes to Harding's 16 million, with the usual diversionary ruses for the farmers, the single taxers, and the drys, plus 920 thousand who came out for Eugene V.

Debs (who doubtless would have had a hard time of it trying to execute his duties from his cell in Atlanta). The Republicans took it with miles to spare on the understanding that the increasingly centralized federal powers, a necessary concomitant of the business of producing a successful war, be diminished under a sweet man who looked like an emperor and carried on his arm the shrillest, frumpiest first lady in the history of the office.

If looks are any sort of cue, no wonder we raged for healing, normal Harding. But the qualities of good nature and sincerity that purchased his Presidency, qualities that stood out on him as palpably as John Adams's will to win and Andrew Jackson's directness glowed on them, turned out to be his tragic flaws. For though the new President surrounded himself with some able men, he also persuaded himself that anyone he liked was as dedicated and honest as he was (and he was both . . . in the political, Pickwickian sense), and he packed the appointments with cronies and crooks. "Warren, it's a good thing you wasn't born a gal," his father once told him. "You'd be in the family way all the time—you can't say no."

A bit later, after Harding himself admitted that he wasn't cut of presidential cloth, when he took off in the summer of 1923 on his forlorn "Voyage of Understanding," an underpowered version of Wilson's quest, it became a commonplace to think of Harding as a railroaded victim who said yes too often and got kicked high in the air against his will, which could only add to the joke of an America so determined on an understated Presidency that it got no President at all.

But Harding wasn't railroaded. He had volunteered for public service—in his often stinging editorials in the Star, in the Ohio Legislature, and as a Senator in Washington, freshman class of 1914. Once nominated for chief executive, he had waged an active campaign, albeit mostly on his front porch, where crowds gathered to hear him indulge in the old-American oratory of the 1800s that still thrilled those whom H. L. Mencken was to term the "booboisie." Harding was a very king of boobs to Mencken, who heaped the contumely with joy in the Baltimore Sun. Compared to Gamaliel, as Mencken called him, even Wilson looked good:

[President Harding] writes the worst English that I have ever encountered. It reminds me of a string of wet sponges; it reminds me of tattered washing on the line; it reminds me of stale bean-soup, of college yells, of dogs barking idiotically through endless nights. It is so bad that a sort of grandeur creeps into it. It drags itself out of the dark abysm (I was about to write abscess!) of pish, and crawls insanely up to the topmost pinnacle of posh.

Mencken's literary sensibilities were of no moment in the socially panicked air of 1919, however, and Harding was a shoo-in. Folks voted not only for him but for his front porch as well; they wanted to move onto that front porch and forget all the supranational despair of the last few years. He got city people as well as the hicks: Al Jolson, as slick an urban upstart as the culture had yet produced, put his name to the official Republican campaign ditty, "Harding, You're the Man for Us." Even the rumor that Harding was part-Negro and would make an Uncle Tom's Cabin of the White House didn't threaten his support to any degree, though a vile and most official-looking handbill purported to detail the facts of the tarred line of the Hardings. No doubt this was what George Harvey was referring to when he questioned the incipient candidate on the question of "impediments." The legend was fabricated by a malcontent in Blooming Grove, Ohio, where Harding was born, and it was to dog him all his life, as would a more substantial item about a woman or two on the side. This Harvey would not have known about, for like the so-called Ohio gang's oil swindles at Teapot Dome and Elk Hills (like, furthermore, the afterbirth of Watergate), Harding's personal life didn't come to light until later on in the era, after the regime in question had ended.

Harding's opposition, of course, had an impediment, the League of Nations, and in this "great and solemn referendum," the League was permanently disposed of as far as the voters were concerned. Two weeks before the election, Mencken caught the ferocious backlash aimed at political crusaders, introducing, as it were, the certain

revealed cynicism that would come to define the twenties for later
generations:

> Today no sane American believes in any official statement of
> national policy, whether foreign or domestic. He has been
> fooled too often, and too callously and impudently. Every idea
> that has aroused him to sentimental enthusiasm and filled his
> breast with the holiest of passions has been dragged into the
> mud by its propounders, and made to seem evil and disgusting
> ... Tired to death of intellectual charlatanry, he turns de-
> spairingly to honest imbecility.

The last word is, if exaggerated, a bull's-eye. Harding wasn't just a
do-nothing, but a know-nothing as well, a cosmetic statesman. For all
his camaraderie with the press, he often horrified reporters with his
unconcerned lack of Oval Office savvy and his apparent, and quite
genuine, ignorance of issues. "Greatness in the presidential chair,"
said Daugherty when he was talking Harding into chasing the
nomination, "is largely an illusion of the people"—a *visual,* he might
have added, could he but read the future, illusion.

Running the country seemed a simple proposition in 1921, when
Harding took office. One's Cabinet did all the detail work—after all,
what are specialists for?—and Harding chose a partly brilliant cabinet.
He named Charles Evans Hughes as Secretary of State, Henry C.
Wallace as Secretary of Agriculture, Herbert Hoover as Secretary of
Commerce, and these were unimpeachable choices. Cheers greeted
also the appointment as Secretary of the Treasury of Andrew Mellon,
"the world's second richest man," who resigned the directorships of
fifty-one corporations to lend his business expertise to the ultimate
business, the federal government. One Cabinet investiture that looked
okay in 1921, that of Albert B. Fall as Secretary of the Interior, was
to cost the deceased President the bulk of his reputation forever after,
and he also blundered in making his political Pygmalion, Harry
Daugherty, his Attorney General, over the objection of virtually
everyone in D.C. A confirmed wire-puller had no place in a
Presidential Cabinet, but here was loyalty if not good sense: "Harry

Daugherty has been my best friend from the beginning of this whole thing," Harding told Senator Wadsworth, who was trying to wise him up. "He tells me that he wants to be Attorney General and by God he will be Attorney General!"

Daugherty's entrée into the ranks in the capital signaled the erection of an omnibus apparatus of wheeler-dealing and larceny, headquartered in what came to be called "the little house on H Street," also known as "the love nest," and so wide-ranging was the ropework of corruption that an annex, "the little green house on K Street," was set up to field the overflow. This was a heyday of cronyism, of poker evenings when government intimates chuckled over the selling of pardons, thefts of incriminating evidence, and assorted grand and petty connivings that they enjoyed. The caravansary at the little green house in particular carried an odor of louche luxury about it, although 1625 K Street was hardly a smuggler's cove, and such orgies as were supposed to be taking place at that address would not likely have escaped detection—by the indefatigable Alice Longworth, if no one else.

One tiny footnote takes pride of place amidst the politicking and the social psychology: the 1920 election was the first event in our history to be monitored on radio, this pregnant occasion being as well the debut of commercial radio broadcasting. It was not the first American election broadcast ever, but the first professionally organized one. (In 1916, Lee De Forest single-handedly ran an election-night special in New York with the cooperation of the *New York American*, announcing Charles Evans Hughes as the next President of the United States.)

This was a methodical operation. The returns fed to Station KDKA in East Pittsburgh by the *Pittsburgh Post* as they came in, a crew of anonymous broadcasters relayed the count to, if not a waiting world, at least to those few who had access to a receiver. A similar experiment obtained that night in Detroit, but this was all but erased by the tantara of publicity from Westinghouse, which presided over KDKA and which impressed connoisseurs of such goings-on with the viability of investing the transmitting channels with news reports, music, drama, and chat. This is where we all pass over into the

modern era of the masscult media: an address by Woodrow Wilson
on Armistice Day in 1923 reached three million people, and Labor
Day of the following year found Robert La Follette kicking off his
third-party campaign for President with the first political speech
specifically tailored for the airwaves, both men thus partly externaliz-
ing the image that before radio shimmered only in the mind's eye—
and television was still to come. William Jennings Bryan, characteristically confusing acts of mortal genius with those of God, called
radio "a gift of Providence"; who better than this master orator could
visualize the potential of telegraphic oration? Much power, now, to
him who secures the airwaves; the date November 2, 1920, incidentally a presidential election but most strategically the commencement
of the national media blitz, ranks as a prime one in our history. Mark
it for a sign of things that were to come, an omen of uprearing
cataclysm in the form of a great marketplace of the mind. Radio and
television, above all, are there to vend.

So, President Normalcy takes office; we'll see how that works out.
The voters' rejection of Wilson, and, by implication, their refusal to
admit that a world was out there, a world that badly needed seeing
to, suggests that the new decade was to be a gambol of busy
beehiving and recreation, all homespun and picket fences, patent
medicines and straw boaters as the great bourgeoisie, having outlawed
hot and rebellious liquor in the Eighteenth Amendment, closed ranks
in grace.

It was not to be, of course, for numerous reasons about to be
disclosed. The first of them—the Harding reason, the national non
serviam—was the ludicrous ambition of creating normalcy simply by
voting it into office. The Red menace had quieted down for the
moment, and inflation, ballooned to capacity, finally sank along with
unemployment as the stock market turned bullish. So far, so good.
But a boom economy is not normalcy any more than a depression is,
and as Sherwood Anderson, Sinclair Lewis, F. Scott Fitzgerald, and
others of their confraternity were about to make clear, normalcy, in
the towns, in the country, and in the in between, was not to be had—
not at these prices, no sir!

TWO

The Found Generation

Self-sufficient villages can resist time and transformation; nations cannot. An isolated culture consisting of arrowheads, fire dances, and an oral folklore can hold back wind, tide, and fortune as the aeons pass, but a civilization, however isolated it wishes itself, will succumb to continuity. "Sometimes with the wind and sometimes against it," wrote Oliver Wendell Holmes—"but we must sail, and not drift, nor lie at anchor." Nothing stops dead, finally, ever, except perhaps, finally, a war, and nothing that resisted control before The Big One was going to lie down and play dead after. The past was still being reconnoitered—the very frontiers had yet to be tamed in the form of land booms in Florida and Southern California—and the future could not be commandeered: even an amendment to the august Constitution, taped on like a spinster's anonymous hate letter to somebody's front door, couldn't effect a ban on liquor.

There was much mooting about of "the good old days," in the early twenties, when the technology of the automobile, the movies, radio, and aviation bedazzled the view of the swells and the villein alike, but all the same, a majority of Americans managed to adjust to the new times with resignation (the old), wonder (the youngish adult), and rude facility (the young). Even the oral folkloric tradition exercised its gift for renewal by fitting trendy new lyrics to the old anthem, "My God, How the Money Rolls In," with the bonhomie of freewheeling nihilism:

> My sister sells snow to the snowbirds,
> My father makes bootlegger gin,
> My mother, she rents by the hour,
> My God, how the money rolls in!

Cocaine was just around the corner, whiskey right where you were, however illegal, and sex, whether free love or at a rate, provided much of the town with its topic. Cheap fiction was judged useful or pointless by the amount of "sex suspense" it bestowed, and the nation's youth were said to be aflame—not in the acceptable tic-tac-toe of the ceaseless generation war, initiated by Cain and Adam and hallowed by time, but in grimy new patterns, guided by the columnist Dorothy Dix, egged on by the storyteller F. Scott Fitzgerald, intoxicated by the movie actors Rudolph Valentino, Clara Bow, and Betty Blythe, who was, especially in *The Queen of Sheba.*

Not only in the hip cities, but out on the land, raging for hip, the would-be sheiks and shebas were in an uproar, at least as their parents saw it. The city of Middletown—it sounds like an adman's cant for the mass market—unfolded its secrets to the sociologists Robert and Helen Lynd in the mid-twenties, and their classic investigation of an American peacetime neither too Northern, Southern, or Western, neither too industrial nor agrarian, neither snail-sleepy nor overbold, *Middletown*, gave voice to what altered life-styles the moving finger had written upon the national scene. The book *Middletown* punctured the idyll "Middletown": cigarette smoking was no longer considered either unwomanly or effeminate; big families with ten or eleven children were looking less respectable and even faintly unsavory, like something left over from the Old Testament; the divorce rate was climbing (41.4 splits per 100 marriages for the first five years of the decade—and this was Middletown, remember, not any of your fancy Babylons of the Northeast); one-third of the high-school graduates were heading immediately to college; people worked only a half-day on Saturday now, the business class sometimes not at all; clothes were more slim-lined, revealing the shape instead of concealing it, and fewer women were making their own; the hail-fellow lodge was losing its grip on the minds of men even as their whilom news hub on the courthouse steps was ceding to the newspapers and, soon enough, radio; and of course there was the ubiquitous flivver, the atom of the new industrial molecular structure.

The automobile might have stayed a rich man's hobby, as it had been at the top of the century, if the man who oversaw its presentation hadn't been determined to turn it out the way God turned out little green apples. In 1906, when the whole thing was still a game and cries of "Get a horse!" de rigueur, Woodrow Wilson observed that "nothing has spread socialistic feeling in this country more than the automobile; to the countryman it is a picture of arrogance and wealth, with all its independence and carelessness." But worldly show wasn't what Henry Ford had in mind, not for worlds. When he upped his minimum wage to five dollars a day in 1914 (other managements thought two dollars inflationary), he wasn't just giving the workers of Detroit a share in his profits, he was creating supply and demand, virtually imposing upward mobility upon the proletariat of the nation, starting with his thirteen thousand employees. "Tomorrow," he might have added, "the world."

They called it "the Ford idea"; they called it plenty of things— paternalism, Socialism, "a magnificent act of generosity." Foot! You can't sell to people who can't pay, and Ford had something to sell, a commodity, a staple, not a rich man's taboo. Somebody had to inaugurate the ball and invite the middle class to it, and if this somebody didn't exactly invent consumerism, somebody certainly found it bashful and promptly filled out its dance card. Ford was a capitalist, after all, and here was this . . . this machine which anyone could use but which Ford was resolved everyone would need. No, they told him, when he started out. No, look: all those . . . those machines on the road will panic the horses. And Ford would tell them right back that there weren't going to be any horses to panic— everyone will drive a car. He made cheap and sold cheap, giving the raspberry to the ornaments and extras that turned other makes into sleek chariots of the ancien régime. "They can have any color they want so [long as] it's black," he said.

That was before the war, and by the twenties, Ford had made his point. He was a force in Middletown, bouncing and rattling down Main Street, connecting downtown with the outskirts and Middletown with Junction City and Jonesville and the outside world across the state line. Perhaps the best-known employer in the history of the world, Ford was mainly known for his passionless, unstoppable assembly line, which was actually the brainchild of Frederick Winslow Taylor. Ford's own lighning flashes tended more to the bizarre than to the pragmatic, such as the "peace ship" sent to Norway in 1915 to mediate a war settlement, an attempted revival of the square dance, and the revelation of an international Jewish conspiracy. Ford often seemed to speak in the megalomaniac voice of the crackpot prophet, and he was all over the place in the twenties, as fresh as a new movie star and as unexpected as a California earthquake.

Whether he was suing the *Chicago Tribune* for a million dollars for brading as anarchism his resistance to the war, or offering to take the property at Muscle Shoals, Alabama, off the government's hands for the mass production of inexpensive fertilizer, Ford was an item, one that recurred, almost monthly, with headlong predilections and kinkiness evergreen. Who was it that wrote a pamphlet, *The Little White Slaver,* denouncing the cigarette ("Study the history of any criminal," he opined, "and you will find an inveterate smoker")? Who believed in reincarnation and the rehabilitation of ex-convicts, recruiting instances of the former in the most innocent accidents of nature and instances of the latter in his factories? Who discovered the superb nutriment of the carrot, gorged upon it, and then, discovering the soybean, discreetly abandoned the carrot? Who promised to discharge any employee who drank liquor? Who said "history is bunk" and claimed that he never read books because they confused him?

Who was the businessman hero of his day? Not Ford; he made too many pronouncements, knocked the props of reason out from under himself too often. The newspapermen adored him—he was always good for a story—and of the readership some liked him and a few admired him, for when all was said and done, could anyone that rich not be smart? Proponents of his causes, such as Prohibitionists, anti-Semites, and folk dancers, were glad he was around while his causes were theirs, and 1923 saw a brief flurry of grass-roots support for a "Ford for President" draft, based largely on the opinion of great numbers of yokels that Ford was not "stuck up," and therefore good leadership material. But reasonable men saw in him a half-dangerous, illiterate lunatic, and even the citizens in the jury box who found for Ford in his libel suit against the *Chicago Tribune* only awarded him six cents damages and court expenses.

It was the car, really—the cylinder, the piston, the power you could walk right up and buy. Sinclair Lewis put his pen on it in 1922 in a novel devoted to the microcosm of the small businessman in an imaginary Midwestern state capital: "To George F. Babbitt, as to the most prosperous citizens of Zenith, his motor car was poetry and tragedy, love and heroism. The office was his pirate ship but the car his perilous excursion ashore." Not even when Ford took over the weekly *Dearborn Independent* to light from its masthead a beacon for the American idea, for "national and international liberalism," was anyone much convinced by his schemes who wasn't convinced already. An ersatz leader, a leader by fractions, no leader at all because a leader converts you to his vision, Ford was, in everything but his machine, a figure of fun. And the machine, too, as it got used to the public and the public to it, was adopted by the amiable derision of folklore. Ford stories were the Polish jokes of their era, though invariably about the friendly car, not the invisible man:

"Does this car always shake like this?"
"Only when it's running."

It sounds like an innocent age, but as anyone out in the towns was ready to tell you, it wasn't. Cigarettes and divorce in Middletown? Five-dollar wages for an eight-hour day? *Only* eight hours? And the younger generation . . . what about that lot? Petting parties, sinful dancing, forbidden (not to mention illegal) flasks of "whoopee water," clothing fetishes like boys' collecting of garters and girls' rolling their stockings below the knee—and this at a time when many older women wouldn't have been caught dying without a corset on. The innocent front-porch sparking of old had mated with the Model T and produced lovers' lane, a black and chaperoneless Baghdad out on the back roads where, so it was rumored, the behavioral code that had done for three generations was shattered nightly. Parents were afraid to allow sex education in the schools, reasoning that anything the kids heard about they'd want to try.

The kids already knew a lot more than any public school sex education course could teach them. They all went to the movies, naturally, taking tips from the Babylonian flashback sequences that kept popping up, often on pretexts that couldn't even be called scanty, in Cecil B. De Mille's films. Some might have read F. Scott Fitzgerald's *This Side of Paradise,* the new "true confessions" magazines, or the novels of Elinor Glyn, Dorothy Speare, and Warner Fabian (a pseudonym of Samuel Hopkins Adams). All but Fitzgerald are forgotten today, but all were vibrant at the time with the slang, the snappy cynicism, and the self-congratulatory yet somewhat punctilious hedonism of the Protestant bourgeois. For testimony, sample this extract from *College Humour* magazine:

> 1st FLAPPER: The boy I'm going with now thinks of nothing but necking.
> 2nd FLAPPER: What can you do with a fellow like that?
> 1st FLAPPER: Neck.

This Side of Paradise's hero, Amory Blaine, endured the romantic crise of the ultracollegiate, lived in riot, flirted and rhapsodized—but, mainly, went to Princeton, taking with him the idolization of romantic collegiate youth. Others, less literary, sought advice in the confession rags; these promised more than they felt free to deliver, putting their come-hither into an explicit table of contents not entirely lived up to in the succeeding pages. "Sex need not necessarily be dirt," wrote one confessions editor of his craft. "Characters may do anything they please but they must do it from some lofty, or apparently lofty, motive. If a girl falls, she must fall *upward.*" This pseudomorality, adopted in the movies after scandal put the heat on, proved to be a gold mine. *True Story, True Lovers,* and *True Romances* were all put out by the health faddist Bernarr Macfadden, who also founded the insidious *Evening Graphic* in New York and generally gave publishing a bad odor, which can't have been easy in that epoch of the wanton tabloid.

On the other hand, these Glyn, Speare, and Fabian books did nothing for the American novel except sell it, scorching the pants off the old morality and latching onto the latest answers as fast as the younger generation, unwrapping its gift for argot, could devise them. The titles, smirking on booksellers' shelves, cried out for the prudence of a secret reading nest—Fabian's *Flaming Youth* and *Unforbidden Fruit,* Speare's *Dancing in the Dark* (which made good all over again early in the Depression as a moderately incomprehensible ballad in the Broadway revue *The Band Wagon,* pop feeding on pop).

It was Glyn who coined a new meaning for a harmless word and entered the lexicon in her story, "The 'It' Girl." It, basically, was personal magnetism, and her readers, who had been wondering what to call it, dashed to the mirror to identify their quotient of It, and would spend hours rating their beaus. Either you had It or you didn't, but, look, you simply *had* to or all life went punk. This was the concern of the sheiks and shebas, this their contemporaneity. Angst and melancholia they left to the nobs of the bohemian elite; Glyn, Speare, and Fabian catered to a middle, quasi-lettered class with promiscuity, dipsomania, and hell-raising, as in this extract from Fabian's *Sailors' Wives* of 1924:

"How much of the local cat-chatter about the Wild girls is true?" asked Rollo lazily.

"They're a pair of pettineckers, all right."

"Meaning what, if anything?"

... "Petting and necking, bushing, snuggling, plain and fancy twining, and all the popular four-arm exercises of the season. Everything but—and I wouldn't bet on the but as far as Milly is concerned."

Much of the cultivation of It consisted of working out a good "line" to go with one's appearance, the more worldly the better, and a good line consisted not of concepts, but of words, pretty words in profile, a line. "Do you think I ought to bob my hair, Mr. Charley Paulson?" asks the wallflowerish Bernice of a gentleman at a country club dinner dance in one of Fitzgerald's stories, using a line worked up for her by her cousin Marjorie. "I want to be a society vampire, you see." This new generation, unlike the highbrows of the day, questioned nothing in life; it all simply occurred, with a little help from one's barber. Code told one how far to go, and with whom, and for what purpose, if any, for somewhere or other—God knew where, though God had no influence over that crew—and almost overnight, it seemed, the flappers and their sheiks had concocted a code. The satirists of literature turned to look (they know the clues to era when they see them), and now The Young People and their code turned up in the work of writers better than Glyn and older than Fitzgerald, as with Booth Tarkington's "incomparable damsel," the heroine of *Claire Ambler:*

> It may truly be said that she did not think about herself . . . nor about anything. She had feelings that she believed to be thoughts; she had likes and dislikes that she believed to be thoughts; she had impulses she believed to be thoughts; her mind was . . . full of echoes of what she had heard and read, and these she usually believed to be thoughts original with her. Words were fluent upon her lips without her knowing or wondering how they got there; yet she was sure they expressed truths and easily became angry, or grieved, if they were challenged.

How did they get so sophisticated so suddenly? "You see I think everything's terrible anyhow," says Daisy Buchanan in *The Great Gatsby.* "Everybody thinks so—the most advanced people. And I *know.* I've been everywhere and seen everything and done everything." Perhaps they'd been reading about themselves in books. This was, after all, quite early in the visual era, long before the ultimate completion of television, and even the kids were reading. Before his first novel was published, Fitzgerald predicted that his fame would be made by "the debutantes," and, going a step further, a cartoon in *Judge* magazine showed a toddler curled up in an armchair, book in hand, addressing a matronly type adjusting the flowers in a vase: "Mother, you've been gypped!" cries the little darling. "This is the expurgated edition." Impressionable but devoted to a brittle cynicism and not unaware of their emerging independences, the younger generation set a tone for the decade, one of its several tones, and like the bohemians of the art world, they indulged in a rejection of tradition, though unlike the artists they offered nothing in exchange.

Debunking, exposing the sham, was the preferred text for rejection and debunkers the preferred prophets. Collegiates enjoined the generation war simply by reading *The American Mercury,* the scurrilous megaphone of H. L. Mencken, "a maggot, a buzzard, a ghoul of new made graves" (the *Tampa Times*), "a moral pervert" (the Knights of the Ku Klux Klan of Arkansas), "a bellowing democrat" (J. B. Priestley). His fellow journalist, William Allen White, likened him, in a lengthy and fastidious metaphor, to a pig, "railing at the whitewash that covers the manure about his habitat." Mencken's habitat was Baltimore, which, he claimed, "bulges with normalcy," but *The American Mercury*'s offices were in New York, the national capital of debunking, and from there, doing Mencken's work like a witch's familiar, the green-covered rag busted the old symbols and taught the sheiks new ones. Naturally, as an agent of upheaval, the *Merc* was the outrage of editorials, Sunday sermons, and college faculty meetings across the land, a ceaseless foe of Mencken's foes, which included illiterates, Village literati, superpatriots, Socialists, capitalists, Fundamentalists, the Ku Klux Klan, drys, prudes, watch and warders, "homo neanderthalis" . . . as he put it, "American piety, stupidity, tinpot morality, cheap chauvinism in all their forms." He was more American than any other American, and believed in nothing but freedom.

An impeccable stylist and canny news reporter, if an erratic literary critic who was likely to lose interest in his discoveries just as they reached their prime and popularity, Mencken more than anyone of his day beat the tempo for urbane comprehension of time and place, of patria. He spearheaded the modern movement to decipher the pandemic kinks of spoken American English in *The American Language*, three huge volumes' worth of regional congeries that remain a classic statement of that unexpected turn of fortune that we are now willing to term American ethnicity. Strangely enough, for someone as dedicated to rebutting the attitudes of the booboisie as Mencken was, *The American Language* sought the flavor of the rank and file, the dumb inventions of folklore complete with folklore's corruptions, misapprehensions, and primitivism.

Nothing owned him, and nothing was immune to his analysis. He occasionally waxed rabid, but for a reason. "Criticism and progress," he once wrote, "to be effective, must be iconoclastic and pugnacious." Most of America thought his writing treasonous, but the wise minority found in his hydrophobic utterances the basis of sane social chronicle. He was tireless in work and abundant with leisure, and everything he did bore the overkill of his Socratic progressivism and the strop of his wit. On one rejection slip he wrote, "This smells like Aimee Semple McPherson's pants."

Mencken and his readership dwelled in the cities or in academe; his targets were, largely, the rubes of the land, but Mencken was really the last of the hayseed's worries. For those many Americans of the early 1920s who looked about them and felt uneasy, dispossessed of something they hadn't known was there but now were certain was missing, the problem clearly seemed to be the new morality of this younger generation, possibly assisted by the evils of life in Hollywood and the strained ethical code brought about by the widespread subversion of Prohibition. There was, as well, clawing at the threads of the moral tapestry, once sewn up so prettily by readers of the McGuffey *Readers*, the New Woman, with her hankering for things she had never needed before. Why now, all of a sudden? Why was everything changing? After all, the war was finished, the Red deported, and the very picture of a Great White Father ensconced in the White House. Things ought to be as they were before, now, quiet-like.

They weren't. And the real problem, the utter change, was the experience of change itself, the omnium-gatherum of revolution that decayed or enriched—depending on how much you liked your life before—virtually all of what the population had taken for granted as the American mode. Jeepers, at each step you took, every time you turned left or right, there was the future going into its dance—not just in the cities of the Northeast, with their rage for transformation, their anterior impulsions and cheesy mix, but in Middletown as well: in Dearborn, Michigan, where Ford put the Taylor system for competitive mass production on the spot and created a demand for his supply; in Atlantic City, where the first Miss America pageant was held in 1921, complete with a one-piece-bathing-suit parade of beauty; on Catalina Island, off the California shore, from which point wireless and land lines carried a telephone conversation to a ship moored three thousand miles away near New York; in San Francisco, where the film comedian, Roscoe "Fatty" Arbuckle, may or may not have raped and murdered a minor actress during a protracted hotel-suite orgy; in Hollywood in 1922, where the film director William Desmond Taylor was shot to death, case unsolved; in the mind of God, speaking for Whom the Protestant Episcopal House of Bishops voted in favor of deleting the word "obey" from the marriage vow; in Tonawanda, New York, in 1923, where twenty-seven-year-old Homer Morehouse strutted eighty-seven hours in a dance marathon, left the floor half-dead with his partner, and immediately collapsed, wholly dead. The future: evil, change.

Middletown, it turned out in 1929 when the Lynds' report was published, was Muncie, Indiana, and there as well as anywhere one felt the world whirling, controlled by chaos. The palpable inroads made on one's piece of mind by the sociopolitical ruckus of 1919 were one thing: that had been a brief era in the first place, over already, and a movement sponsored largely by strangers, not Americans, in the second. But the continued fever of the 1920s proper was another thing, for it inflamed even the simple things in life, "the best things" that, as a song of 1927 put it, were free. Still, it was hard to concentrate on the condign grace of "the sunbeams that shine" ("they're yours!" it developed, "they're mine!") when they were lighting up such outgrowths as feminism, free love, devout late-night carousing, low-down slang talk, or the increasing popularity of seamy literature.

There was another Middletown besides that of the sociologist, a sub-Middletown of lesser area but greater dimension, where time and fortune are less categorical than elsewhere, where tradition abides like an uneatable god and simple tools never turn into artifacts. This was the Middletown of a school of writers who kept in touch with beginnings and rejected not only the end but the middle as well; there was no development, and no present transition, in their span, only continuity. As if in rebuttal to the modern attack on the good life made by *Winesburg, Ohio* and *Main Street,* Willa Cather rose in Nebraska, years before Anderson and Lewis were heard from, to defend pioneers and immigrant settlers from satirists, and though she eventually lit in New York, her work clung like the vine to the stately edifice of unobtrusive villager Americana.

Lacking the humor of Mark Twain before her and the fulfilled mythopoeia of William Faulkner after, she banned technology from her truth, locating a shining Golden Ageism on the plains of the Midwest. No bootleggers, dance marathons, or It intruded on Cather's prosy spring; if anything, the headlong dynamics of the twenties roused the best in her by way of challenge, her back more or less against the wall to defend the things that always were—*A Lost Lady* and *Death Comes for the Archbishop,* two of her finest novels, both came out in the twenties. An early and unpleasant brush with Hollywood in an adaptation of one of her books convinced Cather that the cinema was another example of corrupting modernity, and she consequently withheld her issue from further transformation, keeping her poetic world view from the mainstream of popular art and the national spectator's trance, but adding greatly to its purity. Readers only may taste of Cather, with the elite eye of the mind and heart, and like a very few of the writers of her time, she is still very much in print.

But what did she mean by junking wholesale the ideas of the new, and what was this paradise that she saw out on the unvarnished prairie? Was the real-life countryside so forbidden to petty intolerance, to perversion and anguish and mortality, as the countryside she wrote of? Was the epic of tradition truly as ongoing as she pictured it? "I had the sense of coming home to myself, of having found out what a little circle man's experience is," says Jim Burden, the narrator of Cather's *My Antonia,* revisiting his boyhood home in Nebraska, the home as well of Antonia, the Czech immigrant he loved in adolescence. "For Antonia and me," he goes on, closing the novel, "this had been the road of Destiny; had taken us to those early accidents of fortune which predetermined for us all that we can ever be. Now I understood that the same road was to bring us together again. Whatever we had missed, we possessed together the precious, the incommunicable past."

It may have been incommunicable to Jim Burden, but not to Cather. The past, to her, said it all, and there in the past she found herself in a time of crossing over. What Ford and his fellows sought lay ahead, in the future, but what Cather sought was there already, as it had always been, but as it could not be much longer. Ford saw to that.

Here is why Ford is the polestar of all this, as he was a linchpin of the news business for his obligingly screwball notions, so suitable for quoting: Ford was change, more so than any "new morality," but a change disguised as that old American constant, profitable business. Ford taught automation to the citizenry in this sense, that the machine wasn't a godless monster walled up in some hidden place, but an indispensable piece of the familiar. One rode about in the machine as a matter of course, and one might eventually live surrounded by machines; one ought to think machines; one must will what is necessary. Ford was Doctor Change. He made one feel good about the cure. He made one need to be cured. He made one decay without his medicine. Ford was Professor Change of some university of spacetime where education is a matter of subliminal response, for one didn't recognize what was going on right then—one simply bought a car, and that was that. But one had bought more than a riding machine; one had borrowed a belief in the Absolute. And Ford was God Change, because it was the future and it worked.

In the history of the West, the development of the tool into the machine into the technopolis reads as the history of man, and the last phase more or less begins around the 1920s. Since then, we in America have dwelled in the machine, used it to resurface the texture of our lives. It was power once, demon momentum; now it's an irresistible tutelary, obeyed in toaster ovens and coffee grinders. But to most folks in the twenties, science was tepid study, a vision for people who suffer visions, such as scientists. The laboratory was associated in the popular mind with Thomas Alva Edison, who, as everybody knew, hadn't even been educated before he endeared himself to the nation with the incandescent lamp and the phonograph, domesticated loot (had they but known that the Edison company smithies dabbled in such escalation as the ore separator and electric dynamo, they might have thought him a little less the folk hero).

Edison survived the twenties, just, a living reminder of the humanness, albeit distracted, of the scientist, of the finiteness of technology: and Faust, too, was mortal. Why, it wasn't until the mid-twenties that the "electric" process allowed phonograph records to reproduce a good-sized orchestra with any fidelity to speak of, and not till 1930 did Garbo Talk. Radio had become something of a fad by late 1922, right about the time of the Mah-Jongg craze, but, like the automobile, the "radio-telephony box" was quickly subsumed into the world of the quotidian, a greasy flower in the garden of consumerism. The car and the radio were something to do. One went for drives; one listened. But one didn't really make the voyage; one didn't quite hear the message.

A few there were, however, ready to draw the line against everything foreign and different that was muscling in and baiting their attitudes. They were led, starting in 1915, by a history professor, Methodist speaker, and ex-lodge solicitor in Georgia who dubbed himself the Imperial Wizard of a movement devoted to the preservation of ground-zero Americanism as it obtained in the lower- and lower-middle-class South just before the war, and at least partly inspired by a reading of a book about the old night riders of the Reconstruction. New recruits weighed in at ten dollars a head, four dollars of the membership fee going to the recruiter, so go-getters oiled up their zip, went, and got. By 1924 the national personnel was reputed to lie just short of four and a half million, wielding strenuous political power in Oklahoma, Texas, California, Oregon, and Indiana. The group's periodic festivals grew to spectacular proportions, especially their luminescent nocturnal displays, and an air of mystery was provided by secret jargon and hooded robes. A small boy who happened upon one such scene in Tulsa in 1922 related, "Everyone knelt before the flag and seemed to kiss it. It was awful solemn and spooky. White figures were every place."

The Ku Klux Klan, with its Kleagles, Klavalcades, Klaverns, Kludds, Kloreros, and Koncilliums, and its idiot, murkyglot motto, "Non silba sed anther" (translation impossible), appealed at first mainly to white supremacists in Georgia, particularly those who had seen D. W. Griffith's film, *The Birth of a Nation*, and who had cheered the heroic, nick-of-time Klansmen who galloped in their hoods near the close of the picture to save a white family from slaughter at the hands of savage blacks. There had been fear, when the infant cinema shook its rattle at the common man in nickelodeons and nickeldromes, that the credulous working classes would come under some harmful influence, and indeed the rabble was roused by Griffith's two-and-a-half-hour tale of the Cameron family of South Carolina and their unceasing martyrdom by American Negroes, characterized by Griffith as parasitic cretins. That fervent ride of the old Klan in *The Birth of a Nation*, including a startling shot of the horsemen traversing a hillside in silhouette, proved a locus classicus of the "send in the marines!" climax of the American action thriller, and gave the spectator something to ponder even in that palmy 1915 before Preparedness, the League of Nations, and the Red Peril.

Hindsight suggests that viewings of *The Birth of a Nation* catalyzed the Klan, but in fact the club proved a sluggish, statebound affair until the Imperial Wizard, William Joseph Simmons—also known, in that hospitable ambiguity of the South, as "Doc" and "Colonel"— enlisted the aid of two powerhouse salesmen, Edward Young Clarke and Elizabeth Tyler. It was hard for someone, or some two, with brains and moxie not to smell success in Simmons' little project, what with rural America's fondness for clubs; Clarke and Tyler had brains and moxie to spare. As Arnold S. Rice put it in *The Ku Klux Klan in*

American Politics, the pair transformed Simmons's association "from a somewhat easygoing Southern fraternity of patriotic whites into a violently aggressive national organization of native-born, white Protestants." In another field, the country might have hailed the pair for their "get up and go," their horse sense, their uprearing Main Street moxie. As it happened, much of the country, when the Klan acquired a national profile almost overnight in a binge of newspaper exposés in the early twenties, evinced disgust and horror, and thought it a vicious conspiracy. It wasn't. It was a business.

—with this exception: that its clients took it more seriously than the clients of other businesses. Clarke and Tyler were making money—at the height of their reign as much as $40,000 a month, perhaps more—but whatever their personal beliefs, they were doing what any Babbitt or Gatsby ought to be doing in an increasingly conscienceless boom era, doing well. As for doing good, that was of lesser moment; had Clarke and Tyler been penguins in Antarctica, they might have been selling membership in a secret society uniting penguins against the insidious tern.

But the Klansmen themselves believed in what they were doing. The American tradition of xenophobia—the human tradition of xenophobia, to be fair—has a long history, and the revived Ku Klux Klan can point to progenitors in the 1850s, such as the Supreme Order of the Star-Spangled Banner, briefly influential as "Know-Nothings," so dubbed for their regulation answer to all questions, "I know nothing." What the new Klansmen knew, however, and what they were eager to tell, at least to each other, was that the altered America of the postwar years was being submerged in a slime of mongrel infusions—on the West Coast, the Japanese; in the lower Midwest, the foreign Socialist; in the South, the Negro; and everywhere the Catholic and Hebrew. Don't call it a Southern fetish, for though it started in Georgia, it spread as far afield as Oregon and Maine (to oppose the French Canadian; every state has its woodpile) and virtually owned Indiana, that Booth Tarkingtonland of front-porch sparking, magnificent Ambersons, and Penrod.

Not only local problems but federal ones as well built the Klan big. With gripes about foreigners' low-wage competition as workers, their radicalism, and their slushy moral sense flooding in from constituents, President Wilson had refused to sign an emergency restriction on immigration, but Harding and, later, Coolidge both favored quotas—who didn't, at the time, except immigrants?—and Coolidge's announcement that "America must be kept American" was a shout from sea to shining sea. The National Origins Act curtailed the incontinent inflow of strangers, favoring Northern Europe but unfortunately slapping the Japanese in their elaborate sense of face by cutting them out entirely. Not only the Klan but all America was satisfied with the new quotas, but the professional natives of the Klan stood alone with a further beef: how to deal with the immigrants who were already here.

It was a true splurge of the grass roots, the Klan, a pioneer quest, self-serving, reckless, corrupt, and wicked. Its members, who feared the new America, were the rank and file of the ungifted, small people seeking the satisfaction of self-expression that motivated big people like Henry Ford. Klansmen must have thrilled to Ford's anti-Semitic campaigns in the *Dearborn Independent,* running to such exposés as "The Jewish Associates of Benedict Arnold" and a gala reprinting of an old forgery, the "Protocols of the Learned Elders of Zion," though most Klansmen hadn't likely ever met anyone who was Jewish in their lives.

The incongruity of the Klan was its failure to take hold in the cities of the Northeast, where its message of WASP self-defense would have had some resonance. There, where the immigrant was a fact, where rootless blacks congregated and Catholics held political power, the American Protestant could feel genuinely threatened, and it can't be said that the loutish, teeming masses of the urban ethnic enclaves were an impressive argument in favor of assimilation. But the old cities remained cosmopolitan and transcended, giving way to an occasional race riot, while the stagnant countryside took up the cudgels and, fearsomely at times, used them.

Repression isn't a hobby so much as a reply, and the question, put most severely in the twenties of all eras in our history, was transformation. Folks could only surmise that a heavy Catholic subpopulation would win whole regions of the land for Rome, and they were too used to a subservient black minority to apprehend what it might be like if liberated; of technology they comprehended as little as they did of the flourishing, iconoclastic new bohemia of the New York art world; the monetary system hadn't been changed for many years; the state language was still English. But something was wrong. It *was* different, all of it—or it was going to be. If they didn't unite and take control it wouldn't be America anymore. Some of their guidelines they took from the Reverend Billy Sunday, a baseball-player-turned-evangelist whose every utterance shot him higher up to the Everest of star-spangled imbecility. Said Sunday, among other things, "America is not a country for dissenters to live in." That was good enough for the Klan. The white, Protestant, visionless, repressive American—one of our oldest tropes, ancient yet evergreen—had found himself at the forefront of a backlash, hiding behind a peaked hood and the flag of God, and possessed of a haphazard but ferocious lynch law. What he could see, smell, and touch was all he knew. He loved limits. Having so many himself, he wanted to lend them to others, nolens volens, and he protected the American idea, looking like a ghost come to party with the dance of death. He went native.

The Ku Klux Klan was essentially another version of the country fighting back at the city, from which all the winds of change seemed to billow like fire from Fafner's throat. The country fought hard, massed up for boycotts and the bloc votes that not only swung county elections but which also delivered national Prohibition. The Klan could not be countermanded: the smart thing to do was keep silent—that is, if one wanted to get reelected or just stay alive. J. C. Walton, the governor of Oklahoma, was successfully impeached for trying to control Klan barbarism with martial law, and at the 1924 Democratic Convention, William R. Pattangall, the attorney general of Maine, offered a condemnation of the Klan to be read into the party platform—and lost his post in the following year's election, purportedly through Klan militancy. Yes, in Maine. *He* was surprised, too.

Movements of repression claim something of a tradition in America, as we have noted, but, pace Billy Sunday, the tradition of dissent is just as old. The Klan—whose worst enemy was not the Negro, nor the Catholic, nor even timechange, but nonconformity—was as anti-

American as anything ever will be; Joseph Stalin and the Kleagles of the Klan have more than terrorism in common. As it happened, though, not everyone did keep silent. William Allen White stung the Klan with exposure in his *Emporia Gazette,* the *Baltimore Sun* disclosed skeletons in the closet of Louisiana, where a grand jury awarded incontrovertible proofs of skulduggery with no indictment, and Herbert Bayard Swope ran a series of twenty-one disgusted reports on the Klan in the morning edition of the *New York World.* That paper's circulation rose by sixty thousand one day after the first installment.

It was not outrage from without but worms within that ultimately ate the heart out of the Klan, specifically a wrenching war for supremacy among its leaders and, hotter copy, an episode of 1925 that cast illumination from the fiery cross of justice, not from the wooden totem of a Klonvocation, upon the Klan safehold of Indiana. Showing the true face of Klan mentality more vividly than White or Swope, the king of Indiana, Grand Dragon David Curtis Stephenson, raped and bit twenty-eight-year-old Madge Oberholtzer so brutally that she committed suicide, swallowing bichloride of mercury tablets and then making a complete statement for the benefit of the doctors who were unable to save her. The cause of death, it turned out, was less the mercury than the treatment Oberholtzer had received from Stephenson. The man had chewed her body so badly that in her last hours she was a living vessel of infection.

"I am the law and power in Indiana," Stephenson had said; other gangsters of the era were to rate themselves comparably in the pecking orders of other regions, usually Chicago. Ironically, the immigrant Italian, Irish, and Jewish desperadoes of self-advertising crime evaded punishment in their brushes with the law better than the native-born Stephenson in his. He was found guilty of second-degree murder and sentenced to twenty-five-years-to-life imprisonment. Expecting a pardon from his Klan Kolleague, Governor Ed Jackson, Stephenson got none, and shot back with a happy revenge, revelations of corruption that sent the mayor of Indianapolis, the sheriff of Marion County, and a Congressman to jail. Well, that was three down. And there weren't so many more to go, for by the end of the decade, for reasons that will never be understood except perhaps by the anonymous mob that tossed out their cotton hoods, the Klan had dwindled from the millions down to an estimated nine thousand with no great political base, a regional gaffe, a boondocks craze, the serpent's cast-off skin. With no charismatic leader to hold the Klan together as a national movement, it subsided, a failing business like any failing business, for the true movement needs its *duce,* its human slogan; a business expands and contracts with the fluctuations of the market. Thus the Klan contracted.

Other Americans, however, were finding themselves and going native in less nasty ways. Some little people rejected limits in discovering Coué, as it was known, a philosophy of self-help devolving on the phrase, "Day by day in every way, I am getting better and better." A much brisker program than the est and Essalen of today, this prescription of the French pharmacist, Emile Coué, caught the country with a promise of individual regeneration, available at numerous Coué institutes; others played Mah-Jongg or worked crossword puzzles. All three fads, of which only the last named has survived as a national fancy, were launched by ingenious advertising ploys, another aspect of the new America's "pep." The flotation of the first crossword-puzzle book, published by the tenderfoot firm of Simon and Shuster, based its appeal on the very appropriateness of faddism, suggesting that if 1921 had Coué, 1922, Mah-Jongg, and 1923, bananas, 1924 shall have *The Cross-Word Puzzle Book.*

(Wait a minute. Bananas? What, a food? A comedian? A gangster? None of the above: a song, still recalled today and at the time something of a national crise, "Yes! We Have No Bananas (We have no bananas today!)." Set in part to the Hallelujah Chorus from Handel's *Messiah,* the ditty was inescapable. Everywhere one went, someone else had got there first and was halfway through the third or fourth asinine stanza—"all together now!" came the cry, and the infectious flummery would commence. Eager amateurs devoted some leisure to contriving a tenth, a twentieth, a seventy-fifth chorus; the horror, for those who did not subscribe to the jollity, was like inchmeal strangulation.)

The mass media, an *idée fixe* of the sixties, arrived in the twenties—in the radios that blared "Yes! We Have No Bananas," till the cows came home, prancing; in the adolescent art of commercial promotion such as gave each new fad its send-off; in the ripening persuasions of the movies; in the army of new "specialized" magazines, not least when the house specialty was the slatternly confessions of housewives; and in the newsmen's realization that they could make as well as report the news, a by-product of the personality sell of the late twenties. The word "medium" comes from the Latin adjective for "middle," and so it is with the American media, a stewpot of middle, hogging the center of the road out of fear of the educated, the specific, the divisive, the weird. Grow together now, people, hearing the same music, playing the same games, viewing the same fantasy world on the black and white screen, reading the same scandalous chronicles of idiosyncrasy and sudden death in newsprint.

Only Ford was rich enough to be weird and get away with it, and he also had a reasonable excuse: all-inclusive ignorance. (On the witness stand at his libel suit against the *Chicago Tribune,* Ford was asked if he knew who Benedict Arnold was. "A writer, I think," he replied.) Just plain folks, who heard, read, and saw along with their neighbors, were to be convinced by a Newer Testament, the gospel according to the golden mean of antiweirdness. It has taken decades to invent The Average American, and not till television's rating system did the device earn its patent, but the process really began in the twenties, when take-it-home technology first moved on to the scene.

Not only the Tin Lizzie, the Model T—soon to be scrapped for the snazzier, not-so-Ford-as-before Model A—but virtually any commodity could materialize as a necessity rather than a luxury, provided that the right message were circulated in print and on the radio. It was not too early for advertising and public-relations men to be working up the foundations of their art, minting their outlandish jargon and warning of those hazards of everyday life, B.O., cigarette throat, tooth neglect, and party pooperism. (Tooth neglect made, in one ad, a "wistful onlooker" of a former golf champion, viewed on the sidelines, corrupt and wasted, while men with better-cared-for mouths strutted the green. Worse yet was pyorrhea, to judge from the "four out of five" remiss in their use of Forhan's gum treatment and shown wearing ghostly white masks to hide their invidious mouths.)

There were safeguards and cures, of course, the dramatic healing powers of which were built up incrementally, creating a vacuum that only Orchidew Skin Lotion, or Marmola Diet Tablets, or Beech-nut Cough Drops could fill. "Reach for a Lucky instead of a sweet," one was told in the days before it turned out that both of them were poison. Most creative of the entire field were the ads that dealt with the nonphysical snares of modern living, thus turning even the nonutilitarian into a remedy: "When you meet Cynthia, the college widow, for the first time in ten years and call her Helen ... *be nonchalant* ... light a Murad cigarette."

It was the day of the savvy hustler, birth of a salesman, and wherever consumption was conspicuous, it was obvious that the nation was, if nothing else, prospering. Martin Arrowsmith would be a doctor, and Sam Dodsworth a retired engineer making the Grand Tour abroad, but their predecessor in Sinclair Lewis's oeuvre, George Follansbee Babbitt, was a real-estate salesman, a creature who speaks, by his own admission, three languages—"American, baseball, and poker"—and thinks in terms of Talking Points, Sociability, and the Psychology of Salesmanship. Remember, this was but a fast thirty years before "the man in the gray flannel suit" and "Madison Avenue" entered the folk consciousness as agents of a sinister, Atomic Age infestation, and when Frederick Pohl and C. M. Kornbluth could project a future in their novel *The Space Merchants* in which earth is run by advertising agencies and the precepts of the diabolically hidden sell govern a society of consumers.

The twenties welcomed Sinclair Lewis's knockout arraignment of native brass in *Babbitt*, but this was also the decade that was to give us *The Man Nobody Knows*, by its author's own admission "the story of the founder of modern business" and a two-year best-seller that sincerely compared Christ and the Apostles to the go-getting, back-slapping American businessman. Naturally, it took a man of the future to comprehend the corporate Oz that awaited the entrepreneur sage enough to address the stereotype with stereotypical images, and so it was an advertising man who helped define the genius of his age. Name: Bruce Barton. Affiliation: Batten and Barton, eventually to mushroom into the first half of Madison Avenue's archducal firm, B.B.D. & O. Greatest achievement: furnished—how might an adman put it?—the Semantic Cue Terms and Image Apparel needed for good times to Self-Project as right times.

Barton wrote *The Man Nobody Knows,* subtitled "A discovery of the real Jesus," to be the ultimate expression of the Protestant work ethic's time-honored union with the Godhead. "Wist ye not that I must be about My Father's *business?*" is the book's epigraph, and the italics are not only Barton's, but those of the times, seeking incantations with which to exalt our ancient ideology: man's business is God's work. Presenting the Savior as an outgoing, magnetic organization man (what would they have done about that long hair, though?), Barton claimed that He would have been a national advertiser in the twenties—that, indeed, He was a great advertiser in his own day, if limited to the viva voce promotion of the fortuitous soapbox. "As a profession, advertising is young," Barton explained; "as a force it is as old as the world. The first four words ever uttered, 'Let there be light,' constitute its charter." In other words, a man in business is a man in grace.

This was nothing new, bizarre as it is. The authority that shaped the Massachusetts Bay Colony thought as much, likewise McGuffey and his readers, Daniel Boone, and Henry Ford. It was just that no one had ever delved into the mating habits of God and "the bitch goddess, Success" quite so frontally before. "The Executive" was chapter one, with such glosses on Scripture as "The Outdoor Man," "His Method," and "His Advertisements" following close behind, and Barton gave his spiel the witness of authenticity by working some of his parallels in as newspaper headlines:

PALSIED MAN HEALED
JESUS OF NAZARETH CLAIMS RIGHT TO FORGIVE
SINS
PROMINENT SCRIBES OBJECT
"BLASPHEMOUS," SAYS LEADING CITIZEN
"BUT ANYWAY I CAN WALK," HEALED MAN
RETORTS

So that was the vision of the admen's boardroom, eh? Mark it for a sign of things to come.

However, this is still the early twenties, for the time being, and the media, too, are in the process of finding themselves. The boom hasn't struck yet, Europe isn't making a peep (except in the New York arts scene and an occasional reference in the newspapers to Germany's imminent bankruptcy), and Harding's people are busy at their sport. Bourgeois dinner parties culminate in Mah-Jongg play-offs, and the cry of the "pung" and the "krak" is heard in the land. Crossword fiends go into their trance as they ransack memory for a four-letter word for a Polynesian idol. The fast set whoops it up with renditions of "The Bootlegger's Daughter" and "Don't Bring Lulu" ("You can bring Nan with the old dead pan but . . ."), while romancers hum "The Japanese Sandman" and "What'll I Do (When you are gone?)." And the flaming youth, checking themselves and each other for signs of It or S.A. (sex appeal—what else did they have on their minds?), find themselves, at an average of once or twice a week, and usually unchaperoned, at the movies.

Now that is a world, isn't it? up on that screen? Until the Arbuckle and Taylor scandals a free and uncensored enterprise, the film was a fixture in Middletown, each show dispensing a newsreel, a one-reel comedy or documentary *(Laying an Ocean Cable)*, and the main feature, a Western, perhaps, or a "society" film. Or even, because the new morality entices both those who are living it and those who only heard tell of it, a "sex" specialty. The posters told the public all they needed to know, as in this come-on for *Married Flirts:* "Husbands— do you flirt? Does your wife always know where you are? Are you faithful to your vows? Wives—what's your hubby doing? Do you know? Do you worry? Watch out for *Married Flirts!*"

Indeed. One Middletown movie manager blamed the failure of *Down to the Sea in Ships* on a lack of "heart interest" for the women in a film in which the hero was a whale. The ladies related more efficiently to the sheik, Rudolph Valentino—here was an absolute they could recognize at first view, an innovation of the era that acted like one, that pulled everything along with him like a wave roaring onto the strand with unexpected flotsam: I am the new. The men thought him baroque and effeminate (the men were right), but his air of minatory sexuality held the women, bleating quietly in the dark, with the ideal. "Out of the cage of everyday existence!" cried an advertisement in *The Saturday Evening Post.* "If only for an afternoon or an evening—escape!"

Alarmists assailed the movies for routing the status quo. Not only did Hollywood purvey sex, it was said, but the Cinema's impossible social idyll was too appetizing and would foster upheaval by opening the eyes of the lower orders to the delights of the higher materialism. If *The Birth of a Nation* could stimulate a racist vigilantism, what would be the effect of all those views of the luxurious life in the society films? In a special movie number of the political science review, *The Annals*, the ex-secretary of the National Board of Review, Wilton A. Barrett, rightly judged the movies as a "purveyor of ideas and symbols and secrets" that the beneficiaries of the status quo "did not intend . . . the humble servants of humanity and an exploiting civilization to know."

If films could be a fount of information to all for their very accessibility to all, they were more a stupid shambles of high living, adventure, and slapstick than any reasonable or unreasonable presentation of social contraption. If anything, the movies were a leveling device, like any mass medium, catering to Alexis de Tocqueville's "tyranny of the majority," stripped of variety and nuance in flat and fantastical glamourspeak. Anita Loos's Lorelei Lee assessed the movies' outlook better than most social critics in *But Gentlemen Marry Brunettes,* when she and her millionaire husband Henry mount "a superproduction based on sex life in the period of Dolly Madison":

But when they wrote the scenario we had quite a little trouble, because the scenario writer wanted it to be full of nothing but "Psychology." And the director wanted it to be full of mob scenes and ornamental sets. And Henry wanted it to be full of a great moral lesson. And I did not care what it was full of, so long as it was full of plenty of cute scenes where the leading man would chase me around the trunk of a tree and I would peek out at him, like Lillian Gish. So then Mr. Goldmark, the great film magnet, said, "Why not be on the safe side and have it full of everything?"

Well, what sort of influence could one expect from a place like Hollywood, "this Pollyanna greasepaint pink poodle paradise," as Hart Crane got it, a wasteland in the middle of a desert, an oasis only in hallucination? Many gave way to delirium in the dark; what did they care who made the movies—directors, producers, what? After all, it had been only a few years since the stars were identified by name at all. In the cinema's early heyday of New York auteurism, it was "Broncho Billy," or "The Vitagraph Girl," or even "The Vitagraph Dog," yclept, off-duty, Jean. Not till Florence Lawrence, "The Biograph Girl," decided that she was more likely Florence Lawrence than some Girl and left Biograph for Carl Laemmle were the stars truly stars, people with real lives—terribly real lives, neatly invented by P.R. men, so that it came as a shock, after reading in movie magazines about their tennis game, their collection of T'ang dynasty clutter, their dapper ways, to learn that they were dying of drug overdoses, rape, and anonymous gunplay. For some of them, the funeral at the end of their short lives was the only real thing that happened.

H. L. Mencken claimed, in perhaps the only understatement of his career, that Hollywood had the morals of Port Said, but Hollywood's morals prove less fetching to commentators nowadays than Hollywood's ethic, its pietistic quest of the money grail, almost exclusively in the hands, big studios and small, of Jewish businessmen. Anti-Semites had a field day raising Ned about this point of view, but the producers were only giving the public what it wanted. They couldn't actually *sell* anything that wasn't attractive to the population, now, could they?

Oh, ho, could they now! But we have here not only the P.R. men of commerce, lecturing on the depravity into which tooth neglect and dandruff must lead, but the Hollywood publicity machine, attendant upon the launching not only of each new title, but each new personality, too. Commerce met fantasy when stars were flown in from the Coast to endorse a rota of products in New York, photographed grinning for this company, that; swearing that his or her regal enigma conduced to the use of this item, that. Broadsides purportedly revealed by secret informants threw open the imperious lives of the stars, to be Biblically inscribed by the newspaper columnists or ghosted in confession articles in the magazines. It was a grand hoax, the whole of it, as much a hoax as the movies were themselves.

And, of course, it was all for "real." No one can make a hero, but the coast P.R. men could make gods—Valentino, for example. A former exhibition dancer and gigolo, then a movie extra and bit player, Valentino was thought too Latin looking to charge the ranks of the leading men, all of whom were of a clean cut of jib and a good-natured innocence. But the twenties were to prove neither wholly clean nor even vaguely innocent, and Valentino helped usher in the new times in 1919 with *The Eyes of Youth* as "Clarence Morgan, a cabaret parasite" (so the title cards introduce him) who destroys Clara Kimball Young. Two years later, Valentino truly arrived, this time openly playing a Latin in *The Four Horsemen of the Apocalypse*. On the release prints he was billed with the feature players, but his manifestation of star quality so startled the business, having so startled the public, that Metro recalled the prints and reshot the credits to emphasize the deity. *Uncharted Seas, Camille* (with Alla Nazimova), and *The Conquering Power* followed, but not till Valentino left Metro over a salary dispute did he become what he would have to be, for Paramount, his next home, knew better than Metro what to do with a Latin lover. Paramount made Valentino *The Sheik*.

Now the tango of this our mortal life is enjoined, a short tango at fever pitch, danced down the two-way street of P.R. salesmanship and public purchase. While female audiences watched and wondered at Valentino's resourceful hand-placement, his nostril quivering, and Arabian moues, Paramount signed sheikism into the almanac of fad. The word "sheik" itself caught on in collegiate circles, complemented by "sheba," interior decorators tasted of Middle Eastern savor, pop music took up the refrain in "The Sheik of Araby" and dusted off 1918's "Hindustan" . . . all with some prompting, it seems, from the Paramount public-relations office, using the press who in turn used the public who used them both to whet a thirst for lubricious amusement. Even in attacking Valentino for his cream puff presence, the *Chicago Tribune* was still playing the game.

The newspapers, however, were never as calculatingly manipulative as were the public relators. Feeding rumors to the journals which would later be gravely denied, the P.R. grandmaster, Harry Reichenbach, kept Valentino in the current, even unto concocting a stunt involving the actor's supposedly growing a beard (a false moss was fitted to his chin for public airings), until protests from his fans and a lobby of barbers could result in a gladsome public appearance as the clean-shaven Latin Lover of new. Reichenbach himself coined a term to cover his product: "phantom fame."

Of all the Hollywood phantoms, though, the most gnomic and invincible were those producers, the moguls of fleshly barter, unknown to the general public though their names were easy enough to find in the credits. Here are some names: Louis B. Mayer, Marcus Loew, Adolph Zukor, William Fox, and Harry, Albert, Sam, and Jack Warner. Now, what were they up to, besides making pots of money? Nothing. Making pots of money was what they were up to. The sum of their work is hardly the sum of American art, even admitting that the movies grew to be perhaps the most popular of the pop media, because these men aimed exclusively for the middle, leaving a definition of the shattered edges of us, the angles and niches of the real real lives, to others.

Surely Hollywood was the most potent force in the illumination of America's sexual blackout, forcing the issue by getting it out in the open, but this was an unwitting dividend. The labor might be as variegated and artistic as anything in the country, what with foreign directors (from Germany), foreign beauties (from Sweden and Hungary), and foreign writers (from Manhattan), but this was of small moment as far as the producers were concerned. With something like twenty-one thousand theaters in the United States as of 1925, and something like seven hundred films a year with which to fill them, capital, to the moguls, was all; viewpoint was whatever you ended up with.

Thus it was a simple matter in 1922 for the producers to change the "moral" character of their industry when the public reaction to the Arbuckle and Taylor murder scandals grew shrill: they simply hired the Postmaster General of the United States, Will H. Hays, to front for them at $150,000 a year as the arbiter of morality on the screen. Not only was Hays a Cabinet member of the sterling Harding Administration, he was also a Presbyterian elder in his home state, Indiana, and the head of the Republican National Committee at the time of the Chicago convention that nominated Harding, his suite providing the very first smoke-filled room—altogether, a solid choice, even if he did look like a rabbit.

Quizzed as to what sort of divertissement the self-censoring movie men would now produce, that expert on pop mores, Elinor Glyn, replied, "Whatever will bring in the most money will happen." Under Hays, movies were relatively what they had always been, save that the final frames now tended to didactic repentence, reminding one that the preceding ninety minutes of enervating sex games and commandment busting was to be frowned on. In other words, the ethic had not changed an iota; it was still, after all, money. The producers were well-advised to buy a piece of the rock-solid Harding regime, for the Democrats were in disrepute, and even when, just a bit later, that regime turned out to have been built on a gauze foundation, when Teapot Dome and Elk Hills stank of an oil leak so broad of flow that even a resigned Postmaster General such as Hays was seen to blush in high places, Hollywood had already secured its public sanction.

Besides, there was never any question of doing without the movies in the manner of Prohibition. For all the sociological fretting of experts and prudes, jes' folks were crazy about the cinema; this much of progress went down like home brew. But the movies got very regular very fast, for they had little distinction and needed to please too many people to retain any mystery. Of greater fascination were the movies of life, such as the stupendous Hall-Mills murder case of 1922: a minister and his choir leader, the sexton's wife, found side by side, shot to death, on a deserted farm near New Brunswick, New Jersey.

There's one advantage that real life has over the cinema—it's real, and subject to no Hays office on the question of moral ethic. Reverend Hall was real, Mrs. Mills was real, the position of the bodies, close for touch even in death, was very real, and realest of all was suspicion, which lit on the reverend's widow and her two brothers. As it happened, though, the murder occurred too early in the decade for technology to be able to convey the media dramatization on a national level; anyway, a grand jury failed to bring in an indictment. Remember, this is the era that arrives, that invents itself gradually. Date it from Edison, or Ford, or earlier, or the shake-up that followed the war; connect it to the rampant corruption made necessary by national prohibition, or to isolationism, or to the growth of the city—wherever it starts, it transforms over a period of time, and only after the transformation does the period stand forth in relief as such. The Hall-Mills show had to wait till journalism could accommodate the spectacle—when, to be precise, a tabloid on the prowl for copy in 1926 had the case reopened and played for its every nth of sensation and riddle tease. The press turned every crank of the salesmanship machine for the late reverend and his dark lady of the hymns then. In New York, the *Evening Graphic* ran a contest for the best amateur detection of the culprit, Western Union set up the largest telegraph switchboard in the world to service the newsmen, and although the trial drew nothing like the class of celebrity reporters who attended the shortly succeeding Snyder-Gray case (when the historian Will Durant sat table to table with the revivalist Savonarola, Billy Sunday), this Hall-Mills show did profit from a touch of true-life fantasy few movies will ever contain in the person of the star witness for the state, the unearthly "pig woman," Jane Gibson, littered into court on what one was assured was her deathbed to give testimony on the whole truth and nothing but as to what exactly transpired and who transpired it to whom on the night the murders took place. "Like something brought in from the graveyard" was the *New York World*'s description of her; actually, she was more like something brought in from central casting: "get me a Tugboat Annie type, grizzled and rank, with a heavy regional patois and no credibility whatsoever."

Certainly the jury didn't believe her, and the defendants were acquitted, but not without a telling tour de force from this pig woman. She received mixed reviews from the press, some of whom commended her for her public spirit and others of whom damned her impudence. Still, they had themselves been drawn to the trial; they were one with the mob, or why were they at such length to docket her performance? Her entrance, like that of any Bankhead or Fontanne, caught them at once—jury, onlooker, reporter, the readership, everyone. "All were standing, craning," wrote Dudley Nichols in the *World*. "There simply was something clammy about the whole thing, something begotten of nerves and the smell of iodoform and formaldehyde and excitement long pent and murder and impending death." After three hours of recalling that night, four years before . . . how did she put it?—"the moon was shinin' bright and pretty" . . . she leaned up on her stretcher, confronted the three defendants with the exactness of the sedulous romancer, and cried, "I've told the truth, so help me God. And you know it! And you know it!"

That's what movies were for, even if it wasn't a movie and three people were on trial for their lives, one of them the widow of the adulterous reverend. This was 1926, a little ahead of us yet, into the high twenties, but one can see why the carnival was coming: everything was getting bigger. When each new version of anything has to be not merely better-fangled but of maximum selling power, honesty trickles out like the last drops of blood in an embalmed body and rigor hypis sets in, the metal of hype, the steel gut of overspeak: good, better, most fabulous hype. The buck passes endlessly, but the passing starts here in the postwar years, and it was then, mainly, when advertising and the P.R. language found themselves. They got rhythm.

So may you all. This is the end of that stasis of the old America of nostalgic appeal to many who lived through the transformation and had to, somehow, grinding their teeth and inching into second gear, adjust. The adjustment was twofold: one, that of business to the new markets, and two, that of the people to the new business. It is in such times that one most craves an emblematic patron, an *übermensch* of the solid citizenry, one thing to all men, and that thing is hero. Prismatic, catching the national light to reflect it in the rainbow of national initiative, he defines us, assures us in his nonpartisan applicability that the heroic performance is still possible, that the masterstroke still can be played.

Here, in the early twenties, there is no hero. In Warren Harding we have, effectually, no leader—we knew that when we voted him into the White House. But he was elected in 1920, after that wretched 1919, and we were too wracked by palpable upheaval to want a hero then; we wanted a controller, a backstepper—Normalcy City, not Oz. Not heroics but healing, Harding had said, and sure enough, World War I was the first time we had come out of a war without a national war hero. Perhaps General Wood might have made it had he not incurred Wilson's vengeance for his allegiance to the Preparedness-hungry Teddy Roosevelt; Wood's job went to John "Black Jack" Pershing, who, for all his abilities and his much-mooted refusal to cede American forces to French command, lacked that collective address that the much less crucial but so debonair fighter pilot aces commanded—Captain Edward Rickenbacker, for example. It was a hateful war, and when it was over, nobody—not even Pershing, who was generally supposed by Americans to have won it— looked good.

We free men will have our heroes, especially when the healing of the Harding regime showed itself based more on seeming than on substance. We made passes at worship every so often—Calvin Coolidge, when he "put down" the Boston police strike; and on another end of things social, Nicola Sacco and Bartolomeo Vanzetti, the flagship of the liberal flotilla of causes for much of the decade; and William Harrison "Jack" Dempsey, the heavyweight boxing champion of the world, tarred a bit by the charge of draft-dodging, exculpated in 1920, back on top in 1921, when he knocked out Georges Carpentier in four rounds in Jersey City and then crashing into minor legend in his bout with the Argentinian Luis Firpo at New York's Polo Grounds in 1923, when Dempsey decked Firpo seven times and got blasted out of the ring himself in the first round alone, charging back in at the second bell for victory in what is still remembered as the greatest few moments in the history of prizefighting; and George Herman Ruth, the Babe of the Yankees, fawned over and followed in a time when baseball really was the national pastime and the suspension of a thousand-dollars-a-week outfielder (in 1925, and not Babe's first such penalty, either) caused American manhood to feel something akin to jilted.

But none of them appealed to us as a whole. No state governor, no anarchist, no athlete appeals across the board, as a true legend must. So think of the sky, where the heroes dwell; think of the land mantling westward, hovering north on the lakes, smoldering to the south, fulminating with discovery in the east. Think of it all, a mass of arenas and stimuli: *someone* has to be out there, of a universal likability and the power to unite in some binding American miracle to be shared by all. How will he come, the avatar? From the land up into the sky and down to the people again, of them and yet not quite with them. He ought to come on a giant bird, trained for myth, but a new model bird for a new age, a great technological bird.

Think of the plane.

THREE

Seeing Things from the Underside

> back to the city archy
> and dam glad of it
> there s something about the suburbs
> that gets on a town lady s nerves
> fat slick tabbies
> sitting around those country clubs
> and lapping up the cream
> of existence
> none of that for me

That's Mehitabel speaking, Mehitabel the blasé, blowsy cat of Archy's acquaintance, Archy being a literary cockroach who speculated in free verse, a Spoon Riverite of the city rather than the village—not without, however, a pathos reminiscent of Edgar Lee Masters's Illinois folk. Ah, we're all human. Too weak to depress the shift bar on a typewriter in the office of the *New York Sun*, Archy did without capitals and apostrophes, and his distinctive reflections on life and its livers debuted in 1916 in Don Marquis's column, "The Sun Dial," one year after the *Spoon River Anthology*. (Ever after, typesetters have preserved "archy s" lower case, though Marquis made it clear that this was exclusively the cockroach's exigency, no one else's.)

Archy exhausted himself nightly typing out his vers libre ruminations, one key at a time and headfirst, so to speak, leaving the results for Marquis to find each morning. These whimsical vignettes of the animal nation, like a proper fable, rang life-true amidst the *Sun*'s other, less colorful columns, which were merely life, nothing special. What assortment of humans ever had the range of Marquis's tatterdemalion varmints of the urban whirlpool, such as Warty Bliggens, the toad who could prove dialectically that the universe was created to be the exclusive retreat of Warty Bliggens? Or Clarence the ghost, who hated the spiritualists who gave him no rest ("but wait . . . till the fat medium with the red nose that has my number passes over . . . there s going to be some initiation beside the styx")? Or the ancient roach who grew maudlin in a speakeasy and bored Archy by rehearsing his family tree, including a maternal grandmother "slain by john masefield with a bung starter"? Or the tomcat of theatrical background who took up, briefly, with Mehitabel and who not only played the owl in Modjeska's production of *Macbeth,* but once went on in *Uncle Tom's Cabin* for an indisposed bloodhound? With their coterie of bohemians, wastrels, and petty thieves, Archy and Mehitabel rattled on into and through the twenties, surviving a Depression, another war, another Red peril, and even now are still in print and no less acute on the intricacies of . . . uh, animal behavior.

> give me the alley archy
> me for the mews and the roofs
> of the city
> an occasional fish head
> and liberty is all i ask
> freedom and the garbage can
> romance archy romance is the word

That's Mehitabel crowing, mehitabel of the "toujours gai," one of the many characteristic voices of the times that, while not being anything like unsettling, certainly had no intention of settling down.

The direction, to the many who arrived in cities, green as the
cornhusk, was up, and the city was their escalator. More people lived
in cities than didn't as of the 1920 census, and still more were on
their way. And surely that's mehitabel confabulating there, reconciling
what she was to what she would be, mehitabel the tough, the bitten
and biting, the everlasting . . . the city cat, a new myth.

> maybe i do starve sometimes
> but wotthehell archy wotthehell
> i live my own life

Oh, that's mehitabel all right, *un peu* raunchy as well as *gaie* but
very game, all bohemia in fur. They gathered in the cities, the
mehitabels, and even a few archys—tender bugs, not really equipped
for the tough town—for this was the decade of the cities. We collate
the times with the mores of restlessness and banter, buying time with
a mot, for history, in this age, was made in town—in New York, the
cradle of the "highbrow," where the Democrats met in 1924 for the
most disastrous political convention in modern times (103 ballots to
pick a sure loser), and in Cleveland, where the Republicans met for a
businessman's Eucharist, swift and serene, nominating Coolidge in
one roll call. The cities, and not just those of the Northeast, dictated
the context of contemporaneousness, as with symbolic Chicago, the
former "mud hole of the prairies," now the "hog butcher of the
world" and a mudhole all over again, slick with gangsters, bought
Feds, and the rotten regime of Mayor "Big Bill" Thompson. Chicago,
particularly to Europeans, represented American life in its essence,
but Americans could point proudly to the better influence of Boston,
that flinty Athens of lawyers, sailors, and bluestockings, even if our
Puritan fountainhead was already into its eclipse and suffered a bad
press during the big police strike of 1919 and the execution of Sacco
and Vanzetti in 1927.

Some people preferred the smaller cities, such as Baltimore,
headquarters of H. L. Mencken and somewhat flattered by his
affection for it (Baltimore was London to Mencken), and there were
the new cities, too: Los Angeles, the last city (though founded as far

back as 1781), a barbaric, balsa bijou plunked down in the middle of cow country, beckoning to the East as the West had done for over a century (and as the West still does); and Miami, the next city, the southern tip of a land boom that floated high on bonds, mortgages, and P.R. presentations until the whole damn thing defaulted in 1926.

News is made everywhere, knowing no topographical priority, but we remember the metropolises now more than the Middletowns as being the timeplaces of the twenties, for they were so thought by the Dick Whittingtons of the Middletowns. From the Midwest especially, but from all over, they gathered in the cities to be earnest and to compromise the vulgarity of life with the consolations of art—to flee, in Edmund Wilson's words, "the shame of not making money." They came, leaving rural sprawl to the ministrations of Ford customers, the Ku Klux Klan, and the readers of Elinor Glyn. Small-town, corn-fed highbrows devoured Frank Norris and Maurice Maeterlinck, gorged on atheism and *Jugendstil*, dreamed of writing or painting themselves, up and went. Some, such as Floyd Dell, would pen novels on their coming of age in the sticks, while others would proscribe their pastoral origins and sing only the city, as Carl Van Vechten did in a pride of precious novels, rounding the set off in 1930 with his personal definition of the twenties experience: *Parties.*

From Gopher Prairie or Cabbageville these would-be bohemians would move first to Chicago, and from Chicago, which was quite a place before the twenties but still not Paris, to New York, which was Paris; a few, such as Ernest Hemingway and Sherwood Anderson, actually removed to Paris. Even the nonhighbrows fled east, as did the principals of F. Scott Fitzgerald's *The Great Gatsby*—wealthy Tom and Daisy Buchanan and Jordan Baker, not-so-wealthy Nick Carraway, and the American Dreamer, Jay Gatsby—as indeed, did Fitzgerald himself, too grand for St. Paul and, so it developed, too grand for life.

What had happened in New York that made it so magnetic for the nation's highbrows was a movement directly opposed to the isolationism of the postwar years, dating back to the early 1910s and the influx into Manhattan of the very latest in European artistic experiments. Greeting the avant-garde the way the first men must have greeted the first spring, Americans rushed to judgment when Gertrude Hoffman and her dance corps modeled on Dyagilef's Ballet Russe called in 1911, and in America's judgment, it was good. The Ballet Russe technique aimed at primitivism, presaging modern dance with simplistic design and "natural" plastique, thus reversing the *fin de siecle* tradition of making art as arty as possible. A year later, Max Reinhardt's Deutsches Theater decanted its erotic pantomime *Sumurun* in town, a "whole idea" of conceptual production, with drama, stage lighting and decoration, and music all synchronized for partnership, and then came the famous Armory Show of 1913, the International Exhibition of Modern Art, a feast of cubism and the like as developed by Rouault, Picasso, Brancusi, and Marcel Duchamp, the infamous lewd who descended a staircase of life and art, thoroughly routing the bourgeoisie.

Artistic unity, the clear statement of the tableau, with all the parts coagulated into total form, was the message, and the former citizens of this little farmopolis and that little gotham of a crossroads were quick to read it, though a few sobersides demanded that the Armory Show be closed as obscene and immoral. But bohemia thrives on rejection. The newly arrived artists of New York were incited by Europe to reinvent their lives; continental truth gave them energy and a vague but strenuously intuitive goal. They had thought, in coming east, that they were just moving to a bigger and better place. No: they had come home.

The city has its natives, but it is a hub of educational incongruities, with a different continuity than that of the land. Out on the steppes, except for the helpless dislocation of migrant workers in hard times, the folk stays put. The city, however, thrives not on permanence but on regeneration, and for that the confluence of visitors, the coming and going, is required. The city is there, ultimately, to receive newcomers, and to contain the idols they raise to themselves and to their confrontations, with each other, with strangers, with the account books, with art. Intruders sustain the city.

Imagine how they felt marching in—not the arty foreigners, who just came here to perform and go home, but the Americans, who came to live. Instinctively, they found each other—did they notice that virtually no one who wrote for the fledgling *New Yorker* actually came from New York?—and lived where people such as they would live. Life in Urbantown is short-winded, a scrimmage of contacts: where quarter elbows quarter, citizens regale citizens and thinking collides. For all his predilection for neighborhood, for serrying himself within the clan ranks, for joining up with his like for defense and celebration, man will have to cross the marketplace at some point of every day, and there he hears the news. No such visit is possible in a small town, where the general store or the courthouse steps serve to intensify the unanimity of the region; in the city diversity rules, and it is one of the era's paradoxes that the media laid the cornerstones of their empires in the most diversified and antimedium city in the hemisphere, New York. No matter where movies were shot, where reporters sought the scoop, or where radio stations were licensed, the organization that owned them looked out of its windows over a dirty, teeming sea of people who resisted amalgamation the way the South had once resisted the dissolution of its economy by the North—and in exactly that way, for, just as the South lost its battle, amalgamation is in the offing. Just give us time.

Said Friedrich Nietzsche, "architecture is a sort of oratory of power by means of forms"; immigrants gazing at Manhattan as their boats docked at Ellis Island must have sensed this in the upsoaring obelisks and stupas of the Wall Street forum. But New York's highbrows, some of them, sensed it most keenly, as an expression of upreaching American technology—no! as a statement of America itself, expressed in the language of technology, a *Gesamtkunstwerk* of life. John Dos Passos' novel, *Manhattan Transfer*, in 1925, borrowed the city's concurrence of strangers to weave a book of the living, restless and flustered, in chapters entitled "Rollercoaster," "Revolving Doors," or "The Burthen of Nineveh." He abstracted the disorientation of city life, its loss of man-to-man contact, in the tempos, colors, and smells of characterful anonymity. The city was the new, and so was Dos Passos, but he, at least, could mourn the old:

The leaden twilight weighs on the dry limbs of an old man walking towards Broadway ... Broken doll in the ranks of

varnished articulate dolls he plods up with dropping head into
the seethe and throb into the furnace of beaded lettercut light.
"I remember when it was all meadows," he grumbles to the
little boy.

To Sinclair Lewis, America was the middle-class boobois businessman, to Sherwood Anderson the poor white of the undecorated, dim
little towns, to Ernest Hemingway and Edna Ferber the adventurer,
and to F. Scott Fitzgerald the collegiate of means and manners. To
some others, he was the city itself, the skyscrapers and the work
whistles and the subway and the syncopated dance rhythms, the
objects hurtling down streets, running, stunned, or shambling, the
lights blinking messages, above and around; no awe, it just happens.
   It stank of whiskey, but it sure looked like the goods, New York:
someone must have planned it. Suddenly, everyone grew conscious of
"design"—industrial design was another diversion of the era, a major
industry subclassed within industries—and New York and Chicago,
not tall enough yet, threw up more and better Babels. The Chicago
Tribune Tower, hardly mentioned anymore even by architects, had
been the landmark of its day, and now here was the Chrysler
Building, which babbled in fluent Art Deco and could shoot steam
into the air from its tower to embellish the spire with hovering clouds.
   With regular vibrations from Europe conveying new aesthetics, one
began to feel that the arts connected not so much to life as to each
other—yet life itself, suddenly, was natural art. Who but an artist
could understand the self-expression latent in the barren utility of the
subway, of the carved slabs called office buildings, of the streets hung
with office buildings, undercut by a subway, and crawling with
humankind? "On and on below the toothpaste and the dandruff ads,"
wrote Hart Crane in "The Tunnel," and, aboveground, the composer
John Alden Carpenter collaborated with the designer Robert Edmond
Jones in 1926 on Skyscrapers, a "ballet of modern American life"—
pistons and blue notes, the fox-trot and the welder, all one.
Carpenter's music exhibited the same zealotry for the "popular"
sound that George Gershwin caught in his twenties opuses, the
Rhapsody in Blue, the Concerto in F, and An American in Paris, but

Carpenter swaggered and sentimentalized less than Gershwin, courting the brutal ego under the ebullience of modern life (just as Aaron Copland would later on in the decade). A man who had composed the score for a ballet based on George Herriman's *Krazy Kat* comic strip, complete with the brick-throwing mouse, Ignatz, as Carpenter did in 1922, had sensed too surely the anxiety of the era to hymn the fleet amours of Gershwin's expatriate Paris or to rhapsodize in blue. As sentinels for his passage, Carpenter elevated the raucousness, the pushy burgeoning, the beehive machinery of the consuming god Urbantown and his bohemian prophets of the technocratic age.

Yet even so, Carpenter was no enfant terrible. He could only go so far; it took the pitiless avant-garde to spit the city onto the stage in Confucian bluntness, and one year after *Skyscrapers,* George Antheil's *Ballet Mécanique* squatted, leaped, and thundered from the stage of Carnegie Hall. A concert piece, all *mécanique* and no ballet, Antheil's score took eleven pianos, an ominously large percussion battery, pulleys, thingamajigs, two amplifiers, and a wind machine to perform and had vastly emptied the auditorium by the time it ended, practically blown it empty. In Paris two years before, *Ballet Mécanique* had provoked fistfights and boos from the public, but the composer Erik Satie, a visionary of the neoteric, put his finger on it. "What precision!" he is reported to have said from his box, though it is hard to imagine how anyone could have heard him above the uproar. "What precision!"

That was the ticket: precision. That was the exactness of American urban life, the pointillism of the city anthill—and that was why there was no dancing in this *Ballet Mécanique:* the mechanisms themselves provided the dance as they cogged and clocked. So, behold the machine, precision, was art. Here was raw power to harness, to externalize in music, drama, and literature even as the media internalized it in appliance. While the far-flung people of the farmland and village fought back against transformation, the highbrows of New York, communications city, fought right back in its pursuit. It was civil war, if a cold one. In the theater and literature, in painting, sculpture, and architecture, in music, the trend was to relate to modern dynamics by rethinking the inherited forms. Freud's visit to

America in 1909 and the publication here of his writings gave the creative highbrows a new rhetoric to teach their audiences, especially in the theater, where smother love, infantile regression, and split personality were taking stage in plays cast of both novel and traditional molds.

Expressionism, for the new breed, gave Elmer Rice the vehicle on which to hunt down the technology of business in his play *The Adding Machine,* a surrealistic collage of Freudian trauma and wish fulfillment centered around a hapless nonentity of a bookkeeper, Mr. Zero, beaten down by his shrewish wife and replaced by the more efficient computer. Both Rice's script and the original Theatre Guild production in 1923 were heavily influenced by European experiments, especially in Mr. Zero's murder of his boss when he gets his notice, played in ghoulish flashes of blood-colored light as the stage began to revolve faster and faster, and in the succeeding trial scene, a monologue by Mr. Zero in free association that the court chooses to ignore. Nowadays we take theatrical arraignments of the Way Things Are for granted; then it was news. Broadway gaped at expressionism, at decor and lighting that helped tell the story, but the highbrows pronounced it a good thing. They knew unity when they saw it.

An artist is no more likely to greet a technological take-over than is a barefoot country boy (although the farmer must welcome the machine that helps him hoe that hard road), and among the various revolts of the intellectuals, a pronounced antipathy to mechanization was felt everywhere there were intellectuals to count. If one hears in Carpenter's *Skyscrapers* the vitality of the townsman, much of it does turn on a coarse asymmetry, even an ugliness, that complements the prizefight studies by George Bellows and the city paintings of John Sloan, Thomas Hart Benton, and William J. Glackens, pictures of rush hours and els and intrusive neon, often in an inappropriate calm that by its very strangeness reminds one of how overcrowded this new world would get.

More of the "ugliness" of life came spilling onto the stage in the many dramas inspired by a hasty reading of Freud. Now, *there* was a scientist the laissez-faire highbrows could accept, particularly because they tended to deemphasize or even to discount altogether the dark side of psychotherapy, rating it glibly as a profound "life-art" of self-expression. The enticing prospect of the unconscious mind, especially, attracted the playwrights, for it adapted wonderfully to the free-associative speeches that garnished the decade's theater like alter egos in Bedlam. Eugene O'Neill based his most prolific period almost exclusively on the implications of Freudian dramaturgy, devising a new mode out of the bizarre interior monologues that made his *Strange Interlude* a sensation of 1928, and Sidney Howard dubbed his *Bewitched* in 1924 a "Freudian fairy tale," giving Florence Eldridge some six or seven roles to play as The Girl. In one scene she appeared as the protagonist's mother, in another she was the Goddess of Love, in yet another a sinister sorcerer's granddaughter—the ur-woman portrayed in her several blond- and dark-lady guises.

Because most of Broadway's theatergoers proved bashful about Freudian truth, whether as tragic flaw or wisecrack, much of the new wave fled to the sociopolitically responsive purlieus of Greenwich Village in the so-called Little Theatre movement, a potent catalyst of highbrow theater not only in New York but in outposts all over the country as well—and not only in the larger cities. The Village had established itself as the nation's left bank even before the war, as the haven of *The Little Review* and *The Dial,* magazines of elitist literature—the first eventually deported to Paris for its attempted serialization of *Ulysses*—of Mabel Dodge's famous Evenings, of rebellious painters, writers, and thinkers who rejoiced in a little region all their own where West Fourth Street crossed West Twelfth. Edna St. Vincent Millay lived there, and Theodore Dreiser, but so did Willa Cather; their paths must have crossed as quaintly as did the streets.

Many of the small-town refugees docked in the Village and promptly set themselves to humming along with the isms of the highbrow circuit, for the Village was the *terra cognita* of the highbrow's *tabula rasa,* a place of familiars in which to start over again and know thyself. It was Gilead and the Casbah. It was the eye of the needle and everything was passing through—aesthetes, dadaists, nudists, freethinkers, revolutionaries, camels . . . everything but rich men. It was Dissent City. To the rest of America it was a joke of a place where nothing meant to last lasted more than a week or two, and the Village folk agreed, for nothing *was* meant to last: all was now to change. Even the little magazines that served to introduce the next literary generation celebrated their choice transience, as *1924*, or *This Quarter* (as if there'd never be another issue), or *transition*.

It was at the theater that the Village made its tenets most palpably felt, for the stage was America's most patronized popular art, and therefore the most likely beachhead for an artistic landing. Everyone wrote plays, everyone acted, everyone sewed costumes and passed out programs; whole companies would band together, extempore, at a party, plan a season deep into the night, collapse the next day, and regroup elsewhere by nightfall. Such pioneers in the new theater as O'Neill, Kenneth Macgowan, Robert Edmond Jones, and the fledgling Theatre Guild, then known as the Washington Square Players, introduced themselves south of Fourteenth Street where the air was racy and the gentry defiantly open to plastic disquisitions on technique. Bare stages draped in *je-ne-sais-quoi* were welcomed, as were shadowy silences, unexpected gurglings of music, and vicious, family-devouring mothers.

Europe played Nestor through it all, whether in the form of Pablo Picasso, Max Reinhardt, Sigmund Freud, or Eleonora Duse. When Stanislafsky's Moscow Art Theatre toured the country in 1923, Village thespians rushed north to Broadway, saw everything six times, and never forgot, but rather than mount local derivations of Chekhof, the bohemians of New York turned to American subject matter and style while keeping one eye on the ensemble finish of the Russian team. At the Provincetown Playhouse, a converted stable still standing today at 133 MacDougal Street—still a working theater, truth to tell— O'Neill bowed in town with his one-act plays of the sea, then inaugurated the decade with *The Emperor Jones,* newest of the new, in which grisly jungle drums accompanied the dissolution of a resilient, adventurous black into a slobbering, terrified bush nigger, an atavistic exorcism in reverse. Out in Middletown, it was certain death socially to be thought highbrow; in New York, nothing else would do. But if the highbrows took themselves seriously in creation, they lived for jibe and joke. Once, when trapped in stalled traffic in an open carriage with Alexander Woollcott, Dorothy Parker rose to her feet and, blowing kisses to the pedestrians hustling around them, cried, "I promise to return one day and sing Carmen again for you!"

Even the impromptu city has its organized reactionaries, and though no Ku Klux Klan ever attempted to bottle up the bubbly in the new waves, the equally vigilant if more law-oriented watch and warders were kept busy trying to blitz a host of "offensive" drama from O'Neill to Mae West, not to mention James Branch Cabell's novel *Jurgen*, a coy, chivalric fantasy set in Cabell's private Oz, Poictesme. *Jurgen's* phallic metaphors set off John S. Sumner, Anthony Comstock's successor as chief of New York State's Society for the Suppression of Vice, and at his behest the book was banned, though not for long. What with all the fuss, the public appetite had been whetted for this *Jurgen*, whatever it was; Sumner had created a need as deftly as an adman hawking wares. Cleared by the courts in two years, *Jurgen* hit the bookstalls again with, naturally, even bigger sales than in its first issue, but the prurient had to wade through Cabell's flirtatious euphuism to get to the juicy bits, and Mencken's prediction that *Jurgen* would "long outlast its day" proved to be one of the Sage of Baltimore's less applicable sententiae.

So, in the cities as well as elsewhere, there were Babbitts opposing the highbrows, even if they could make little headway in New York (where the local Prohibition enforcement laws were dismantled in disgust by the state legislature as early as 1923). The Babbitts would have been better advised, though helpless, to oppose Henry Ford, for Ford represented change in an epical way that a Eugene O'Neill or a John Dos Passos could comprehend but never abet in their uncozy corners of the art world. This modern America, symbolized by New York, looked as if it were going to blow our constitutional continuity off its pins, to forge ahead too hastily to keep our traditions intact—such traditions, that is, as had survived the collectivism of the federal war on the Southern states in 1861. A rootless America—this was the nightmare, a correct nightmare: ultimately, it came true. Federal centralism was to turn despotic in the thirties, and media tyranny, less open if spectacularly tentacled, would be sovereign by the late fifties. But in the twenties, the revolution was being run by industry, not by art. Art, after all, is not an American priority, but business is, and business, a code word for God from Harding to Hoover, fired the crucible. Ford, the most apparent businessman of the technological turnover, is the man to shake one's fist at—or worship—not O'Neill with his paranoiac interior monologues and his audiences of, at most, a mere ten thousand a week per play. Ford, however, was Merlin, and Ford rode Pegasus, and Ford held the Promethean fire.

Ford was a Babbitt, wasn't he?—born and died in the unmetropolitan area of Dearborn, Michigan; not much educated and self-made, *very* much made, the utter pattern of upward mobility; a man of by no means conventional but at least not disreputable attitudes, except perhaps for his arrant peace pleadings during Preparedness. A fool, we say now—yet his endorsement of the Republican candidate in 1924 was considered a crucial boon by party satraps.

The mythology of the Babbitt is so very clear—his origins, his initiations, his quest. He was parochial, Midwestern, an apostle of the men's lodge, the automobile, and the status quo, and his goal was a familial-social-financial success. The highbrow cosmology is less easy to pin down; even such learned professors in the college of transformation as H. L. Mencken and Sinclair Lewis were hardly the bohemian highbrow enshrined in the twenties. Mencken was as regular in his habits as any farmer, and the heedlessly loudmouthed Lewis was frequently known to behave like something out of a Sinclair Lewis novel.

All these highbrows, near highbrows, and Babbitty highbrows had one thing in common with each other that set them apart from the rest of the nation: they made the dark voyage, the true quest for something not yet invented or known about—and they made it alone, while the Babbitt only acted from within a mob. One way or another, however, the passage had to be made. Even Warren Harding, the President of Normalcy, encouraged the crescending newness, in addressing the lame-duck session of the Sixty-Seventh Congress in 1922: "There will never again be precisely the old order. Indeed, I know of no one who thinks it to be desirable. For out of the old order came the war itself."

Harding wasn't anything like a Progressive, but he did surprise the pundits by recommending that the United States join the World Court and by making overtures to such minority interests as organized labor, blacks, and even the radical left. He wheedled the steel industry into setting an example by reducing the working day from twelve hours to eight, asked Congress for a law abolishing child labor (to replace one struck down in 1922), spoke out harshly against the inequality of Southern blacks to a segregated audience of shocked whites and startled blacks in Birmingham, Alabama, and, when he pardoned Eugene Debs, invited him up to the White House for a talk. "Mr. Harding appears to me to be a kind gentleman," Debs told the press after their meeting. "We understand each other perfectly."

Ha! No highbrow would have said such a thing. Harding understand the demimonde and its covenant with the future? Harding, the Babbitt president? Maybe a kind and generous Socialist like Debs could unbend so—who knew what hieratic potpourri boiled in *his* head?—but the bohemians of this glittering era were of brittle stock, and they found bending difficult. It was an inbred, a nearly incestuous, community, regaling itself with japes about how everything outside of New York was Bridgeport and then bounding away to dinner with Woollcott or the Lunts or Noel Coward and then off to the theater, opening night, and right after to Fifty-second Street to one of the forty-odd speakeasies clustered between Fifth Avenue and Broadway, and of course there were those luncheons at the Algonquin. What a crowd!—Dorothy Parker, Robert Benchley, George S. Kaufman, Harold Ross, Alice Duer Miller, Marc Connelly, Heywood Broun, Neysa McMein, Robert E. Sherwood, and Edna Ferber, when she wasn't feuding with Woollcott. They knew each other so well they must have felt as if the men had all married their sisters. Later on, the whole crowd, more or less, was associated with Ross's wee babe *The New Yorker,* but that wasn't until 1925, when the twenties were shifting into high gear.

Anyway, that lot wasn't all of literary New York, with their newspaper columns and their short stories and their fastidious one-liners. Some bohemians weren't even bohemians, such as Willa Cather and Edith Wharton, and an awful lot of straights neither bohemian nor Babbitt thrilled to the expressionistic malevolence of the German film, *The Cabinet of Dr. Caligari*, in its showing here in 1921, and to the hollow reverberation of T. S. Eliot's *The Waste Land* a year later. Getting the gist of the times from the art of the times, even in so limited a locale as New York, is a touchy business. Who *are* the artists, and what are they up to? Do they aim to comment on their times, merely express their times in instinctual unreason, or did they just happen to be there, chatting, at the time?

Cather, Wharton, and their *commère*, Ellen Glasgow, had been there before the time, in fact, whereas it is the younger confraternity such as Fitzgerald, Lewis, Dos Passos, and Hemingway, all of whom started in the twenties, that most resonantly recall those days for us. Fitzgerald with his debs and beaus and young marrieds, his rich boys and flattering runoffs of Zelda, Lewis with his small towns, Dos Passos with his city, and Hemingway with his desperate émigrés hyperventilating in Europe—this, we believe, was the "lost generation." Gertrude Stein coined the phrase in a conversation with Hemingway, translating it from something her garageman had told her. Just like that, she said it: "Ernest, you are all a lost generation." And Hemingway replied, "Really?"

It sounded right at the time, considering how depressingly empty the rooms always looked when the decorations were pulled down, but since then baleful eyes have been turned on that . . . that silly excuse for raucous behavior and melancholia. Malcolm Cowley likened it to "telling what a hangover one had at a party to which someone else wasn't invited," and Dorothy Parker later ridiculed it, as she tended later to ridicule everything she had known, written, or been. "Gertrude Stein did us the most harm [with that term]," she reported in the *Paris Review*. "That got around to certain people and we all said, 'Whee! We're lost.' Perhaps it suddenly brought to us the sense of change. Or irresponsibility. But don't forget that, though the people in the twenties seemed like flops, they weren't. Fitzgerald, the rest of them, reckless as they were, drinkers as they were, they worked damn hard and all the time."

Still, Stein had a point. She was an original, a charmer, and a positive influence on Hemingway, Sherwood Anderson, and many writers who read her in the decades that followed. Living in Paris as she did, at the famous atelier at 27 Rue de Fleurus, she remained unknown to the stay-at-homes in New York, but Hemingway carried her words around with him to quote to others, for they were distinctive words and begged to be spoken. Most people write better than they talk; Stein wrote as she would have talked had she been a cubist Marx Brother with a degree in psychology, which is exactly what she was. Write, she would tell the writers, about the here and now, "the thing seen by everyone living in the living they are doing."

Not everyone did. John Erskine wrote one best-seller after another about no one living—*Adam and Eve, The Private Life of Helen of Troy, Penelope's Man, Galahad: Enough of His Life to Explain His Reputation*—and though Edna Ferber's career took off with stories about Emma McChesney, a traveling saleswoman—very here and now—soon she was dealing in romance and historical adventure, in *So Big*, with its affair between a bond salesman and a painter, and in *Show Boat* and *Cimarron*. "Fantasy," sniffed the highbrows, who preferred the realistic war novels, such as Dos Passos' *Three Soldiers* or e. e. cummings' *The Enormous Room*, expressing the disillusionment that the war had brought to town and country. Later in the decade came the most brutal of them all, Erich Maria Remarque's *Im Westen Nichts Neues* (No News from the West), translated here as *All Quiet on the Western Front*, and generally referred to as *All Quiet*, all the rage for what it told that folks were willing to believe. So that's what it was like after all in the trenches? Remarque didn't so much amaze his readers as express graphically what their husbands, sons, and sweethearts had already told them—or what they had seen themselves. *All Quiet*'s relevance, for a time, elbowed Zane Grey out of the picture in places where Zane Grey was read, and though a film version of Remarque's novel did not appear until 1930, even then its strongly antiwar sympathies (not to mention the celebrated final shots of the hero's death, the accusing looks of his comrades, and the fade-out in total silence) made it far more successful than its jingoistic coevals, *Hell's Angels* and *The Dawn Patrol*. Not only the highbrows, but the lowbrows, too, could make telling tales of their art.

Willa Cather's war novel, *One of Ours*, won the Pulitzer Prize in

1923, but it was a strangely virginal army and spruce battlefield that Cather pictured. Her suggestion that the protagonist's death, with his boots on, saves him from a retrograde existence back home in a ruined, modern world was taking the romantic viewpoint to the far side of Sir Walter Scott. Moreover, Cather's distaste for this ruined modernity took the form of a rather preposterous slam at the household goods and machinery that supposedly swindled the country idyll of its purity: "The farmer raised and took to market things with an intrinsic value . . . in return he got manufactured articles of poor quality; showy furniture that went to pieces . . . clothes that made a handsome man look like a clown. Most of his money was paid out for machinery—and that, too, went to pieces . . . a horse outlived three automobiles."

As many critics pointed out, Cather had got that backward. The machine coolly replaced *The Adding Machine*'s poor Mr. Zero, yes, but it went far in easing the burdens of agrarian life. As for technology's peddled shoddy, it simply wasn't so, and Carl Van Doren's analysis of the literary "revolt from the village" summed up the new cynical attitude toward countryside "purity" of the many who, like Cather herself, fled the open spaces for New York. Realists accused Cather of telling the reader what he wanted to hear, but actually America seemed to prefer the gory naturalism of the tougher war narratives to *One of Ours*—so much so that Laurence Stallings' and Maxwell Anderson's raunchy play about Marine Corps life, *What Price Glory?* was one of Broadway's biggest hits in 1924. Some thought it a rejection of heroics, others cheered its warty bravado; both were wrong. *What Price Glory?*, the most outspoken product of the artists' war on war, was neither for nor against heroism, and neither accepted nor disavowed it. It simply dropped the Leathernecks, as the former Marine Stallings recalled them, onto the stage as a backdrop for the sadomasochistic friendship of Sergeant Quirt and Captain Flagg, developed in unmistakably post-Freudian language that almost everyone managed to mistake. The authors thought they had written utter realism, but the spectators pounced on the violent high jinks and used them for escape. *What Price Glory?* was taken as a high point of popular comedy, and its final line, Quirt's "Hey, Flagg, wait for Baby!" became a catchphrase of the day.

While some highbrows were rebels and some escapists, there was a third, rarer subgroup, the highbrows of popular art, crossing the bar from the good, the beautiful, and the true over into the meretricious, the plebeian, and the no less true. Led by the critic Gilbert Seldes, commentators began to notice the values in the creative echelons that lay beneath the drama, the symphony, and heroic verse. As a matter of fact, there were no American symphonists of note at all at the time (though Charles Ives had been busy—and unheard—for two decades, and though Aaron Copland, Roy Harris, Walter Piston, and Henry Cowell were shortly to materialize with a dapper tradition worked up almost over the weekend), and Stephen Vincent Benét's attempt to reconnoiter the epic in *John Brown's Body* impressed some people less favorably than did the adamantine concoctions of Amy Lowell and the imagists. But lo, there were George Gershwin and Jerome Kern, bemusing at least some critics' aptitude for pigeonholing, and the perceptive depths of such endeavors as George Herriman's comic strip *Krazy Kat*, Charlie Chaplin's screen comedies, and Fanny Brice's stand-up routines in Florenz Ziegfeld's *Follies* revues appeared to sophisticate the simple formulas of mass entertainment with the interior resources of art.

Seldes's book of 1924, *The Seven Lively Arts*, set in motion an awareness of our democratic American art, perhaps the first such awareness we have had. Songwriters, comedians, and comic-strip artists were seen, suddenly, as functionaries in a ritual that drew the public into the fundamentals of its identity as the advance guard of an ideology. The harum-scarum lyrical violence of Krazy Kat and her/his (Krazy's ambiguous gender was never extrapolated) beloved brick-throwing mouse, the ragtime naïveté of Irving Berlin and the lazy blues-blowing of Gershwin, the ghetto pragmatism of Brice, Al Jolson, or Eddie Cantor . . . was it art? came the question, and if so, did it conduce to a statement about this agglomeration of localities? Or was it only the hot-truckin' city talking us up? Did Carpenter's *Skyscrapers* ballet root at the initiative of the exploding nation, or was Carpenter only playing the hurdy-gurdy of metropolis? Like Gershwin, Carpenter drew heavily on blues and syncopation—now, that's city music, sure as rain come on washday. Carpenter once named Irving Berlin's "Everybody Step," a ragtime dance number, as music of the highest order, adding, "the music historian of the year 2000 will find the birthday of American music and that of Irving Berlin to have been the same."

But Berlin's "American" sound, including the quotation of a musical phrase from Stephen Foster's "(Way Down Upon the) Swanee River" in "Alexander's Ragtime Band," was entirely the result of an upbringing on the Lower East Side, for this was a time when those of non-English descent first made themselves a significant component in the culture, though their sense of nation was undeniably informed more by the dissenting city than by the "neighborly" town. Alexander Woollcott in his biography of Berlin claimed that he metamorphosed into melody "the roar of the elevated, the frightening scream of the fire engines . . . the cries of the fruit vendors and push-cart peddlars," and so on, but as the historian Mark Sullivan pointed out, how different might the course of American music have been had Berlin given ear to "the twanging of banjos in Alabama, the summons of church bells in rural Ohio," or even "the cry of the hog-caller across the rolling Kansas plains." Oddly enough, this was exactly the experiential panorama that characterized the music of Berlin's contemporary Charles Ives, but they were humming Berlin's "Shaking the Blues Away," not Ives's "The Housatonic at Stockbridge."

This was the debate of the twenties in bohemia—one of them, at any rate. Who were we, exactly, especially as recorded in our popular art, whether that "popular" referred to the folk-cultural aesthetic that informed it or simply the large audience that supported it? With delight, or scientifically, not caring what they might learn, or in horror, analysts turned to examine the movies, where the vectors of Popular found their terminus. There they found a more florid world than that addressed by Irving Berlin—and, indeed, the netherworldly tropes inhabited by Rudolph Valentino, Mary Pickford, and Gloria Swanson at the time look ridiculous to us today. But Chaplin's dauntless, sentimental tramp is still remarked on as a ghost of the American spirit then and now, and did that ghost ever breathe then! Surely there couldn't have been much identification on the part of Chaplin's willing audience with a pratfalling underdog who amounted to the visual equivalent of gibberish, but the man was doing something right. His film *The Gold Rush* in mid-decade cleared a profit of 5 million dollars worldwide on an outlay of $750,000, two-fifths of the take going to Chaplin.

Whatever drove the moviegoers to seek what they sought in Chaplin, one can easily see why the highbrows took to him, for dwelling on the underside of life as they did, they promoted a fellowship of the underdog; naturally, they would look to their fellows when raising up heroic emblems, and so it was with the underdog Chaplin. In the pages of the leftist *New Republic,* Stark Young offered his nostrum for abnormalcy by urging great roles of modern drama upon Chaplin, and there were those who argued that America's clowns were our Hamlets, transcending the mode of Popular to formalize a wholly native art technology of commentative fantasy. Was it possible? Even a certain spirit of St. Louis, T. S. Eliot, by then removed to England (and one who surveyed the scene from the topside of things, the Anglo-Catholic highbrow), noted that Chaplin "escaped in his own way from the realism of the cinema and invented a *rhythm.*" Ah. So it was art, after all!

Not everyone joined in the huzzahs for man-in-the-street artistry. Ring Lardner, whose ear for the buckles and lulls in the native voice was second to no contemporary ear, penned a story called "Rhythm," about a pop composer who nearly lets himself be destroyed by the intellectual applause of highbrow critics, and, with George S. Kaufman, dispatched the industrious clichés of songwriting in the comedy *June Moon.* Anyway, the general passion ran more to defacing fame than erecting it. The American publication in 1922 of Lytton Strachey's rather less than worshipful *Queen Victoria* heralded the real work of the decade: debunking. It wasn't a particularly new idea, certainly. Like *archy and mehitabel, Krazy Kat,* Freudian drama, Dorothy Parker's quips, and much else that feels so "twenties," debunking took off before the war—but it flowered, with a weedy smirk, just as the decade began to roar.

The word "bunk" derives from the 1850s, when a politician of Buncombe County, North Carolina, habitually made a fuss over his local options by vowing that he was "bound to make a speech for Buncombe." The term was too rich to die. Sometime after the turn of the century "buncombe" and its alternate, "bunkum," turned to "bunk," and when William E. Woodward's satirical novel *Bunk* came out in 1923, everyone was ready for a revival. Woodward not only put the word back into currency, he also took the trouble to limn the flagrant mediocrity of everything in America that needed debunking. *Bunk* pictured the successful promotion of a book entitled *The Importance of Being Second Rate* through the forced proliferation of Second Rate Clubs, which inspires the fictional author to live a pilgrimage of debunking.

Real-life authors, too, heard the call. Woodward himself debunked George Washington in a to-some-eyes libelous biography, while Van Wyck Brooks condemned the technocratic bias in *The Ordeal of Mark Twain*. Sinclair Lewis punctured the evangelist game in *Elmer Gantry;* Thomas Beer demoted Louisa May Alcott, Frances Willard, and Henry Adams in *The Mauve Decade* in what may have been the most elegantly vicious prose style of the era; on the stage George S. Kaufman and Marc Connelly exposed Hollywood's cardboard-character symbols and the crassness of American middlebrowism in *Merton of the Movies* and *Beggar on Horseback;* George Jean Nathan decertified the money-grubbing vanity of Broadway in his witty drama reviews and Dorothy Parker exercised her quill scalpel on the highbrow, the "authors and actors and artists and such," concluding

> People Who Do Things exceed my endurance;
> God, for a man that solicits insurance!

She didn't mean it, not really. The men that solicited insurance stoked the impatience of the intellectual set, and the novelists among them were happy to speak for them all by spaying the self-esteem of the businessman, calling him America's loudest symbol and a lot of bad names. Yet what, in truth, did this smart set know about the business world? How well informed were they, one sometimes has to wonder, about anything but their smug, smart little lives? For every H. L. Mencken, taking his politics seriously and compiling the three rich tomes of *The American Language* for scholarship's and passion's sake, there were ten of George Jean Nathan, whose stand on politics, scholarship, and, for that matter, passion, he himself defined in terms that most of bohemia understood: "If all the Armenians were to be killed tomorrow and if half of Russia were to starve to death the day after, it would not matter to me in the least. What concerns me alone is myself, and the interests of a few close friends. For all I care, the rest of the world may go to hell at tomorrow's sunset."

So it went for so much of bohemia that one must be prepared to accept its infrequent forays into sociopolitical militancy with some skepticism. They were apolitical, these highbrows, because liberalism was an artistic creed, not a social warranty, not really. Their only movement was the art movement, their resolution that of art forms; theirs was the comity of the outcast, of the prophet of controversy, and they would make the world safe not for democracy but for outcast prophets.

In establishing a context for this specific bohemia of this specific period, one must remember that a high percentage of the nation's readers and theatergoers thought bohemians inessential. The ideas of a Sinclair Lewis or a George S. Kaufman could always be dismissed. How many evangelists read Lewis's *Elmer Gantry?* How many Midwestern Babbitts saw themselves in Kaufman and Connelly's *Beggar on Horseback* as Fred Cady, proprietor of the Cady Consolidated Art Factory, where a novelist, a songwriter, a magazine artist, and a poet, locked up in cages, dispense prefabricated artware by the time clock? ("What will you have," asks a Cady guide, showing tourists through the factory and stopping to watch the artist, "a cover or an advertisement?" "What's the difference?" replies one of the group. "There isn't any," he is told.)

If novelists and playwrights couldn't shake the world, philosophers and historians were taken seriously, not least because decades of liberal contentions came to a head in the twenties to dare the Establishment. Since the publication in 1899 of *The Theory of the Leisure Class,* Thorstein Veblen had been someone for the money bosses to regard with an anchor to windward, and 1923 brought his *Absentee Ownership and Business Enterprise: The Case of America,* one chapter of which found the roots of a greedy capitalism in small-town America and attacked it as root and trunk in terms at once more harsh and widely applicable than those of a popular novelist such as Sinclair Lewis.

All right, now. Where was the conservative political spokesman to debate Veblen? There had been enough of them at the time of his *Theory of the Leisure Class,* when Progressivism stimulated an intellectual balance of power among the political scientists. But the open forum was closing up in the twenties, almost as if the preceding decades of conspiratorial inventions by the radical Left had tempted the more colorful theorists and bereft capitalist tradition of its Aarons. True, there was Irving Babbitt and George Santayana, the humanist and the Burkean, but theirs were not the voices most prominently heard, and conservatism in the twenties seemed to be constituted not of elected principles but of greedy pie-jaw on "private enterprise." It was Lincoln Steffens, John Reed, Walter Lippmann, and John Dos Passos whose phrases rang with the conviction that passes, in default of rebuttal, for truth. Starting now, the highbrows of the Left won't really be challenged until the conservative revival of the late forties.

Of course, someone had to stand up to the charges put forth by the blatant beasts of Anglo-Saxonism that continued immigration would destroy America. Madison Grant's *The Passing of the Great Race,* Lothrop Stoddard's *The Revolt Against Civilization,* and C. W. Gould's *America, A Family Matter,* all published in 1922, used the recently instituted Stanford-Binet I.Q. test to conclude that because immigrants from southern and eastern Europe scored in lower percentiles than those from Nordic countries (many of whom had been over here longer), they were genetically inferior.

This was much too early in the history of Stanford-Binet data to utilize a complete set of variables in assessment, and the pioneers who were settling city ghettos in the company of their own were as yet a generation or so ahead of the cultural assimilation so necessary for reasonable performance on an I.Q. test. But the Anglo-Saxonists pounced on the test scores as proof of genetic inferiority; in their hands, scientific method was quoted rather than practiced. Unfortunately, the liberal opposition was no more scrupulous than the bigots. Heading the attack on the tests in the *New Republic,* Walter Lippmann invoked the Left's instinctual superstition that anything

that distinguishes a segment of the population is intrinsically coun-
terproductive. His arguments against genetic deductions—against any
interpretation of the tests at all—bore as much respect for scientific
inquiry as did the anti-Semitic diatribes of the Anglo-Saxon alarmists.

Thus the convulsions of development felt in technology, communications, and art often took on a sociopolitical slant, even an
ideological one; no wonder the Babbitts saw it as one great
subversion of tradition—no wonder the highbrows saw it as one great
redemption by chaos. Some highbrows even reasoned out their
assaults on tradition, working up theories on the matter of the
restructuring of society with a diligence that their apolitical brethren
of Art For Art's Sake regarded as excessive. Not only Veblen, but
other thinkers rode roughshod on the businessman symbol, whether
as middle-class entrepreneur or plutocratic technolandlord. Veblen
looked to science, John Dewey to novel socialistic so-called prac-
ticalities, and Charles Beard to a revaluation of America's economic
origins—but they all called for utopian revisions, for federal institu-
tionalizing and interference.

Even lacking a charismatic spokesman to provide it with the
lightning phrases and applied ideology with which to refute Veblen,
Dewey, and Beard, the business community knew what words to call
them, and the highbrows of the Northeast and the universities are still
the whipping boys of the anti-intellectual. As Richard Hofstadter
points out, "egghead" replaced "highbrow" in the fifties, with an
even direr nuance; in the twenties a highbrow was the girl who didn't
get asked out on dates—in the Eisenhower era, an egghead was the
bleeding heart who undermined our position in the cold war. "Why I
Never Hire Brilliant Men," an article in an issue of *American*
magazine in 1924, hymned the torpid stolidity of the true man of
affairs. "Business and life are built upon successful mediocrity," it
claimed, anteceding Bruce Barton's picture of Christ-as-businessman
in stating that "the greatest organization in human history was twelve
humble men, picked up along the shores of an inland lake."

In an age of such holy business the separation of the nation's
minds and the nation's accountants was acute. More than their
professions opposed them; they spoke different languages. How could

the highbrows understand that the businessman identified not with Mammon, nor yet with Christ, but with the Protestant virtues inculcated in American youth, the uprightness and moral fiber and dynamic manliness of competition? A successful mercantilist was less a rich man than he was a sturdy man, of a certain cut of jib, and business as usual meant that Christian probity worked. The Babbitt-God propounded by Barton in *The Man Nobody Knows* was simply a clumsy way of updating the work ethic of the Protestant farmer.

Even a businessman could debunk, as witness Henry Ford's famous dismissal of history as "bunk" (although he recanted later, explaining that he didn't mean that history was bunk, only that history was bunk to him; it makes about as much sense as anything he said). Ford's gift for verbalizing the contemptuous outrages of the ignorant in exactly their language was one base of his on-and-off popularity, but he attracted favorable comment from some surprising quarters. Was it really *The Wall Street Journal* that asked, "Why Not Ford for President?" in 1922? (It was, perhaps only to keep the forum open.) And what could the onetime city reformer and later convinced Communist Lincoln Steffens have been thinking of when he reverenced Ford as a fellow traveler? "Radical" was the word he used, praise enow from Steffens, whose autobiography featured a picture page headed "Dictators" and displaying photographs of Lenin, Mussolini . . . and Woodrow Wilson. Apparently, the intellectuals could wear blinders as naturally as did the anti-intellectuals, for in seeing Ford as a custodial father of the workers, Steffens was mistaking the man's moonstruck Midas touch for profit-sharing techniques.

But Steffens was not one's common-or-garden highbrow. A determined, if peaceful, revolutionary, he had few counterparts except in the world of such artists as Eugene O'Neill or Robert Edmond Jones, who would feed theater hunger, no other kind. The profile of New York's highbrows showed itself most aptly not in politicizing, but in debunking and larks, which is why the Algonquin Round Table is better remembered than anyone's social conscience. "The class struggle plays hell with your poetry," John Reed had said, drawing the line between the highbrows and militant liberalism.

No, all bohemia's sport was satire, the classier grade of debunking, and a satire aimed at the American way; it drew the elite together as surely as did *The New Yorker*, or a Shaw premiere by the Theatre Guild, or the City itself, a golden city then, for all the trash and trollops, for all the craving in the eyes of the many who arrived not to enlist in bohemia, but to work. There was so much more to the American art scene than many of those snappy New York highbrows would ever understand—Edward Arlington Robinson, Ezra Pound, Carl Sandburg, Robinson Jeffers, and Vachel Lindsay in poetry alone. "How fur ye goin'?" the truck driver asks of the hitchhiker who leaves, not enters, New York at the close of Dos Passos' *Manhattan Transfer*. "I dunno . . . pretty far."

But New York's highbrows could see into the distance when they had to, say as far as Boston, where the decade's choice debunking of Americana centered around the arrest, trial, and, finally, execution of two immigrant anarchists, Nicola Sacco and Bartolomeo Vanzetti, for the robbery and murder of a factory paymaster and his guard that occurred in South Braintree, Massachusetts, on April 15, 1920, just after A. Mitchell Palmer's Red raids had ground to an embarrassed stall. It was not inevitable that the murder evidence point to two of the nation's least savory inhabitants, sworn subversives who weren't even citizens—but, this being the much-mooted age of the "little person," with idealistic republics sprouting up in traditionally anti-democratic European terrain, it was inevitable that the cause of Sacco and Vanzetti capture the hearts of the highbrows. The case, very slightly in doubt, became a crise of unbelievable proportion, blown up at first by the organized Communist network and then inherited by gullible city liberals.

The highbrows who weren't totally apolitical made this their field day, both in street demonstrations and in the newspaper columns they controlled (Heywood Broun went so far in his vituperative attacks on American justice that even the distinctly liberal *New York World* found it politic to accept his resignation and print an apology). Now we understand why they were so entranced with the art of Chaplin and Berlin all along. It was the "little person" syndrome, the thrill of helping someone from the ranks edge out—provided he stays "little"

in word and deed—thereby supposedly "fooling" capitalism. Bad cess
to the peasant who achieves true American money-power, such as a
Joseph P. Kennedy, and worse cess to the success who started out
with The Advantages; these are not for bohemia. There was no
glamour, for them, in a wealthy scion who made good, such as Cole
Porter; one never heard Porter credited with the miracles they were
ascribing to that ghetto kid, Berlin, though Porter was in fact a vastly
superior musician and a lyrical wag whose verses made those by
Berlin look like a cycle of lumpen proverbs.

Sacco and Vanzetti were to become the star puppets in an anti-
American spectacular produced by the radical Left, in association with
unwitting liberals, and one couldn't have asked for an apter string-
master than the judge, Webster Thayer, juridically meticulous but
garrulous with editorial snorts and point of view. "Hearken to your
verdicts as the Court has recorded them," said the clerk, following
protocol, when the jury found both men guilty. "You, gentlemen,
upon your oath, say that Nicola Sacco and Bartolomeo Vanzetti is
each guilty of murder in the first degree upon each indictment. So say
you, Mr. Foreman? So, gentlemen, you all say?" "We do, we do,"
replied the jury, and suddenly Sacco shouted, "*Sono innocente! Sono
innocente!*"

Then it began. Though all mention of it had been omitted from
the trial, Sacco's and Vanzetti's political creed was no secret, and this
made it easy to believe, if one was inclined to, that the pair had been
railroaded for their anarchism. Two opposing interpretations of the
case, both bigoted, informed popular opinion: one, that as anarchists
they deserved to die, and two, that as anarchists they had to be
innocent martyrs. Between these facile viewpoints resided the educated opinion, which was, at first, that the two were probably guilty—
certainly, the evidence against them was very damaging. Unfortunately, Thayer's performance at the bench and an *almost* reasonable
doubt hung the case in the air while a global campaign of anti-
American bedlam from the radical Left was put into gear.

Demonstrations and outbreaks of violence inflamed European cities
in 1921 for months, especially where the Communists were best
organized. A quaint irony is that the anarchist era had pretty much

ended in Europe by then, and even as the Reds turned Sacco and Vanzetti into pawns, Stalin was slaughtering Russia's many thousands of anarchists without even bothering to leave their fate in the hands of a jury. But anything that could cause unrest in the United States was useful to the Left, which had thus far been unable to provoke much of a cause out of Sacco and Vanzetti at home. In Europe, however, the mobs were steered with a deft touch. Not just protests, but grenades and bombs were hurled at the authorities, and as the agitation moved to Central and South America, we, the isolated, began to take notice.

They were unlikely heroes, Sacco and Vanzetti—"nameless in the crowd of nameless ones," in Vanzetti's sometimes quite touching prose writings; except to highbrows, political revolutionaries, and the Italian community, they were never heroes at all. Of the two, Vanzetti was riper for election to the halls of martyrdom for his sweet disposition, always useful in the presentation of crucified idealism. But, after all, while dissent is a convention of democratic life—or, better, an essential, to keep thought free—do we really need the dissent of anarchists, or any dedicated subversives? Had the issue been simply one of political iconoclasm, the two Italians could have been shipped back to Italy with no questions raised about due process that now can never be answered. But the subjunctive is an idle picnic in the writing of history; what happened is all. And what had happened was that two men had been killed, the solution of the case leading to Sacco and Vanzetti. The affair should never have become, as it immediately became, that of two political executions, but rather that of two men found guilty of crimes they might not have committed after all. This was not our Dreyfus case: Dreyfus was innocent. No one knew, for sure, about Sacco and Vanzetti, a shoemaker and an odd-jobber unable to explain why they happened to be carrying firearms when they were arrested, including the dead payroll guard's revolver, still loaded.

The European ruckus put the business in the wrong light, making of the two Italians victims not of a possibly flawed legal adventure, nor even of xenophobic anxiety, but of American money bossism, as if the business interests needed this immolation to secure their influence over the people. Scott Fitzgerald's Gatsby, enthralled by Daisy Buchanan, commented that her voice was "full of money." Now the rest of the world heard the rasp of banknotes in the voice of America, although no one took the trouble to hear any quality of expression in the cool, clean murder of the paymaster and his bodyguard.

Squelched appeals for a new trial kept Sacco and Vanzetti in prison for years, while hordes of highbrows fulminated and contributed to a defense fund. Besides Heywood Broun's angry series in the *World*, there were two plays by Maxwell Anderson and one by Elmer Rice on the theme (all three after the execution, however), and such card-carrying highbrows as Edna St. Vincent Millay, John Dos Passos, Dorothy Parker, and Robert Benchley joined picket lines as the case continued to grow, becoming the prime rite of intellectual passage of a whole highbrow generation. As anyone who grew up in Middletown then can tell you, the pair was guilty; anyone native to highbrow circles would call him a liar. It was not the money bosses who resisted clemency for two convicted murderers. "It was also the doctors, the lawyers, the shopkeepers, the farmers, the workers," as Granville Hicks observed. "The battle was between the intellectuals and everybody else."

The defense changed hands in late 1924, from Fred Moore, a strutting caballero from California, summa cum laude in getting justice for radicals on the coast, to William G. Thompson, very old Boston and the best P.R. imaginable for this gauntlet run for underdogs, though the hard-line Left of course denounced this resumption of bourgeois procedure, recommending direct action by the workers. More and more, however, the "right" people were changing their minds about the case, coming out in print and telegram for a new trial, a commutation of sentence, or a pardon. The converts to the cause give one something to think about, for these were no knee-jerk dupes of the fifth column: historians Samuel Eliot Morison and Arthur Schlesinger, Rabbi Stephen Wise, Jane Addams, Alfred Landon, Robert La Follette, H. L. Mencken, the *Atlantic Monthly* (which ran an indictment of the trial by Felix Frankfurter), three-fourths of the graduating class of the Harvard Law School, and finally even Alfred Dreyfus himself. The mail of Massachusetts' Governor Alvan T. Fuller grew so heavy that his assistant started to throw it all out as it came in.

Probably what convinced the prodefense activists was Judge Thayer, who had volunteered for jurisdiction in the first place and showed himself too prepared to teach a lesson to these "arnychists." It was Thayer whose prerogative it was, under state law, to order or refuse a retrial; Thayer refused, forever dooming the two Italians' court hearing to be remembered as one supervised by an interested party, for a second trial, given the prosecution's evidence, would most likely have returned a verdict of guilty.

With anti-Thayer outrage still mounting, Governor Fuller stepped in with a personal investigation and decided to hand a final decision over to a three-man committee headed by the president of Harvard, Abbott Lawrence Lowell, an upright man troubled by the popular confusion between the arguable miscarriage of justice in Thayer's court and a deliberate frame-up of radical opinions. No friend to radicalism, Lowell was, however, a great believer in opinions, in the freedom to hold and assert them. (One such that he himself asserted was in favor of a U.S. participation in the League of Nations, a premise he debated in Boston's Symphony Hall with that archparliamentarian and even more arch anti-Wilsonian, Henry Cabot Lodge.)

Lowell, of course, had read Frankfurter's explosive article in the *Atlantic,* the first response from the Establishment in favor of Sacco and Vanzetti, and he accepted Fuller's assignment, assuming that he would probably not be able to uphold Thayer's jurisprudence. Serving with Lowell were Samuel Stratton, the president of the Massachusetts Institute of Technology, and Robert Grant, a combination probate lawyer and light—very light—novelist. The panel, in all ways respectable, was neither liberal nor conservative, nor cut wholly of Boston cloth, for though Stratton, like Lowell, was an academic, his academe was technology and he hailed not from Back Bay but from Illinois farmland, a mingling of urbane highbrow and scientific bumpkin.

The Lowell Committee convened, reading a transcript of the trial, checking out the scene of the crime, and interviewing some of the jurors as well as the convicted men. By June of 1927, Sacco and Vanzetti were world-famous; the radical Left couldn't have wished for a happier infamy. European countries that would have been under German domination if the hateful capitalists hadn't bailed them out were screaming for a pardon for the condemned pair. Royalist periodicals waxed as shrill as Red rags, and H. G. Wells suggested the coining of the word "thayerism" to cover the "self-righteous unrighteousness of established people." Then the Lowell Committee made its recommendation: Sacco and Vanzetti were "guilty beyond a reasonable doubt."

Renewed demonstrations followed, both for and against the decision, a vain appeal to U.S. Supreme Court Justice Oliver Wendell Holmes was made on the front porch of his summer home, the house of one of the jurors was dynamited late one night with, miraculously, no injuries, Boston was harried with pickets, and Sacco and Vanzetti were electrocuted on August 21, 1927—a technological death, a very modern death—and no one will ever know for sure whether they were innocent or guilty.

So many confessions, confidences, and contradictions have surfaced since then regarding the case that its ambiguities are cloudier today than before. Fred Moore, the first counsel for the defense and no enemy of radical causes, came to believe in their guilt; even the archanarchist Carlo Tresca told Max Eastman that Sacco, at least, was guilty. When the crack historian Francis Russell wrote his book on the case, *Tragedy in Dedham,* in 1961, he had an up-to-date ballistics test made on the bullets and on Sacco's pistol, only to confirm findings made at the time of the Lowell report.

"Revenge our blood," wrote Vanzetti in 1927; the highbrows would have liked to. How easily convinced they were that injustice had been done, how quick, they, to point a finger—but when has the intellectual elite ever stood behind a winner? Give them rather a Chaplin or a Berlin . . . now you're talking: underdogs they can deal with. They stood by complacently while Wilson dissolved before their eyes, giant lapsing into blob, trying to enforce the peace program he was mandated to enact—and the same disenchantment was in the air shortly before John Kennedy was assassinated, for that "underdog" president, like Wilson, was acting too much the winner. Of course they adopted Sacco and Vanzetti. It was their war, the intellectuals and the bohemians against the world. "All right we are two nations," wrote John Dos Passos, from the losing side, combining the non-punctuation of Gertrude Stein with the unqualified self-awareness of the rebel.

America's self-image, tricky enough in the hands of Sinclair Lewis, George S. Kaufman, and Ring Lardner was not looking all that rosy as of the Sacco-Vanzetti controversy, and while few habitués of the boondocks were aware of Northeast urban angst, those who computed our worth in the data of art and thought were increasingly shaken by what they felt they saw. But why, one wonders, were they so fetched by these two intruders who had only degeneration and riot to offer America, when the grisly beating, castration, and lynching of Wesley Everest in the I.W.W.–American Legion confrontation in Centralia in 1919 made no effect on them?

The reason why is that they scarcely knew about it. Everest was a fast newspaper item; Sacco and Vanzetti were a campaign. Their trial had passed, at first, without much notice, just another murder trial. It was the publicity generated by foreign bile and a growing awareness of the case over the course of seven years that brought the matter to fever pitch—advertisement, in other words, exactly the sort of advertisement that builds up a presentation, whether for Luckys, Forhan's gum treatment, or radical emblems. Sacco and Vanzetti were Communist puppets, though opposed to communism as well as to capitalism, and today they remain liberal puppets, the strings ever ready to be pulled by liberals who haven't taken the time to examine the record. Like Julius and Ethel Rosenberg, who helped Klaus Fuchs steal the atom bomb for Soviet Russia, Sacco and Vanzetti are names the city emblazons on walls to keep the Trouble current. This is the underside of bohemia, the unreason of the highbrow—not the rigorous scruples of a Morison or an Addams, concerned over the wayward happenstance of criminal prosecution, but the hell-clicking *savoir dire* of artists devoted to overthrow, one way or another. They're all in it together: all art is subversive. Match the epic achievements of Eugene O'Neill, perhaps the sole genius our theater has produced, with the short forms of Dorothy Parker, little stories and poems, veering from satire to sensibility in the space of a pun, or with the novels of F. Scott Fitzgerald, in one of which, *The Great Gatsby*, he came closer than Lewis or Dreiser to an understanding of the romantic contraption of the American quest. Fitzgerald himself was prone to more infantile romances, such as the "lazy beauty" that the hero of *This Side of Paradise*, Amory Blaine, saw in Ivy League fraternity, but he could project the grander view onto others. He writes this on Gatsby's final page, of America's first explorers: "For a transitory enchanted moment man must have held his breath in the presence of this continent, compelled into an aesthetic contemplation he neither understood nor desired, face to face for the last time in history with something commensurate to his capacity for wonder."

A romantic in the inelastically realistic city, the New York brought to life so convincingly without a shard of romance by Dos Passos? But then Fitzgerald does admit that his characters are Westerners: "Perhaps we possessed some deficiency in common which made us so subtly unadaptable to Eastern life." Some Midwesterners adapted, some didn't; some Midwesterners couldn't even breathe until they had gained the Eastern metropolis. Its paradox was the heart-on-sleeve earnestness of people whose daily life conduced to hardhearted debunking, and its consolation was its embrace of the new and the self-expressive. "I was once a vers libre bard," Archy the cockroach relates, "but I died and my soul went into the body of a cockroach . . . I see things from the under side now."

Ah, yes, in the city even a cockroach could make waves.

FOUR

⊰✠⊱

"My God! That Means Coolidge Is President!"

"The rich get rich and the poor get children," chortled a song of 1921—now, that's real normalcy. What did our elected normalcy get us? As of 1923, when President Harding dropped dead in San Francisco, normalcy had tendered a stepped-up "enforcement" of Prohibition, a breakthrough for an eight-hour day in industry, the five-power Arms Limitation Conference that rolled back warship stockpiling, a signed armistice, finally, with Germany and the late Austria-Hungary, the Federal Highway Act, an economically conservative Supreme Court, and the biggest scandal to blacken the name of a chief executive in the nation's history, coining a byword of big-time corruption unrivaled until "Watergate."

Like Nixon's gaffe, Harding's was known by an item of topography that quickly came to symbolize a philosophy of federal pollution and wholesale arrogation, "Teapot Dome." This was not a building but a queerly shaped butte in Wyoming that arrived as a godsend to political cartoonists. Always sparked by the latest strange device, they borrowed the teapot contour of the hill en masse to perk up their sketches for what they assumed would be a few weeks. It lasted seven years.

The saga of Teapot Dome wasn't easy to follow at the time, late 1923 to early 1930, for it came out slowly and indistinctly, in excerpts of the whole truth, and after the first few disclosures newspaper readers tired of it, calling it Democratic scandalmongering and demanding surcease. Then, suddenly, the trickles of evidence began to run less silent and deep; the seepage of revelation metamorphosed as a spill, splashing odium upon the high and low in Washington like a geyser aimed by some Jeremiah. Now the public left off complaining and turned, fascinated, to the Congressional hearings in Washington where they learned at last what normalcy begot—larceny on the grandest scale imaginable, millions bought and possibly murders committed. And the name of normalcy was Oil.

By 1923, President Harding had some little inkling of what his great good friends had been doing under his nose, but what else could he have expected? When he moved into the White House he handed out scores of posts to little corporals of money bossism. Any business that paid its way was good business; so thought the Ohio gang, who systematically looted every department and situation it had access to. Payoffs, boodling, favors—these were the wages of patronage, which the partly innocent Harding had understood as a perquisite of federal power. Every night was old home night with the Ohio boys, and business was usual . . . usual for state machines. Like good old boys, they made the decisions over cards, the very picture of small-town grafters amidst the shirt-sleeves, "Scotch" jokes, toothpicks, spittoons, and—a novel touch for the postcard—bootleg whiskey. Charles Forbes, Harding's appointee to head the Veterans Bureau and a major figure in rumors circulating D.C., later described a typical poker session in the White House library, unwittingly putting his itchy finger on what passed for government in Hardingville:

During the game Ned McLean [a millionaire dandy and owner of the *Washington Post*] announced that Jack Johnson, the prize fighter, was about to be discharged from the Federal Penitentiary at Leavenworth, and either Ned or Lasker [Albert Lasker, the chairman of the Shipping Board] exclaimed, "Why, his old mother used to work for me and he has a fine of $1,000 hanging over him and can't pay it." Ned McLean said: "Albert, I'll give $500 and you give $500 and we will pay his fine." The President spoke up: "Don't let that worry you; I'll remit the fine." And the game went on.

This same Forbes was using the Veterans Bureau to retail construction contracts for government hospitals that would never exist and was peddling surplus war supplies, mainly untouched hospital equipment and drugs, for pennies on the dollar. Forbes had grown so heedless with power that finally even Harry Daugherty, the Attorney General, and one who was almost certainly wading heavily into the muck himself, advised Harding to replace Forbes (who, it later turned out, had misappropriated over two hundred million dollars). Shortly after Daugherty's warning, a White House visitor took a wrong turning and chanced upon an open doorway through which he saw the President bouncing a man against the wall and shouting, "You yellow rat! You double-crossing bastard! If you ever—" . . . It was Forbes, of course, who was immediately packed off to Europe, where he resigned.

Too late: the Senate had already called for an investigation of "irregularities" in the Veterans Bureau, and a sinister note was added in the suicides of two Ohio gang gophers, first Charles Cramer, who had served as general counsel for the Veterans Bureau, and then Jess Smith, a glad-handing, minor-league bandit in the Justice Department and a sidekick of Daugherty's. Harding's heart weighed him like a stone as he made ready to stump the country on his "Voyage of Understanding," one of America's last sieges of the old in-person communion of politico and folk that radio and television would make unnecessary. Indeed, Harding dropped one foot into the future in St. Louis, where his speech at the Coliseum was heard not only by the ten thousand Rotarians in attendance, but by a nationwide radio audience as well.

Harding was planning to run for a second term the following year, and with reports of a growing small-town movement to back Henry Ford, the President determined to consolidate his position from the back of his railroad car, the *Superb,* on the World Court, Prohibition, the capital and labor ruckus, and the eight-hour day. Everywhere, in cities and towns, people came to see, and spirits were high. Farmers brought wives, children, and lunches and looked at the king like cats, waitresses in Yellowstone National Park climbed onto the running board of the presidential car and let loose with a guitar serenade, and when the party boarded an army transport to take in Alaska, the people on shore broke into "God Be with You (Till We Meet Again)," and the navy band obliged with the indispensable, "Yes! We Have No Bananas."

Photos of Harding on this continental tour show a man older by more than the three years that had elapsed since he took office; one thinks of a similar voyage of understanding undertaken by President Wilson to preach his particular peace to the nation. Those who were with Harding remarked on how depressed and nervous he seemed, afraid to be alone, and likely he was thinking less of the term that might loom ahead than of that which faltered now behind him, a past like a minefield detonating on its own initiative. In his autobiography, William Allen White recalled the shattered Roman he encountered at the White House shortly before the trip to the West; this Caesar had come to believe the soothsayer's warning. "My God, this is a hell of a job," Harding told him. "I have no troubles with my enemies, I can take care of my enemies all right. But my damn friends, my God-damn friends, White—they're the ones who keep me walking the floor nights!"

This Caesar may have been assassinated, too, in San Francisco after the Alaskan jaunt. His friends poisoned him, or had him poisoned, according to rumor—or his wife, maybe, to save him from disgrace. Anyway, it was a suspicious death, an attack of ptomaine from crabmeat that others had eaten without taking ill, a high fever, a gradual recovery, and, suddenly, death. A cerebral hemorrhage was the medical interpretation—Mrs. Harding refused to allow an au-topsy—and back east in Massachusetts, Henry Cabot Lodge got the news and blurted out, "My God! That means Coolidge is President!"

A Famous Moment in History—ours, at least—finds Calvin Coolidge taking the oath of office at Plymouth, Massachusetts, by kerosene light in his father's house at 2:47 A.M., his father being a notary public (it later turned out that the senior Coolidge had no authority to administer a federal oath and the ceremony was quietly reenacted in D.C.). It was Coolidge luck, all right, as Bill McNutt had foreseen at the Chicago convention, and how Lincolnesque the setting—the open Bible, the kerosene lamp and its suggestive shadows, the simple country furnishings. Guido Boer's painting of the moment, heavily influenced by El Greco and McGuffey's *Readers,* shows a drab and humorless man, his eyes staring glumly downward as if at some unpleasant duty to be gotten out of the way.

Coolidge didn't look like half the president Harding had appeared to be, though his starchy demeanor and stingy, almost pointillistic speech habits gave welcome evidence that the Puritans were in and the good old boys of the poker parties were out—for by now D.C. was screaming with scuttlebutt and the ill-considered innuendo that was then known as "roorback." To the general public, who had no access to the grapevine and still revered the man they thought Harding was—the man Harding basically *was* after all, at his best—it was simple tragedy, though they were willing to give Coolidge a chance.

Even less of a doer than Harding was, Coolidge nonetheless willingly inherited his predecessor's programs. Soon enough, the personality came out from behind the cool front just as normalcy began to turn into prosperity, and Coolidge, as they used to put it, made a hit. His dictum, "More business in government and less government in business" sounded even better than his papal "there is no right to strike against the public safety" bull of the Boston policemen's adventure, and the country put off mourning for Harding to rally for Coolidge. Tirelessly apathetic to the agricultural community and an initiator of literally nothing in his six years in the White House, Coolidge had a favorite saying: "If you see ten troubles coming down the road, you can be sure that nine will run into the ditch before they reach you and you have to battle with only one of them"—clumsily put, but it worked for Coolidge. The acerb and laconic lawyer from Massachusetts wasn't likely to inch big business into his lap with poker nights and good times, the way Harding could, but he didn't have to, ever. His first emergency in office was a threatened coal strike, a very serious proposition considering how unpopular coal strikes were getting (there had been two in the decade already). But the miners ran into the ditch with the eight other troubles, for Coolidge presented the situation to Pennsylvania's conservationist governor, Gifford Pinchot; Pinchot mediated the dispute successfully and Coolidge came off looking jes' fine.

The tenth trouble, the one that has to be battled with, was the mess left by Harding's cronies—only Forbes and two suicides so far but much more to come. Once Teapot Dome really got going, the cleanup ought to have toppled the Republicans from power, and might well have done if the Democrats hadn't been so deteriorated by disunity and lack of leadership. As Harding's vice president, Coolidge could not logically expect the public to except him as independent of the scandal about to be unleashed (he had, in fact, no connection with the Ohio gang empery), but this is exactly what happened. No doubt the rigid Down Eastness of Coolidge *en grande tenue* added to the boom that carried his name, and the fact that he wasn't mentioned in the years of trials and hearings kept his reputation as sound as a bank. He had the air of a well-to-do but mainly honest businessman, and he lived the idea that business, for Americans large and small, constituted a kind of Calvinist beauty, that his was the business character, and that a man who succeeded in business had courage, ambition, stick-to-itiveness, and a steady hand when the going got rocky.

Now, that must be what saved Coolidge and built him big. Some historians, we know, were questioning the true identity of this "character"—did morality or just plain greed inform it?—but Coolidge, in his Spartan plastique, treated the nation to an exhibit of the "good" capitalism, the "private vices" that made, in Bernard de Mandeville's venerable dictum, "public benefits." Even when posing for the cameras in Indian feathers, hayseed overalls, and other local regalia, Coolidge retained his dour, bald eagle character, cut with not the slightest dram of earthiness or ease.

Alice Longworth observed that he looked as if he had been weaned on a pickle, and in 1933, when told that Coolidge had died, Dorothy

Parker asked, "How can they tell?" Tart and short-winded, often viciously witty, Calvin Coolidge proved to be everything the era he presided over was not—flat, unnuanced, inactive, and untroubled. He didn't leave the White House a rich man, but many of his constituents got rich while he was in office, and though it was all to blow away before the decade closed, while the sun was shining and the hay being made they named the paradise after him: "Coolidge prosperity."

Yet, with all the wild webbing of the joy sampler being threaded in those mid-twenties, in Gershwin musicals, Hollywood romances, and Hollywood farces (not to mention Hollywood orgies), in slumming in Harlem nightclubs, in bootleg hooch and sensational murders, in urbans giggling at rurals and rurals glaring at urbans, the whole thing was overshadowed by a gluttonous oil spill known as Teapot Dome, an apocalypse of such scummy magnitude that only an era as cynical and self-protected as the twenties could have handled it.

Oil: a very neoteric loot, whose arrival in the great world of international barter had begun under the conservationist movement of Theodore Roosevelt's Presidency. As "liquid gold," it was vital in the foundation of a modern navy. Rather than abandon all the petroleum resources of the West to the collection of private exploiters, Roosevelt's successor, William Howard Taft, had public oil lands set aside for the Navy's future use in 1909 and the years just after at Elk Hills, California, at Buena Vista, California, and at Teapot Dome, Wyoming. There was some controversy over the rights of prior claimants to these lands and over the possibility of neighboring drilling draining off the Navy's hypothetical oil—Buena Vista had been rendered useless for both reasons—but nothing specific was done until somebody struck it big almost on the border of the Elk Hills reserve, whereupon Congress placed the disposition of the three tracts in the hands of the Secretary of the Navy. That worthy was Josephus Daniels, serving in Wilson's Cabinet, but before he could move, the Wilson Administration had ended and Harding's team was brought in.

Harding replaced Daniels with Edwin Denby, an honest dimwit who was easily convinced by the Secretary of the Interior, Albert Fall, to cede the oil lands to his department. It was Fall's intention to hand Elk Hills and Teapot Dome over to private development in return for both a percentage of the oil and steel storage tanks, to be built and thus filled when and as the Navy required.

This was not exactly the act of a conservationist, but then Fall wasn't one and never pretended to be one. Moreover, it did make some reply to the question of how to deal with Japan's growing potential as an enemy, a potential enriched shortly thereafter when the Immigration Act of 1924 excluded the Japanese from citizenship and inspired a raft of "Hate America" rallies and a "Humiliation Day" in Tokyo, and suggesting that storage tanks of oil at Pearl Harbor would not be inopportune. So Fall's maneuvering of the two oil lands into his department and then into the private sector was, if irregular, debatably acceptable.

Only problem was, Fall took a personal profit off the top— $269,000 for Teapot Dome and $100,000 for Elk Hills.

For a man who had joined Harding's Cabinet almost $150,000 in debt and eight years behind in his taxes, Fall had turned into a rather conspicuous consumer on his ranch, Three Rivers, in New Mexico, the consumption taking in a hefty extension of the property, new roads and landscaping, irrigation projects, and a hydroelectric plant. Meanwhile, tales of the signing of leases relevant to Elk Hills and Teapot Dome circulated out of the Navy Department office and into an outraged oil industry. Even the common man had gotten wind of a shift in tempo at Teapot Dome: Senator John B. Kendrick, of Wyoming, was being inundated by letters from his home flock asking for some explanation of what was going on at Teapot Dome.

It was bound to come out, and it did—at first as belated formal announcements of the leases in the spring of 1922, and later as the focus of what got to be known as the "Harding" scandals. It wouldn't have reached the public with so much verve if the culprits hadn't been so colorful, but gangsters do have their fascination. Will Rogers called it the "great morality panic of 1924," but in its ponderous evolutions and witness-stand shivaree, it was more of a circus, and one not without its wild animals and clowns. As Mark Sullivan saw it, "In the fauna of American society, they belonged among the genera of the grizzlies and the bison, the Hereford bulls and the timber-wolves." So fetching was the assemblage that nearly everyone who writes about them succumbs to metaphor. Sullivan goes on to cite the Teapot Domers as Napoleons, Cromwells, and Medicis of the modern era. He calls the liars "magnificent liars," the good guys "eminent on the side of virtue": "Those who were weak were spectacularly weak, those who were strong a little too strong for an age that has left the Napoleons behind it."

The ringmaster of the Senate subcommittee hearing on the oil leases, and no little hero himself, was Thomas J. Walsh of Montana, slow and canny, all eyebrows and mustache, and as upright as God. A Democrat, Walsh was charged by some critics as a reckless defamer of Republican incumbency, but as the file of villains grew longer and their villainy contained not only in larcenous doings but in open contempt for Congressional procedure, reasonable men had to concede Walsh's rapt devotion to fair-mindedness.

Certainly, Walsh had some tricky steers to rope. Besides Fall, his two most inscrutable witnesses were the two men who were awarded the leases by the Interior department, Edward L. Doheny and Harry F. Sinclair, money bosses of the old school, summa cum laude in everything that, one presumes, goes into the amplifying of personal fortune in the cutthroat arena of petroleum. After hearing inconclusive testimony from both naval and scientific viewpoints on the advisability of Fall's having leased the oil fields, Walsh called both Doheny and Sinclair, from whom he learned only that the leases were in the best interests of the government. Period.

Meanwhile, Harding had died, putting something of a damper on the Senate hearing, and Walsh's subcommittee seemed to have bogged down embarrassingly . . . until Fall was asked to make some account of the sudden financial exuberance that had obtained on his ranch in New Mexico. Fussing with the national crepe, the public pricked up its ear: oil bored it, but a tale of ill-gotten gains was something else again—and lo, like a key suspect in a thriller, Fall began to Act Strangely. On the question of his unexpected wealth, he at first stalled for time, then promised to send his son-in-law to speak for him, and finally, that promise not kept, he sent the subcommittee a lengthy missive explaining that he had borrowed $100,000 from Ned McLean, and containing the statement, "I have never approached E. L. Doheny . . . or H. F. Sinclair . . . nor have I ever received from either of said parties one cent on account of any oil lease or upon any other account whatsoever."

And that, friends, was noose and gibbett and all. This Ned McLean, Edward Beale McLean in the indexes, was a flighty though not truly dissolute heir to the *Cincinnati Enquirer* (in which connection he had made Harding's acquaintance in Ohio), the *Washington Post,* numerous businesses, and an unspendable fortune. McLean's wedding present to his wife Evalyn, an heiress of comparable standing, was the Hope diamond, as big as a small fruit, and a repertory trope of the day, combining wealth, idleness, and the romance of a curse. McLean, in all, might very well have lent Fall $100,000. But as it happens, he hadn't, and though he seconded Fall's story, he immediately panicked, hid out in Palm Beach, and purchased every hurdle money and influence could place in Walsh's path. A. Mitchell Palmer, he of the Red raids, was acting now as McLean's lawyer in that elastic ethic of the politicos that keeps them popping up in the annals, playing one part in this saga, quite another in that. (Still, it must be admitted that party loyalty kept the Democrat Palmer intriguing exclusively with Democratic Senators on McLean's behalf, leaving the Republicans to McLean's Republican attorneys.) The telegraph McLean found therapeutic, and he kept the keys clicking with messages in ridiculous codes (Walsh was identified in one of them as Jaguar, an insightful image); this, of course, is the clown number in the Teapot Dome show.

Walsh went down to Palm Beach himself to question McLean; McLean persisted in upholding Fall's alibi. But it turned out that while McLean *had* given Fall checks totaling $100,000, they were returned to McLean uncashed. So there had been no loan after all. No sooner had Walsh returned to Washington to read McLean's gibberish telegrams into the record and announce that Fall's swag was yet unexplained—thrust, so! and parry—than entered the Roosevelt family, flags to the breeze: Theodore, Jr., Archie, their wives, and, of course, Alice Longworth with husband Nick.

An employee of Harry Sinclair's company, Archie Roosevelt volunteered himself as a friendly witness in the matter of a large amount of money that Sinclair might have passed over to Fall. Roosevelt, it must be stated, did not represent the run of witness that Walsh's team got to hear and which the nation got to read about daily. Felons and stooges of all types came, spoke their piece, and went, bestrewing D.C. with chapters and verses of avarice. Everyone involved was beginning to look like an unretouched photo of himself—and through it all, there was Coolidge, saying nothing publicly, though his boiled-beef-and-cabbage temperament let loose with fury enough when the press was elsewhere. "There are three purgatories to which people can be assigned," he told Herbert Hoover, one of the few Cabinet members left free of taint, "—to be damned by one's fellows; to be damned by the courts; to be damned in the next world. I want these men to get all three without probation." Even so, Coolidge kept to his secret keel, refusing to replace Denby and Daugherty at popular behest; Denby, however, resigned anyway in something of a daze, and Daugherty was finally fired only for failing to cooperate with another Senate investigation highly interested in Daugherty's Justice Department. Coolidge replaced Daugherty with Harlan F. Stone, who provided one of the lasting contributions of the decade by ousting the unspeakably crooked head of the Bureau of Investigation, William J. Burns, and turning the bureau over to J. Edgar Hoover.

Eventually, the truth about Fall's new fortune came out: Doheny and Sinclair had paid him off for their leases, which they explained were loans. By this time, it didn't matter what word one applied to it—loan, bribe, whatever—there had been too much lying, too much corruption in other cantles of Harding's Washington, for anyone to quibble over what Fall had done that was proper and what improper. All of Fall looked bad, and with Fall, Harding. But not Coolidge.

Moves were made to cancel the leases and the three principals of the case, Fall, Doheny, and Sinclair, went to trial, Fall ultimately being fined $100,000 and sent to jail for the better part of a one-year term; similar rewards awaited Charles Forbes and a few others of Harding's appointees. Through it all, incredibly, the efforts of these and other nasties to evade detection escalated even while they were in the searchlight and all eyes upon them. Under investigation, Harry Daugherty had offices ransacked and Senators hounded; an attempt was made to frame Senator Burton K. Wheeler, Daugherty's archfoe, in a hotel room with some doxy; and Sinclair, while being tried for contempt of the Senate, commandeered henchmen to tamper with the jurymen's sense of justice or, that failing, their health. Given these tactics, the two suicides of 1923 and Harding's death began to take on ever more unnatural colors. Were they, one wondered, what one had been told they were? Maybe Harding had been poisoned, after all.

Some innocent people, too, were smeared in the melee, most notably the Democrats' logical candidate for the coming presidential election, William Gibbs McAdoo. Had the party been stronger, it could have cried oil and swept into office, but the apparently imperturbable Coolidge rose above it all so matter-of-factly that, on second thought, maybe no Democrat whatsoever could have won. Having done nothing to earn popular support except make prominent noises after two prominent strikes (four years apart) were settled without his help, Coolidge, the jaundiced custodian of the lares and penates of New England thrift, was taking the cake.

It was Harding who bought it all. They still recall him as the one who gave himself, his friends, and the exchequer entirely over to all sorts of lubricity. Books, a play, and a movie sensationalized his regime, and as late as 1931 came *The Strange Death of President Harding*, an absurd scoop revealing lurid motivations behind the deaths and suicides of the Ohio gang regulars. It was penned by an insider—Gaston B. Means, the most unappetizing malefactor of all in Teapot Dome and a man to whom lying came as naturally as speaking. Means had impressed the Senate committees with his affable, oh, so helpful testimony on a variety of Teapot Dome–related matters until it dawned on them that he was nothing but false witness, loud, long, and loving, every word a swindle. Means got two years and a $10,000 fine for what little of his past turned up in the record, yet readers fell for his theories on Harding's death when his book came out, so pillaged and defaced was the President's memory then. They thought him the worst rascal ever elected, not understanding how much of his apparent culpability was a guilt of association and of too free a use of the spoils system. He had done what was often done: your friends helped you, you helped your friends. How was Harding to have known that he had such . . . friends?

So the dead President ended up a repository for the sins of the party, and Republican continuity was challenged but not necessarily blasted by the Democrats. A political cartoon during the 1924 campaign presented what seems to be a vaudeville turn by elephant and donkey, lyric sheets in hand. The quivering elephant is muttering new lyrics to "It Ain't Gonna Rain No Mo' "—"O, we ain' gwine steal no mo' "—while next to him the donkey screams out, "But how'n the 'ell kin the country tell 'you ain' gwine steal no mo'?' " Obviously, the opposition would make much of oil in the election of 1924, but this opposition was first going to have to reconcile its Western with its Eastern wings, its drys with its wets, its Kluxers with its civil libertarians, its Protestants with its Catholics—in short, its rural backlash with its urban progressives. This opposition was also going to have to conquer the Republicans' realization that in Coolidge they had no mere substitute incumbent but a winner on his own.

We joke about him now, about his narrowness, his social ungraces, his utter lack of initiative; they joked about him then—that's how much they liked him. He spoke in a sort of peremptory drawl, like the quack of a distracted duck, and few were they who truly admired him, but he looked smart and offered security. He was honest, solid, and had the "right ideas." No matter how far off the deep end they might stray, he was there still as he was, heading the corporation. Someone was minding the store.

What they didn't know about was how calculated the routine was. Coolidge was no dummy, if no intellectual, but in a nation as varied as this, there is no panacea or platitude, no matter how simple, that at least one whole region won't hold against one. "The things I never say never get me into trouble," he once pointed out, and except for the veto he exercised, the public Coolidge seldom had an opinion. When he left the office in 1929, people who had lived through a great era of presidential style in the persons of Theodore Roosevelt and Woodrow Wilson (though style took too much upon itself in Wilson's last days), hailed the totally unenterprising Coolidge as one of the greatest Presidents ever. For about nine months.

No one knew that Coolidge prosperity was ahead in 1924, though the depression of 1921-22 was obviously very much over, what with cars, stoves, "bus. op.'s" and Florida and California land grabbing to clog the advertising pages of the magazines. Coolidge was the available man in Republican terms—especially since Henry Ford had put the kibosh on his own potential by coming out for Coolidge—and the party convention in Cleveland radiated confidence in the voters' ability to separate the G.O.P. from Teapot Dome. Even as the Walsh hearings and the concomitant headlines kept the outrage before the eyes of anyone who could, and was willing to, read, it was evident that Coolidge not only wasn't suffering from petroleum poisoning, but that he was regarded as the antidote.

Those were the days when the Republicans still held sedate, what you might call Republican-style, conventions, and Cleveland saw none of the manipulating and filling of rooms with smoke that obtained in 1920 in Chicago. It was fleet and friendly, save for a flurry of holdouts from agrarian Progressives in Wisconsin and the Dakotas, and once Charles G. Dawes was picked as Coolidge's running mate, there was nothing left to do but wait for November and win.

Coolidge did win, of course, by a landslide slightly less effusive than Harding's, because the Democratic party had almost ceased to exist as a political entity. The Democrats' convention amounted to a kind of marathon dance of pigheaded, kamikaze sectarianism, and live radio broadcasts carried the message of discord to a nation that hadn't seen real leadership in years. True, it hadn't wanted to, but four years is a long time for a democracy to spend without a hero. For many, Coolidge would do, but he was no hero, and for some others, there was Robert La Follette, Al Smith, William Jennings Bryan, and William G. McAdoo. There were also two survivors of Harding's Cabinet, Andrew Mellon of the Treasury and of some hifalutin tax dodges for his fellow hifaluters, and Herbert Hoover, of Commerce, still remembered for his brilliant stint in picking up the pieces of Belgium that the Kaiser had left between the Scheldt and the Meuse and for rehabilitating most of the rest of Europe as well. But these were partisan idols, captains of blocs, not of a people.

The Democrats who met in New York held, willy-nilly, a two-party convention, split down the middle by the urbans and the rurals. The kingpins at the head of the two armies were Al Smith for the former and William McAdoo for the latter, each prepared to fight it out to the wall, through the masonry, and beyond into nowhere if necessary. Smith, the governor of New York State, was a slicker from Tammany Hall, a wet, and a Catholic; McAdoo, an ex-New Yorker and Wilson's son-in-law, was now a dry Californian of appeal to the Protestant agrarian West and South, unfairly tarnished by Doheny in the Teapot Dome escapade. It would be one or the other—the city machine or the camp meeting—but given the strong feelings aroused by Smith's religion and his distaste for Prohibition and by McAdoo's Fundamentalist, dry following, it could be neither. It could be no one. It would be nothing. Satiric editorials in the press advised the delegates that the only way to save the party was not to hold a convention at all.

Two weeks after the Republicans hit it off so discreetly in Cleveland, the Democrats arrived in, of all places, New York City for their siege in the old Madison Square Garden on Twenty-sixth Street. A circus had preceded them, and another circus engaged them for seventeen days of animal riots, slapstick hoopla, and popcorn anarchy. "Just wait, those are Democrats down there," said an American reporter to an Englishman who noted how calmly the first day went, and the uproar came soon. Demonstrations for and against almost every speaker's motion made it difficult even to hear each disaster as it occurred, and perhaps only the presence of the unflappable Senator Walsh as chairman saved the event from dissolving in a total shambles.

It was shambles enough as it was. Half of the delegates were for Prohibition, the KKK, and McAdoo, the other half for Repeal, denunciation of the KKK, and Smith. Amidst the cacophony of nomination jamborees and attempted censures of this or that special interest, there were few of those moments that even today can thrill the convention attender with a comprehension of the ripe vitality of American democracy (or do they still set it up in the smoke-filled room?). Walsh, with his keen moderation, was the hero of the hour for hours on end, and Franklin Roosevelt had his moment of grandeur when he nominated Smith in the famous "happy warrior of the political battlefield" speech. The saddest spot in the whole two weeks belonged to William Jennings Bryan, who attempted to harmonize the congregation in a lackluster harangue that only served to pull it farther apart. Rural, dry, and all for McAdoo, Bryan was a leader, all right: speaking more or less for Buncombe Country, he led his half of the flock right out of the communal pasture.

Most significant in the carnival misfortunes of the convention was a vote on a plank in the platform concerning the Ku Klux Klan, whether to condemn it or not mention it at all. The balloting on this issue provoked so much internecine brawling, anti-Klaners behaving as much like a lynch mob as pro-Klaners, that Walsh lost control of the hall—yea, even the indomitable Walsh—and when the tally was counted, the vote stood at 541 3/20 in favor of condemnation and 542 3/20 against—Klan support via tacit approval had carried by a single vote. Will Rogers called it "the day when I heard the most religion preached, and the least practiced, of any day in the world's history."

Less hairsplittingly schismatic but much more spectacular was the vote on the candidate; the count teetered now to McAdoo, now to Smith, with neither one in a decisive majority. Names came, names fluttered in the ozone for a poll or so, and names went, while logrollers squawked and delegates squabbled and the Democratic National Convention slouched toward Bethlehem to be dead. There was but one footnote of consistency throughout: Alabama voted invariably for a favorite son, and, as it opens the alphabet of states, day after day radio listeners heard each new ballot take off with Governor Brandon of Alabama crying, "A-la-ba-ma! Casts! Twenty-four votes fo-or Oscar! W.! Underwood!" What with all the other states rooting about frantically in one possibility after another, Alabama's steadfastness became one of the great radio memories of the era, passing into folklore as a vaudeville catchphrase and a standard "warm-up" line at megaphones and microphones.

Coolidge's campaign slogan, "Coolidge or Chaos," was going to sound awfully apropos. Was this the promise of the Democratic party, this unbending pluralism? At length, totally cashed in and disillusioned, the delegates found a compromise in John W. Davis, the former ambassador to the Court of St. James's and more recently a successful Wall Street lawyer (as a sop to Bryan, Wall Street's severest critic, they gave the vice-presidential nomination to Bryan's brother Charles, the governor of Nebraska). The final ballot, a sort of crawling stampede to Davis, was the one hundred third.

Not only Democrats' hopes, but those as well of the few surviving Progressives, were dashed when Robert La Follette saw the Republican Convention turn so readily to Coolidge. It had long been La Follette's intention to be President, but though he was the best thing that had ever happened to Wisconsin, he was defeated in every attempt to extend his influence beyond the Senate. No doubt it was too much for a man who backed such radical measures as federal ownership of railroads, renunciation of the use of court injunctions against workers in labor disputes, and legislative leverage for the farmer to expect to be more than a regional leader, but on the other hand who but a lone-wolf noncompromiser like himself could tame the rampant dishonesty of state machines and federal inertia? "Alone in the Senate" was the title of a chapter in his autobiography; it might have read "Alone in the Nation."

In failing health, and knowing for certain that nothing short of cataclysm could save Progressivism from the obituary of makeweight promises in future campaigns, La Follette took on Coolidge and Davis on the Conference for Progressive Political Action ticket, with Burton K. Wheeler, another dissident Senator, as his running mate. La Follette had to make more of a fuss on far less of a financial outlay than his opponents, but the press regarded it as copy that a man of his stature should join the grand contest, and there was little patronizing of the third-party procedure then as there is now. Still fumbling with the infant apparatus of nationwide personality-sell, the newsmen kept Fighting Bob in view, and, in addition, many prominent liberals—the same names as would shortly be associated with protesting the Sacco-Vanzetti trial—endorsed the C.P.P.A. ticket. Furthermore, as mentioned earlier, La Follette was smart enough to open his campaign on Labor Day with the first political talk ever made exclusively for radio broadcast.

Unfortunately, the candidate was not an effective radio speaker. His flair for gesture, his living presence that exampled the respectability— the morality—of dissent, was lost in transit; the voice alone did not carry. George Washington had noted, in words as applicable before as after the technological revolution, that "the people must *feel* before they will *see*," and this same La Follette who could stir their feelings in life was unable to adapt his style for the airwaves. Not long after, some others as individual as he made radio their weapon—Goebbels, Churchill, Huey Long, and Franklin Roosevelt, for example—but they had to discover its secret first. One didn't simply march up to the microphone and "be" into it, the way one debated in the age of bombastic oration, but then that was all La Follette would permit himself, ever, anywhere. He always just was. Not so much in the twenties, but more and more as time passes, the lesson of the media will be that nothing natural ever quite goes over, for natural tends to the humdrum, and this is the commencement of the age of Bigger and Better. Striving for effect through the prism of the mike and the lens, one can only achieve effect, but effect is all one asks of it; time and technology were closing in on the La Follettes as surely as the bad taste of war closed in on Progressivism's appeal to the social conscience and Doing Good. And this much had La Follette understood about the shifts in a public servant's address of the public, that he must launch a presentation on radio. But this much was radio going to change things around, that man had to accommodate himself to it, for it would never accommodate itself to man.

La Follette died a year after the election, but not before he had embarked on the last telling splurge of a third party until recent times, winning a bigger percentage of the popular vote than George Wallace did in 1968. He didn't stand a chance of garnering a majority mandate, or even a winning minority, yet he chanced it, knocking his exhausted body over the hill to the churchyard, a *mens sana* in a *corpore insano.* How could he have reached the nation? The Progressives spent $221,000 on the campaign, the Democrats $800,-000, the Republicans $4,000,000. La Follette's supporters noted with sinking heart that both the leading parties were offering "Wall Street" candidates, and even the farmers were swayed away from "their" man by a slight incline in the price of wheat in late '24. Anyone with half a brain and a family to raise had to admit that Coolidge prosperity looked like prosperity for all. The tenor of the postwar ban on altruism and the retreat to the self-interest of normalcy was going to serve for another chorus.

"More business in government and less government in business," Coolidge had proclaimed, a reference to the guiding hand of Andrew Mellon, Secretary of the Treasury from 1921 to 1932. The Mellon idea was a thriving American economy based on uncurbed stock speculation and a collapsed European economy based on accountability for war reparations (Germany) and war debts (England, France, and Italy). "They hired the money, didn't they?" was Coolidge's summation of policy. He was right; they did. But some economists point to Europe's sagging rather than our bulging as a contribution to the protraction of the Great Depression, not to mention the panicky fiscal nowhereness of Germany that helped negotiate the coming of fascism and another war. Throughout the twenties, Congress took steps to turn Mellon's muscular laissez-faire into a humane capitalism, refining his tax breaks to include some of the subelite brackets. The aim was to make more money available to the rich to expand the mechanics of economic flow, at the same time encompassing the consumer to devour the supply.

No one can say what La Follette or Davis—or, since a miss is as good as a mile, the Communist candidate of '24, William Z. Foster, who pulled 33,361 votes—might have done at the helm, but Coolidge's lack of advance leadership is a matter of record. Later on, in 1927, William Z. Ripley predicted a downturn in the economy in a book he called *Main Street and Wall Street.* "The house is not falling down—no fear of that!" he wrote. "But there are queer little noises about, as of rats in the wall, or of borers in the timbers." At Coolidge's invitation, Ripley, a Harvard professor—and they *know!*—

visited the White House to enlarge on his views. Came the moment when Coolidge asked Ripley what he, the President, could do about all this. Given the laws as they stood, Ripley told him, he couldn't do a bloody thing; it was up to the states to deal with it. And that was all Coolidge wanted to know: it was just another trouble running into the ditch that he could turn his back on.

Boy, things had really swiveled around by the time Coolidge was triumphantly borne back into the Oval Office, having polled nearly twice as well as Davis (as in 1920, the Dixiecrat South was about all that kept the Democrats on the map). No longer the robber barons of the trust-busting days, business leaders had become respectable again, the very agents of earthly grace. Much of this can be accounted to the "good times"—good? Hell, they were like living in a wallet—but much of it also can be traced to the careful work of P.R. revisionists such as Bruce Barton, who so nimbly mated church and business in *The Man Nobody Knows*. Coolidge put the final stamp on the premise: "The man who builds a factory builds a temple."

Not that men like the Kleagles of the KKK or a Midwestern opinion molder such as William Jennings Bryan ever bought Wall Street as a positive force, but Bryan was dead and the Klan dying by middecade, and, besides, why complain when matters were progressing so swimmingly? The Walsh hearings on the Ohio gang went on into 1928, turning up snakes under rocks in D.C. from the Hill to the recently reclaimed Foggy Bottom, but the scandal began to be looked on almost as a signet of a wild and daffy era, as if the sexual and youth revolution, the artistic outcries, Prohibition's organized crime, and this high-level corruption as well were all bells on the same sleigh ride.

Isolationist and punch-drunk on local prosperity, Americans looked up to no one and asked few questions. In his campaigning with La Follette in '24, the vice-presidential candidate Burton Wheeler underscored our want of leadership by debating the issues of the day with an empty chair—a stunt, but a telling one. "President Coolidge," he would say to the chair, "tell us where you stand on Prohibition." And of course there was no Coolidge, so there could be no answer. "Tell me, Mister President," Wheeler would continue, to the chuckles of the crowd, and garbling some of his facts, "why was it necessary for Congress to act before you dismissed the Secretary of the Navy who had allowed the Navy's oil reserves to be turned over to the Secretary of the Interior, knowing this Secretary of the Interior was frankly in favor of turning over all the nation's natural resources to private exploiters? Tell me, Mister President, why is it you stood behind Harry Daugherty?" And naturally there was again no answer to questions many others would have liked to put to Coolidge. And then Wheeler would beam at the people, and the people would respond with a cheer of appreciation. What a laugh.

But that *was* Coolidge sitting in that chair.

FIVE

Doin' the New Low Down

Speako Deluxe, Joseph Golinken's painting of the inside of a Prohibition era speakeasy, shows bright and beautiful people in evening clothes ensconced around an elliptical bar manned by suave-looking waiters. A touch of Art Deco sets the scene off just so; light bathes the den, and though everyone in sight is breaking the law, nothing could look less forbidden. Men and women, wise and witty, are at their social sport. "The putting of the fear of God in the minds of those who fear neither God nor man is the chief function of good government"—the Reverend Clarence True Wilson, secretary of the Methodist Board of Temperance, Prohibition, and Public Morals.

Robert Benchley once walked the north and south lengths of Fifty-second Street between Fifth and Sixth avenues counting speakeasies. He put the total at thirty-eight, which will have included Jack and Charlie's at 21 West as of 1929, but not Belle Livingstone's Country Club nor Texas Guinan's Three Hundred Club, the Club Intime, the El Fay, the Del Fay, and Salon Royale (to name a few of her many) nor Helen Morgan's place, though all were nearby in the West Forties and Fifties. This neck of the woods was New York's pride of Prohibition, compact of the best music, the most swank personalities, and the safest booze. There was no danger of chancing "jake foot," blindness, or alcohol poisoning at Club 21. "I call it legalized murder and the Government is an accessory to the crime"—Edward I. Edwards, Senator from New Jersey.

It was, of course, a different story across the country, where the improvisational settlers of the Prohibition frontier used whatever was to hand in the brewing of elixir in the "beer flats," "blind pigs" (bars with blank fronts) and "shock houses" of the slums and in the drugstores of the rural districts. A necessary ingredient in all sorts of industry, alcohol could not practically be legislated into extinction, so the government contrived a number of denaturing and poisoning processes to keep the plants supplied while discouraging the human throat. Bootleggers found it relatively easy to divert the denatured alcohol from its sources, dye it and flavor it and bottle it. And sell it. In 1927, the death toll from the imbibing of "liquor" containing poisoned alcohol stood at 11,700. "We're big business without high hats"—Dion O'Banion, florist and gangster.

Licensed to kill, federal Prohibition agents were less omnipresent than toxic hooch but much more agile. They were barely, if at all, trained, recruited by unsympathetic or even vindictive authorities, and often fired at themselves by strangers: not astoundingly, they proved as dangerous as any bootlegger, and waged a bloody war against, on occasion, anything that moved. No governmental figures on innocent people shot down by federal agents on mere suspicion of violation came near to the truth. The official death count for such accidents was 173; *American* magazine, however, chalked up 1550 fatalities. "Come on, suckers, open up and spend some jack!"—Texas Guinan, speakeasy proprietor.

Guinan's snazzy approach is the one best remembered now. The speaks were lush clubs or heavenly dives; bootleggers and gangsters, colorful roughnecks; the federal agents amiable savants; and the times the best of times. Whole cities turned scofflaw in the happy anarchy that a democracy must indulge in when its laws get too stupid to obey, and the whoopee was immense. Hosts and patrons grew so inured to police raids that they could navigate through them sleepwalking; at Texas Guinan's, whenever a Fed would rise up to announce the arrest, glass or teacup in hand as evidence, the band

would go right into "The Prisoner's Song" and Texas would bawl a
festive insult. A smash musical with a Gershwin score, *Oh, Kay!*,
hymned the wild life of the rumrunner with sitcom and schmaltz
("the difference between a bootlegger and a Federal inspector," one of
its lines ran, "is that one of them wears a badge"); two Feds, Izzy
Einstein and Moe Smith, won renown for the cute getups and ruses
under cover of which they sneaked into joints ("There's sad news
here," was Izzy's way of broaching the announcement that his quarry
was under arrest); a concerted drive by U.S. Assistant Attorney Mabel
Walker Willebrandt to close New York down cost her office $75,000
in bar bills and netted only $8400 in fines, to the town's delight;
thousands of cameras snapped the communion of merry patrons
waving teacups of gin while bartenders grinned like family retainers:
nothing but fun. It wasn't Prohibition that was taken for granted, but
the spoofing of it. Taken for granted, too, was the sly pragmatism of
many law enforcers and the lack of moral hangover over having
shattered the sanctity of this democracy's most precious endowment,
the Constitution—the sanctity of which had first been shattered by the
most arrant contempt for personal liberty in the history of the
document, namely the Eighteenth Amendment to it ("the manufacture, sale, or transportation of intoxicating liquors . . . for beverage
purposes is hereby prohibited"), and then by its enforcement equipment, the Volstead Act. "Cops like dough and law is just tricks"—
anonymous, a Chicago bootlegger.

The rape of the population's respect for law that was accomplished
during Prohibition has since entered our folklore. What did the
twenties do? They did roar, nothing else: again, nothing but fun and,
oh, maybe a little death. Turn in all the fun for examinations of
managing policy or artistic insurgence or scientific achievement and it
wouldn't be the twenties anymore. For reconnoitering the times,
twenty acts of Congress, ten prize novels, and fifty patents together
equal one gangster movie, and *now* you're talking—literally talking,
for the gangster movies didn't come in until the thirties when
technology discovered Hollywood and gave it sound, and when, as
well, the twenties had fallen away and hard times wanted to hear
more about the black knights of the lawless frontier.

The gangster show is a significant item in Prohibition's several bequests, and it strikes closest to our ambivalent awareness of how often the hoodlum business connects to the straight and narrow. In a typical such number, *The Roaring Twenties*, of 1939, James Cagney is nabbed by the Feds while unwittingly delivering bootleg booze to speak owner "Panama Smith." "Buster, who da ya know?" the lady asks him as they're escorted to court. "I know a lawyer," says Cagney, and she replies, "It'd be better if ya knew a judge." It isn't the twenties talking, true; it's just hearsay, but of all that was, it's what's mainly left.

To capture what was we move from New York, playground of the highbrows, to Chicago, the El Dorado, Vatican, and Calcutta of Prohibition, for it is Chicago, which Nelson Algren described as "a joint where the bulls and the foxes live well and the lambs wind up head-down from the hook," that birthed much of the lore of the American twenties. There were gangsters and speakeasies and riotous city rooms and entrenched police corruption all over the land, but Chicago usurped the whole shebang as an enterprise primarily native to Chicago. New York remains the focus of the artistic energies of the time, and insidious science lurked in hangars and unmarked laboratory complexes from here to there, but for many onlookers, Chicago symbolized the blunt athleticism and even the sweep of the era as a kind of Wall Street of the national thirst.

No tong of desperadoes ever fought so hard and openly for their territory in New York as did the gangs of Bugs Moran, Klondike O'Donnell, or the Genna Boys in Chicago, nor so brazenly patrolled the polling places at voting time, nor felt so little compunction about enjoining extramural skirmishes in pedestrian traffic, as did the desperadoes of Chicago. Chicago was where a tough on the rise went to make bad, as young Alphonso Caponi did, and in its perversion of the Horatio Alger idea, Chicago and its millionaire racketeers impressed some critics as baring the crude essence of capitalism's acquisitive heart for all to see, the gangsters being no more than unduly forward businessmen with the lucrative fiefdoms, assistant yesmen, and competition one looks for in industrial circles. But this sounds like a spoilsport canard from some highbrow radical; gangsters

had much more in common with fascism than with upward mobility—
although they did show how easily a determined minority could bend
democratic freedom into a land's end of presumption.

It was no accident that Chicago was the country's prize enclave of
gangsterism, and Caponi knew what he was doing when he quit New
York, where juries occasionally convicted gangsters, for the queen of
the Midwest, where they didn't. He proved in his long career that he
was the most efficient of Prohibition's scofflaws, moving in, taking
over, and making the queen his whore, and there had to be a reason
why so tenacious a reptile didn't attempt his rise at the Northeastern
water hole adopted by his immigrant family when they arrived from
Italy. New York was wide open, but it was no pushover, and Caponi,
restyled Capone, headed for the one true gangsterville at the invitation
of Johnny Torrio. Starting out as a bouncer in one of Torrio's
brothels (situated on the state line, it had an entrance in Illinois and
an exit in Indiana), Capone took Chicago, clearing upward of fifty
million dollars a year and owning outright the suburb of Cicero by
being as ruthless as his fellows but a bit brighter. It could only have
happened in Chicago: New York just wasn't that cynical.

Chicago was that cynical. It had long been, at least in the words of
Alderman Robert Merriam, "the only completely corrupt city in
America." Reports of the free-living low-lives who hustled it, when it
was still a frontier crossroads, for the ill-gotten gains that the twenties
would dub "ice" and "gravy," filtered back to the East like a slap in
the face, for from the beginning, the law was no law. Again and again
citizens complained that the official civic arm was not protecting the
innocent from robbery, murder, and the minutiae of organized
turpitude, but then for a Chicago policeman to arrest a blackguard
would have amounted to conflict of interest. A book of 1893, *If
Christ Came to Chicago*, recounted a tale one was to hear throughout
the following century, of "solid" citizens hooked up to crime rings
hooked up to a bought constabulary hooked up to larceny hooked up
to the political machine. As the Prohibition chronicler Kenneth
Allsop relates, "In one six-month period of 1906 there was a burglary
every three hours, a hold-up every six hours, and a murder every
day."

Chicago's history is unquestionably a violent one; the town was also the seat of America's earliest brush with the original Marxian escort, dating back to the subversive and trade unionist Lehr und Vehr Vereine of the 1870s, and, of course, the Haymarket Riot of 1886, a landmark of bomb-throwing labor violence, occurred in Chicago. No other spot on our map offers a more patent illustration of the inadequacy of public opinion or state law to control evil, or of the ease with which evil might make cause with the prevailing structures for power, security, annd continuity.

Yet Chicago and its corruption have become withal a joke, a national sarcasm bordering on the chummy, and a byword for the scapegrace frivolity of the twenties especially. Legends that reconstruct the era for us are mainly the legends of Chicago, voluble with the screech of change on the brakes of tradition, and favoring the raw, rich scorch of chaos and the tumult of the dance dives. Chicago was the newspaper town, urgent with headlines, a man's town—"stormy, husky, brawling, City of the Big Shoulders," Carl Sandburg called it—as if only here in this entrancingly wide-open city could virility and ingenuity and potency prove themselves; one isn't surprised to learn that the *Chicago Tribune* was the country's most outspoken censor of Rudolph Valentino's ambiguous biology.

But there was also the feeling that Chicago was too virile in the wrong way, too pushy, too deranged by power to want the ethics, as well as the fruits, of progress. New York, shooting skyward, was the very pattern of progress, but Chicago, the palace of ice in the kingdom of gravy, was more like a jet-propelled sewer. Edna Ferber, who saw the American continent as a mad plateau of romance, hit upon a telling simile in 1926 in her novel *Show Boat,* wherein she gave Chicago as the counterpart to the Mississippi River, torrential and ruinous, unharnessable, and no man-built city but a natural force subsuming men. The big river, in her view, is "a tawny tiger . . . lashing out with its great tail, tearing with its cruel claws, and burying its fangs deep in the shore to swallow at a gulp land, houses, trees, cattle—humans, even, and roaring, snarling, howling as it did so." Chicago, later in the book, is "only the Mississippi in another form and environment; ruthless, relentless, Gargantuan, terrible. One might think to know its currents and channels ever so well, but once caught unprepared in the maelstrom, one would be sucked down and devoured."

This is strong aspersion from someone such as Ferber, who had a soft spot for adventurers and adventurous places. But she drew the line at Chicago, and there were those whose artistic reaction to the place ran more closely to disgust than horror. Europeans especially excoriated Chicago as a centrus of American mores, a typical rather than exceptional spot. Bertolt Brecht, to take an admittedly extreme example, chose Chicago as the perfect setting in which to expose what he took to be the fallacy of benign capitalism in his play *St. Joan of the Stockyards,* with its saintly radical maid and its meatpacking villain Pierpont Snouter. Brecht really got to exploit Chicago: he also borrowed it for his and Kurt Weill's louche musical play *Happy End,* and then supposed a phantasmal city where everything goes and the only crime is not to have money in his and Weill's opera, *Rise and Fall of Mahagonny City,* this Mahagonny being modeled on Chicago (although as usual Brecht laid the exact location in that private Atlantis of his somewhere in between Surabaya and Berlin).

In a way, Brecht's twentieth-century, pressure-group spiel is just a through-the-looking-glass extension of Europeans' wonder at the free commercial culture. As a Communist, Brecht was bound to present the defective side effects of a political and social openness that, frankly, no European is ever going to understand, from Alexis de Tocqueville to Dino de Laurentiis. But Brecht's tarts and hustlers of a kind of Chicago remind one of such thoughts as these, voiced by the *London Daily News* in 1853 in honor of the visiting Cornelius Vanderbilt: "America . . . is the great arena in which the individual energies of man, uncramped by oppressive social institutions or absurd social traditions, have full play, and arrive at gigantic development." It sounds almost like the satiric invention of an anti-American, in mock praise of Chicago. To Americans, the city on Lake Michigan embodied the worst (to a very few, the best) aspects of American life; to Europeans, Chicago was America in little.

With its entrenched foundation of municipal corruption and a traditional laissez-faire on the part of a traditionally helpless citizenry,

Chicago and the bandits who would throng to it in the twenties were waiting for a deal like Prohibition, which could net them the countless millions being paid across bar tops and in drugstores. And in a way, not only Chicago but the whole nation, too, was waiting for Prohibition—or it should have been, for the signals of its coming had been transmitted loud and clear for decades.

Usage has it that the national dry code was put over on a people distracted by the war effort and rushed into law so suddenly that drinkers had no time to mobilize for resistance. In actuality the drive for a national ban on alcohol had been flooring the gas for fifteen years after half a century of careful motoring, and Prohibition was finally set up in the Congressional elections of 1916, before the United States entered the war. The National Woman's Christian Temperance Union, founded in 1874, and the Anti-Saloon League of America, founded in 1895, were absolutely dedicated to their cause— capable of creating, or killing, messiahs and kingdoms. The W.C.T.U. defined itself as "organized mother love," and these mothers and their allies argued that liquor causes poverty, marital distress, and negligence, and that wherever a saloon was built, brothels, gambling dens, and a slum directly followed. Misperceiving the meaning of the word "temperance"—which is drink in moderation—they lobbied for total abstention, and they weren't about to leave the choice up to the individual. One uses the word "lobby" here in the Pickwickian sense; no Roman lion ever lobbied for raw Christian the way the drys lobbied for Prohibition.

Here was a true tyranny of the majority, but it didn't even require a majority to accomplish Prohibition, just a precisely concerted minority that knew how to use letter campaigns, speaking tours, and blackmail to achieve its aim. Local option to go dry or wet by county had long been the norm, but the drys worked unceasingly to grasp whole states, and by the 1900s their goal of a national moratorium left only two bottles to cork: one, dry federal Congressmen to back it, and two, dry state legislatures to endorse it.

No one is better qualified to present the modus of the dry lobby than Wayne B. Wheeler, head of the Anti-Saloon League of America, a champion marplot and a "powerful, determined, cunning realist" as characterized in Lincoln Steffens' autobiography. "I do it the way the bosses do it," Wheeler told Steffens, "with minorities. There are some anti-saloon voters in every community. I and other speakers increase the number and the passion of them. I list and bind them to vote as I bid. I say, 'We'll all vote against the men in office who won't support our bills. We'll vote for candidates who will promise to. They'll break their promise. Sure. Next time we'll break them.' And we can. We did. Our swinging, solid minorities, no matter how small, counted."

So what if the reform candidates the drys forced on whole constituencies were inexperienced, incompetent, or even unwell? They were dry, and that was what counted, that alone. Trading on whatever was in the air—a hatred for Germans, say, that could be translated into a war on beer, or a promise of economic and social salvation to a depressed area, or the domino theory: beer leads to rum leads to alcoholism—the drys led their crusade through the districts so minutely that every vote, built up in the aggregate, began, as Wheeler says, to count. They pleaded, they wheedled, they harangued, they threatened. And they appealed to voters' lambent Christian righteousness: "Don't you want to end the distress of the wine widow and her starving children? Close the saloon and bring her husband home!"

In the cities, tavernkeepers and restaurateurs preferred to let the husband make up his own mind, but to the ladies of the W.C.T.U., freedom of choice was a rationale for evil—and a city evil at that. Ultimately, Prohibition may be viewed as another instance of the rural-urban conflict, a draft on the somehow never quite closed Puritan account believing itself to be a reform movement, collectivism masquerading as Progressivism. The National Wholesale Liquor Dealers' and the Brewers' Associations fought back with bribery and the boycott, but they were unable to tap a vein of wet fanaticism to counter that of the drys. No doubt many of the Prohibitionists were only doing what they took to be good, but the vindictive aspect of the program came out in the late twenties, when it was obvious that besides being unenforceable, Prohibition had wreaked an appalling devastation upon the land in the way of law, order, and human life. Many drys registered second thoughts then, but many others openly declared their willingness to fight the issue to the wall at any cost. In 1929, when told of how six Feds broke into the home of a suspected bootlegger, clubbed him down, and, as his wife leaped to his side, blasted her with a shotgun, Ella Boole of the W.C.T.U. commented, "She was evading the law, wasn't she?"

Whence this frenzy for repression, this hatred of one's fellow citizens for doing what had been done as a matter of course, camaraderie, and medicine for 250 years? Since when did an American reform movement have to raise the guillotine? In the early 1900s, there was some identification on the part of drys with Progressivism, especially since the brand-name Progressive Senators of the Midwest and West either were dry themselves or beloved of dry constituencies. But Progressivism, a distinct species of reform activity emphasizing the idealism of a politico who acts for the little man against the money boss, signifies an opening up and a giving out, not a taking away. There really were two branches of Progressivism, one Eastern, relatively intelligent, and moderate—Theodore Roosevelt and Woodrow Wilson—and the other Midwestern or Western, populist, and rabid—Robert La Follette and William E. Borah (note that the moderates rather than the rabids tended to the presidential). Neither strain turned on denial or centrism, as Prohibition did, and no Progressive, with so much at stake on the national agenda, ever was willing to barter all values but one for the one, as Prohibition did. Furthermore, Progressivism was basically a Republican development, while Prohibition, though having loyalty to dryness alone rather than to any political philosophy, eventually assumed control of the Democratic party, which testifies to its populist appeal.

Georgia went dry in 1907, Oklahoma later that year, fast followed by North Carolina, Tennessee, Mississippi, and West Virginia—the Dixiecrat and Fundamentalist countryland, in short. By 1910, state and local option had dried ninety-five percent of the land in area, two-thirds of the population. Only the cities and the states with a bulk urban polity held out for demon rum, but the drys got a break with the passing of the Seventeenth Amendment to the Constitution in 1912, providing for the direct election of Senators by popular vote, and incidentally giving every dry and his *idée fixe* a personal veto to apply to wet candidates. Working with their signature agility, the drys pushed their men into office at the polls in 1916, aided by the women's vote in the eleven Western states that had adopted sexless suffrage.

The rest was simply denouement. The Lever Food and Fuel Control Act of 1917 outlawed the use of foodstuffs in distilled liquor to conserve grain, and a few months later came an eighteenth amendment to the Constitution, national Prohibition in toto—"don't you know there's a war on?" Sneaking under the wire as a contribution to the war effort, the ban on liquor had marched right into Congress and now stood ready to check out the vote, and woe to the man who was slow with his aye. Mother love, Christian charity, bighearted Progressivism . . . now it was calling itself patriotism: "Stay dry for victory!" But as the *Washington Times* saw it, "Every Congressman knows that if the ballot . . . were a secret ballot, making it impossible for the Anti-Saloon League bosses to punish disobedience, the amendment would not pass."

The wets weren't down yet, however, and the cynicism that professional politicians carry about with them in inexhaustible supply told them that there was still a way out. It was mighty Senator Penrose of Pennsylvania who spoke up for demon rum, who rallied wet Congresmen fearful of dry retribution for nonsupport, and who dealt the amendment a telling proviso: the required ratification by thirty-six states had to be accomplished within seven years. Experience told the pols that nothing happens that fast in those men's democracy, but experience had nothing to do with the Anti-Saloon League. Wheeler and his machine got the Eighteenth Amendment ratified in thirteen months, and Wheeler himself drafted the enforcement law, known as the Volstead Act after Andrew Volstead of Minnesota, who introduced it in the House of Representatives.

The manufacture, sale, and transportation of liquor was banned as of midnight, January 16, 1920, which gave the offending industry a year in which to dissolve and sell stockpiles to would-be drinkers, for one was legally entitled to continue to own and drink liquor purchased before the cutoff, and one could even apply for a permit to transport his hoard if he moved. The last hours of wet America—in those places, that is, that hadn't already gone dry under local option long before—were a dog race of nick-of-time and too-late gambits in unloading the remnants of the trade. The first hours of dry America were a party for drys. "We will turn our prisons into factories!" proclaimed Billy Sunday at a mock funeral for John Barleycorn. "Men will walk upright now, women will smile, and the children will laugh. Hell will be forever for rent!"

Meanwhile, a federal judge suddenly ruled that liquor troves stored in warehouses (as opposed to home) were liable to seizure, and frantic wets scrounged up every form of locomotion known to mankind to cart their bottles toward home and federal sanction. Liquor dealers faced a myriad of contretemps nationwide in the act of shipping their surplus abroad, for they had all waited for the eleventh hour and there wasn't enough transport to go around. In California one despairing winegrower committed suicide. Across the hinterland, meetings of the W.C.T.U. sang their ever-popular and now so fitting ditty, "A Saloonless Nation in 1920," while in the cities, sardonic resignation prevailed in the establishments of carousal; waiters dressed in black and salon orchestras played medleys of farewell songs. And in Chicago, bare minutes after Prohibition took effect, organized crime celebrated the new regime by pinching two legal consignments of alcohol and highjacking a third lot from less well organized criminals. "Who's Johnny-on-the-Spot?" chortled a song of 1930. "Red hot Chicago!"

Naturally it would be Chicago that squashed the embryo of a dry new world when the eggshell was scarcely broken, but all over the country wets furtive and open, amenable and sadistic, made their arrangements for shattering the spell of Prohibition on a continuing basis. This law was tyranny, and antiauthoritarian dissent is an American specialty, our heraldic urge: we resisted. Until the Twenty-first Amendment legalized liquor again in 1933, a vast public opinion, the safety in numbers, and plain common sense lined up on the side of the bootlegger . . . and the widespread purchasability of the law's enforcement agents didn't hurt. There were a few untouchables—the Eliot Ness team in Chicago, for example, or the zealots of the Coast Guard who patrolled the notorious Rum Row, a maze of shining sea and rumrunners from Portland, Maine, to Charleston, South Carolina—but most Feds were easily bought because in most cases they weren't selling out to anyone whom an American would class as a criminal.

Said H. L. Mencken, in late 1926, "The business of evading Prohibition and making mock of it has ceased to wear any aspects of crime, and has become a sort of national sport." And E. B. White suggested an outright nationalization of speakeasies, so that "the citizenry would be assured liquor of a uniformly high quality, and the enormous cost of dry enforcement could be met by profits from the sale of drinks." At first, many moderate drinkers accepted Prohibition with a sheepish guilt, conceding the possibility that the moral argument held water, so to speak, after all. But many others, law-abiders in all but this—people who respected codes and never told lies and believed in the white Protestant God—simply refused to go along with the project. Soon these part-time sinners convinced the sheep to join them, by their example, in disobedience. For some, it was a form of voting.

This improvised electorate made its stand mainly in saloons, technically underground but easy enough to locate, and home brew provided a very civil disobedience plus the distinctly American cultivation of do-it-yourself multiformity, with about as many recipes, or variations on recipe, as there were home brewers. "Bathtub gin" is the term that has lasted, but a wealth of pioneer contraptions created a whole folklore of fermentation, much of it centering around wine, to those of recent emigration from Europe a virtually indispensable beverage. Those who were not in touch with the public domain could apply to the stores, where live demonstrations of timely gadgets told the prospective buyer what natives of Tennessee and Kentucky had known for generations. "Yes!" the store clerk would exclaim, in that way they have of starting out at a thousand and surging to a million, "you simply dissolve this flavored brick in a gallon of warm water, chill, and voilà! a delicious grape beverage! But be sure not to store this liquid in a cool, dry place for exactly twenty-one days, for then it would turn into wine! And, *whatever* you do, *don't* apply this handy cork containing the rubber siphon hose to the neck of the bottle—that procedure would only be used to induce fermentation! Also, be careful not to shake the liquid faithfully once a day, because that, too, will help turn the juice."

One of the decade's discoveries was that it wasn't as easy as it sounded. Again, let us hear from Mencken, a determined foe of repression who wasn't going to let the Volstead Act deprive him of his beer. In a letter to a friend, he wrote:

> Last Sunday I manufactured five gallons of Methodistbräu ... but I bottled it too soon, and the result has been a series of fearful explosions. Last night I had three quart bottles in my side yard, cooling in a bucket. Two went off at once, bringing my neighbor out of his house with yells. He thought the Soviets had seized the town ... I shall make dandelion wine if I can find a dandelion. But down here they are not to be trusted. Dogs always piss on them. And, now and then, a policeman.

We tend to respect people who break rules, who just go ahead and *do*, don't we? It's an outlet for the fascination with anarchy that hovers dimly in the back of our minds, and has sparked whole genres devoted to the outlaw in our popular arts. For a century the Western reigned on the nation's stages to extol the trail of the lone-wolf adventurer and his confrontation with nature untamed, latterly turning to a confrontation between good adventurers and bad. The Western is still with us, but meanwhile we have developed a taste for the urban Western, with Thompson submachine guns in place of muskets and imported names erasing the Boone and Crockett of yore.

As Chicago's gangsters rose to prominence, social critics jumped Frederick Jackson Turner's "frontier" theory of characterological purification and produced its corollary: if the taming of the West had created an American race of the self-sufficient fittest, as Turner proposed, it had also created a reckless morality of the take and a law of the gun, likewise self-sufficient. For Coolidge, however, the descendants of the old West were the new businessmen. "The frontier still lingers," he said. "The hardy pioneer still defends the outworks of civilization."

The popularity of such films as the aforementioned *The Roaring Twenties* and the excessively bloody gangster cinema of more recent years keeps social critics busy making a comparison between the racketeer lords of the twenties and the robber barons of the late 1800s; "a syndicate is a syndicate," they tell us, "whether headed by a Rockefeller or a Capone." Americans worship wealth, and how one gets it is, to Americans, a quibble, or so the story goes. But this equation doesn't take into account the rise and fall of the plutocrat's public relations, nor the differing temperaments of differing localities. It is true that the Chicago gangsters, who won exhaustive "personality" coverage in the press in their day, were looked up to by some few Chicagoans as exemplars of muscular capitalism, as robber barons of a more ethnic era. But what has become of that benighted worship today? It is gone—yet the businessman-king of *Forbes* and *Fortune* magazines remains a potent symbol today.

Even in the twenties, the businessman had evolved from the ghoulish, invisible monopolist of the trust-busting era into the stalwart Nestor of public service in the twenties, beneficent and available for group photographs, and he has retained a certain qualified eminence since. Not till the Depression got under way were the critics of capitalism much heard, for in the Teapot Dome years such symbols of courtly money power as the wise Andrew Mellon, the humanitarian Herbert Hoover, the honest Calvin Coolidge, and the omnipresent Henry Ford inspired emulation rather than hatred. Weathering hard times and the overextended populist administration of the thirties and forties, the industrialist-banker-lawyer still claims top-rank respectability when elections are held and appointments made, while gangsters are looked upon as what they are, depraved and conscienceless looters.

Yet even now the lure of adventure, of masters and the vanquished, lingers in the folklore of organized crime, and much of it is contained in the sound of "Chicago." One reason for the city's brief heyday as a crossroads of "heroic" adventure was the attitude of the press, particularly in the leverages applied to the unofficial circulation war between the newspapers of the town, the *Tribune,* the *Evening Post,* and the *Herald and Examiner.* The vicious criminal proved a tangy subject for investigation, denounced in editorials to soothe civic outrage, and vaunted in the news columns to tempt civic curiosity. As much copy as news, with their aliases and argot, their proclamatory nicknames (Frank "The Enforcer" Nitti, Julian "Potatoes" Kaufman, Jack "Greasy Thumb" Guzik), the outlaws filled Chicago's newsprint, fulfilling a contract between editors and readers that gave the former revenue and the latter a vicarious tour through forbidden hedonism.

That is a key word, hedonism, because for all the visions of Willa Cather's romantic farmers, sensing their tiny span in the epic, and for all Sinclair Lewis's small-townish businessmen, falling out of touch with the land and unaware of all but the money hustle, there is another twenties world view to take in. It, too, has its chroniclers, totems, and heroes, and it even has something the others didn't— theme music, shortly to be heard here. Unlike Cather's pioneers and Lewis's Babbitts, the bawds and gaudies of Chicagoland had neither a past nor a future to calculate: they were the present, and the tone of their time was turbulence.

It can't be denied that the Prohibition period was greeted by a widespread amusement at its circuslike giddiness as well as an anger at its lawlessness. Despite the constant rain of bullets that fell upon Chicago, heralded by a screech of brakes and a mass dodging into doorways or jackknifing behind automobiles on the part of those in the vicinity, the experience was taken as a carnival in which the fairgrounds were all freak show and corruption tore the tickets. After a failed attempt by Mayor William E. Dever to reclaim the city with a reform program, the former mayor, "Big Bill" Thompson, was merrily voted back in (thanks in some degree to the gangsters who hung around the polling places, urging folks to weigh their choice as a matter of life or death) to resume his reign of unbridled misrule.

"Big Bill the Builder" was his slogan, and he was probably the most destructive man of the decade, as bad as all the mobsters put together, for he was a living testament to the wages of status quo sin and his wages were very, very high. (Strongboxes unearthed in his home after his death in 1944 revealed a dragon pile of $1,750,000, not easily accounted for by his $22,500-a-year salary as mayor.) With his professional politician sleaze, his cowboy hat, his cartoony lies,

and his ridiculously irrelevant tirades against Britain as an answer to
any criticism of his administration, Thompson was a true signet of the
defiantly wet epoch, much more so than Texas Guinan and the
"Hello, sucker!" that welcomed patrons to her speakeasies or than
New York's nervy annual revues, the *Follies,* the *Scandals,* and the
Vanities, that merged seminudity with weisenheimer comedy and
innocent "cheer up, who needs money?" ditties. To the rest of the
country, gaping in disbelief when Thompson was returned to office, it
appeared as though most of the population of the nation's second city
lived the way the picture of Dorian Gray looked.

So it appeared to honest Chicagoans, too. Every so often a lawman
or a reporter would be "bumped off" (as the lingo had it); stinging
editorials, whinnies from the police commissioner, and, sometimes,
posted rewards from a newspaper or two for information leading to
the apprehension of the guilty would follow. Time and again the
victim, supposedly silenced in his war on crime, would turn out to be
just another cog in the machine of swindles and payoffs. "Who killed
McSwiggin?" was the bellow of a wounded citizenry in 1926 when
Assistant State's Attorney William H. McSwiggin was machine-
gunned to death—that is, until the leads in a baffling and ultimately
unsolved case began to point to young McSwiggin's apparent collusion with the Capone mob. Rumor had it that McSwiggin's father, a
policeman, confronted Capone only to turn away in tears when the
felon offered him a revolver and bid him shoot if he thought Capone
was really guilty.

Sodom was destroyed because it couldn't produce ten righteous
men; it's a wonder that Chicago still stands. Americans, eyes eager
and grinning, fled there from other places to dance, drink, and shove
each other, to watch how black blues singers moved and to adopt the
look as their own, the music as their anthem. Mobile America, land of
communications, sang and danced up a dead end in Chicago. It was a
war zone of boundless egoism, a sort of self-help program that
dispensed with the formula of a Coué in favor of direct action. The
immigrant and second-generation Italian, Irish, and Jewish gangsters
who struck the citizenry as the pepper on the cake, vulgar but jaunty,
were expressing the upward mobility of the fast buck, nothing less—

but nothing more—and a barrage of analysis in the media turned them into celebrities. After all, don't immigrants have to work harder at whatever they do to win acceptance? Al Capone especially was the subject of ceaseless surveys by Fleet Streeters, to the point that he finally felt as harassed and spied on as any movie star. His occasional passes at philanthropic presentation were a source of headlines; so was his hurried getaway from a football game at Northwestern University, where he and his henchmen were literally booed out of the stands.

Hot copy, that was Capone, hotter than Ford and Coolidge combined; like them, he was ultimately just another winner. True, they outsold their competition, while he slaughtered his, but glamour is in the eye of the beholder, and the press can acclimatize the most unacceptable behavior to a kind of familiarity by sheer habituation, just as poison is disarmed by regular dosage. A Broadway hit of 1928, *The Front Page*, gave theatergoers some comprehension of the cahoots between a carefree public and a nihilistic press, both of which register nothing but the scoop: to *The Front Page*'s heedless reporters, a Capone is a pawn in a chess game mated by headlines, and responsibility a dead language, neither spoken nor understood. They're all in it together in *The Front Page*—the sheriff, the mayor, the policemen, the reporters, and the editors—lying, bribing, fixing . . . anything to sell editions, win elections, and just keep floating.

The Front Page's authors, Ben Hecht and Charles MacArthur, had both seen action on the Hearst beachhead in Chicago and thus learned firsthand how the bandwagon runs, and how symbols of one kind or another are manipulated by the press, whether in league with or opposed to the pols. Indeed, when the advertising agencies began to set up shop, the people most often hired as copywriters were ex-newspapermen, already experienced in the methods of what was then known as "ballyhoo," the hard sell. Hecht and MacArthur's front pagers know the ropes if not the rules, and as the curtain rises they are seen awaiting the execution of a cop killer, whose crime and punishment are being turned to everyone's advantage. The mayor has garnered reprieves from an obliging governor to postpone the hanging till just before the local election, neatly providing the wedge of a law-

and-order ticket, and, as the condemned man is an anarchist, Red fever provides the thrust of the incumbents' targeting. "Reform the Reds With a Rope!" is the slogan of the campaign—and it doesn't hurt the "Negro vote" any that the slain policeman was a black.

Not surprisingly, *The Front Page* was set in Chicago, so the farcical free-for-all on stage could only mirror what the audience took to be the real free-for-all of Chicago in life. Doling out the passes for the execution, the sheriff limits them at two per paper, angering the reporters:

> McCue, *City Press:* What do you mean, two for each paper?
> Sheriff: What do you want to do, take your family?
>   .....
> Wilson, *American:* The boss wants a couple for the advertising department.
> Sheriff: This ain't the *Follies,* you know. I'm tired of your editors using these tickets to get advertising accounts.
> Endicott, *Post:* You got a lot of nerve! Everybody knows what *you* use 'em for—to get in socially.
> Murphy, *Journal:* He had the whole Union League Club over here last time.

Two years before *The Front Page,* another Broadway hit, suitably named *Chicago,* jeered not only at the conniving con men of officialdom and newsland, but at everybody else, too—the System. Like *The Front Page* a testimonial from the city room, *Chicago* was the work of a former reporter on the *Tribune,* Maurine Watkins, and also like *The Front Page,* it helped set a tone for slick burlesques of the Prohibition era's morality from the pop media. In *Chicago,* a heartless murderess named Roxie Hart learns the strategy for playing the press, its readership, and judge and jury the way an ingenue learns technique. She even rates a kind of star billing as "The Jazz Slayer," thanks to the avid attentions of the newspapers.

Ah, yes, finally: here's jazz . . . and right where it belongs, too, in a rubric for a criminal who's going to get off scot-free. What reverberation the word had then, jazz—the jive and juke of it, the insensate gambol, that sound and that dancing, rising up out of ragtime and nowhere to assert itself in the city of the big shoulders as a leitmotif for egotists. Sex and slang named it, from black patois (to jass: to copulate) into the dictionary; derelicts played it while classicists fumed; wastrels, above all, adored it—they were playing their song. Fats Waller defined it best: "Man, if you don't know what it is, don't mess with it."

Wise words. Pure jazz is a special item, made by elitists for elitists; "jazz" as popularly applied broadened out to include just about anything that one heard with a bass fiddle stalking below and a saxophone prancing above, the hot lick of musicians who hoisted "axes" (their word for their instruments) to pop tunes in clubs where patrons debunked Prohibition, spending jack and themselves. They were soloists, these musicians, gadflies of tone living a code as hit or miss as that of the gangsters. Drugged, alcoholic, down and out when they weren't on the bandstand, they respected only one truce, that of keeping to a steady tempo for the benefit of the dancers. No matter what the intention of a composer or lyricist—no matter how chaste or sophisticated—two seconds into any song they played, every song was jazz. That's how it was.

From the south it rolled up the Mississippi to Chicago, shrilling that law and order was a lie—and jazz, too, could lie: A nation of debunkers (and what did we debunk?—business, art, government, the past, the present, all) needed the music that debunked. Late at night, in the cities and towns one could hear the idle riffs of some combo fading away but still holding to it, impromptu, stalling for time till closing, hating daylight. Primitive man sought the essence of a thing in its word, and some cultures believed that to name a thing was to command it; the word "jazz" was magic in just this way. Today we say "Jazz Age" and invoke the whole era, from Teapot Dome via *The Great Gatsby* and The Sheik to the market crash—but what *is* jazz? Folk art, American mode, the sound of gin singing . . . something, but something indigenous and savage and, like Chicago, the essence of a thing—the essence, perhaps, of us. To name it was to conjure up a store of associations; thus the Jazz Slayer, confession and exculpation at once, for if jazz demands surrender, how can the helpless compulsive be guilty? Roxie Hart, murderess of Chicago in Watkins's play, learns to jazz, and Roxie Hart is acquitted.

Pietro Mascagni predicted that jazz would kill opera, and John Philip Sousa thought that it would eventually disappear, but Paul Whiteman, the bandleader who styled himself "the King of Jazz," called it "the folk music of the machine age," and of the three only Whiteman was proved correct. Jazz and Ford, they were coevals. And they hated each other.

Jazz is apparently an outgrowth of the extemporized honky-tonk piano style through "creole" syncopation and solo virtuosity, loose, staccato, and anonymous, but its folk origin is of lesser import than its wild folk acceptance. Like Prohibition, it had been building up to a national explosion, through ragtime and the dance crazes of the 1910s, and when it finally arrived in the twenties, the speakeasy world was ready. They came together, bootleggers and jazzmen and the prominent advocates of the new morality—and all of these got along just fine, being of an unfastened character that Ford would not have understood. Jazz, it was said, made one lose control, but no: jazz was just something to hear while one lost the control that one was determined to lose anyway.

Part of the swank of those days stems from the emphasis on wet personalities. Such noisy drys as Billy Sunday and Wayne Wheeler don't have the lure nowadays—and didn't, really, then—that Jimmy Walker, Texas Guinan, or Al Capone possess in the piecing together of the mystery of Prohibition. It is true that Sunday won a huge following from people as sold on bigotry and repression as he, but his name by itself lacks the reverberations of Walker and Capone. And who importunes the memory on behalf of the twenties more than Texas, the "Padlock Queen," Mary Louise Cecilia Guinan, the former movie cowgirl and then sucker-baiter from Waco?—Texas who ran a fleet of clubs in Manhattan, sailing one into infamous report as soon as the authorities docked another. "Three cheers for Prohibition," Texas once remarked. "Without it, where the hell would I be?"

Tender enough to give way to tears at Rudolph Valentino's funeral, Guinan was all the same as brassy as they come. It was her type of woman that replaced the wistful, truehearted maid of pastoral America and the old morality, the Frances Willards, Louisa May Alcotts, and Lillian Russells. When a jury found her not guilty of "maintaining a nuisance" at her Salon Royale on West Fifty-eighth Street, someone in the courtroom cried, "Give the little girl a great big hand," a phrase Texas herself was known to use on occasion.

It was not a naive era, and the jazz that held forth at Guinan's many haunts and at those of less familiar Guinans seconded the mores of the times. In *Processional*, a Theatre Guild attraction of 1925 billed as a "jazz symphony of American life," striking coal miners, radical organizers, Ku Kluxers, and just plain citizens were presented accompanied by a lithe combo, as if only jazz could set the tempo for contemporary drama—even one set in the open country of West Virginia. According to *Processional*, jazz had been received into the culture and was here to stay, jazz and its people. It was our problem and our consolation—in Vachel Lindsay's eyes, "our most Babylonian disease."

And it was the key with which even serious composers thought they might unlock the secret doors of America. George Antheil, he who almost blew off the roof of Carnegie Hall with *Ballet Mécanique*, wrote an entire opera in 1929 in the doo-dah of jazz, *Transatlantic*, an absurd burlesque of business, money power, and politics. Of course it took place in New York, and of course its ecstatic finale tendered dawn on the Brooklyn Bridge, with the cast intoning a jazz hymn to the workday, though in fact the Czech lyricist-composer Ernst Křenek had already superseded Antheil's effort with the even more absurd opera *Jonny Strikes Up the Band*, which foretold the subversion of European art by a corrupt black American jazzman. This worthy was seen at the finale astride a globe of the world, jiving on a violin while red-white-and-blue-clad choristers acclaimed him and his blasphemous music.

Strangely, though the character of dissolution and cunning was evident to any jazz-hater who listened, America's pop music was undergoing a bizarrely sentimental stage in the twenties, trilling innocence and flirtation in both lyric and music. "(This is my) Lucky Day," sings a fellow who found his girl, courting her with "Tea for

Two" and "(Kiss me, dear) What D'Ya Say?," then toddling off with
her to "My Blue Heaven." Even the great Gershwin, the nation's
little Fauntleroy expounder of the new sound, aspired to great heights
of sissy susceptibility. His gutsy "Nashville Nightingale" fell by the
wayside, but scores of couples fell in love to the pristine "Somebody
Loves Me," with its sweet, caressing blue note on "I wonder *who?*"

They were still tripping the waltz then, although such dance fads
of the late twenties as the Charleston and the black bottom struck a
livelier pose, and while the hoodoo of the black blues singers chimed
in with a less naive strain, few people were in the audience when
Bessie Smith launched into "Nobody in Town Can Bake a Sweet
Jelly Roll Like Mine." Only in the seedier dumps of Chicago, each
with its jazzy theme song ("The Sunset Café Stomp," "The Royal
Garden Blues," and the more ambiguous "Twenty-ninth and Dearborn"), would one hear Bessie, and when the voices of the mainstream such as Kate Smith's did attempt to level with the "low
down," it would be via something like "Red Hot Chicago," from the
musical *Flying High,* backed up by the "poop-oop-a-doop!" of a
vocal quartet and about as low-down as Calvin Coolidge's vest. Oh,
the song does make some effort to address the low down on a
personal level in its verse, pitched in the minor, but as soon as the
chorus gets going, it's all vo-de-oh-do and the superficial self-
congratulation of pop-tune sollipsism. "Blue singers," Kate warbles,
"those heart wringers who sob ballads to the nation"—but how many
of her listeners had heard the blues, the true blues? No matter: "Who
furnishes the lot?" Kate continues, with oomph, "red-hot Chicago!"
That was about as deeply into it as the brand-name American songs
cared to go.

The smart city folk could always seek out the Negro quarter to
absorb the aperçus of jazz; the sizable towns had their own private
Chicagos just across the tracks, and there the white man made himself
intelligent of the real McCoy. On Broadway's stages, lush revues
celebrated the fetish of the black in terms that Stephen Foster would
have kenned ("Pickin' Cotton," from one of George White's *Scandals*
shows, opened with an evocation of "darkies," "lazy weather," and
"Simon Legree," assuring its audience that "cotton pickin' is a kind

of a spree"), but the in crowd slummed up to Harlem for the more
apropos "Empty Bed Blues" or "You Been a Good Ole Wagon
(Daddy, but you done broke down)."

That Bessie Smith—now *there* was a jazz slayer for you. She
understood what it was all about; in her records, one hears a
comprehension of era, even of incomprehensible Chicago during
Prohibition. "Any bootlegger sure is a pal of mine," said she, and
that does make more of a statement than "Pickin' Cotton" can. But
the most complete statement of all these passes at the new lowdown
was the lowdown itself, just jazz, manning the baton in the jurisdiction of pagan joyland. With Bruce Barton and his messiah businessman on one side, and Billy Sunday and his Fundamentalist drys on
the other, there had to be a midpoint, spitting pretty between the
profane and the sacred, and of course that midpoint went right to
extremes and blew jazz at them both.

But weren't the sacred and profane blowing their own jazz back?
What were the media and their "presentations" if not a planned jazz?
What was this punk superstition about immigrants and liquor and
science if not instinctive jazz? "Even when she loses, she wins with
her smile," opines a tennis player about a gorgeous model flashing a
gorgeous grin in an ad for Colgate ribbon dental cream—isn't that
jazz? "From beer to rum to skid row," shrieked the drys—now you
have jazz! And what about our Coolidge businessmen? Didn't they
fall right in with the beat when Barton purveyed a Christ who had
apparently retired His opinion of the money-changers to fill the
temple with commercial poesy? Look, they were all tooting their
horns one way or another. In the ateliers of the highbrow, where
debunking was croquet, everybody was subject to satire, and satire
was the best jazz of all. Satire took the jazz out of those Roxie Harts
who socked the System for sport, and out of the publicity machine
and ballyhoo, and out of the younger generation and their new
morality, and out of the money bosses and their corporate arrogations.
Satire took the jazz out of jazz.

Bunk and debunk, question and answer at once, jazz could survive,
but Prohibition could not. It wouldn't be dead until after Franklin
Roosevelt took office in 1933, but even in the twenties Congress was

refusing to vote up the requested appropriations for enforcement of the Volstead Act, resentful as it was over the incontinent haste with which the drys had forced state ratification of the Eighteenth Amendment; obviously, both houses were waiting for public opinion of the bad side effects of Prohibition to mount to a mandate for repeal. It took thirteen years, mostly because of the fanaticism of the diehard—or, rather, dienever—drys, and because so many otherwise regular citizens found jazzing Prohibition just as much fun as not having it at all.

Down with Prohibition, then, and down it went; repression wasn't what the Constitution had in mind. This was just the sort of factionalism that the Founding Fathers hoped to write out of law. They knew what mobs can do. "Poor reptiles!" Gouverneur Morris had called them. "They bask in the sun, and ere noon they will bite, depend upon it." And what a sore they left. Prohibition's encouragement of disdain for lawmaking and law enforcement drew the land closer in tone and tempo to Chicago, to the essence of the thing, to its callousness—in the cruelty of federal enforcement—and to its anarchy—in the collusion between judicial authorities and organized crime. Worst of all in this national swindle called a law, was the blow to the tradition of state option, a crucial premise in the structure of our government, but one that had been breaking down since the dynamic business interests of the North and West mobilized the abolitionist movement into an economic war on the static South, and which was to disintegrate further in the devastating centrism of the Roosevelt Administration during the Depression.

At least we didn't lack for self-expression while it was going on, did we? Self-expression by authority flouters, underworld money demons, and flamboyant musicians was there for all to hear, each a contribution to the chorus yet each dedicated to delirious egotism. If they weren't doing violence to each other in the streets or in print, they did it to music in speakeasies. Naturally, it took a Quaker to see the Light. "What the Prohibition situation needs first of all," said Jane Addams, "is disarmament."

Objective Addams was one of the few well-known Americans of her day who had no jazz to grind whatsoever, not a note, though she, too, lived in the city of Capone and Bessie Smith. A sociologist, crusader against war, many times authoress, and a cofounder of the first social-working community settlement center in the United States, Hull House, Jane Addams was as much a part of the scene as anyone. Her voice must be accounted for in the din as one of those exceptions that smashes the rule. Calmly shepherding her flock at Hull House through the years, questioning the justice accorded Sacco and Vanzetti, serving as the president of the Women's International League for Peace and Freedom, and sharing (with Nicholas Murray Butler, the president of Columbia University) a Nobel Peace Prize in 1931, Addams forms a kind of trinity with Bessie Smith and Texas Guinan—the activist, the artist, the "personality" . . . three drafts on the account of new American womanhood. It is most reasonable not to choose a favorite from among the three, but while Bessie lives in song and Texas has passed into a bit of legend for her "Hello, sucker!", Addams, one notes, gets mentioned in books, but not folklore. Yet she, in her dissent—like Smith and Guinan in theirs—is one of the decade's great stars, neither news nor copy at the time, but one for the history books. And, just to confuse the issue, who gave her what she got?

Red-hot Chicago.

SIX

Timon and Athens

"Only connect!" is the fulcrum of a stunning passage that occurs midway through a stunning novel of 1910, E. M. Forster's *Howards End*. "Only connect the prose and the passion, and both will be exalted, and human love will be seen at its height. Live in fragments no longer. Only connect, and the beast and the monk, robbed of the isolation that is life to either, will die."

Why a quotation out of Forster, from another country and, besides, that time is dead? Because now that we have jazz, the elixir of bunk and debunk, we must see just how far this alleged American isolationism went in the twenties; for somehow our more patent withdrawal in the thirties, caused by the self-possessed housecleaning of poverty and the reaction against fascism, has been stretched to accommodate the reigns of normalcy and prosperity as well.

What is this isolationism? Traditionally dated back to President Washington's Farewell Address for want of a more obvious linchpin, it rejects "entangling alliances" while not curtailing commercial contacts. Much of what Washington said has since been anointed as oracular sacrament, even if John Adams thought it all "a strain of Shakespearean and Garrickal excellence in Dramatic Exhibitions." But Adams as well as his successors, Thomas Jefferson and James

Madison, adopted Washington's foreign policy, and James Monroe's Secretary of State, John Quincy Adams, engineered the converse of the Farewell Address as the Monroe Doctrine: not only should we not entangle ourselves thither, "they" were not to trouble us or our neighbors on this side of the globe. Adams, who as an envoy abroad had seen the insidious kingdom machines of European diplomacy at firsthand, added something practical to Washington's theory about American involvement in Europe: Europe's leadership conduced to politesse and dice play, and was as worthy of trust as a keg of dynamite on the roll.

If the proclamations of Washington and Monroe codified tradition, however, one doesn't need a tradition to feel dubious about Europe, and isolationism in the average American circa 1920 was largely a question of xenophobia, cheap-jack patriotism, gut reactions to newspaper headlines, and occasional minor acts of destruction (such as defacing the facade of a delicatessen). Anyway, Washington's advice had been undermined in the imperialism of the 1890s, when our manifest destiny had, too long before, bumped its nose on the Pacific Ocean, and in the election of 1900, when William Jennings Bryan's defeat was blamed largely on his anti-imperialistic platform, and again a bit later, when President Theodore Roosevelt spoke to Congress of an American role in the course of the world's fortunes. "Our place," he said, "must be great among the nations." To reach that place, we found it necessary to entangle ourselves in Cuba, the Philippines, Haiti, Venezuela, Colombia, Nicaragua, the Dominican Republic, Panama, and various Pacific islands. Thus was a tradition upended, and then overthrown in the specious neutrality of the first years of the war, the "big one," by which time France and, especially, Britain were regarded as our hereditary allies and their travails ours. But who exactly so regarded them?—most Americans had no love for either. Indeed, the armistice signaled a rampant folk isolationism, as we have seen, one based as much upon distaste for our allies as for our enemies.

Ours is a culture within a civilization, sharing inevitable consequences of commerce, art, and faction. What's an ocean or a tariff these days? They just add time or freight to the connection. Avoiding partiality in our foreign affairs was a great idea, given the likes of foreigners, but by 1900 transformation had purchased new scripture—the writ was power, and we had that power. Most Americans just weren't aware that we were using it.

For most Americans weren't ready to become citizens of the world in the twenties. The lure of tradition and the fear of change kept them from reestablishing tradition within the new global context, as technology so clearly demanded of them. World leadership was to have been the natural extension of domestic Progressivism, but the former reformers of the electorate had had it with all that—look what happened to Wilson. Rather than face an international future, they tried to order a false present rooted in the past, erecting deadends at every crossroads.

(One contrary voice spoke out, however. "Where there is no vision, the people perish," said the spokesman for the future, quoting Proverbs as he presented his case in *The Saturday Evening Post*. He was a brigadier general in the Army, William Mitchell by name, and his vision was air power. Naval warfare, he stated, was a thing of the dead; a trained air force could smash battleships and raze cities, and Mitchell attempted to prove his case by conducting air bombing tests on a fleet of anchored warships off the Virginia Capes in 1921. But the people were not impressed, and neither was the Army, which court-martialed the persistent Mitchell in 1925 after a board appointed by Coolidge found no substance in Mitchell's vision.)

No one was ready for aviation, really, in the twenties—whether for peace or war—except in the form of short-hop stunts, which is why a nonstop flight from New York to Paris in 1927 will seem like the gesture of the age. Too remote a technology to be housebroken like automation and radiotelephony, aviation was "wildcat stuff" except when the flying aces of the war lent it the human character requisite for public enthusiasm. That gallant "Eddie" Rickenbacker and his gang posing for the Kodaks in a frozen strut, leaning on their fighter planes, ready to do—that was glamour, something any consumer might buy. Otherwise, aviation was kept at suspicion's length by many Americans, a source of feats and daring but rather extra and possibly even useless; its potential for passenger and material transport was scarcely mooted, and the hazard of flying the mail was proved by constant mishaps.

No one was ready: this is isolationism, too. It's risky enough to turn one's back on unignorable developments that one *knows* are out there, but it can be just as foolish to fail to discern what cannot be known and has to be conjured up out of technological romance. With our last frontiers all accounted for, the only way to go was up, yet despite an occasional speculative article such as those by Billy Mitchell, enjoyed but not truly received, flight was fantasy, a conceit for the daredevil hustlers of adventure who fitted themselves out in scarves and goggles like men from Mars on their way to a prom. "Sometimes with the wind and sometimes against it . . . but we must sail."

The wind, in this era, does nothing but change—though we have already seen much resistance from reactionaries—and most of the principal figures who inhabit these pages are deputies of transformation. It obtains not only among scientists and artists, ever committed to renewal, but in Middletown as well, as for example when Warren Harding made his totally unexpected presidential appeal in Birmingham for black equality—the first time such an issue had been so treated by the chief executive, and at that without public pressure.

One must understand—for they didn't then, and what excuse have we for not understanding fifty years later, with our hindsight and perspective?—that there was no debate on isolationism, no doctrinal dialogue. The withdrawal into one's private America was a given, at least to the man who was neither immigrant, radical, nor highbrow. We were all presumably doing what came naturally, whether as doctors, bootleggers, writers, or pols, and maybe it just isn't natural to set up a booth in the international forum. For a depiction of the national temper, we can apply to a short story written by F. Scott Fitzgerald in 1922, "The Diamond as Big as the Ritz."

Here is where we meet the beast of Forster's metaphor, in the person of Fitzgerald's Braddock T. Washington, the richest and most secret man in America, whose estate in Montana is built on a giant-size diamond (*bigger* than the Ritz, as it happens). Staffed with black slaves and laid out in the most fabulous splendor (by a chap from

Hollywood; "he was the only man we found," says Braddock's son, "who was used to playing with an unlimited amount of money"), Washington's estate is withheld from detection through the murder or incarceration of intruders. Interestingly, the only threat to its glorious isolation is the increasing use of aircraft.

Braddock Washington, who ultimately attempts to bribe God when aviators invade and destroy his sanctuary, is an exaggerated locus classicus of the money boss, not a businessman so much as a scavenger—a beast—hoarding a fortune too huge to be spent by his next thousand descendants. While this fantastic zillionaire locks himself away in a modern El Dorado, his countrymen locked away their minds, and Fundamentalism was one of the closets they slunk into. We have met the beast; now comes Forster's monk, or, rather, the antimonk, in the person of William Jennings Bryan, chief counsel for the prosecution in a test case set up to try Fundamentalism on its own turf, Dixieland. This was the famous "Monkey Trial" of John T. Scopes, a high-school science teacher and athletic coach who volunteered to sit in the dock while Bryan argued against Darwinian evolution and Clarence Darrow, for the defense, argued against Bryan.

Scopes' days in court were sponsored by the American Civil Liberties Union, which had been eager to put the state laws against the teaching of evolution in public schools on the line and into Constitutional jurisdiction. The intention was to establish a precedent for free thought via the appellate court, and tiny Dayton, Tennessee, offered itself, through Scopes, as the inaugural battlefield, with the understanding that even the persuasive Darrow would not be able to defeat Fundamentalism in its own bailiwick. As any Bible-shouter could have told you, man was man and a monkey was a monkey, no matter what you had read to the contrary in depraved European books. At the very midpoint of the decade, July of 1925, scores of reporters and newsreel cameramen hastened down to Dayton from the North to catch the act of the century, "Absolutely Not, Mr. Darrow, Positively So, Mr. Bryan," and to learn if the heartland of America were going to connect, only connect! with the twentieth century at last.

Isolationism had taken the hard line before World War I (and would do so again before World War II), but that was when many lives were at stake; great mistaken measures—like a war—call for great outcry. Peacetime, however, and keeping that peace, call for a forward advancement and open eyes. These were lacking in the twenties, but then so was outcry. If Fitzgerald's devouring beast on his colossal diamond is the worst sort of crittur, he is nonetheless a quiet one, and the citizens of Dayton, expected to be revealed as lynch-mobbing monks of ignorance, surprised the city reporters with their good nature and sense of humor, and their lack of violent reaction to the idea of evolution. Much to the disappointment of H. L. Mencken, who had arrived in Dayton with hopes of savaging the booboisie in his reports, few of the vicious, Klan-mentality Fundamentalists could be found on either the jury or in the gallery; on the contrary, Dayton apparently pressed the indictment on Scopes just to get a little flutter from the national press and to enjoy a spell of tourism. In fact, few citizens of the town were more popular than Scopes, who had coached Dayton High's football team to its first respectable resistance of Baylor High School, its traditional rival in Chattanooga. Dayton didn't win, but at least it didn't suffer its usual massacre.

Scopes was popular, too, with the national press via his cause, and much humor was had at the expense of Tennessee law. Bryan they singled out for special treatment. Luther Burbank noted that Bryan's skull "visibly approaches the Neanderthal type," and one Rabbi Joseph Silverman of New York gave thanks for evolution, "for without it we would not have a William Jennings Bryan; he would still be a gorilla." Don Marquis's Archy, explaining the matter to someone on the planet Mars, announced that the donnybrook stemmed from whether the grandfather of man was "a god or a monkey." It should make more difference what he is now than what his grandfather was, offers the Martian. "Not to this animal," Archy replies—"he is the great alibi ike of the cosmos."

The American Civil Liberties Union came in for some distinctly unlighthearted condemnation for its part in setting the whole thing up. The *Detroit Free Press* termed the Union a "bolshevist-loving aggregation" and denounced the trial as jobbery by "a gang of professional poseurs, wind-jammers, self-advertisers, and self-exploiters." And it can't be denied that self-exploitation was the aim of some Daytonians, assisted by 120 reporters, numerous Holy Rollers and demagogues down from mountain country, and even two chimpanzees, one named Joe Mendl and the other, Big Joe. (One had expected a Darwin, yes? But onward.)

So there were real-live as well as metaphorical monks on view in Dayton, as befitted the proceedings. But the star monk of all was that killer-diehard of Fundamentalism, William Jennings Bryan, the "prairie avenger, mountain lion" of Vachel Lindsay's verse, as relentless as ever in address and exhortation. ("Bryan, Bryan, Bryan, Bryan," Lindsay goes on, by no means overstating the case.) Boy, did that Bryan have opinions! Here was the monk of ignorance, sure, or of repression, or of obtuse tradition, or, perhaps, of fear; who knows? His own newspaper, the *Commoner,* defined him, for he was the only begotten commoner, the last celebrity of the vanished America of aggressively humble, anti-intellectual, Bible-shouting populism. Progressives more reasonably progressive than Bryan had kept him from the glory (in three unsuccessful presidential campaigns, among other things), but this stint as attorney for the prosecution in Dayton was to be his ultimate achievement. He would defend "revealed religion" against the blandishments of the jazzing atheist Darrow. Never in all his speechifying triumphs of the 1890s—not even in his stupendously belligerent "You shall not crucify mankind upon a cross of gold" speech that won him the Democratic nomination at Chicago in 1896—did Bryan command such locomotive righteousness and agility in debate as when he took the stand to suffer Darrow's demolition of Biblical literalism. Technically, Bryan's side won the first round in the battle over the teaching of evolution in public schools (Scopes received a token fine), but whether or not Bryan's performance can be rated an achievement, it was at any rate his ultimate adventure: he died a few days after the court adjourned.

Darrow, the attorney for Darwinian inquiry, was the biggest thing Bryan had battled since the gold standard. Ten months before he defended Scopes, Darrow was in Chicago to plead the case of Richard Loeb and Nathan Leopold, Jr., the rich-kid "thrill murderers" who had dispatched a thirteen-year-old boy for, apparently, the fun of it.

Undaunted by a virulent and clamorous public opinion—yes, even in red-hot Chicago—Darrow in his summation spun out one of the classic attacks on capital punishment for one of the classically indefensible crimes in our past. Nothing was not useful to Darrow's argument; the man who would shortly rip with abuse into the Scripture now made use of the story of Abraham and Isaac (in connection with a New Yorker who had played Abraham to his infant son and was acquitted), and dared to say that the families of the victim of Loeb and Leopold were to be envied in comparison with the families of Loeb and Leopold. "Great wealth curses everybody it touches," Darrow said at another point—*anything* to save his clients from the noose and to challenge the custom of capital punishment for capital crime. He succeeded, too; Loeb and Leopold got off with life imprisonment.

Technically an agnostic rather than an atheist, Darrow represented everything that Bryan hated in the urban intellectual, even if the two did pose amicably in shirt-sleeves and suspenders for the photographers, Darrow looking no less the country cousin than Bryan himself. Their confrontation, Bryan undergoing Darrow's cross-examination under the trees whither the court had adjourned because of the humidity, was the climax of the trial, and, in J. C. Furnas's words, Darrow "took him apart like a dollar watch." Countering his foe's questions with epithets and holy utterance, Bryan rekindled the old stormy era of the Bryans for the twenties to note—as if America's staunch background of evangelical camp meetings and circuit riders needed any bolstering.

Bryan had plenty of company in his wish to face Darrow down, but for all his moxie, Bryan was arguing from a ludicrous premise in affirming his idea of the "truth" of the Bible. One doesn't seek naturalism in that book any more than one does in the *Iliad* or *The Divine Comedy.* Bryan's and Fundamentalism's mistake lay in literalizing a work of art meant to abstract situation rather than describe it, to mythologize through suggestion—and this literalization, too, was the mistake of isolationism in that it accepted as fact what was really no more than belief. We hadn't been "isolated" for years, and thinking us secure in a safehold didn't make us so.

Thus Bryan, defender of the faith, found himself forced out on tenuous limbs to maintain the trunk. As reported by Charles Michelson in the *New York World,* Darrow invited Bryan to extrapolate on Jonah and the whale—did Bryan accept that as written?

> BRYAN: When I read that a big fish swallowed Jonah I believe just that. It doesn't say "whale."
>
> . . .
>
> DARROW: Do you think that fish was made for the particular purpose?
>
> BRYAN: I don't know, and, unlike you, I do not guess.
>
> DARROW: When we guess, we have a chance to be right. You haven't any opinion as to the creation of that fish?
>
> BRYAN: No, sir, but one miracle is just as easy for me to believe as another.
>
> DARROW: Me, too; it would be just as easy to believe that Jonah swallowed the whale, wouldn't it?

All right we are two nations. It was a hot day, and the court had convened in the open air, but despite the stifling weather, the crowd attended the proceedings with animation, cheering impartially for both men at moments of bravura. After all, it was seldom that two of the big leaguers played Dayton, Tennessee. The trial had been a jolly business up to this duel of titans, but in the ninety minutes during which Darrow had at Bryan, the air turned nasty as Darrow repeatedly scored and Bryan suffered the strokes. From Jonah they progressed to Joshua and the sun standing still, to the Flood, to the Tower of Babel, to the Creation. And Bryan could not make it stick, could not "prove" his Book. Sensing the rout, not only of his case, but of his work, his life—you have to understand how big a man Bryan had been, and how big his belief; he *had* to win, but he was losing—he finally rose up from the chair, red and heaving with sweat, to denounce Darrow's method, Darrow's work, Darrow and the many Darrows, but Darrow cut in on him like the Lord smiting Nebuchadnezzar, "I object to your statement!" Darrow roared. "I am examining you on your fool ideas that no intelligent Christian on earth believes!"

The crowd leaped up in a riot, everything at once on all sides—rage, confusion, defiance, nervous laughter. Bryan had lost. The attempted culmination of his life had turned out to be only the last of his many defeats, though technically the prosecution won. In his report for the *St. Louis Labor*, Paul Anderson wrote, "It was profoundly moving. To see this wonderful man . . . this man whose silver voice and majestic mien had stirred millions, to see him humbled and humiliated before the vast crowd which had come to adore him, was sheer tragedy, nothing less."

Bryan died, but Fundamentalism didn't, though the A.C.L.U. carried the battle into the high courts (unsuccessfully). The worst of it was the party held by the foreign press at the expense of the American profile, which, like Bryan's according to Burbank, was indeed looking rather Neanderthal. The Ku Klux Klan, the Red raids, the Sacco and Vanzetti trial, Prohibition, and Chicago were all beginning to fall into place. It just couldn't be much of a country if such rampant ignorance felt so comfortable with itself, and if no leadership was there to educate and guide. Except . . . and this brings us to the hero of this chapter, the man who tried to bring the exile America back into some dialogue with the rest of society, and the prime mover in America's connection of the prose with the passion.

We know the names of the twenties—Harding and Coolidge, Hoover and Mellon, Eugene O'Neill and John Dos Passos, Babe Ruth, George Gershwin, Garbo and Chaplin, and such. However, there are less popular but equally salient names, and one is that of Charles Evans Hughes, lawyer, reform governor of New York, U.S. Supreme Court Justice, Republican candidate in the very close election of 1916 (lost, really, through a small diplomatic error Hughes made in California, but for which he would have been better remembered as our twenty-ninth President), very nearly the American Civil Liberties Union's attorney in the Scopes Trial, and, for our purposes here, Warren Harding's Secretary of State.

Often ranked with John Quincy Adams and William H. Seward as the historical elite of the State Department, Hughes was an anomaly in the Republican brotherhood of the post-Roosevelt days, a doer who did without the rhetoric of the crusade, and a man of reason, integrity, thunderbolt efficiency, and open nonpartisanship. Under him, the State Department was run for America, no party. "I am the only politician in the department," said Hughes.

He was a superb politician, but greater as a progenitor of statesmanship midway between the rustic wariness of the young republic and the infatuated secrecy of more recent years. Contending that countries have the right not to risk international humiliation, Hughes favored discreet negotiations but not secret agreements. He knew, always, that he represented a people rather than a regime, yet in those years Hughes, in his judicious way, was the most important man in the world. While the beast and the monk reveled in their domains, the Secretary of the State Department quietly connected, single-handedly laying the groundwork for the first global peace program that might have worked, defter than the League of Nations and, of a sort, distinctly disentangling.

If only in commercial terms, America was on the cusp of a far-reaching domination, both to the south and the east, though the Far East remained inscrutable and irksome even when bowing, especially since Japan had the ears of diplomats—to the detriment of China and its protectorate, Manchuria. The situation was further complicated by the forenoted Immigration Act of 1924, when the beasts and monks of Congress excluded the Far East entirely from the revamped quota system, instilling in the Japanese a rabid hatred of America that built into a frenzy in the 1930s. (Even Coolidge, on Hughes's advice, remonstrated with them for some token inclusion of Japan, but this was not to be.)

Only two years earlier, Hughes had put over the foreign relations coup of the era in the Washington Conference on the Limitation of Armaments, a pioneer bid at nonproliferation and, incidentally, the occasion of D.C.'s coming out as an international capital. It was a debut by fiat rather than fact, perhaps, for the ten-mile square was no Paris, but all the same it marked an encouraging show of strength for America in its would-be role as all-knowing mediator. This was the core of Hughes' work, to negotiate a peaceful future for America by negotiating one for the world, and in its way this meant renewing the Monroe Doctrine in modern—i.e., technological-global—language.

So, to the forceful embrace of America, the fraternal arbitrator, came the great naval powers (minus Russia, of course) to confer in Washington, at the time the sleepiest capital in the Western world—a sort of Dayton, Tennessee, of capitals. Custom, not to mention common sense, had always settled the national hub within the natural hub of the social-commercial-artistic center, but D.C. reversed the usage that produced London, Vienna, Stockholm—or, rather, the usage that adopted them after they had produced themselves. D.C. was a capital trying to turn into a city rather than the more usual city turned into a capital. Even St. Petersburg, a logical parallel, had managed to acquire a regal set of social and artistic sensibilities in a matter of years after its founding, but the D.C. of 1921 struck the diplomatic missions of Great Britain, France, Japan, and Italy (Belgium, the Netherlands, and Portugal, as colonial interlopers in the Far East, also attended) as the most provincial little cow-town capital imaginable, Bonn being some decades ahead of their acquaintance.

The biggest crowd of international journalists ever to cover a Washington event assembled with the dignitaries in November of 1921. To some of the more astute analysts, Hughes's conference represented a poker session of the Far East, aimed primarily at leveling intrigues of treaty and conquest from Sakhalin to the Philippines; to a few others it meant a possibly suspicious gambit on the part of America to thrust its, to foreign eyes, barbaric normalcy upon the oceans. On the other hand, it might be viewed as the opening salvo of a new burst of Progressivism, curing the world's ills with moral legislation, for the roots of Hughes's peace plan lay within homegrown American movements, some fancy, some quack, and some liberal, all organized to outlaw war forever. The supposition was that governments are amenable to war and only frown on certain practices of it (such as losing). The intention was to get them to renounce it regardless of practice.

Hughes was less naive than that (though he depended too much on the honor system and failed to incorporate enforcement measures in his treaty); his method was to roll back the frenzy of naval expansion. Not only was this in itself a reversal of every foreigner's policy, but he also dropped his bombshell on the first day of the meeting, virtually in its first minutes, smashing precedents of style as well as program. As vitiating and shabby as were the money-grabbers and the technophobes, those beasts and monks, so was Hughes advanced and vital.

This is how it went. They met on November 12, 1921, in Continental Hall, overlooked by a balcony of reporters, V.I.P.'s, and rubbernecks. Solemnity prevailed at first, for the Tomb of the Unknown Soldier had been dedicated in Arlington Cemetery just the day before, and disarmament was after all a direct outgrowth of the war that had originated several such tombs, and uncountable graves. A Baptist minister opened the conference with a prayer, followed by an address from President Harding, who was tendered a cheer by the gallery that shocked the delegates but did make things a little less starchy. Then came Hughes. Rather than launch a series of windy speeches, he announced his objectives right off—a ten-year naval holiday, with big sea powers limited to a parity based on existing tonnage and the needs of minimum security, but including a wholesale scrapping of ships already built or in construction. Hughes was specific; the United States, he said, would junk thirty battleships, and before the delegates could recover their wits, he told them what Britain and Japan would have to give up, naming boats that were the pride of the fleet. Grins turned to gapes, and the gallery exploded. There were ovations for Hughes and for France's Briand, which Americans mispronounced as Brỳ-and and which William Jennings Bryan mistook for a populist demonstration and rose to acknowledge, his face washed with tears and his body immediately pulled back down by embarrassed neighbors.

Never could anyone recall a diplomatic conclave so lacking in millstone punctilio and so encouraging for the press to publicize. Within hours the world read the news that war had suffered a setback, and as it was Saturday, Hughes's plan got an extra day in which to sink in and win worldwide public backing before the delegates could meet again and anyone get away with a rebuttal. Nice timing. In one afternoon, the main event was over, Hughes by a knockout. "This is going to be a bum show," Ring Lardner was quoted as saying. "They've let the hero kill the villain in the first act."

"Bold Conference Plan Impresses British and Japanese" ran *The New York Times* headline that Sunday—a typical *Times* understatement. A British observer, one Colonel Repington, came closer to the mark: "Secretary Hughes sunk in thirty-five minutes more ships than all the admirals in the world have sunk in a cycle of centuries." Under Hughes's scheme, a ratio of 5-5-3-1¾-1¾ held, respectively, the United States, Great Britain, Japan, France, and Italy at a firm par, and further aggressive incursions in the Pacific were severely limited. The usual infighting, skulduggery, and interceptions of coded telegrams expected of an international congress obtained for twelve weeks, but ended in 1922 with seven treaties of various sorts, followed by the comparable infighting of Senate ratification, delayed but delivered a year later. Most significantly, Hughes had organized an international procedure for disarmament talks, one invoked as shortly thereafter as in 1927—alas, disastrously—in Geneva.

The landing of the statesmen at the eager backwater of D.C. puts the parochial folksiness of America in some perspective. Compared to the magisterial futurism of the Disarmament Conference—to the foresight and energy of Hughes—the carryings-on of the beasts and monks in their continental fortress appear much less gala than ghoulish, and all the good humor of Dayton fades behind the savagery of the Ku Klux Klan, the repressiveness of the Prohibition militants, and the nihilism of their protégés, the Prohibition gangsters. Too, there were the outcriers to denounce the Disarmament Conference as an entangling alliance—but unlike some disarmament talks of recent years, which tend to put a misleading, suicidal construction on the strategy entailed by the word "disarmament," Hughes's round table did not surrender our defenses, but rather attempted to control the offenses of potential enemies.

This aim at peaceful independence for the United States—an unencumbered détente—also lay behind Hughes's intention to enroll us in the World Court. That body had to be considered apart from the League of Nations, which administered it, for the latter remained an explosive issue. After the popular hostility shown it just after the war, Americans took to regarding the League with benign neglect on the condition that it not be brought up seriously again, and most politicians forbore mentioning it, though Hughes kept up disengaged but interested relations between Washington and Geneva.

In truth, American participation in the League of Nations would have been a dangerously entangling venture. Though it was nothing like the rubber stamp for certain terrorists, slave traders, and cannibals of the Third World that the present United Nations has become, the League nevertheless boded ill for U.S. interests and even with our help, most likely would not have been effective in containing fascism in the thirties. Another reason why the League had to get along, lamely, without American cahoots was offered by our foreign minister at Berne, Joseph C. Grew. "We have too many discordant elements in our own country," he wrote in 1924, "and an American member of the Council and the Assembly could never properly represent the country as a whole. Every position he might take with regard to European politics would infuriate some national element at home."

The World Court was another matter, for its protocol was less importunate than that of the League. By 1926, both houses of Congress had approved a U.S. adherence to the Court with a number of reservations. One of these, relating to our right to veto advisory opinions on matters of American interest, was not acceptable to the Court (its members having no such right themselves), and that was that. Neither of the two major parties in the election of 1928 promised to resume negotiations in the matter, and though the question was reopened by both Hoover and Roosevelt, the United States never did assume an active cotenancy in the tribunal.

Perhaps we didn't deserve a Hughes at all. As it was, his programs in naval retrenching, in Latin-American fellowship, in stabilizing the Far East needed another Hughes to carry them through, and Hughes's successor under Coolidge, Frank B. Kellogg, wasn't quite it. Kellogg and his superior, Coolidge, we deserved; they made it look easy by falling into grooves cut by others and largely doing nothing, but importantly. Indeed, there is little to remark in American foreign policy of the late twenties except to note that Coolidge took more afternoon naps than any other President in history.

On the other hand, there is more to Coolidge than is easy to spot, and while he had no constructive policies, he could move with force when necessary, an unambitious but never a weak man. A case in point would be that little storybook kingdom of crises, Nicaragua, an American cryptocolony since 1850 and a protectorate of "dollar diplomacy" as of 1914, though the Senate Foreign Relations Committee made such a to-do that Secretary of State Bryan had to offer the Nicaraguans a treaty that omitted any suggestion of intervention and customs control (both parties also ignored the censure of the Central American Court of Justice). Vital for its situation on the Panama Canal route, Nicaragua was therefore vital to U.S. interests—fateful phrase, that—but as the domestic scene down there had proved surprisingly tranquil for some years, American forces withdrew in 1925. Civil war immediately broke out, with all the feral riot to which that part of the world is so finely tuned, and the country suffered four different "presidents" in thirteen months. When U.S. marines were called in to restore order, a storm of controversy erupted in the press; in response, we get a rare view of a forgotten Coolidge, as brusque as ever but dynamic now with the threat behind the language, a man of some fire. Assuring Congress that the government had proprietary rights along the harbor line to the canal as well as American citizens to protect, Coolidge promised to exercise his powers to protect U.S. interests "whether they be endangered by internal strife or by outside interference." He then sent Henry L. Stimson to Nicaragua to conclude a peace settlement, a coalition government was set up, and American forces withdrew again in 1933 after training a native national guard.

Coolidge's credo of meeting trouble when it arrives but instigating nothing is an old political philosophy—Abraham Lincoln knew it well. But these were parlous times for not meeting trouble when it's halfway here, and certainly Coolidge's substitution for a hefty disarmament policy, the Kellogg-Briand Pact, was no legitimate replacement for the international disarmament talks that fell apart in Geneva in 1927. So hot ran the popular distaste for the likelihood of another war that Coolidge was virtually coerced into doing something to head it off—and now, man!, not then.

The French Foreign Minister, Aristide Briand, got the ball rolling with an open letter to the American people recommending that their two nations join in proscribing war as a recognized expression of national affairs; the enthusiasm on these shores, from the media, private foundations, and Congress, demanded some compliance from the State Department. The result was the Kellogg-Briand Pact, its point to "outlaw war," and its effectiveness nil. But its reception was joyful, especially since Kellogg had convinced Briand to make the treaty multilateral and to delete any commitment for armed assistance in case of attack. Unlike Hughes's naval disarmament, however, with its teeth-pulling measures spelled out for each mouth, Briand's brainchild, signed by fifteen nations in Paris in 1928, expressed wistfulness but no real determination to alter the ropes: war goes back as far as man and will grow old with him, so why not sign a little paper, eh?

Who deserved Coolidge the most—unscrupulous nationalists, grasping investors, snout-poking do-gooders, or ranting liberals, who would suddenly go all sentimental on you when you enlisted them for the revolution? Fitzgerald's Braddock T. Washington earned his Coolidge by amassing his storybook stockpile and fearing/hating everything but himself, and both the Fundamentalists and Kleagles earned their Coolidge by trying to turn all the lights off. This was a time when flexibility counted most, when disasters of later decades might have been circumvented through the indulgence of a little foresight, or, at least, the indulgence of the few who had it, but no dice. Hughes's foreign drive was creative and original, but the folk preferred one routine and reactive, and Hughes, the hero of this chapter, cedes to the beast, the monk, and to Coolidge, the hero of this era until something better came along.

Actually, Coolidge wasn't their hero; he was just as far as they thought they needed to go into the domain of action. One can hardly blame Americans for not wanting to mess around with Europe, and for having tired of making the sacrifices of reform—but someone should have told them that the age of entanglement had dawned whether they liked it or not. Détente is something one seeks not for fun, but for survival; it was already high noon as of the twenties, and the gunslingers called trade, communications, and imperialism were toting their shooting irons and looking restless. The memoirs of a jazz-age president should read like gangbusters, wrapping the most delicate diplomacy around tough talk and ultimata, yet Coolidge's autobiography plays back nothing but lackadaisical self-satisfaction. Those acid cuts he supplied in life, the jazz of Coolidge, at least had a tang, but they reveal less about the man than about his age: "They hired the money, didn't they?" ... "Farmers have never made money; I don't believe we can do much about it" ... "The business of America is business" ... "Our first duty is to ourselves."

Our first duty is indeed to ourselves, but we carried out that duty better under Theodore Roosevelt, when we freed Panama from Colombia to cut a canal through it, or under Taft when we withdrew oil land from the private sector just in case the Navy might need it someday, or under Wilson in the Clayton Anti-Trust Act, supplementing the Sherman law with the provocative statement, "the labor of a human being is not a commodity or article of commerce." God knows, Taft was no doer (he himself admitted he was much happier as Chief Justice of the Supreme Court than as President, passing on the difficulties of other men instead of inventing his own), but that was all right then because the momentum of Progressivism swept him and the nation along anyway.

But the war had killed popular Progressivism, and recommended chief executives with less cheek than Roosevelt and Wilson. Isolationism needed Coolidge, not Hughes. Things were going to stay the way they were, see? Why, even liberals thought the twenties looked good. Lincoln Steffens reckoned that "big business in America is producing what the Socialists held up as their goal; food, clothing, and shelter for all." Or Walter Lippmann: "The more or less unplanned activities of business men are for once more novel, more daring, and in general more revolutionary, than the theories of the progressives." Not only business, but slam-bang, closed-door ignorance was in fettle, as when William Jennings Bryan announced that "all the ills from which America suffers can be traced back to the teaching of evolution. It would be better to destroy every other book ever written, and save just the first three verses of Genesis." All right we are one nation, rising like a comet on the arc of a bunkum boom.

Hughes was ready to take the world but we, it seems, were not, and the reason is less xenophobia than its corollary, moral superman-ship. Rich was good, famous was good, local was good—all rich, any famous, our local—and anything less lacked character. Foreigners were less, being poor, anonymous, and foreign, and Americans mistook foreign immigrants for foreign stock, as if the whole outside world were nothing but ghettos of pushcart vendors, spaghetti makers, and gardeners, illiterate in gibberish, and as if they hadn't all just been dangerous enough to drag us into the latest, not the last, of their intermittent wars.

Well, there's no novelty in backward thinking around here. Hopeful make-believe is still with us, still determined to withstand the natural process by which the invisible entanglements of technol-ogy and commerce "only connect." As far as entanglement goes, we already had it, inescapably, and neither the richest beast nor the stubbornest monk could get around it. Yes, American business—or should one say, American character?—was sufficient unto the day. But look what happened tomorrow.

SEVEN

Roaring People Roar for People

They called for jazz; they called for tales of love and death; they called for heroes. We return now to the cold facts and to the twenties, about half over but just getting into form, gaining new stars with each new headline as old stars die out and old loves stale. The death of the age was Bryan's, for even the highbrows sympathized with the sad finish of this Great Commoner, cut down as he was under the steel rhetoric of Darrow at the Scopes Trial; what an end to greatness! But the funeral of the age belonged to Rodolpho Alfonzo Pierre Filibert Guglielmi di Valentina d'Antonguolla . . . Rudolph Valentino.

One hundred thousand people viewed the body at the Campbell Funeral Parlor on Broadway and Sixty-seventh Street, while radio and the press blasted each other and the nation with scoops about the death, most of them exaggerations, ecstasies, or hoaxes, such as the "composograph" cut and pasted up by the *Evening Graphic*, using faces out of the celebrity file and unknown models' bodies to reveal Enrico Caruso receiving The Sheik at the gates of heaven. It was late August of 1926; it was hot; it was muggy; it was about to rain buckets; it was inconceivable that Valentino should have died—he was only thirty-one years old and at the top of his career with the release a few weeks earlier of *The Son of the Sheik* (Valentino played both parts, looking like hectic twins). An inflamed appendix and two gastric ulcers had brought him down at New York's Polyclinic Hospital: inconceivably, it was true.

When the news broke, American womanhood slumped over the kitchen table, all purpose in life wasted, and in New York the crowd outside Campbell's indulged in one of the worst riots New York had seen since the century began. By noon of the appointed day, Lincoln Square looked like the anteroom of hell. Thousands of people stared lifelessly at the undertaker's front door, waiting for a signal to move. A squad of auxiliary police hung around unconcernedly. Suddenly the sky broke and the rain poured down, and the crowd tore for shelter, pushing at each other, venting their frustration at the long wait for Campbell's to open. Mounted police charged the mob, but everywhere they contained it, it slithered away and reformed, charging Campbell's, charging each other, going into hysterics. Women lost their shoes and fell to the pavement, moaning. Under the pressure of eyes and noses, the plate-glass windows of Campbell's gave with a shower of cutting edges while cameramen dodged in and out of the fracas, turning to snap a picture wherever they heard a scream, clicking away; first the broken window, then the mob, then the window again, where two women had been shaved along a ragged suture, then the mob again, clawing at each other, breaking glass, tearing up the side streets to head back around corners and into the fray once more, all for Rudy.

Inside Campbell's, the coffin itself, encased in bronze, had been covered with a thick plate of glass to protect the body from fans unto death and souvenir hunters. Having got the riot under control at length, the police instituted a fast-moving line for the rest of the week—an average wait of three and a half hours for a look of three seconds. These last riters were mostly women, naturally, acting as if they'd lost a husband instead of a stranger, but there were a few men in file, amateur Latins who eyed the corpse, according to the *New York World,* "with a cynical kind of interest, as if they would discover some secret within the casket." There was, however, nothing to learn there. Any secret yet to be ciphered lay up on the screen in

Valentino's flicks; that was the true Valentino, the essence of a thing. This, in the bier, was only a man, an ex-tango dancer, blackmailer, and second-rate actor, and a dead one at that. True, Valentino's funeral did prove the biggest event in the career of Valentino's following, far bigger than his emergence in *The Four Horsemen of the Apocalypse* and his ascendance in *The Sheik*. Valentino had outdone himself by dying. As the *World* put it, "Rudolph Valentino alive never drew such a crowd as did Rudolph Valentino dead."

On the other hand, Valentino's funeral was the best-handled publicity stunt of the day. P.R. men for the actor, for his studio, and for the undertaker worked their tongues off getting the right coverage and "materials"—the latter would include an impressive long shot of the funeral cortege, distributed so far in advance of deadlines that one newspaper reportedly had it out before the procession could be set in motion—and much money was made by all involved. Poeticizing the tragedy, a song entitled "There's a New Star in Heaven Tonight" was rushed into print and performance, and a hasty search was made for last words to quote, settling at last on "Let the tent be struck," which seemed appropriate considering how closely Valentino's persona was bound up in desert rendezvous. But the phrase had unfortunately seemed just as appropriate to Robert E. Lee, who had already used it on his deathbed. "I want the sunlight to greet me" was adopted instead.

Best of all the promotional effluvia were the stars who haunted the funeral services at St. Malachy's on West Forty-ninth Street—fame calling to fame to pay dues—such as Douglas Fairbanks, Mary Pickford, Texas Guinan (weeping copiously for perhaps the only time in her adult life), and the definitively vivid Pola Negri, the Polish bombshell. Negri was the hit of the funeral, single-handedly providing a large share of its many noises, now ordering a pall of four thousand roses, now fainting photogenically at the coffin, now announcing that she and Valentino had been secret lovers of late, now threatening to enter a convent. Negri made her contribution as well to the lore of the last words: according to her agent, Valentino's final statement was "Pola, I love you and will love you in eternity." (There were to be yet more last words. The memoirs of Valentino's ex-wife, Natacha Rambova, printed excerpts from conversations which Rambova claimed to be having with Valentino from The Beyond.)

The public amassed to pay its own sort of dues to celebrity. Just two days after they tore up Lincoln Square for Valentino, they were cheering for eighteen-year-old Gertrude Ederle as her victory convoy moved up Fifth Avenue from the Battery to 108 Amsterdam Avenue, where the Ederles lived. Unlike Valentino, Ederle had done something—swam the English Channel, the first woman to do so and in record-breaking time besides—rather than been something. But immediately the news broke, she was turned into someone who *was,* specifically, lovable, unspoiled, German-American "Trudy," hyphenated for immigrant interest, nicknamed for democracy, and showered with money offers—to endorse products, to appear in vaudeville, to try the movies, even to swim.

The crowd that turned out to view Ederle's parade was greater than any that New York had seen in the recent past, greater than Pershing's and the Prince of Wales'; and though the police again had trouble keeping order, this crowd never got up the mob action they had effected for Valentino's body, even if they did trap Ederle inside City Hall for a half hour at the bottom leg of the festivities until police reinforcements permitted her exit. Speeches and splendor, gifts and offers to rent one's celebrity while the halo was still glowing, compliments from the great and the little were the spoils of those who stood out, often for whatever reason, from the crowd. If the press made a business out of selling the last and then the next new face, the public was buying all it could handle. Merchandise doesn't move in a vacuum.

Anyway, there had to be more to the popular profile than gangsters and politicians. People Who Did Things may have exceeded Dorothy Parker's endurance, but most newspaper readers were duly impressed. Ederle, a young woman of no special presence (on the chubby side, in truth), had done the relatively impossible, not only as the first of her sex, but clearing the old record by nearly two hours. The wonderful access to her feat was that, unlike flagpole sitting, aviation, or sensational murder, the essence of the act—swimming—was something ordinary, within the ken and experience of most Americans. This would be Babe Ruth's secret, too, perhaps—that he was doing what other people did, only better and with flash, only with human flash, like any good old guy from down the block, only the best. Others, such as Shipwreck Kelly, Charlie Chaplin, and Mae West would come to prominence for their very specialness, but what made the real heroes living gods for the folk, what so arrested the attention and made the favorites not chance amusements but leitmotifs of American life, developing along with the nation and lasting as long as the heroes were willing to last, was the *routine* glow of their specialness, their universal likeness. Perching on flagpoles for record spells made Shipwreck Kelly famous, but it also made him a joke, something to turn up in soigné patter songs in *The Greenwich Village Follies* and something for (the) hoi polloi to salaam with derisive wonder. Similarly, Chaplin and West were freaks to respect or indulge, but freaks nonetheless, without the peculiar leverage that tells the masses instantly who's real and who isn't.

Something attracts them. Something reminds them, they believe, of them—a way of standing, or the texture of voice, or a quirk in one's résumé that reassures them, or a phrase that seizes their passion. "For what, Trudy?" Ederle's trainer had said, trying to talk her out of it eleven hours into the channel; "For what, Trudy?" the crowd shouted as the cavalcade drove through the cheering and surging and thrilling and adoring—nothing weird about it, just good-natured appreciation. For what? For the adoring, of course.

So, there was more to the public response than debunking, and there were values after all to inculcate and live up to. It wasn't cynicism that batted Babe Ruth into the nation's consciousness when baseball was The Sport, nor was it only his gift for accumulating precedents in the matter of the home run. There was no airwave camaraderie in the twenties, no talk shows or personal appearance spots for the revelation of electronic veneer; only stage and movie people got to portray themselves. Yet that in itself brought people closer to other people, for everything was live—almost, if you leaned into it enough, a one-to-one encounter. The Babe was experienced firsthand, lored over in sports columns, yes, but there to view on the field. He was known, the Babe was, and since familiarity often enough breeds affection, he was not only admired but liked, not least because of his numerous scrapes with the authorities—coaches, team owners, and policemen alike.

The Babe broke rules, and they loved him for that. It was seldom that he made curfew, for each new stop on the road in season meant another girl to look up, and when a reporter once tried to pump Babe's roommate for details of the interior Ruth, the roommate was unable to answer. "I don't room with him," he said, "I room with his suitcase." Babe once even spent a day in jail for speeding, in 1921, getting released a little after that afternoon's game had already begun. The news had spread, and again there was that crowd waiting outside the station house; already in uniform, Babe was hustled out a back door, conveyed up to the Polo Grounds by motorcycle brigade, and cheered uproariously when he trotted onto the green. If it wasn't one crowd, it was another.

An orphan from Baltimore, big but plain and ill-proportioned, Ruth was no Beowulf or Arthur; his appetites were more to flesh than stone, more to the prosaically urban rather than the outdoors of myth, and thus the legend grew. His very ordinariness, like Ederle's, was what made his feats so inspiring: it could happen to you. When the Yankees bought him from the Red Sox in 1919 in a sophisticated deal sounding like $100,000 but ultimately totaling $400,000 in notes and interest, Ruth was being acclaimed as the greatest hitter in the history of baseball, and the records and new records that he set throughout the twenties made him something better, the greatest hitter in the future of baseball. The Babe's unbeatable tally of sixty home runs in a single season, in 1927 (it was beaten, finally, in 1961; it took that long), was treasured by lesser men in the stands not because of P.R. presentation, but because there was nothing to have to worship in an imperfect man, nothing intimidatingly fabulous or masterful about that barrel-stomached dub in the outfield. They laughed when he tripped over himself chasing a pop fly, booed when he threw dust in an umpire's eye and got thrown out of the game, and huzzahed when he shot another and another over the fence. It was the most natural respect in the world.

Fame, they say, yields celebrity a restless spotlight, always hoping to move on to discovery. But Babe Ruth kept on being king even after he had retired and remains the king today, long after he died and his sixty-homer bequest was broken on the diamond court by Roger Maris (albeit by only one homer more than Ruth's sixty and at that in a season richer than Ruth's 1927 by eight games). Novelty it is that flickers early on; a real American accomplishment, made in "American" terms—accessible, human, a fact rather than a principle—endures with the allegedly fickle public.

On the other hand, Gene Tunney didn't think so. In 1928, when he was the world's heavyweight boxing champion, he lectured at Yale one afternoon on Shakespeare—for Tunney was the bookworm of fighters—and chose *Troilus and Cressida,* perhaps the most difficult item in the canon, on which to preach his lesson. "Shakespeare," Tunney announced, "was a sport," echoing from another vantage the reductive procedure of Billy Sunday's "Jesus could go some." Heywood Broun caught Tunney's act and wrote, "Go-getters sit in the seats of the mighty. Harvard, I trust, will counter by asking Babe Ruth to tell the boys at Cambridge just what Milton has meant to him." Such irony rolled right past Tunney, who lacked it himself. Everything he did was on the level; maybe that was the trouble. At Yale, pointing out how quickly Achilles becomes a forgotten man while sulking in his tent, Tunney compared that hero of the Trojan War to two heroes of a later and even more bitterly contested war, Wilson and Pershing, both of whom were already in eclipse (though for more potent reasons than some fickle public: there was nothing fickle about the way the public hated the names associated with the sending and leading of the Yanks and drums over there). Tunney's moral: "to cash in while I can. And it is quite applicable to this day and age."

And yet, only seven months earlier, Tunney had fought one half, unquestionably the more intriguing half, of the most terrific boxing match of its day, a controversy which is still being worked out in working-class taverns by men who weren't there. No, fame is not necessarily so transient as all that. They couldn't quite replace Valentino with Ramon Novarro, Antonio Moreno, or Ricardo Cortez, either, though they tried hard to do so with the same P.R. network that had created the ideal of the Latin lover in the first place. Nor could Tunney replace Jack Dempsey, even as he took the title from him and retained it in a return match a year later.

It doesn't work that way; the public isn't fickle except when novelty overbids its contract. This is the paradox of the communications media, the paradox of the twenties when the communicating picked up its habits, for the P.R. satraps still seem to think that anything can be sold, anything at all in the right campaign. The truth is that almost anything can sell for a nonce, whereas only true goods last out the weekend. But there is another paradox contained within, a fun house catch in which art is not life but makes life, and that is that anything can come to believe its own promotion, and live up to it, and thus tumble into its own fantasy like Alice down the rabbit hole. "Kid," said Babe Ruth to Red Grange when they crossed paths for the first time, "don't believe everything they write about you." Such advice is extraneous out in the real world, where a Warren Harding knows Warren Harding's limitations and where a Calvin Coolidge wisely stays out of trouble (they called him "the man who crushed the Boston police strike"; he himself knew better). But politicians, like businessmen and highbrows, don't get Created the way celebrities do, celebrities who need only the one good break, who land and vanish, and who don't have to go as far as involving themselves importantly in a pattern called a war to fade from the scene. Celebrities have to believe so the public will believe, at least if they intend to last.

Tunney, whether he believed or not, lasted, despite retiring but one bout after the big one, "The Battle of the Century." Dempsey lasted, too, though said Battle was his last, his best, and according to one view of things, altogether his, even if Tunney took the official decision. These are doers we're speaking of, men of a certain limited action. Tunney made a few passes at principle, for his intellectualizing and humorless demeanor defeated sportswriters' powers of profile. . . . "I'll lick any man who checks his brains in the dressing room," he once said, robbing the sport of its brute spontaneity. Dempsey, however, was all fact, easygoing offstage and a savage in his trunks.

Asked, in the light of Tunney's Yale adventure, for his personal slant on the Bard, Dempsey replied, "Sorry, never had the pleasure," which was more like it and all that one needed to hear.

Still, the collegiate Tunney had bested Dempsey for the world heavyweight title in Philadelphia in 1926—a terrible match, the undertrained Dempsey breaking down to living bits in pouring rain in front of another crowd ... that crowd again, watching, 121,000 people taking in the collapse with even more fascination than that with which they attended lyings-in and triumphal processions. But then this fight was the fact itself, not an aftermath to a fact. "There never was a more deliberate butchering of a champion," claimed Hype Igoe of the *World,* "never a cooler man in gleaning a heavyweight crown. I'm sure Tunney felt sorry for him. He took the battered king that was in his great arms and, folding him to his breast as if he had been his own mother, Tunney whispered something in Dempsey's ear. I don't know what it was. I don't want to know. It was some sacred little thing, an unusually kind word from a conqueror to a beaten man." As Dempsey had creamed Jess Willard in 1919, so was it now with him, but there was no replacement, and Dempsey remained Dempsey, loved still in defeat, urged up from the mat, so to speak, by that crowd, who knew a winner when it saw one, even when it saw one lose. What was Tunney? A college punk. Just let Dempsey at him, just once more for sure!

The return match in Chicago, 364 days later, was a great moment for the teeming public, a very factual moment. Even with every spare reporter giving the fight all his concentration, it seemed as if the newspapers couldn't give the event enough coverage, couldn't supply that crowd with enough of the human-interest minutiae that kept it happy. Such was the curiosity that thousands at a time were paying to get in to see Dempsey's and Tunney's training sessions, making a fact of a mere preliminary, and *The New York Times* dubbed them "The Thrill Hunters" in a leery editorial: "No future chronicler of our times can fail to note that people will contribute about $3,000,000 to see two men fight for something less than forty-five minutes and even at that, most of them couldn't see all that well."

That much was true. The arena, Soldier Field, was blocked out for tickets of five to forty dollars, the forty-dollar "ringside" seats being way back of the V.I.P.'s and press and the five-dollar bleacher seats being, according to a local joke, in downtown Milwaukee. They came anyway: even people who had had their own share of mob appreciation showed up—Douglas Fairbanks, Charlie Chaplin, John Barrymore, Al Jolson, Jim Corbett, Mayor Thompson—along with a few men who could have bought and sold a mob ten times over, such as Otto Kahn and Charles Schwab. Twelve hundred reporters were dispatched to write up the bout, and the New York Central ran thirty-five special trains to Chicago, with the Twentieth Century Limited spanned out to seventy-seven pullman cars. Best of all, radio broadcast made sure that everyone could be there: now you could join up with the crowd without having to leave home and riot in the rain.

That, ultimately, was what radio was for, to open up the ends of public events so that they could reach beyond one place and time, to placate the thrill hunters with those facts they required at long distance. An estimated sixty million people tuned in to the Dempsey-Tunney rematch on eighty-two stations, and tension had been nicely honed by all the media ruckus and editorials and gentlemen's wagers and the daily tales on what the two fighters were eating, thinking, and, in Tunney's case, reading (he finished *Of Human Bondage* the afternoon of the fight), and by the flap over a nasty letter from Dempsey to Tunney accusing the latter of unfair play anent their match in Philadelphia the year before. Breath was so bated that ten radio listeners died of heart attacks in all the excitement, seven of them in the seventh round, the seventh round that passed into the annals as both history and bunk virtually as of its occurrence, the infamous seventh round of the Long Count. Now, that was a fact, all right—even advertisement couldn't have built it any bigger than it already was. The Long Count was so real it made legends look measly.

Unlike another famous controversy of the decade among boxing fans, when Dempsey may or may not have smashed Jack Sharkey a fast one below the belt in the play-offs for this very match with Tunney, the Long Count was witnessed free and clear by everyone in the arena, so everyone who was there, plus everyone who had heard it on the radio, and everyone who read of it in the papers or just heard tell about it had an opinion. There were only two opinions: either Dempsey deserved the title, or Tunney deserved the title. That simple.

The disputation stemmed from an Illinois state law, the only such law in the nation, that the fighter who perpetrates a knockdown must retire to a neutral corner *before the ten-count can commence.* The referee naturally reminded both Dempsey and Tunney of the rule before the first bell, but in the heat of the ruction a fighter who, as Tunney had put it, "checks his brains in the dressing room," might easily lose track of a state law.

Tunney was lithe; Dempsey was ruthless, impatient with his adversary's stylish sparring propriety, eager to slug it out. But Tunney was in control and setting the tempo while the onlookers noted Dempsey's form and fury, waiting for truth. They had to wait through six rounds, while the excitable and often ambiguous sportscaster Graham McNamee kept the radio listeners up to blows and expectations as what after all was the decade's top-hole grudge match went to flab and point scores. But then, at the seventh bell, Dempsey imposed his own rhythm on Tunney, driving him into getting it on . . . pounding his head—then a hard left to the stomach—now Tunney fights back because now at last it *is* a fight—"like a couple of wild animals," McNamee observes—a terrific right from Tunney—Dempsey staggers—no! a hard left from Dempsey and Tunney staggers—Dempsey crouches—Dempsey prepares—Dempsey releases—the—greatest—left—swing—in—boxing—history . . . and Tunney is down. That is a fact.

But state law and the neutral corner are facts, too, facts which Dempsey forgot. He stood over the fallen Tunney, waiting to sock him when he rose, but the referee got to Dempsey and pushed him aside in the direction of a neutral corner and then, only then, began the count. The Long Count. At nine, Tunney got up. The match continued, Tunney taking the decision, the champion still. But, said some, had the fight occurred anywhere else, it would have been a knockout—Tunney really got something like sixteen seconds, not nine. But, said others, like any smart boxer, Tunney deliberately waited till nine to rise to collect himself. What sixteen seconds? The count was nine when Tunney got up, wasn't it? Well? Wasn't it?

McNamee, incidentally, did not narrate the Long Count as well as he might have done, and there was some confusion out there in radioland—as announcers used to phrase it, forgetting, or perhaps simply refusing to admit, that they themselves were the ones in radioland—until the gong signaled that the ten rounds were over and the judges conferring on the decision. "Yes," McNamee avowed through the tension, "Tunney, I feel sure, retains his championship because at the last moment Dempsey was practically out on his feet. And, ladies and gentlemen, I assure you there were no fouls in this fight. There were no fouls here. There was nothing questionable that I saw"—it sounds as if McNamee doth protest too much, as the poet quoth, but just then the boxers were called to the center of the ring, Tunney's arm was raised, McNamee let out a whoop, and it was all over. All except for Dempsey's appeal of the Long Count, overruled by the Illinois Boxing Commission, and the heated arguments that have taken Dempsey's side or defended Tunney's ever since.

Well, whomever one finds for, that was some fact, anyway; that was something being done, all right, like Ruth and his homers, like any number of sports events that took us neither forward nor backward but were, at bottom, forms of action. Athletes, even when they functioned as personae first and sportsmen second, were doers, achievers, whether of a "because it's there" geste such as swimming the English Channel, or a peak performance on a regular basis, such as the Babe's annual precedent. But it was all the better if their real lives were identifiable as ordinary-but-special, like Ruth's, rather than totally surrealistic, like Valentino's. No, those movie people all dwelled in halls of Montezuman freakiness, and while that crowd, yes, would indeed turn out for anyone, it preferred the men and women it could place with its inner eye, other Americans like itself.

In other words, doers, for the mirror must reflect the ideal. Babe Ruth was the great doer, a teamworker but a star as well, ace-high even in the context of the Yankee batting combination known since 1919 as Murderers' Row—Frank "Home Run" Baker, Bob Meusel,

Roger Peckinpaugh, Ping Bodie, Wally Pipp (later joined or replaced by Lou Gehrig, Earle Combs, Mark Koenig, Tony Lazzeri) . . . and Ruth.* This was the great ground-zero of American enterprise, men pulling on the same rope, but each not without his own distinguishing grip—collaborators but winners, like the gentlemen of the business community. Valentino was as nothing compared to them; he wasn't even real; he had no fact. Ruth was real, a virile guy where Valentino was suspect, a man who worked with his hands where Valentino worked hardly at all. Ruth was witnessed and quoted, a known quantity; Valentino was more likely *experienced,* and that mainly by women, a mystery. Best of all, Ruth had the right quotient of sentimental belief and cynical hooliganism expected of a hero, but Valentino had none of this protective coating so useful for exhibit by the media. How wounded he had been by the *Chicago Tribune*'s editorial entitled "The Pink Powder Puff," that recommended the suppression of Valentino before "the ancient caveman virtues of [the American male's] forefathers are replaced by cosmetics, flopping pants, and slave bracelets." Not that such a thing could have been said about Ruth, but if he did indulge in an occasional tantrum, mostly he just laughed things like newspaper editorials away to the wind.

America has always had its stars, one way or another, but one does note that in previous centuries they tended more to the leadership professions, statesmen and generals and such. The escalating heterogeneity of the population, both from foreign immigration and from domestic mobility—added to the widening hours of middle- and lower-middle-class leisure—changed all that by enriching life with professions of neither social nor political influence, professions for which the leadership caste signaled a new turn of character and a new relationship to the population. Less prosy than statesmen, less responsible than generals—and yet more communicative of populist grandezza than the most outrageous demagogue or the most informally

---

* The addition of the remarkable Gehrig to the lineup (as of 1923), combined with Ruth's ever-elaborating dialogues with statistics, has located Murderers' Row, in the folklore, in the late twenties; however, the term was coined in 1919—just *before* Ruth was traded to the Yankees—by the cartoonist Robert Ripley.

harum-scarum brass hat—these latter-day heroes are as likely to belong to the pointillistic episodes of the sports world—to the knockout, the end run, the homer—as to the tapestry of presidential or senatorial prevalence, and by the time the technological media had caught up with it, fame was ready to fly. Gradually throughout the 1800s, but with more particular haste from then on and at the gallop after the big war, fame and fame making not only collaborate, but enter into so fine a symbiosis as to lose track of where the fame leaves off and the making of it begins. Often enough the fame proper is abandoned as a reckless drawback and production is all. There are no more heroes today than there were a hundred years ago—but there are many, many more celebrities.

How right Alexis de Tocqueville was, back in the days of statesmen and generals, to predict that egalitarian democracy must inevitably depreciate to a lifeless, leveled society of neither depths nor quotients, file upon file of brutes screaming for fodder—for that does seem to be the future awaiting Western Europe—but how wrong he was to see it latent in the American plan, for our *égalité* is one of ethical conscience and law, not of character or "need," and the personal dissent of eccentricity, perverseness, or distinction remains one of our great traditions. "Lost in the crowd," was De Tocqueville's apprehension of any given American: "Every citizen, being assimilated to all the rest, is lost in a crowd, and nothing stands conspicuous but the great and imposing image of the people at large." Nonsense. Even admitting that De Tocqueville's brief visit to these shores occurred at the time of Andrew Jackson's Administration—the first importunately democratic regime in our history and what amounted to a derailment of what some of the mob-hating Founding Fathers had in mind—America was never like this. De Tocqueville can't be expected to have taken media blitz into account, but even before the fame makers were making it, this specific democracy was going out of its way to perceive the men and women whom God's grace, practical advantage, or happenstance have delivered from mediocrity.

Must one even debate the existence of an American aristocracy, with King Babe, Count Dempsey, and little Princess Trudy holding their levees on the High Street for all to see? Whether it be wisdom, or talent, or looks, or ambition, or dumb luck, some are more gifted than others, and gifts will win prizes here. "Pick up the first hundred men you meet," John Adams once wrote, "and make a republic. Every man will have an equal vote, but when deliberations and discussions are opened, it will be found that twenty-five, by their talents, virtues being equal, will be able to carry fifty votes. Every one of these twenty-five is an aristocrat in my sense of the word, whether he obtains one vote in addition to his own by his birth, fortune, science, learning, craft, cunning, or even his character for good fellowship and a bon vivant."

The last sums up the case for Babe Ruth. Winning is prizeworthy, and it does matter, very much, that one has come out the winner—but it does, too, matter exactly who one is on the way to the tape. This is the truth of the winner, *his* fact, and this is why game scores, yardage, and precedents were the smallest fraction of the sportswriter's copy. After all, didn't Bruce Barton pen *The Man Nobody Knows*, his "discovery of the real Jesus," to save Him from that lack of truth now referred to as a low profile? In his introduction, Barton recalled his childhood image of Jesus, "a pale young man with flabby forearms and a sad expression." What was this fogy compared to Daniel— "good old Daniel, standing off the lions"—and David—"with the trusty sling that landed a stone square on the forehead of Goliath"— and Moses—"with his rod and his big brass snake." Personality is all: "They were winners, those three," cries Barton—and who would know better than an advertising man?

Noting the crowd's rage for this certain truth, the press obliged with as many instances of it as could be found, and, discovering that a paucity of truths lowered circulation, they determined that there would always be much dissemination of truth, whether they had simply to report it, embellish it, or start out from scratch with concoction. The effect, in all three cases, was the same, for jazz is jazz, whatever the truth may be, and the jazz of winners was the form of jazz most highly acceptable to the great American readership. Societies of men will have aristocracy, and the aristocrat of choice will lead them. This is what the crowd wants, waiting and watching, massing up to cheer for heroes because that's what masses do. Like Edmund Burke, they want facts: "I must see the Things; I must see the men." Ruth and Dempsey the crowd could see. Any one of the spectators might have nudged Pontius Pilate, pointed, and said, "That, since you ask, is truth."

Where exactly an opera singer fitted in with the program of seeing the Things was anybody's guess, for while opera singers tend to portray themselves somewhat sensationally anyway, they had little attraction for the general public, being foreign, highbrow, fat, and so on. But apparently somebody recalled how broad a following the recently retired Geraldine Farrar had boasted, and accordingly somebody rooted about for a second Farrar, a Middletowner who would wow the critics and take the Met by storm, an American beauty voice packaged for glamour. And somebody thought he had found just the one in Kansas City; thus begins the three-year career of Marion N. Talley.

Her middle name was Nevada, which is a great beginning, and she was only seventeen, which is copy, but other than the legend of a budding country girl scaling a cultural Olympus, dutifully built up by the press with the usual touches of myth in her résumé, Talley had nothing going for her. Neither glamorous nor even much talented, she had a sweet, natural, high soprano but little musicianship, less sense of style, and virtually no stage experience—the sort of person who stands out in a community sing. But Kansas City helped launch her, and New York carried the ball; even the simple formality of her audition for Giulio Gatti-Casazza, the general manager of the Metropolitan Opera, was reported as if she had invented new notes. Gatti, one of the last of the golden age entrepreneurs—when opera, so they say, was opera—knew even before Talley had opened her mouth that her name was already so hot that its addition to the posters couldn't help but sell out for a season or so no matter what she looked like, sounded like, or did on stage. When it turned out that she could sing after all, Gatti nodded sagely and sent her off to Europe for refining while the publicity mill kept her name and likeness before the public.

Remember, media blitz travels a two-way street, and the audience has its own personality-vision needs to satisfy, needs that fluctuate on their own schedule—note the easy transition from the expansive, Midwestern burgher, Harding, to the detruded Puritan, Coolidge, within the same administration. While the public will buy overbilled goods, the product must appear to correspond to the image they apprehend. In Talley's case, everyone was truly hoping for another Farrar, not least because intellectuals had been so damning of America's Main Street meretriciousness and lack of artistic emprise, and Talley's debut as Gilda in *Rigoletto* was a smash. It was already a smash before the curtain went up, when scalpers did a land-rush business and ticketholders, presold on Talley's glory, entered the auditorium as if they'd been let into what is known in Texas as hog heaven. Act One, in which Gilda does not appear, went by in a fever of hot flashes and chomping at the bit, not unlike those at the first six rounds of the Long Count fight; in Act Two, Talley's entrance was greeted by an ovation, her duet with Rigoletto was awarded with an ovation, her duet with the tenor was treated to an ovation, and her mediocre "Caro Nome" got the biggest ovation of all.

The aficionados and critics were not impressed, but the public, which can see but can't hear all that well, was so enthralled that it patronized the outré double-bill of De Falla's lurid *La Vida Breve* and Stravinsky's china figurine *Le Rossignol,* two operas no one wanted to hear, simply because Talley turned up in the latter—how right! how like life is art!—as a miraculous nightingale. Still, a gullible public is a fickle public when the subject of worship is without fact. Invented by the press as a diamond of the soil, Talley ran out of promotional glitter early on—and lo, it came out that she didn't even care all that much for singing. Back to the farm she went after three years with the Met, for a celebrity who lacks the public embrace is nothing but the latest sensation, an inadvertently planned obsolescence. A photograph of Talley—for the photo is essential in the twenties; the crowd must see—posed on her tractor and looking cheerful, closes her episode.

Sensation would do until the real thing came along, however. We've witnessed a lot of staying power from people like William Jennings Bryan and Henry Ford, people who can span eras, or invent them, and we've seen, too, the more colorful but less dense demarcation of the strictly period folk like Texas Guinan. There is a third phylum of heroes—weekenders, these, here and gone as fast as it takes the papers to profile their vagrant fascination. These are the inhabitants of Sensation City: crackpots, shrewd purveyors of fad, visitors from abroad, defendants in murder trials. Figures of fun is what this group entails; there isn't a doer in the bunch. The public attended to the endurances of Alvin "Shipwreck" Kelly on his flagpoles as one does a dog act, and the only point of interest in Kelly's record-setting stints in the air (seven days, one hour by 1927) was exactly how the indignities of life are accommodated during a nonstop exile atop a platform barely big enough to sit on (answer: "excess fluids are poured down a pipe running alongside the flagpole"). Even the materialization of a romance between "the luckiest fool alive" and a worshiping flapper didn't make Kelly all that human, perhaps because they met on his flagpole during a sitting in Dallas (she was hauled up to him on a rope). But Kelly was no dope. He preferred engagements above hotel rooftops, where publicity for the hotel called for an advance contract and where a suitable fee could be collected from rooftop gazers. Needless to say, there were plenty of those: crazy is lucrative.

Kelly volunteered for discomfort; Floyd Collins was a victim, and in his two weeks of fame he distracted the nation with a human predicament instead of a stunt. Yet the news media made hay with Collins exactly as they did with Kelly. Ballyhoo was becoming the standard term for what the press and the advertising and P.R. powers wrote and how they wrote it, and ballyhoo was just another name for jazz. The luckless Collins, trapped by a rock slide in an underground passage at Sand Cave, Kentucky, got front-page treatment, and as rescue operations proceeded, the suspense ran hot in print, and that waiting crowd took up its post at the site, held back by state troopers and barbed wire. No one knew much about Collins—nothing at all before the *Louisville Courier-Journal* started running a day-to-day report on the rescuers' progress and little enough after—but even without the personal fact, he was someone to worry over. He had . . . informality. This is not the informality of the merely everyday, or of the self-conscious democrat, but an informality of media promotion that portrays only certain facets of any given personality, those that inspire an elemental, one-to-one response in the audience. Informality appeals to what is basic in our tastes and robs us of knowing about what makes us, whoever we are, different. Babe Ruth's homers were his fact, one that set him apart even in the unceremonious world of baseball—but his sex drive and his resistance to authority, played up by sportswriters: this was his informality, his reduction to human terms, his connection to us. Informality tells us, "It could happen to you," and it reaches everywhere, to the Babe in his day, to Floyd Collins in his moment. But it reaches so blindly, or perhaps instinctively, that messianic politicians, drastic ball-players, movie actors, and victims of natural disaster all step forward in the same dance. Even God isn't exempted from this reductive approach, as in this excerpt from the wit and wisdom of the Reverend Billy Sunday: "Jesus could go some; Jesus could go like a six-cylinder engine, and if you think Jesus couldn't, you're dead wrong." Me and Thee, Lord.

For once, there was no way to *see* the man when Floyd Collins got locked in his earthly prison, but that didn't stop the press from feeding him to a readership daily with the breakfast egg. The cave-in that held Collins held him fast, but the *Courier-Journal*'s reporter was small enough to climb in and talk to him; thus, through the thrill of the interview, Collins talked with the nation. A doomed man, closest to death of all the quick, Collins became a source of worry and wonderment and, until his time ran out, a celebrity. What a fortune he would garner in endorsements, personal appearances, and movie roles, if only the rescue team could pull him out.

Several different plans proved fruitless, including a scheme to drag him loose at the cost of his foot, which had been mangled in the cave-in anyway. But food, at least, was pushed through to him, and to keep him connected with the waiting world, copper wire was led through to Collins to burn a light bulb for him; it was hoped that the illumination would in some dim way cheer him up. As time went on he resorted to prayer, or so the newspapers said. "O Lord, dear Lord, gracious Lord, Jesus all-powerful," he was quoted as saying, "get me out of this if it is Thy will, but Thy will be done."

Outside, the crowd held to its vigil, and souvenir tents, snack stands, and the usual petty hustling followed the crowd, along with some rumors that local officials with an interest in tourism were deliberately taking their time about the rescue technique. Two and a half decades later, Billy Wilder based his movie *Ace in the Hole* on the Collins adventure, pointing up the money-take and copy-crazed chicanery of ballyhoo, and Wilder insisted that the ugly grubbing he portrayed derived straight from chronicle. In his film, the Collins runoff dies in his trap, and that much, at least, did happen. Before the rescuers could get to Collins, a second cave-in cut him off from the outside, and when they finally broke through, the man was dead. *The New York Times* gave it a three-column headline, for whether or not it was ballyhoo, it definitely was news: FIND FLOYD COLLINS DEAD IN CAVE TRAP ON 18TH DAY: LIFELESS AT LEAST 24 HRS: FOOT MUST BE AMPUTATED TO GET BODY OUT.

The press had been careful about the death of Coolidge's son, Calvin, Jr., the year before, when the sixteen-year-old-boy died of blood poisoning contracted from a tennis blister, but for Collins they held a freak show. There could be no informality about the President and his son, no human display—though the stony Coolidge's startling crack of emotion was regarded with reticent bemusement from coast to coast—but the insignificant Collins was natural-born fodder ("something to be consumed," as Webster has it), copy corn. How quickly the pressmen had adjusted themselves to the times, how altered, they, from the sanctimonious arbitrators who spent much of 1919 waxing wroth on sociopolitical doctrine, on booms and strikes and on being right or left. Almost to the month, 1919 marked the last year of the good old newspaper, from sprawling city room to hand-me-down country press, and the commencement of Bigger and Better, when the flat news medium gave up its centuries-old business of helping to guide the nation and became more like just another business, a folding Ford, a perfect pocket Ford, on the loose to guide the upsurge of technocratic P.R. The newspaper looked at radio, and it must have been thinking, Look what that thing gets away with— music, news, and chat all done up so professionally as to seem the reason for radio's being, and thus slightly obscuring what quickly became the upfront purpose of radio, selling. Unlike the newspaper, which until the twentieth century was rather casual about the placement and appearance of its advertisements, radio was meticulous in its delivery of the sponsor's message (by the late twenties, anyway), and in seeking a national market it happily fostered a national midpoint to which it proposed itself most generally. This the American newspaper had never attempted to do. Its sectionalism, its rank and rapscallion candor of locale, was its rectitude, for in editorializing for Buncombe Country, it protected the curiosities of the cultural panorama, reserving dissent for the God of the country and the man of the town, and never the twain should have had to meet.

The celebrity, however, changed that around with his fact and his informality—that is, with his heroic enterprise on one hand and his average-Joe humanness on the other. The time when the anti-Federalist press of Jefferson's Virginia debated with the Federalist press of Hamilton's New York was not a harmonious, but a vigorous, age, for while there is strength in union, there is stimulation in discord. But as of the twenties, the communications and P.R. media took an active part in the presentation of a national personality. Whether it involved the staying power of a Babe Ruth or the eighteen-day contraption of a Floyd Collins, it was demographic gold. Synergic with these heroes and victims, some of whom achieved informality but many of whom had it thrust upon them by reporters who knew how the answers were supposed to run (that's why they asked the questions), the press gathered up the criteria of American-hero folklore—the log cabin, the self-reliance, the lucky strike, the phrase that rings, the doing, the fact.

The aim of this hero jobbery was to create a readership. The vigor of faction was slipping out of the national routine, culturally if not politically, yet the result would never be harmony: just because we bought the personality of the week didn't incline us to lower our dissentient frontiers any more than we had ever done. Letting the communications industries unite us with the promotional package, we took celebrity at their definition, losing sight of the born leaders who take their own time to surface.

And what imbecilic creatures, sometimes, were put over with the public's too-willing collaboration. Ruth didn't need the press to triumph and Collins was a fluke of sympathetic suspense, but, oh, the sleazy marginalia of the big-business newspaper circa 1926. In a matter of a few years, the newspaperman had turned from the pontificator of troubled 1919 into a heel-clicking, upstart "younger generation" of sybaritic caterers, bagmen of the media whorehouse and far more out of control then any sheik or flapper known to Elinor Glyn. True, the scrofulous newspaper was hardly a novelty in the United States, but before the twenties it had been the exception; now it was proving the majority rule. Even the scrupulous *New York Times* devoted twenty-two thousand words in two days to the Ruth Snyder-Judd Gray murder trial, one of the more festive adventures of 1927, and everywhere—not only in the new and frankly disorderly tabloids—editorial and letter pages were down while photographs, sports and crime news, and the lowdown on low-lives were way up. The death of the educator Charles William Eliot, one day before that of Valentino, was not nearly so emblazoned upon the nation's tabulature as was the passing of The Sheik, for Eliot's forty years as a great, progressive president of Harvard, the magic he worked with graduate schools in the arts and sciences, his labor on the college preparatory curricula of public schools, and his editing of the famous "five-foot shelf" of classics had, for the general public, no reverberation to compete with the jerry-built pseudohero of the Hollywoodland romance.

"Oh, f'r a Moses!" cried "Mr. Dooley," the Irish publican wag created by Finley Peter Dunne to provide an urban counterpart to Will Rogers' sly hick commentary on time and place. "Oh, f'r a Moses to lead us out iv th' wilderness an' clane th' Augeeyan stables . . . an captain th' uprisin' iv honest manhood agin th' cohorts iv corruption an' shake off th' collar riveted on our necks by tyrranical bosses! Where is Moses?" Moses certainly wasn't to be numbered among the sensations of the day, the flagpole sitters, movie stars, gangsters, and assorted minor perverts built big by the honchos of cultural charisma. Neither Harding, nor the accidental Coolidge, nor the soon-to-be landslided Hoover offered the presidential style of the public Moses, and if our political leaders were no leaders, and a Moses such as Charles Evans Hughes, fact and all, hadn't the informal associations to connect with the people while he connected with the future, what could one expect of our ephemeral dandies except beasts and monks? In 1925, William Allen White, one of the last of the old-time crusading newspapermen, summed up the case against the new journalism in his obituary in the *Emporia Gazette* for Frank A. Munsey, known as "The Grand High Executioner of Journalism" for his practice of taking over and ruining respectable organs of community polemics. Capitalizing on "the talent of a meat packer, the morals of a money-changer, and the manners of an undertaker," wrote White, "he and his kind have about succeeded in transforming a once-noble profession into an 80 per cent security. May he rest in trust!" But to similar criticism of *its* procedure, the *New York Daily News* had a ready answer: "Newspapers print the news. That's why they're called newspapers. That part of the news happens to be scandalous is the fault of the people who make it, not the fault of the papers."

What jazz. It was in the emphasis on how much of which news to advance that culpability lay with the papers, especially such as the *Daily News*, William Randolph Hearst's *Daily Mirror*, or Bernarr Macfadden's *Evening Graphic*, aptly known as the *Porno-Graphic*. No Moses would have done for these exponents of backstairs journalism, for the Moseses don't abide the rules of play—that's what makes them what they are. For the tabloids, persona grata was someone like Edward West Browning, "Daddy" to the readership, a man out of slick folklore, a "big spender," a "butter-and-egg man," a "sucker," a tintype of mores espied through a keyhole, the door about to be forced open and the cameras hungry to click. ("The big butter and egg man, from Crackertown, P.A.," ran a song of the day, connecting the Brownings and their didoes to the supply and demand of pop art.) A wealthy real-estate operator with a yen for nymphets, Browning played Humbert Humbert to teenage girls whom he called his protégées and whom Walter Winchell of the *Graphic* dubbed "keptives," and as such provided the tabloids with copy parfait, not only never running out of the sauce but actually peaking in exploit, building up to a marriage with a hefty, doll-faced Lolita of fifteen years, Frances Belle Heenan—"Peaches" to Daddy and Peaches to the nation.

Having made the acquaintance of the boys in the pressroom on earlier outings, Daddy had a direct line to fame and the boys had a direct line to Daddy. He loved the attention, loved putting himself to print, even loved the crowd that swarmed around the newlyweds when they arrived, notification made and celebrity collecting its residuals, at Grand Central Station in late spring of 1926. Much was made of them. Every incident in the courtship and every quotation of bliss from one or the other of the couple appeared in print in widely varying ways; and, of course, it only added to the thrust of the exhibition that Daddy was an enthusiastic practical joker and given to cutting what might gently be called an odd swath about the boudoir. The sexual side of his butter-and-egg eccentricity did not come out till later, but it had long been clear that Browning would go the limit to hold the limelight, whether it meant showering his bride with heaps of candy, flowers, and knickknacks, or spending an afternoon with an unhousebroken African honking gander.

Yes, Daddy was everything that the press could have wished for in a subject—and don't think that the haughty *Times* left it all to the *Graphic* to report—but he really reached for, and grasped, the paper moon when Peaches tired of his carryings-on and left him at their temporary bower in Queens, the Kew Gardens Inn. Peaches, of course, had a mother—what baby-faced, dimpling, gold-digging flapper did not?—and Mrs. Heenan added to the picture that so-useful cliché, the Hateful Mother-in-law. The Roman farceur Terence would have known what to do with Mrs. Heenan, and the *Graphic,* too, had its method, the composograph. Just as it had offered Caruso welcoming Valentino at the pearly gates, so now did it propose the comparably edifying image of Daddy and Peaches actively occupying the bedroom while old lady Heenan lent an ear to the closed door.

Not surprisingly, Browning's immediate reaction to his wife's self-demobilization was to contact the newspapers, and thus commenced the last stage of his cumulative saga; it was the biggest thing to hit daily circulation in weeks. "Money isn't everything after all," was Peaches' diagnosis of the affair, wading out of the Kew Gardens Inn amidst a caravan of trunks and cases. HAS CINDERELLA'S LOVE DREAM CRUMBLED? asked one tabloid, and CHARGES RUN PERVERSION GAMBIT answered another as an array of disclosures and counterdisclosures were vomited out of the *News, Graphic, Mirror,* and *Journal,* all "by" either Mr. or Mrs. Browning. It is to be expected that no one version bore much resemblance to another, even when assigned to the same by-line, for unlike Babe Ruth and Jack Dempsey, the Brownings had no fact, no essence of a thing, and one could make any assertion about them, any at all, and still conform to the general outline of their exposition. The Brownings weren't what they "were," nor what they were perceived to be, Pirandello-fashion, for like Valentino and Floyd Collins, they were by-products of a production line, the Big Spender and the Baby Doll Flapper cutting a slapstick swank. Valentino represented a sort of ecstasy to women and a sort of dissolution to men, but Daddy and Peaches were a bang-up folly of the best sort, and one thing to everyone, a national travesty. "Why does Peaches sit on the beach so much?" Texas Guinan would demand of the assemblage at her latest speakeasy. Why? "To keep her tail from Browning!"

Yet the crowd that haunted the comings and goings of Daddy and Peaches was the same crowd that doted on any and all celebrities. "Heroes," villains, freaks, the doers and the done—all seemed to have been procured on the same conveyer belt, at least as far as that crowd was concerned, that crowd and its eyes, ready for focus. Perhaps George Washington was wrong after all to say that people must feel before they will see—wrong, at any rate, for our time if not his. These people saw more than felt; there was no time to feel; everything was happening so fast; but one didn't hear them complaining about it, did one?; and seeing was feeling. The crowd was there, inevitably, to check out the famous, the media's aristocrats, to take some measure and arrest a definition of some image. For what, Trudy? For what, now, Peaches, suing her benefactor for separation and alimony on grounds of mental cruelty? Covering the trial in late January of 1927 in White Plains, Damon Runyon noted a caboodle of baby carriages parked outside the courtroom in the snow, babies bereft while mothers observed the sacrament of fame: "grandmotherly-looking old women; stout, housewifely-looking dames; and skittish looking janes stood all morning and all afternoon on their two feet . . . a gray-haired old wowser and child wife attracting more attention than the League of Nations."

And the trial itself! The *Graphic* exercised its penchant for the composograph daily to keep up with the revelations of the Brownings' connubial exploit. What with Daddy loping around on all fours and making animal noises in his weird pajama costumes, Daddy throwing telephone books at Peaches through a transom, Daddy getting Peaches to pose for numerous publicity photos, Daddy bringing home nudie magazines for Peaches' storybook hour, and Daddy—or some-one—heaving acid at Peaches shortly before the marriage, the *Graphic* had its work cut out. The African honking gander proved a composographer's godsend as a kind of Aesopian commentator, pointing up the moral of jazz as the tabloid, of all twenties inventions, best could. "Woof! Woof! Don't be a goof!" honked the gander on his first appearance, alluding to Daddy's nocturnal dog imitations (sure enough, there was Browning, somehow, on all fours in his pajamas), and the best of the series had Browning menacing a moderately disturbed Peaches while the gander explained, "Honk! Honk! It's the bonk!"

That it was. At length the judge dismissed Peaches' suit, granting a separation but no alimony, and the next display of fad and foible, the Snyder-Gray murder case, quickly displaced the Brownings, for without the fact there is no continuity, no real fascination for the crowd. How much more stimulation the impossible Bryan had held for them; now, that was a true informality, there, and much fact: Bryan was a doer. Had the land not got so emancipatedly modern in places, mostly cities, Bryan might have been a winner as well, and would have had more than just Prohibition to crow over in the twenties, would have mustered a more personal stake in federal issues than he did—although nothing would have kept him from making a fool of himself at the Scopes Trial. It wasn't time on his hands that drew Bryan to Dayton in the summer of '25, but rather an unwillingness to admit that the city and its corporate-technological-highbrow evolution had played ducks and drakes with the God-fearing town. And the city had won.

The city has no informality—not, at least, the right kind. The city is invasive, inhuman; this the Dos Passos school had taught us. But the city had fact aplenty, for besides the seeing crowd, the city had the artists, and they are the great manipulators: they can make people feel before they can see. No longer simply a gathering place for country gentlemen, hostal for the occasional congress and convention and charmed with reasonable amenities, the city had become its own congress, hostile to outsiders, unreasonable, a New York or a Chicago, not a Boston or a Charleston. In the new city the highbrows gathered; the question is, whom do the highbrows choose?—besides the cultural underdogs, of course, for, being undersiders, they cheer for their own. When Peaches sued Daddy, the highbrows of Urbantown were preparing to make a last stand on the picket lines for Sacco and Vanzetti in perhaps their one serious moral undertaking of the decade, but in this the highbrows were no crowd seeking fact and informality. No tabloid, no radio could sell the highbrows a celebrity, but they themselves can sell, and thus one asks, whom did they choose to sell?

To pick an instance, the true life of art usurped the hoax life of news in 1928 in Sophie Treadwell's *Machinal*, an expressionist play based on the murder of a magazine editor, the trial of his wife and her lover, and their subsequent execution. "The Sash-Weight Murder" it was called, the "murder in Queens," the "crime of the Tiger Woman"; Damon Runyon called it "the dumb bell murder," and he comes closest, for no two criminals ever were so crude in operation and so transparent in their guilt. MOTIVE MYSTIFIES POLICE. A stranger, said Ruth Snyder, had broken into the Snyder home in Queens Village, tied her up, stole her jewels, and killed her husband, but the jewels were found under the mattress of her bed and her story, on repetition, jelled into an aspic of contradictory versions. Finally she admitted that her lover, Judd Gray, pulled it off. RUTH BREAKS—NAMES PARAMOUR. Gray was in Syracuse, where he claimed to have been on the night of the murder, but police found the stub of a train ticket in the wastebasket of his hotel room, a round-trip from New York to Syracuse. RUTH—JUDD BARE ALL. Notice the first names, the gladhandling informality of the approach. To us of now, it's the Snyder-Gray case, but to them in the twenties, it was Ruth and Judd, the dumbbell murderers.

And to *Machinal* and Broadway, when Sophie Treadwell adapted

Snyder's story for the stage, it was just Young Woman, surrounded by such as Husband, Mother, Telephone Girl, Stenographer, Filing Clerk, Nurse, Doctor, Judge, Jailer, Priest . . . for Treadwell saw more clearly than Ruth and Judd, and to her it all reduced to the fact of the machine, the life-consuming momentum of life. The noises of Today assaulted the ears throughout Treadwell's play—steel riveting, typewriters, telegraph clicks, a black blues singer, religious chant, the elemental jazz combo—and for dialogue she adopted the sequential egesta of free association to indict devil System for the traps it had laid for her heroine, traps of marriage, then murder, then judgment. And, of course, the reporters were on hand to frame the headlines at the trial. "Murderess Confesses," says one, trying it out. "Paramour Brings Confession," offers another, and " 'I Did It!' Woman Cries," a third. Treadwell even led her protagonist right up to the electric chair, though the current was thrown in darkness. The *Daily News* had disclosed the actual event to the crowd in a front-page photo the day after Ruth Snyder's execution, blurry and overenlarged but unmistakably the real Ruth unmistakably being electrocuted.

Still, the highbrows had mostly rooted for the new; typical of them now to debunk it, to smart it with their plays and books and call it a tin party. Many of them showed America their backs and left for Paris, and some who stayed did a lot of grumbling. In 1922, willing to prove that America lacked not only heroes, but poets and thinkers as well, Harold Stearns edited *Civilization in the United States,* a compendium of essays by experts on how there wasn't any, and legend has it that Stearns took ship for Europe the week he handed in the manuscript. Even V. L. Parrington's brilliant and contentedly American *Main Currents in American Thought,* the first two volumes of which came out in 1927, only went up to the end of the nineteenth century, as if there were nothing more to say after Mark Twain and William Dean Howells. The very study of modern American literature was looked upon as a jingoistic ruse in the English departments of many universities, and it seems that the nay-sayers were being heard from more than those with ayes. In an article on the literature of the twenties, published anonymously in 1926 in the anthology *American Criticism,* Edmund Wilson mildly admitted the odd first-rate work, but generally dismissed the entire period as "polyglot, parvenu, hysterical and often only semi-literate. When time shall have weeded out our less important writers, it is probable that those who remain will give the impression of a literary vaudeville: H. L. Mencken hoarse with preaching in his act making fun of preachers; Edna St. Vincent Millay, the soloist, a contralto with deep notes of pathos; Sherwood Anderson holding his audience with naive but disquieting bedtime stories. ... Let us remember, however, that vaudeville has always been an American specialty."

So debunking was still in style; maybe all that prosperity was making the highbrows giddy. They would have no heroes, it appears—no f'r a Moses—even as the folk dashed from pseudohero to pseudofreak and that crowd waited around to see. What was it that made so many of the cultural commentators such bad sports? The "caviar sophisticates" whom *The New Yorker* claimed as its readership laughed as easily at Will Rogers as at Edna Ferber, and they took neither seriously. They laughed at Coolidge, too, of course, though the sword is mightier than the pen. And Coolidge did not laugh, even as he, too, heard the jazz, and heard right through it, and figured it out. Asked what he made of the modish debunking of George Washington then in season, President Cal looked over his shoulder out the window. "Well," says he, "I see the monument is still there."

Too many Americans were not sufficiently aware of the monument: too many new ones were going up. Of a sort, the Chrysler and Empire State buildings replaced the federal debris in the capital, where architecture was held to a height, for uprushing modernism demands its emblems, whether in a ballet called *Skyscrapers,* in a fight/trial/crime of the century of a pattern called a scoop, or in the skyscraper itself, Bigger and Better, moxie, pep, It. Coolidge saw staying power in Washington—i.e., tradition—and he was right about that, but one does pick up new traditions along the way, and part of Bigger and Better meant burning up one's staying power in the lightning flash of total exposure. Freaks came and went at the gallop, but freaks hung around as well. What of Aimee Semple McPherson, the Canadian revivalist who dared test her fact nationwide and managed to survive, though the McPherson logorrhea in the press did grow a deal less grandiose once the corollary of her fact was revealed? Five thousand, three hundred packed her Angelus Temple in Echo Park, near Los Angeles, to hear Sister Aimee preach her "Four-Square Gospel" Sunday nights, and others crowded the eighty-odd branches of McPhersonism that stippled the West Coast, but many thousands more heard her and her cataclysmic spectacle on Radio KFSG, Los Angeles. Until the May afternoon in 1926 when McPherson wandered into the Pacific Ocean and vanished, none knew whither, she was one of the most powerful women in America, an entrepreneuse of intuitive showmanship, an actress of some looks and no little dimension, and, it turned out when she turned up from her six weeks' sabbath, a creature of shatterbrained vulnerability about her personal life.

The woman who was clever enough to make Fundamentalism manifest in pageant upon pageant should have come up with a better story than the one that McPherson tried to sell when she heaved out of the Arizona desert with a yarn about having escaped from kidnappers. Foolish, McPherson, not to have been prepared for the cynicism of the pressmen, who checked her story lovingly, religiously, even, with glad little cries as the four-square Sister proved to be just another redheaded adulteress, much of her binge having been spent in the arms of Kenneth Ormiston, her radio manager. Defending herself from scandal with tenacity, courage, and an extra-heavy on the "Stand Up, Stand Up for Jesus," McPherson weathered the storm, her revival intact, and, strangely, she went right back into her rut of fame, escaping the freakhood of someone like the much-married and not dissimilar Peggy Hopkins Joyce.

Aimee Semple McPherson really was the essence of a thing; she was a doer, and she could go some, all right. Maybe she could even have saved the soul of Texas Guinan, as she once offered to do, for Sister Aimee was a smart operator, and it takes one to save one. A visiting minister spent one Sunday night at McPherson's Angelus Temple, and this man *knew*—they shared the same bag, didn't they?— and he put his finger on the particular informality that served the feverish ejaculations of the singing sinners at McPherson's Jesus circus. "Aimee is Aimee," he said, "and there is none like her. . . .

No American evangelist of large enough caliber to be termed National has ever sailed with such insufficient mental ballast. The power of McPhersonism resides in the personality of Mrs. McPherson. The woman is everything; the evangel nothing. . . . To visit Angelus Temple . . . is to go on a sensuous debauch served up in the name of religion."

A free society is a competitive society by nature more than design, and De Tocqueville missed the boat on his "great and imposing image of the people at large." Individuality, however vainglorious, ostentatious, or conniving, remains both the religion and the business of American culture; we, the democrats, admit the competition to admit the winner, to detect the aristocrat (for which read celebrity), whether he be wealthier, wiser, more valorous, more gifted, more asinine, or just luckier than others. The winners are interesting because we all reckon to be winners somehow: if not one of the gifted, then one of the lucky. Oh, f'r a Moses—every Moses at all!

There's equality for you, in the lesson of informality, which teaches that any man can be a king. Even better, every king must be a man: this is our informality. The highbrows, codifiers of the culture, had analyzed this informality in their appreciation of the forms of popular art—but highbrows, too, need a Moses. "I really didn't have any answer to it all," said Sinclair Lewis, looking back later. "I only knew that the answers could only come from free men."

Problem was, the answers were coming from the free and most uproarious P.R. media and their reading, listening, and watching, carved-into-a-medium America. Since the mob believed the jazz, jazz took belief upon it, and began to think that it actually had a fact: I am thought, therefore I am. Jazz was a lie, but jazz had credibility; thus the joke doubles back on itself and the lie confesses truth. We of today can with our hindsight expose the lying, but they of the twenties knew how to *accept* the lie without actually *believing* it—this, perhaps, is the worst, the most cynical jazz of all. George Follansbee Babbitt's rationalizing argot, Billy Sunday's Bible-braying hogwash, the Ku Klux Klan's and the Prohibition cabal's "reform" movements, Bruce Barton's prating of a theology of business, Harding's oil slick of normalcy . . . all ended up not as mirrors for liars but as mirrors seeking a reflection that could *align* with truth, a seeming without substance. Coolidge addresses the newsmen at the Gridiron Dinner in 1923: "The boys have been very kind and considerate to me ... They have undertaken to endow me with some characteristics and traits that I didn't altogether know I had. But I have done the best I could to live up to those traits."

Truly, the boys of the media had the jazz down pat—but they had their rules, and celebrities, even a president, must go along with the game. Woe, woe on any Moses who rejects the informality issued him to confirm his fact, or who won't show himself and portray his essence. Yet this Moses, to *be* Moses, will not submit; that's what a hero is. A celebrity uses the machine. A hero vanquishes it.

"Suppose the machine shouldn't work?" asks one reporter of another, gazing at the electric chair at the end of *Machinal*. Replies his colleague: "It'll work. It always works!"

EIGHT

⟳⟐⟲

The Very Ideas

Those were names and faces of the day in the last chapter, both the name and the face, *always*, because the public had to see and photography was the thing. Now let us have the ideas, and don't be surprised if faces keep irrupting into the disputation, for it becomes harder now to separate the facts of a theoretical point of view from the fact of the celebrity, since both meet at the root, in symbol. Ford, for example, God Change and The Eccentric Uncle, does not parse into neat sections of promulgator, businessman, and news copy. How much of the copy devolved on the business power? How much of the business power depended on the fame? And where does promulgation of symbolic function (i.e., the automobile) start and instinctive business sense (i.e., the automobile) end?

It all connects now. The thing is that it didn't always connect—that's what must be noticed. Break down the images of Ford's predecessors in leadership into their constituent parts? Easily done! Paine, Jefferson, Edmund Randolph or so—no machine bound their pictures up in their functions, no way to mix feat with fact, because the machine hadn't been invented by then, and in that sense Ford and his fellows have no predecessors. So differently were things perceived in this modern age, so viciously symbiotic the infrastruc-

tures of system, that it is as if one daren't even compare that old
America with this, mustn't raise the spell of traditions and destiny, so
discouraging is the comparison between the promise and the forgetting. "The great and imposing image of the people at large," with a
concomitant death of the regions, of dissent, of meritocratic leadership, is on its way.

Why so? Well, the paper media have much to do with it, especially
now in the twenties, when they discovered the Confucian outworks of
jazz, but there is also radiotelephony, the dry run for the absolute jazz
of television and, when it first got started, a quite innocent and
noncommercial enterprise not unlike the citizens band amateurism of
a later day. There were no commercials on radio in the early twenties,
no significant tie-ins between the music business and what records got
played over the air, and few big-name entertainers with their big-time
hustle. Radio was a sundry enterprise, feeling its way and making
room for all in that easygoing way of an idea that hasn't got to be
vital yet. It had no focus whatsoever, not even a haphazard, well-
intentioned but continually collapsing focus. It had no focus. Some
stations were well-financed, others wonderfully makeshift; some became popular immediately, others vanished after a week or so. In
Wilmington, North Carolina, WBBN was licensed simply to give an
electrical shop an opportunity to demonstrate its radio sets to
prospective customers, for the store was only open in the daytime and
Wilmington's stations only operated at night. Ergo, WBBN: when a
customer asked for an illustration of the ware, a clerk would dash
upstairs and WBBN would put on a program. News, crop and
weather reports, studio performances of opera or recorded dance
music, political harangues, or drama . . . whatever a station scheduled
on a given night, that was radio, and such public as had accumulated
by 1921 and '22 enjoyed it all.

Success would eventually lead stations to seek a medium to play to,
the medium of expression mating with the medium of reception, but
at first the unruled world of the airwaves opened, rather than limited,
radio's horizons. It was a good thing, like the automobile, and like
the automobile it made the regions more accessible to each other, for
long-distance listening was a perquisite of those pioneer days. To

name one instance, the need for more and more records to play inspired the discovery of so-called "race" records, particularly those of Ethel Waters, Mamie Smith, Ma Rainey, and Bessie Smith, singers not at first known outside of the South and Chicago, not to mention the band records of Ford Dabney and W. C. Handy. The ramshackle brilliance of the blithes and the blues from combos and "comediennes" (black vocalists never being billed on the record label, for some reason, as vocalists) introduced radio listeners to a new habit, influencing the tone of American popular music to such depth that its seeds have yet to be charted today.

But if the dissemination of music was radio's major service, the presentation of news was its devil: how free was its speech to be? Radio was a public utility—but it was also a business. The acute historian of communications, Erik Barnouw, reports on the flap over broadcaster H. V. Kaltenborn's broadside over WEAF, New York, criticizing the manner in which Secretary of State Charles Evans Hughes rebuffed diplomatic overtures from the unrecognized Soviets in 1924. As Kaltenborn saw it, foreign commissar Maxim Litvinof's approaches had been "tactful and carefully phrased"; Hughes's answer: "Abrupt." As it happened, Hughes and some V.I.P.'s were tuned in to Kaltenborn that night, and the follow-up treated (public) radio as it would not have treated the (private-sector) press: Hughes refused to countenance such criticism over the wires of WEAF—which happened to be owned by the American Telephone and Telegraph Company—and under this unofficial federal pressure, Kaltenborn's news program got the ax.

Ah, the business connection. A.T. and T. was only too willing at the time to cooperate with the government on the shaping of policy, but then the government, in the person of Secretary of Commerce Herbert Hoover, was likewise eager to cooperate on the maintenance of the airwaves with the forces of the industry. Hoover was a strict constructionist on the matter of tradition, yet there was no precedent to guide him in the administration of this latest wonder in the age of wonders, the Radio Act of 1912 not having foreseen the incredible growth to come. Progress won't wait; why should man?—for progress is how man lords it over nature, the ridiculous standing still of God's earth. Progress is man's universe, and progress has no seventh day. Forward!

Progress, in this case under the guise of commercial advertising, arrived on radio in 1923–24, shyly, like a bride in a marriage of political convenience, amortizing the cost of the growing demand for name professionals to replace the amateur entertainment. As of the Democratic Convention of 1924, when the nation heard approximately one-half of its democratic procedure brawl away to nothingness in Madison Square Garden, radio was the sensational latest issue of the Ford idea, the something for everyone, the treat-turned-necessity, an interpreter in the language of symbols: and now, full speed ahead for the norm. Suddenly, the entertainment business noticed that it had been neglecting one of its most natural children— actually radio was more in the way of being a godparent—and the pros moved in along with the sponsors to pay for them. Will Rogers reportedly got a whopping one thousand dollars for a single appearance on the (note the name) *Eveready Hour,* and in 1925 the physical culture nut and scurrilous publisher Bernarr Macfadden ran an early-morning exercise program on WOR, Newark, meanwhile buying the time outright so as to push his *Evening Graphic* and *Physical Culture* magazine. Thus came jazz to radio, money jazz, and enter the rapport of focus, for fledgling radio had won its business wings, and business abhors a vacuum. While secret negotiations, lawsuits, and federal arbitration tried to unravel the tangles of a hobby made over, overnight, into a billion-dollar commodity, consumers went happily off further to domesticate the machine. The question was no longer should one buy, but which to choose—the De Forest Radiophone ("How many miles did you go last night?"), the Mercury ("The Stradivarius of radio"), the Newport ("makes every day a Christmas"), or perhaps the Melco Supreme ("Aladdin had his lamp, you have the Melco Supreme").

The coming of advertising to radio precipitated quite a controversy, but that was for Hoover and the industry to straighten out; the public regarded it, if at all, with remote amusement. P.R., like the celebrities who panned out with staying power, just was—don't ask. Even Henry Ford finally had to capitulate to P.R. in 1927 when he brought out his Model A in response to the shifting tides of the consumer sea he himself had helped to flood. The Tin Lizzie had been foundering in competition, undersold by the Whippet, demoded by the Erskine, and outrun by the luxurious Moon. This new model, the A, conceded to the revolutionary market with a choice of four colors (including "Arabian Sand"), modified gadgetry, a self-starter, a rumble seat, a shatterproof windshield, and, in the week just before the car was announced for display, several million dollars' worth of P.R. flotation. The rabble could not have been more roused. With local pride and a touch of historical perspective, the *Denver Post* trilled, "There has never been more public excitement in Denver except at the time of the famous robbery of the United States Mint," and, as usual, the auxiliary police had to be called out to control that eternal crowd eyeing agog at Ford showrooms around the country. Of course, the music industry was glad to oblige with a christening in song, "Henry's Made a Lady out of Lizzie," adding to the melee of spin-off patents in this pattern called a civilization.

Well, if Ford could advertise, Ford who always said that a solid product was its own advertisement and who more than anyone begot the dynamic for modernism, radio could advertise, too—radio *must*—and the rise of radio advertising didn't hurt the radio boom in the least, not when the Rose Bowl of 1927 (Leland Stanford versus Alabama) was presented on a nationwide hook-up presided over by the ever quasi-reliable commentator Graham McNamee; not when *True Story* magazine got up a dramatic series based on its louche exclusives; not when the constant play of dance records in strict beat provided the wherewithal for home partying; and most especially not when *Amos 'n' Andy* was to be heard. The last named was the biggest thing to hit the airwaves since the 1924 Democratic Convention, fifteen minutes a time in the ongoing adventures of two black stereotypes, the innocent, put-upon Amos and the domineering Andy, proprietors of the Fresh-Air Taxicab Company of America, Incorpulated, in Chicago.

Two men, Freeman Fisher Gosden and Charles J. Correll, wrote the scripts and at first played all the parts in the now-dead art of burnt-cork humor. On one episode that found the principals in court for a civil suit, Andy was about to take the witness stand when his lawyer informed him that he could say "I don't remember," if necessary, on a rare occasion. So, of course:

BAILIFF: Raise your right hand.
ANDY: I don't remembeh.
BAILIFF: Raise your hand!
ANDY: Yessah, yessah.
BAILIFF: Do you solemnly swear that the evidence you are about to give in this case is the truth, the whole truth, and nothing but the truth, so help you God?
ANDY: I don't remembeh.

Amos 'n' Andy hardly makes the opening up of the cultural mosaic such as was spurred by the airing of Ethel Waters' and Bessie Smith's records, but the show did contribute vastly, good or ill, to the foundation of a radio market. Heedless of their poverty, carefree in a slum, Amos and Andy connected the now with an assumed folklore of then, transplanting the watermelon patch to Chicago's South Side and transporting the radio listener to a nonexistent heyday via some very funny scriptwriting and a crooked focus. This was the decade in which the American theater discarded "reality," indicting it for the consolations it withheld that art, too, was no longer always going to supply—in *The Adding Machine, Craig's Wife, Rope, The Hairy Ape, All God's Chillun Got Wings, Strange Interlude, What Price Glory? The Show Off, Machinal, Roger Bloomer*—and in the realm of black subculture, Eugene O'Neill's *The Emperor Jones* and DuBose and Dorothy Heyward's *Porgy* hit the nail on the head for atavism and ghetto poetry. But like the movies, radio aimed not so high, sizing itself up as too broad a concern to scale the peaks of elitism. Drama educated the public, and ofttimes its daring brought it to the poorhouse or, in the case of Edouard Bourdet's lesbian study, *The Captive*, to judgment in court. But God, when the theater succeeded, how stunning, how long the art in this short life, how brazen to grant the vision to see, just for once, the ideas instead of the faces. Sometimes one must see the Things, not the men.

Radio had its little educations, mostly in the realm of the highfalutin vocal concert, but radio peaked—and radio knew it—in *Amos 'n' Andy*. Even Herbert Hoover, promoted from Commerce to the Presidency at the worst moment in America's recent history, was an *Amos 'n' Andy* buff. Gosden and Correll were invited to the White House to enlarge on their mode and repeat some of their best lines and Hoover apparently offered a few himself. *Everybody*, it seems, was tuning in to the show, rearranging his schedule to accommodate that fifteen-minute slot regularly every evening. Oh, yes, much accommodation nowadays, hereabouts, for if the machine is truly the ego of man on the climb, men must acculturate the flight on an all-or-nothing basis. You must change your life.

We've already seen some resistance to the machine earlier in the decade, both from the philosophers of the raging cities and from the folk of the land, each group for his reasons. Some feared too prodigal an emancipation, some a devouring control, and some few a theft of the humanist spirit, yet the constant in all three cases was precision. There was an exactness in the new rhythms of American life, no matter how grand the scale of conveyer-belt production, competitive marketing, or epidemic communications; alas, it was not the exactness of clarity, of cultural definition, but rather that of union—for it was in that grandness of scale that lay the forced convergence of diversities. In the automobile, in jazz, in the cinema, and now in radio, we have seen ourselves attitudinized in generalities, subject to a focus that uses only what is "viable" to the showman and the huckster. This focus was, simply defined, a force for conformity. It prescribed rather than described, and didn't so much disclose our natural unity as a people as lay an artificial one upon us with salesmanship, a consensus rented out to consumers. Precision *ought* to be the prerogative of individuals—that is the true precision. But we had too little of the true precision in the twenties. Jazz had a technology—that was the focus of the age—and the focus of jazz was lies.

It didn't have to be so, for it was not technology that was at fault but the popular forms that it took. What an astonishing vehicle radio could have been, to pick one example, with its intersecting communication, its instant relevance to the moment. As mentioned earlier, think of Woodrow Wilson called up from his infamous obscurity in

1923 to deliver an Armistice Day message on a hookup of WCAP, Washington; WEAF, New York; and WJAR, Providence. Nearly a corpse then, one arm helpless and features twisted, buried alive with the dead of "his" war, he spoke into a microphone in the library of his home at 2340 S Street, haltingly, almost in a whisper, and with audible prompting from his wife. "That is all, isn't it?" he gasped out after a pause, still on the air. He had reached the largest audience ever to receive a human voice at one time, three million people, and the next morning Wilson painfully hobbled out onto his porch to be greeted by an estimated twenty thousand, most of them veterans of the army that Wilson had commanded. Cliché would have it that "No, they had not forgotten," but cliché is wrong. They had wanted to forget him and they had done so; this stuttered address on "The High Significance of Armistice Day" reminded them of the man they had admired before international Progressivism got shot out from under him. There were no autograph seekers in this crowd; for once, those who would see the men attended on leadership more than celebrity.

Scanning the eager faces before him (though his ruined vision couldn't possibly have made them out), Wilson was at first too moved to say more than the minimum—we are without microphones and loudspeakers now, without commentators and announcers and patents and commercials and insincere sincerity and all that jazz; we are at one of the last moments of the America that had been for 150 years—and this was too brightly spiritual a moment to cut off with the minimum, a moment too redolent of recent fact, the fact of leadership and history. Whether one approved his ideals or not, Wilson himself was truly one of the giants of the age, and he must have sensed all this, too, for as he was leaving he turned around to face the crowd again and spoke. Something of the old Wilson flashed up and outward as he talked, with the old Wilsonian eyes burning disgust for those who couldn't, as he, know the road and take it. "I am not one of those who have the least anxiety about the triumph of the principles I have stood for," he said. "I have seen fools resist Providence before, and I have seen their destruction, as will come upon these again, utter destruction and contempt." A radio talk the night before had drawn them to see, but only now, in point of fact and person, did they understand and know what words (and, later, pictures) on the airwaves can only suggest. This was Wilson at last, the idea of Wilson, and the idea of America, and he told them on his porch, "That we shall prevail is as sure as that God reigns."

Precisions, false and true: that was the twenties, and its central conflict conduced to the battles between the two, between ballyhoo and honesty, the cosmetic mechanism and the real machine, between whoopee and art, between progressivism and fad, between Jesus shouters and the moral ethic that is God, and, some pages to leeward, between the most adored man in America and the adoration, for he wouldn't abide its reductive focus and they wanted to hate him for that.

Precision: what Erik Satie had descried with delight in George Antheil's *Ballet Mécanique* on its passionate Parisian premiere. "What precision! What precision!" Writers, too, were making a name for an almost mechanical exactness in their work, such as Gertrude Stein, Sherwood Anderson, and Ernest Hemingway, all three occasionally sounding like three gradations of the same voice, and all influenced, bafflingly, by the neoclassical revival in France. But note that one needed Satie's revolutionary ears to hear anything at all in Antheil's bag of wind, as New Yorkers discovered when *Ballet Mécanique* came to Carnegie Hall in 1927. Americans didn't hold a row over Antheil, as the French had done; however, everyone agreed that a much more useful artistic precision than that of music's enfants terribles was that of the cinema, where the science of the sound track was concocted and gradually revealed, with little success, until the facts already accumulated in the dossier of Al Jolson forced the sound panic in *The Jazz Singer* in 1927. Now all movie actors had to sing, or at least talk. Strangely enough, not all of them could.

On the question of sound in the cinema there was almost no dissent at all. The only major holdout, besides the speechless actors, was Charlie Chaplin, who forced the issue with two anachronistic silent features in the thirties, *City Lights* and, contemptuously, *Modern Times*. Dissent, however, is meaningless in popular art, for it is in the very nature of a popular medium that it subscribe to popular priorities, and the pop arts are ever in motion to bulldoze dissent and plow it under. Indeed, the pop in our culture is so pronounced that one can easily mistake it for the American rhythm, though this would miss the ingrain of tradition that informs the work of not only the mainstream but of the individualist elite as well, from Melville through James to William Gaddis.

It's a fallacy, this picture of an overstimulated America that can't sit still, for we've seen plenty of sitting still earlier in these pages, a downright clamping down in the chair, muscles tensed, for fear of removal. Yet the restless curiosity is there, too, complementing tradition by way of getting it to renew, which tradition must do periodically, and since the twenties were the first years to celebrate the desertion of the static towns for the avid cities, we must note the rhythm and take a report on it from Gertrude Stein, even if she wasn't there while it was going on:

> I am always trying to tell this thing that a space of time is a natural thing for an American to always have inside them as something in which they are continuously moving. Think of anything, of cowboys, of movies, of detective stories, of anybody who goes anywhere or stays at home and is an American and you will realize that it is something strictly American to conceive a space that is filled with moving.

Stein, of course, was a highbrow, so precise a one that she passed the era in Paris, highbrow country, and we know that many of the highbrows were alarmed by what they foresaw in the focalization of modern life. Perhaps the ultimate in the defining and then debunking of the American rhythm was Harold Stearns' aforementioned *Civilization in the United States,* subtitled "An Inquiry by Thirty Americans" and published in 1922. We've had debunking earlier on in fiction and biography, but that was the more ostensive and raucous heel-clicking of the gaming generation. Here now is the cooler voice of the idea-makers. Stearns' compendium offered specialists' opinions in fields from the arts and sciences to politics and business on the state of American culture: Lewis Mumford, H. L. Mencken, George Jean

Nathan, Conrad Aiken, and Van Wyck Brooks were among the contributors, as was Stearns himself, arraigning America's matriarchal past for having "feminized" and, ultimately, sterilized the home culture. It was not, significantly, the spirit of America that so discouraged Stearns, but rather the stifling qualities of its institutions, its self-congratulatory democracy that demands all men be brothers: "Such an atmosphere of shadowy spiritual relationships, where the thinness of contact of mind with mind is childishly disguised under the banner of good fellowship . . . will become as infested with cranks, fanatics, mushroom religious enthusiasts, moral prigs with new schemes of perfectability, inventors of perpetual motion, illiterate novelists, and oratorical cretins, as a swamp with mosquitoes. They seem to breed almost overnight . . . we welcome them all with a kind of Jamesian gusto, as if every fool, like every citizen, must have his right to vote."

Stearns, however, saw hope in the younger artists, who, he expected, would connect to the mighty Whitman in restoring a muscular intellectuality; most of his colleagues were less sanguine. Unfortunately, they were also premature, for this was the decade when the American arts at last upped and admitted that they were arts all right, long hair and penetrating and even avant-garde. Van Wyck Brooks, on American literature in Stearns's book, announced that "one can count on one's two hands the American writers who are able to carry on the development and unfolding of their individualities, year in, year out, as every competent man of affairs carries on his business." Oh, yeah? To say this, in the age that saw the unfolding of such individualities as those of Sherwood Anderson, John Dos Passos, Sinclair Lewis, e.e. cummings, William Faulkner, F. Scott Fitzgerald, Ernest Hemingway, Thornton Wilder, Marianne Moore, William Carlos Williams, Robert Frost, Hart Crane, Archibald MacLeish, Harry Crosby, and John Crowe Ransom, is hopelessly *avant la lettre*. But the unfolding was still getting under way in 1922, when Stearns's collage came out, and only science came off reasonably well.

Stearns had imposed no surveillance on his contributors, so the prevalent cynicism earned credibility by its sheer spontaneity, but we of today want to see the clash and color of the philosophy of the twenties, not the standard-make scoffing of *The New Yorker*-cartoon highbrows. Busy being disgruntled and paving the way for diatribes from expatriates, *Civilization in the United States* was too limited in scope, sparing the long view with its eyes only on New York (and patches of Boston) and its back turned on a subcontinent. Stearns's biggest blunder was the engagement of the caramel composer Deems Taylor to survey American music, for this late romantic browser who ordered his toots and tootles out of Wagner and Humperdinck as if off a menu wouldn't have known what was American in music if he had seen it coming down the pike playing "Yankee Doodle" on fife and drum. Other than the very apparent John Alden Carpenter and George Gershwin, American music had not emerged into the purview of the Taylors, and while Gertrude Stein had her emissaries taking the word home from Paris, Charles Ives, Carl Ruggles, and Henry Cowell had to fight for every inch of what little yardage they gained, for there is such a thing as being too imposingly modern, and of dealing too portentously in the true precision of nonconformity when the gathering drift of life calls for the false precision of consolidation.

Now it happens that all Western music was learning precision at this time, but neoclassicism was slow to assert itself in the United States and the public quick to scare. "You goddarn sissy-eared mollycoddle—" said Ives once to a concertgoer who was hissing Ruggles's titanic *Men and Mountains,* "when you hear strong masculine music like this, stand up and use your ears like a man!" But though the time fixed and refixed itself on individual celebrity, it was the situation of fame and not individual distinction that captured the spotlight. "For what, Trudy?"—not for iconoclasm, certainly. So it was in life, and so in art. The peculiar focus of the highbrow claimed Stein, and she was heard, but Ives was virtually unknown and unheard during the twenties, though the major portion of his work was already behind him and though there is no longer much question that he remains America's greatest composer.

Strange, then, that a figure so very much out of it as Charles Ives should take up space here, but if Ives didn't suit the age and the age didn't suit him, he actually defines it better than many of its more blatant offspring. His was a true precision, both of life and art, in his orthodox New England existence and his dissentient composition, urging the fastidious dialectic of neoclassicism even before Igor Stravinsky, in Europe, caught on. Talk of your lone-wolf adventurer! Part country bohemian, part highbrow-businessman, Ives looked, acted, and sounded like a respectable, wealthy insurance salesman—which is what he actually was—while his music came out of his spare time as if from another dimension, or Mars. Hell for leather with defiance, Fundamentalist with hymn tunes and belief, weird with zigzag meter and polytonality, Ives's is the most wonderfully imaginative music ever penned. Across the nation, the town was taking on the city and the businessman repulsing the highbrow. But here, in one, was both sides, Dorothy Parker's Person Who Does Things melded with The Man Who Solicits Insurance. A New England transcendentalist, a moral aspirer, in whom the shock of America's entry into the war resulted in a nervous breakdown, Ives links the culture of the twenties to the golden age of Emerson and Thoreau, meanwhile retailoring their romantic optimism for the forms-within-forms of neoclassicism. He took music apart to its particles, to quarter-tones and free-associative allusions, but his frame, especially in his songs, was traditional America, in the rhetoric of the camp meeting and the Chautauqua, of places and events, types and heroes: "The Anti-abolitionist Riots," "Central Park in the Dark," "A Yale-Princeton Football Game," "General William Booth Enters into Heaven," the three "Harvest Home" chorales, and the ecstasy of the God fear in "Give Me Jesus."

Ives had no use for the musical establishment and it returned the compliment, but if Deems Taylor didn't know about Ives, *we* must; if he wasn't famous then, he *was* happening—had already, in fact, happened. His music correlated the primitive and the abstrusely intellectual with, as John Kirkpatrick put it, "a transcendentalist's faith in the unity behind all diversity." That encompassing unity was Ives's precision, that his route to cultural definition, a much grander one than radio's.

Technically, Ives was not one of the decade's principals, neither an archetype like Valentino or the flapper nor a qualified participator like the more "acceptable" composer Aaron Copland nor an operator like Ford or Coolidge (oh, yes, Coolidge was an operator; his operation as the high priest of the business cult was the institution of a sacred stasis), but in that very default Ives puts the false precision of the day into some relief. Even better, in his expression of the most basic American cultural traditions within the most modernistic musical framework, Ives personifies the essential friction of the twenties. The will of the age was resistance, but the tempo was change and the dynamic was precision. Could we maintain our traditions and our individuality even as we succumbed to technological transformation and to the evil accuracy with which P.R., radio, and journalism closed in on us with their universalizing focus? Besides the folk hordes of the countryside, resisting change out of superstition, only the highbrows, they!, held their ground and fought back with their own more potent but less mighty precisions.

Harold Stearns delivered the manuscript of *Civilization in the United States* and hit the whale road for Europe, but most of his confreres stuck it out, and even those who followed Stearns abroad came back. (Stearns himself, far from flowering in civilized France, began rather to dissolve; Malcolm Cowley recalls people espying him asleep in a café and saying, "There lies civilization in the United States.") "America is what one makes of it" is a simplification of what many expatriates told each other, and the strain of making it under the pressure of so many businessmen, lowbrows, and fat kitten flappers turned them liberal the way milk turns, souring in disuse. Waiting it out in Paris, Kay Boyle spoke of an "American conspiracy against the individual" in a congeries of expatriate musing in *transition* magazine in 1928; Boyle's phrase is just another term for the conformity implicit in focus. Some few highbrows turned to the political Left for guidance, but there they found merely another conspiracy against the individual. The bohemian freemason of the unfettered soul, the carrier of no cards, discovered in the real Left an alternative focus wired to Moscow, and backed off to reconsider ragtime and the hymn tune, describing himself, in John Dos Passos' words of conservative epiphany, as "just an old-fashioned believer in liberty, equality, and fraternity."

The national will was resistance, but the highbrows and the machine—what a dubious pair, you think; no, sometimes they were lovers—bulled the tempo of change, battling with the will for right of way. The town, where no highbrows were and where the machine slipped in as the simple economics of the roadster and the factory, had its focus, its gathering together and outlawing of dissent. It had the Klan, for example, a focus of the town against the city, at least to its members (to its superKleagles it was a business and occasionally, as in Indiana and Oklahoma, a political plant). There is nothing new in this, for the Klan was simply a reprise of an older Klan and a discriminatory third party such as the Know-Nothings. Why, one might even want to call the venerable two-party system a double-knit focus, except that parties are coalitions, drawing dissent in centripetally while retaining the factional edges, whereas focus is centrifugal, tossing everything out but the common center, the medium. Focus was of no great moment before the machine retooled it for long-distance running, and focus, the machine of the business media, was born in the twenties.

It almost comes down to *Amos 'n' Andy* versus Charles Ives, the false against the true, and even as the machine favored the false, romanticists of the machine found the true, and were heard. The highbrows, too, had their technology, and if Sophie Treadwell could use the clockwork paranoia of expressionism to damn the System in *Machinal,* Eugene O'Neill found the myth in mechanism in his play *Dynamo.* Reproducing the psychological soliloquy that had made his *Strange Interlude* one of the more improbable theatrical events of 1928 and his heroine, Nina Leeds, one of the most fully realized characters of the era, O'Neill turned a year later in *Dynamo* to the story of a repressed young man in whom guilt turns into obsession and mother love into machine love after the death of his mother. Conceiving the great god electricity as the true mother of us all, O'Neill's Reuben Light welcomes the embrace of the light god, the hydroelectric hummer purring in the plant:

It's like a great dark idol . . . like the old stone statues of gods people prayed to . . . only it's living and they were dead . . .

that part on top is like a head . . . with eyes that see you
without seeing you . . . and below it is like a body . . . not a
man's . . . round like a woman's . . . as if it had breasts. . . . A
great, dark mother! . . . that's what the dynamo is! . . . that's
what life is! . . .

"Eyes that see you without seeing you"—one might apply the phrase
as well to the crowd that shoved and surged, looking for a fact, or,
better, to the false precision of the focus media, to its close-ups
without exactness, its blurred photo of Ruth Snyde 's electrocution
and its ghostwritten "confessions" of Peaches and Daddy. It was just
that system of inaccurate vigilance that highbrow technology battled
in the twenties, whether in O'Neill's bosomy dynamo or Treadwell's
hateful System contra machine, or in Hart Crane's great poem *The
Bridge,* "our Myth, whereof I sing!" and very pro.

One must remember, though, that much of the highbrow's opposition to science was predicated on an unreasoned fear of the dark; like
any Kleagle or Fundamentalist, he reckoned to abolish what he could
not comprehend. Using as a point of departure the debunking of the
businessman that heralded the highbrow chatter of the early twenties,
some liberals proceeded to indict the machine civilization for an
alleged heedless cruelty, fearing, for example, that the Stanford-Binet
I.Q. tests would reveal what was plain enough anyway and needed no
proving: that some people are smarter than others. Stanford-Binet's
identification of some of John Adams's natural aristocrats, of an
American elite, was of course directly contrary to the tenets of the
antimeritocratic Left, which dubbed the machine, extraneously, as
inhuman.

We've seen something of these forensics earlier on, when the I.Q.
test was coming off as Exhibit A for the racial resistance of Anglo-
Saxonism, but here in the late twenties the war took in all the
technology of modernism, for the technophobes had begun to realize
that not only I.Q. tests, but dynamos, bridges, and even office
equipment were in league to crush the humanism of the ideal man of
old. And if the technophobes were humanists, it stood to their reason
that the machine and all its children were materialistic—especially

radio, with its *Eveready Hours* and fitness sessions sponsored by Bernarr Macfadden.

So the highbrows, too, could mass up in their little resistances, but the highbrows had missed the point. It was not the machine, not science, that threatened humanism, but the paceless splurge of machinery, the osmotic absorption of the robot mentality. Systematization, not science, it was, that threatened to corrupt the life-style. To see it in perspective, one had to distinguish between the true and the false focus—between, in other words, the nuances of individualism and the universals of conformity—even if our several prophets of the art world were in no agreement on where the road to individualism lay. For some, the age of systematization was false altogether and strangled individuality, while for others it was true and interpreted individuality, and off into the future rode the highbrows, fighting all the way, while the ordinary citizen was content to buy a car and a radio, or perhaps two cars—that was his share in things to come, for things had already arrived.

Let us realize that this machine of contention was not a matter of simple mechanics, an undebatable boon to mankind, but one of the ideology of mechanics, the practice of machine thinking in man, as if, having invented the devices, he was now attempting to turn into one himself. Some critics accused man of using the machine to turn himself into God—a fat materialist idol with a dynamo for a heart squatting on a toaster and worshiped by consumers. Others saw man turning himself into a slave.

The question of individuality, therefore, burned sore in those days as it never had had to before, and on Broadway an American production of Karel Capek's *R.U.R.* in 1922 chilled theatergoers with a look at a world ended by the men-slaves built by the men-gods. The title is an abbreviation for Rossum's Universal Robots, the business that begins the end by populating the globe with oppressed androids; Capek himself coined the word "robot" from the Czech *robota* (work), and the robots were literally a working class that finally takes over the world and murders all its humans, except for one suddenly very useless man, a builder unable to divine the scientist's formula for the synthesis of life, and thus powerless to give the robots

the only thing they need, future generations. One part speculative
fantasy, one part melodrama, and one part social polemic (almost
certainly a comment on Soviet Russia), *R.U.R.* blasted the brave new
world much more tellingly than could such local traditionalists as
Willa Cather with her briefs for the farmer.

Once, geometry and music were thought to be the patterns of the
universe, but geometry had grown up into technology, leaving music
behind in the world of nonutilitarian embellishment, and now, as if
by signal, much of the changes in life remarked in the immediately
postwar years began to fall into place as plots in the new pattern of
the universe. Those who looked at things instead of at people heard
the awful tempo of change and surrendered to the will of resistance
side by side with the booboisie in the pitiful hope of repulsing the
future inevitable. The machine had taken it all, they thought, as
radio, as the skyscraper, as Art Deco and industrial design, as P.R.
promotion and serial production on the assembly line ... as
organized crime, some said, or organized capitalism, or anything else
in life now, for everything else was imposing organization upon the
regions and dissenters, affiliating the nation in electronic symbiosis.

Yet there were those—poets, mostly—who found a romance in the
machine, in the almightiness of it, the riddle that breaks time and
space, the chaotic energy that heats those city lights. No, not Cather,
nor Wharton, nor—especially—Dos Passos; the chapter titles of his
war novel *Three Soldiers* charted the agony of his hero, a composer
who turns deserter in horror of systems, an agony shared by many
Americans still. "Making the Mould" shows the training camp,
"Machines" and "Rust" show war, and at last "Under the Wheels"
shows the deserter apprehended like a bird caught napping on a
railroad track, the manuscript pages of his latest composition blowing
away in the wind as M.P.'s lead him off.

Making the mold ... who, though, made it? Were we rough-
hewing a purpose, or being sucked into one, like the customers at
Texas Guinan's, afraid not to be big spenders? Man or machine—
choose now, said a few. But who, mostly, cared? Zane Grey, not Dos
Passos, was the best-selling author of American fiction in the twenties,
and Grey's chapter titles showed no systematizational, debilitating

machinery. Grey's heroes rode horses and confronted air, earth, fire, water and each other, and the cities they entered consisted of a six-street grid, not even enough for Middletown's commercial district. A popular film of the day meant no futuristic tract such as Fritz Lang's *Metropolis* but an excursion into such adventure as that outlined in the adaptation of Vicente Blasco Ibáñez' *The Four Horsemen of the Apocalypse,* in which Rudolph Valentino, as an Argentinian playboy, abandoned the sweet life in Paris in the cause of civilization by enlisting in the war and dying a thrillingly doom-laden death. In the theater, the imagination was most fired not by the robot revolution of *R.U.R.* but by Jerome Kern and Oscar Hammerstein II's musical version of Edna Ferber's novel *Show Boat,* in late 1927, the first national epic in American musical comedy, taking the denizens of a floating theater through the years from the cakewalk and story ballad up to the Charleston to set them and their little tragedies against the ceaseless transcendence of the Mississippi River. Billy Mitchell had borrowed the Bible to warn that where there is no vision, the people perish, but his vision, air power, was rejected by the times: the will of the age was resistance.

Even a vision as ripe as that which inspired Crane's exhaustive apostrophe to *The Bridge* (written during the latter half of the decade and published in 1930) was outlawed by the national preference for flagpole sitters and comparable flotsam. Crane's synoptic strophes presented this Bridge as the gateway to limitless potential via our rich traditions, the "steeled Cognizance whose leap commits the agile precincts of the lark's return," the girders man-built yet bigger than men, jutting from city to prairie, the pageant of technology that doesn't enslave but frees men, if man would only comprehend. "I think of cinemas . . ."

Similarly, the composer Carl Ruggles gazed out on the western expanse that *Civilization in the United States* could neither unveil nor accept. Ruggles thought of no cinemas, however. "Great things are done when Men and Mountains meet," a line from William Blake, actuated Ruggles's tone poem *Men and Mountains,* even less complaisant to the average ear than Charles Ives's work. This was the "strong, masculine music" that Ives referred to when silencing a hissing dissenter at a concert of modern American composition, and this was the vision of the heretic, never to be embraced by the community—and why should he have expected to be? What a cacophony, this *Men and Mountains,* its brass signaling to phenomena of the national impulse too prodigious for conventional transmission, for the tasty urban blues of Gershwin or Copland.

Ruggles did not expect the embrace of anyone, not of his fellow highbrows and certainly not of any Babbitt. For his part, Babbitt had never heard a note of Ruggles or Ives, and his idea of a writer was someone like Zane Grey or John Erskine—a best-selling author, otherwise what's the point of trying to sell at all? At a speech made before the Zenith Real Estate Board, Sinclair Lewis's Midwestern, middle-class, median-audience avatar, George Follansbee Babbitt, the original of his race, offers his own reductive focus on the artist: "In America the successful writer or picture-painter is indistinguishable from any other decent businessman; and I, for one, am only too glad that the man who . . . shows both purpose and pep in handling his literary wares has a chance to drag down his fifty thousand bucks a year, to mingle with the biggest executives on terms of perfect equality, and to show as big a house and as swell a car as any Captain of Industry."

Oddly enough, Lewis pictured his primal Babbitt as a secret heretic himself, no highbrow but a man of more open mind and fewer untested slogans than he was willing to show. The conformity—the focus—that he himself supports is false even to him, but Babbitt is more the joiner and less the individual, and after a few discouraging attempts to discard the mask, for which disloyalty he is cast out by his fellows, he dons it again with even greater fervor, Babbitt the Solid American Citizen, the Sane Citizen, the Standardized Citizen— all in his own ungainly words.

But Hart Crane and Carl Ruggles were not about to let a Babbitt's amalgamating congruities put them off their myths of men, mountains, and machines. Romantic America, splayed, spread-eagle, from the Pilgrims' Athens through Bible-and-corn country to the Pollyanna pinkpoodle greasepaint paradise in Hollywood, aggrandized and movin' on in forced march, nation of the big shoulders, heaving its hammers from ocean to ocean ... this America is in many ways nothing but romance, for all the hardheaded neoclassicism of its Machine Age Jazz-precision. Romantics, lacking heroes, must invent them, and that was the need that provoked the sifting of facts to see the men; that is what it all amounts to.

What was to be left of individuality amidst such focus?—this, surely, is the romance of modern America (c. 1919-), for, pace De Toqueville, it was as individuals that we settled, as individuals we constituted a government, and as individuals only we survive. Though the three Republican Presidents of the era were all chosen symbolically to promote ideologies of resistance, everyone else of any standing whatever offered no symbolic statement, just that old fact and a little informality. Babe Ruth, Jack Dempsey, Valentino, Texas Guinan, Mary Pickford ... none of them was interchangeable as to type, none an incarnation of an ideal so much as a container of fact, celebrity taken in adulterous affection, a magic mirror of the bunk of history.

—Except for one man, the Moses soon to come. And he didn't want to play. Just watch what we did to him.

NINE

Shamefaced for showing curiosity about such a louche affair but eager despite themselves, Americans gazed at the photograph of a six-year-old girl who was purported to be the illegitimate daughter of Warren G. Harding, trying to discern some likeness in her features that would recall to them the leonine burgher of the early twenties, the man who had proclaimed normalcy. It was 1927, and the muck of the twenties' Watergate, Teapot Dome, was flowing wide and free, with legal action under way in Washington. The peripheral particulars were coming sensationally to light—Harding's adultery, Harding's "strange death," Harding's orgies of drinking, gambling, and, it was hoped, worse.

All three aspects of the revised Harding image took form in the popular media, his adulterous liaison and consequent offspring most spectacularly in what must be America's all-time underground best-seller, Nan Britton's *The President's Daughter*. Written by the woman in the case herself, this was the book with the photo of Elizabeth Ann (Harding-) Britton, Nan's bastard daughter by, apparently, the twenty-ninth President of the United States. The author dedicated her prolix volume "to all unwedded mothers and to their innocent children whose fathers are usually not known to the world." While there wasn't a publisher to be found who didn't think that the book would make a fortune, there wasn't a publisher who was willing to touch it. Even *Cosmopolitan* turned down the serial rights, though its editor read the manuscript, utterly captured, in one marathon sitting. Britton finally decided to publish it herself, fighting down attempts at censorship both direct and oblique. John S. Sumner of New York State's Society for the Suppression of Vice, which had been making a habit of filling paddy wagons with the casts of the occasional daring play, failed to stop publication of *The President's Daughter,* and if most newspapers refused advertisements for the book, a denunciation from the floor of the Senate gave it some publicity. Booksellers and reviewers, too, turned up their noses, but Britton's autobiography-*cum*-polemic on the Fallen Woman slowly became a secret seller.

It was Mencken, not astoundingly, who broke the gentlemen's silence with a review in the *Baltimore Sun,* and then the dike burst. Up from under the counter and onto the best-seller list it came, a secret no more. "It is an astounding romance," reported Harry Hansen in the book column of the *New York World,* "a tale that even if all names were erased would sweep the country as the story of a woman's tremendous preoccupation with love and motherhood, one of those documents that could hardly have been concocted out of a blue sky, that must have been lived."

A book of the sort that comes out at just the time and seizes the day, *The President's Daughter* collated much that belonged, loosely, to Daddy and Peaches, Valentino and Elinor Glyn's characters, relimning them all in a soap-opera fresco as real as life. Britton did not stint on the citation of chapter and verse that make confessions ring like the church bell, as in this scene of love and passion set in a coat closet in the White House, the players in the comedy being the authoress and Harding:

The windowless cubby hole was pitch dark—and perhaps better so. For the two who outside had seemed so heartwarmingly handsome and respectable began kissing feverishly, lips pressing against lips. For a few minutes this seemed to suffice, then the man's heavy body bent forward, crushing the girl hard against the wall. In answer to an unspoken signal, the hands of each furiously began exploring the body of the other.

The President's Daughter by no means marked the end of the disclosures of crime and lubricity associated with the late President. While Senator Walsh's committee finally ended its hearings in May of 1928, shortly after the oil leases of Teapot Dome and Elk Hills were successfully challenged by the government and their cancellation upheld by the Supreme Court, the pop media took up the story, seeing, as they see so well, the fictive possibilities in the fact of leadership. Samuel Hopkins Adams, the author (as Warner Fabian) of some of the most risqué sheik and flapper novels of the decade, beat Nan Britton to the best-seller list with his novel *Revelry*, a thinly disguised piece *à clef* based on the D.C. gossip about the Ohio gang. Harding turned up as President Willis Markham, the house on H Street was "the crow's nest on Blue Street," and Daugherty, Fall, Ned McLean, Sinclair, Doheny and other henchmen of Teapot Dome were pictured, along with Alice Roosevelt as Edith Westervelt, who undertakes to reform the heedless chief executive in a plot line even more implausible than those of Valentino's movies. Adams even had an explanation for Harding's death—suicide to escape the shame of exposure. A bit later, when *The President's Daughter* had made itself spectacularly scenic in the nation's bookstores, Maurine Watkins, the author of the satiric farce *Chicago*, adapted Adams's novel for Broadway, and Hollywood, too, was happy to borrow the property.

Meanwhile, a Harding memorial had been completed in Marion, a huge marble drum to house the tombs of Harding and his wife, who had joined him in death in middecade. But Coolidge, according to Hoover—still the Secretary of Commerce, surviving the vagaries of Republican scandal with dispassionate industry—"expressed a furious distaste" at every mention of the mausoleum and refused to dedicate it, President to President, in the acknowledged custom. There had, however, been a ground-breaking ceremony at the laying of the cornerstone, which Nan Britton threatened to attend with her daughter; neither of them ultimately showed up, but what a heyday the press would have made of that little junket, had it come to pass.

These are only a few instances of the fruit of Teapot Dome harvested throughout the twenties and on into the next decade with abandon: accusations, confessions, court fights, lies, and truths, and some further Teapot Domery from Harry Sinclair pursuant to his trial with Albert Fall for criminal conspiracy in the negotiation of the Teapot Dome lease, when Sinclair arranged with the William Burns Detective Agency to meddle with the jury. In short, the nation was getting a raunchy inside look at the constitution of its leadership, for besides the simple outrage of the oil swindle, Teapot Dome as crimeplace, there was all the attendant uncovering of the many other swindles of the Harding team, of Forbes and the Veterans Bureau, of Daugherty and the Justice Department, of the pokerizing housecarls of big-time, small-town money rape, Teapot Dome as way of life. Worst of all was the parade of Ohio-gang low-lives that marched through the twenties as Walsh and his fellows unmasked them and as they unmasked each other, everything from thieves and fixers to murderers and unwed mothers, Teapot Dome as state of mind and Washington, D.C., as Chicago.

Leadership, American leadership, suddenly began to look like a lot of bad news from the West, even in an era that had outlawed leadership for the duration of normalcy. Politicians were exempt from the quick satisfaction demanded of celebrity, but the true leaders of the political arena have more fact than any number of celebrities put together; think of Bob La Follette, perched on a wagon in the midst of the folk to harangue them about Eastern credit and railroaders, about the cures for what ailed them. La Follette makes even Babe Ruth look puny, for despite his magisterial self-belief, La Follette carried the informality that addresses the many, and we know how little truck he had with the jazz of the day. If there had been an antidote to jazz, La Follette would have applied it, as he applied the tourniquet and poultice to the Midwestern farming community. But there is no such antidote other than the truth, and the sinewy limits of truth-telling are as nothing in combat with the molasses flexibility of jazz, stretching to cover any eventuality and replicating of itself like an amoeba. "I can't give you anything but love, baby," croons the millionaire vocalist: if you can believe that—and we did—you'll believe anything. And once you're taken in, you don't stand a chance.

Some leaders learn to tame jazz to their ends, and no one of recent days who intends to be prominent could possibly be so without using the system. Back before the forced conformity of focus ripped the edges off of things, a leader was expected to bring his own precision to the job—and what is precision in a politician but individuality? President Wilson refused the help of jazz even when he was battling for the League of Nations on his cross-country tour; journalists, those experts on jazz, advised him to offer some token of homage, in each city, to local veterans of the war, to speak of their part in it to win them over. But Wilson had an idea on his mind. It was peace that he was pleading, a very specific peace; he would give the idea, not flattery, and they would have to hear. He would find no place in his speeches for such cheesy appeal.

Now, that was a true leader, even in defeat, a hero born to resist compromise as few politicians can. But since Wilson, American leadership felt hollow, and maybe only in the late twenties could one begin to feel the lack of guidance. After the creative federalism of Theodore Roosevelt and Wilson, we had thought to take a breather from the ideology of activity, but one can't, not for very long, not even in a period so content with itself as the twenties grew to be. Maybe one didn't realize it until the Walsh hearings had laid bare the depth of Teapot Dome, or until *The President's Daughter* came out. Or perhaps one changed his mind at a performance of Watkins's play *Revelry*, with its presidential suicide. Eventually one had to wonder why the nation could not produce a social leader the way it produced standouts in other fields, such as sports, murder, and gaudy eccentricity. One began to long for a leader and to ponder why Calvin Coolidge was the President of the United States. (That's simple. Coolidge was President because he was Vice President when Harding died. And he was Vice President because he was "the man who crushed the Boston police strike." And he was thought to have crushed the strike because he sent a famous hard-line telegram to Samuel Gompers when the strike was over. See, that's all Coolidge was—a man who sent a telegram.)

This is why Charles Lindbergh, Jr., was so celebrated when he made the first fully transatlantic flight in 1927, by himself, in a plane that he designed especially for the trip. Even amidst all the media hoopla that mantled Lindbergh as pigeon droppings cowl a statue in the park, one could tell that here, for once, was a true precision of the doer, the dissenter who does it alone, no compromises, none of your gimcrack golems fabricated of twaddle and informality. One had to look carefully, though, for the press did everything it could to bend Lindbergh and his plane and their flight, which was their fact, to the rules of play.

See how calmly he wanders into the book—and we so keyed up for a hero. Why fuss about it? Lindbergh wandered into the twenties in the first place. Anyway, he hated fuss, for fuss turns so fluently into that tiresome focus that makes fame into sameness, that hectic conjugation of jazz—to hype, to spiel, to consolidate—when all Lindbergh wanted to do was test his pluck and be the first to do something that was waiting to be done. There will be fuss enough as it is, for his pluck was up to it, and since one Lindbergh was worth a thousand Daddy Brownings, the inhabitants of the twenties suddenly had someone truly deserving to be roared about—for once in the whole bloody decade of Coolidge, Ford, Capone, and Valentino, a genuine fact—so the roaring had to find some scale out of mind on which to gauge itself. This is what it is: Lindbergh flew the Atlantic and everyone went absolutely crazy.

What Harold Nicolson was to call "the Lindbergh religion" began shortly before the takeoff from Roosevelt Field near Westbury, Long Island, but Lindbergh himself more or less begins in 1926 with the renewal of the Orteig Prize offered for a nonstop air jaunt between New York and "Paris or the shores of France" in either direction. Raymond Orteig, a French hotelier, had proposed his $25,000 award in 1919 (the year in which two Britons flew from Newfoundland to Ireland, less than two-thirds the distance between Paris and New York). No one had won the contest in the five years for which it ran, and Orteig was prevailed upon in the name of Franco-American relations to renew it. It was announced that a champion pilot, René Fonck, had a good chance of taking the prize in a special biplane built for him on Long Island by Igor Sikorsky.

Lindbergh, too, was a pilot, a courier on the St. Louis–Chicago mail run, and in his unobserved way no minor champ. Certainly he had the cool, fate's-just-a-word capacities of the daredevil who, if he doesn't get killed, ends up a champion. In those days aviation was still a quite hazardous venture even for experts, but Lindbergh was rich in the tricky bounces of happenstance from which one either rises up, proving that man is a better word than fate, or sinks down forever, proving nothing. Once, kept by fog from landing in Chicago, Lindbergh discovered that a smaller gas tank had been substituted for the one he thought he was flying on. Since he couldn't arrange a safe landing on the reserve, he had to abandon the plane in the air when the engine died and parachute to earth through the murk. Good enough; such things happen—except Lindbergh had not cut the switches on the plane, and, as it nosed down, a last dollop of fuel slipped into the carburetor and started the machine up again. And it came right to him. As if in an episode from some highbrow's technophobic novel, the airplane devised and controlled by man headed at its master of its own accord, descending at the rate of the parachute's descent, and slowly slided past Lindbergh in a spiral pattern. Both man and machine ended up in separate cornfields, the former unhurt, the latter crashed. At least the mailbags were safe.

Learning of the Orteig Prize, on its reinstatement, Lindbergh realized in a flash that there was no reason why he could not cop it himself, providing he could get some financing behind him and providing as well that he could convince a reliable aircraft firm to sell him exactly the plane he wanted for a long-term flight. Other aviators were announcing themselves as Orteig competitors, including a few stars of the profession, but their plans tended to involve elaborate designs, crews, equipment, and glitz; Lindbergh's scheme was stripped down for reason, not romance—and he proposed to fly by himself. Such men as René Fonck and Commander Richard Byrd were the great white hopes, and they had no trouble finding backers and engineers. Lindbergh, however, was nobody, and he had trouble outfitting his project. The Fokker people thought Lindbergh's idea for a single-engine plane more than a little preposterous, and they demanded approval of the operating staff: scratch Fokker. The

Wright-Bellanca people, whom Lindbergh thought made the best single-engine then devised, were represented by a perverse middle man who played power games with the unknown contestant: scratch Wright-Bellanca.

Presumably these lordly companies saw no potential in Lindbergh, which testifies less to Lindbergh's rawness than to their shortsightedness, for others were impressed by the strength of character and expertise that radiated from Lindbergh as color steals out of the diamond. His experience and his grasp had already sufficiently impressed a number of businessmen in St. Louis to back him in the pursuit that would redound not only to America's standing but to that of St. Louis as well. Soon enough Lindbergh located a firm that was willing to meet his innovative requirements on the construction of the plane, the Ryan Aircraft Company in San Diego.

Time, meanwhile, was running out. Other fliers were already seeing to final details and waiting for clear weather, so Lindbergh raced out to San Diego to give Ryan Aircraft the once-over. It was a light one, for he and the Ryan people saw eye to eye early on, even on the wild idea of a solo flight. But Lindbergh was used to going it alone; not depending on others meant not getting caught in others' mistakes. For $10,580 Ryan built Lindbergh the plane he needed: *his* weight the pilot's allowance (170 pounds), *his* the idea for where to position the gas tank (in front of the cockpit rather than behind, blocking the pilot's view but safer in a crash), *his* priority on what instruments to take (no radio, for one thing, to save on weight), *his* miles to go the basis for the size of the gas tanks (3,400 statutory miles from New York to Paris), his plane. He called it *The Spirit of St. Louis*.

Not heroics, but normalcy, eh? Not experiment but equipoise? Not submergence in internationality but sustainment in triumphant nationality, all in Harding's own words? Well, that hadn't lasted long, for experiment was calling the shots and our nationality was not all that triumphant, though it certainly was tooting its horn. Heroics can be very refreshing, and there couldn't be any harm in a little Franco-American internationalism, providing it went no deeper than a plane ride from here to there, preferably manned by one of us. Off our rudder now, like a plane gone careering in the clouds—like

Lindbergh's plane outside of Chicago, playing one-way chicken with him when he was parachuting to earth—we could have used the stability that heroics provide, the sense of being greater than the medium image of a people at large, of having qualities, symbols, traditions, aspirations. Normalcy and prosperity: what were those, anyway? Incantatory fluff, more of that jazz. Why, we really hadn't been a nation since Wilson and the war.

Still, we had our romance; nothing proves it so well as the Lindbergh cult, for with all its mechanical wow and international flutter, it most enraptured the public as a feat, the kind that reminds Americans that a few land first where the many can follow. Wilson, too, had led, and Bryan, and La Follette, and Hughes (who by this time was back at his law practice on Wall Street preparatory to his being named Chief Justice of the Supreme Court by Hoover in 1930), and except for Hughes, one of the first citizens of the nation but of less romantic address than the others in the marketplace, all were gone. Eastern and Midwestern Progressivism had gone with them, we know, but something else besides—spirit.

So, what leadership denied us, romance supplied, not least in the popular arts, one of our most vital traditions and often of a truth not equaled in the middle- and lowbrow arts of other nations. The sheik and the flapper were ceding place to the hero in the literature of the late twenties, as if social satire were at last trying to posit a social ideal—as if we at last were ready to receive one. Hart Crane's mythologizing paean to *The Bridge* might perhaps have surfaced in 1920 instead of in 1930, but it would have felt less apt then; we would not have contemplated Crane's bridges into time and space then—the will, remember, was resistance, not action. But how flat is normalcy compared to myth, and how retrograde the acts of even a home-run king or a savvy revivalist when set aside the cresting genius of the man who can meet the mountains.

Oh, yes, the throaty purr of the jive was as strong as ever. Nothing socks out that old informality like Irving Berlin's song of 1929, "Puttin' on the Ritz," which reduces the universe to a dance floor and morality to a strut—yet how much more potent a conception was Edna Ferber's novel *Cimarron* with its stupendous hero Yancey Cravat, frontier settler, newspaperman, lawyer, righteous murderer, oil man, soldier, poet. God, did ever a man live so big as that one, even in Oklahoma? But 1929 was a year for American mythologizing, what with Ernest Hemingway's *A Farewell to Arms,* Thomas Wolfe's *Look Homeward, Angel,* and William Faulkner's *The Sound and the Fury* and *Sartoris.* By then, the break with normalcy was complete.

From normalcy to romance in a bare decade! Ah, but Americans have always been romantics masquerading as realists, as the "norm." Indeed, we (maybe inadvertently) elected a romantic-realist as President in 1928, for somewhere behind the starchy, so very sensible facade of Herbert Hoover lurked the soul of the man of action. Hoover looked as stolid as Coolidge, but he talked action, not resistance. As Secretary of Commerce from 1921 to 1928, Hoover held possibly *the* Cabinet post of them all, for this was at root an age of commerce, old commerce transformed and new commerce invented. If as President he had the misfortune to see the tradition of laissez-faire crumble under him in a depression that couldn't wear itself out in the traditional manner, Hoover did know a tradition of individualism when he saw one. Thus his book of 1922, *American Individualism:*

> If we examine the impulses that carry us forward, none is so potent for progress as the yearning for individual self-expression, the desire for creation of something. Perhaps the greatest human happiness flows from personal achievement . . . But it can only thrive in a society where the individual has liberty and stimulation to achievement. Nor does the community progress except through its participation in these multitudes of achievements.

Personal achievement: aye, we'd been getting little enough of that since the war. "Democracy," opined Hoover, "must stimulate leadership from its own mass." Well, we had surely stimulated *something* from our mass—flagpole sitters, marathon dancers, movie stars, prizefighters, religious hopheads, ethnic stereotypes. It wasn't enough; it was the essence of nothing.

Aviation stimulated Lindbergh, and this innovation stimulated tradition. His background was one steeped in lone-wolf achievement, for his father, the senior Charles Lindbergh, was a Midwestern farmer and lawyer who joined the Progressive insurgent circle in the House of Representatives in 1906 as a Republican from Minnesota (some circle that was—a chorus of soloists). Nonpartisan, insatiably honest, a tireless worker, and a fanatic for stoical self-reliance, Lindbergh *père* violently opposed the Eastern banking establishment, writing a book on the subject, *Banking and Currency and the Money Trust,* and opposed as well American entrance into the war. In these stands he was not unlike his brother Progressives of the agrarian Midwest, and these were popular issues, but Lindbergh demonstrated his penchant for iconoclasm by taking up the battle between the Roman Catholic Church and the anti-Catholic Free Press Defense League. Acknowledging the Church's baleful history of oppression and censorship, Lindbergh introduced in the House a resolution calling for an investigation of the controversy.

By 1918, when young Charles was sixteen, his father was running for governor of Minnesota in one of the most basely behaved political contests of modern times. Catholic resistance, money bossism, most newspapers, and the Red scare (often suspicious of Progressives and their attacks on big business) united not only to defeat Lindbergh but to harry him out of his campaign. Mob violence and lenient law enforcement made a mess of speech rallies, and Lindbergh was shot at, stoned, arrested, and vilified in terms usually reserved for Robert La Follette in the washrooms of Wall Street. And he lost the election. But he never saw fit to retire, and had offered himself as a third-party candidate for governor when he was felled by an inoperable brain tumor in 1924.

Of such stock came Charles Lindbergh, Jr., and maybe after all Lindbergh doesn't start with the Orteig Prize but in his childhood, growing up absurd and straight-arrow in the care of a man as courageously principled as ever a man was. Of such stock, inevitably, comes more of the same: conformists may raise nonconformists, dissent scared into the children through seeing dull close up, but nonconformists always breed their own kind, for that is a strength that surrenders to nothing and knows only what strength can do. "He'd let me walk behind him with a loaded gun at seven," Lindbergh later wrote, "use an axe as soon as I had the strength to swing it, drive his Ford car anywhere at twelve . . . My freedom was complete. All he asked was responsibility in turn."

Lindbergh's call didn't draw him to the political theater. He had seen the airplanes soaring over Minnesota in his boyhood, and his ambitions were too wild to settle for something that had restrictions. From his father he inherited much, not only the implacability which compromisers call ego (and which other strong men recognize as character), but also a suspicion of war policies, problematic relationships with women, and a tendency to self-righteousness. From nowhere he discovered a love of flight—that was his progressivism—and by chance it was just at the time when flight had yet to be brought into the public consciousness. Unlike the automobile and radio, flight hadn't been moored in Middletown.

Unlike the automobile and radio, flight belonged to individualism, to *personal* achievement. Here was no machine for the consumer, no mob's toy—not only because there was simply too much money involved in the purchase and maintenance of a plane, but because even those few who could have afforded the splurge and rode the air as their neighbors rode roads, didn't. Flight was not just expensive, but strange, and the few men involved in it in the twenties—mostly ex-wartime flying aces—only contributed to its strangeness with the way they moved, and dressed, and were. There was romance in what they were about, in the effortless serenity of the cloud ride described by those who had taken it, and in the comradely valor displayed by such movies as *Wings*, with its extravaganza of air combat seen above, below, and at the level, biplanes nosing above and across, banking in a smashing glide, pitching over in surrender. The sky, the freedom, the plane! Flight was a contraband of nature, another boon that had to be stolen for man—but not like the automobile, not invented: flight was already there. Was this the unfeeling machine, the soulless god who struck humanism from the record and frightened the highbrows? No, flight brought its own humanism, its own poetry and myth-making; flight was not the machine, but man the doer, gloriously overreaching himself in the trackless frontier of heaven. One couldn't even call it a rich man's perquisite, as one once had done the automobile, for the barnstormers and mail pilots who flew the planes were fliers, not capitalists. Indeed, what were they?—native strangers, libertarian voyagers of the stateless skies, individualists by their very profession. Here were heroes, all right, standouts with the rough edges to cut through focus, for any substance of personality throws that pressure for conformity off its kilter. It didn't happen often, even then when the consolidation of communications hadn't yet congealed on us, but when it did ... well, look what a riot they held for Lindbergh when he broke through the barrage of murder raps and flagpole sessions in the media with one lightning stroke of a lone-wolf, undebunkable, focus-smashing deed of individualist precision. We were hungry for the truth of that precision, though we hadn't much realized it. Perhaps Coolidge fooled us with "his" prosperity, as normalcy had fooled us.

Still, every now and then, truth would scrimmage with focus and win a yard or two. There was one such moment in the radio broadcast of the Democratic Convention in 1924, a few seconds when a real look at what was accidentally slipped in with the jazz. Not that the jazz had broken down—the jazz will never break down, remember that—but that humanity accidentally came popping out of the box during what was intended to be a quiet moment in the proceedings. The WJZ channels were carrying the convention program, hosted by Major J. Andrew White, an old hand; White's assistant, Norman Brokenshire, was a newcomer to the field and possibly not aware that WJZ got the okay to air the convention on the promise that anything untowardly would be blinked out (as if the Democrats' ceaseless failure to decide on a party trajectory weren't untowardly enough). But came this lull and White had gone out, leaving Brokenshire at the mike, and suddenly a fight broke out on the floor. As Brokenshire later recalled it,

"Wanting to do well for the glory of WJZ, I concentrated on the fight and let everything else go by. I explained that one whole delegation had blustered across the aisle to register a complaint, following with a blow-by-blow eye-witness account of one of the finest donnybrooks I'd ever seen. Delegation signs were banged on opponents' heads, chairs and decorations destroyed: I had a ringside seat."

It didn't last long. White returned, hurriedly signaled the operator to cut off, and the studio threw something else into the breach, anything . . . no, something soothing, for God's sake (Keith McLeod singing "Traümerei," as it happened, but the point had already been made, the violence heard). In that short episode America was shown what lay behind the hoopla of "fact," and amidst the pro- and anti-Klan jokes then in circulation, the imitations of Smith and Bryan, and that delighted adoption of Governor Brandon's "A-la-ba-ma! Casts! Twenty-four votes for Oscar! W.! Underwood!" as a satiric hocus-pocus of the day, there was the horrible revelation that one majority was just as tyrannical as another. And just as precise.

Similarly, Lindbergh's thirty-three-and-a-half hour solo flight from Roosevelt Field to Le Bourget airfield in Paris tendered not the belittling informality of the celebrity but the formal absolutism of achievement. Interest in the young Midwesterner was mounting when he took *The Spirit of St. Louis* from San Diego to New York, with a morning's respite in St. Louis, but he was far and away outclassed in mediaspeak by his competitors, some of whom were war heroes and past record-setters in aviation. On the other hand, a reporter couldn't help but notice the possibilities in the unvarnished Minnesotan and his proposed solo. Such attention as was paid him disgusted Lindbergh for its crassness and intrusive irrelevance. "Do you carry a rabbit's foot?" he was asked. "What's your favorite pie?" "How do you feel about girls?" Ordering him here and there to pose for pictures and daring gasoline fumes with their cigarettes, the minions of the press gave Lindbergh his first taste of the consistency of American fame and of the pretenses that brewed it. One had a lucky charm, a favorite pie, a feeling about girls, a wise saying, a determination in ten words or less: a celebrity's résumé. Not so naive as his newcoming might suggest, Lindbergh had noted the way of the world and specifically planned on the assistance of publicity, but he had not realized how stupid reporters could be and how misleading their reports.

"For what, Lindy?" they might well have asked him; why was he doing it? There was the $25,000 of the prize money, of course, plus the inducement of being able to implant himself in the profession as an aviator of note, and possibly the dim lure of stapling worlds together at the towers. Mainly Lindbergh was doing it because he knew he could. His confidence, along with the testimony of performance, gave a kindred confidence to his countrymen, a confidence of originality and achievement. Given the twenties and what it had represented before Lindbergh's venture, it was as if he had brought them back from the dead.

The dark horse, Lindbergh arrived in New York in mid-May of 1927 after some Orteig hopefuls had already made their attempts, none successfully, for April had indeed been the cruelest month. The huge, trimotored Fokker intended to take Commander Byrd to Paris crashed on a test flight with its designer Anthony Fokker, at the helm, injuring everyone aboard except Fokker. Scratch Byrd (temporarily, at least). Then the Wright-Bellanca, which like the Fokker had been denied Lindbergh when he had first set out to buy a plane, came to grief even after setting a new world record for nonstop flight on a test run: the plane dropped a wheel on a takeoff and had to make a crash landing. Scratch Wright-Bellanca. Worst of all, the end of the month brought the permanent scratch of Lieutenant Commander Noel Davis and Lieutenant Stanton H. Wooster, whose plane, the *American Legion*, went down on a test flight in Virginia, killing both pilots.

Each big or little disaster served to key the public up even more. The continual test flights and arrivals of Orteig contestants turned into a daily series in the papers, though the front page was yet occupied by the Snyder-Gray murder trial, and it would take more than the abstraction of what an aviator or two *might* accomplish to turn that bonanza out of the limelight. Then, suddenly, the gyre turned and flight took the headline. On May 8, just as the trial was winding up, and while somebody named Charles Augustus Lindbergh, Jr., was still in San Diego completing his trial runs in *The Spirit of St. Louis,* Charles Nungesser and François Coli took off from Paris for New York in a Levasseur biplane, *L'Oiseau Blanc.* They were skilled airmen, much versed in the language of flight from having conversed in it with German aviators during the war. Their *White Bird* would make it. They would be the first.

Never saying die, Lindbergh turned in San Diego to check out an alternative project to cross the Pacific. *The White Bird* had by all accounts crossed the Atlantic, and as it headed southwest over the North American coastline, newsmen and radio announcers brought the land in on the excitement. Programs were interrupted with proclamations and special editions generated to arouse the public, and a crowd was already gathering at the Battery in lower New York. *The White Bird* was sighted off Cape Race by one of our destroyers! *The White Bird* was passing Portland, Maine! *The White Bird* is over Boston! An ecstatic French newspaper even published the news, prematurely, that *The White Bird* had landed after a few festive circlings of the Statue of Liberty.

All lies, or wishful thinking. Something may have been spotted winging over Portland, but it wasn't *The White Bird*. In fact, Nungesser and Coli not only didn't make it to New York, but were never seen again, and to this day no one knows what became of them. They and *The White Bird* had vanished, presumably forced down and into the ocean in some mishap, and the glory of being the first man to fly the length of the Atlantic nonstop was still up for the taker.

On May 21, 1927, Charles Lindbergh took it.

TEN

We

It was like a very few other days in a lifetime, a day that so stands out in one's memory that one recalls forever after exactly what one was doing when one heard the news. Amazing that one man's one exploit could contribute so much self-respect to a nation of people who had never met him, but so it was. It was heroics, but it was healing as well—you can have both at once, and normalcy was a lie.

"He made it!" Where were you when you heard? All right we were one nation, and the will of resistance had to yield to the tempo of change in the fact of the solo, the dissent, the smashing through of shibboleth and sensation—even as it made a sensation of itself—by one man who would have none of what the focus salesmen were selling. It was an outgoing act, going out of borders, shrinking the world and prizing the machine, but if Lindbergh thought of himself and his plane as "we," to America it was all Lindbergh, a hero.

Yet it was a technological fact, wasn't it? Lindbergh piloted the plane, but the plane flew—that was the miracle of it, for despite the short-lived charisma of the fighting aces of the air during the war and the proliferation of flighty exhibit in the popular media (typical reductive touches: in the musical comedy *Going Up*, the author of a best-selling book on aviation turns out never to have been in the air himself, and in the film *Live Wires* a plane is used in a nick-of-time stunt to get a football hero to the big game), the flying machine was the most resisted of all modernism's marvels. Such was the general dispassion for the possibility of human flight that the mathematics and astronomy professor Simon Newcomb's "scientific" dismissal of it in 1901 in an article in *McClure's* magazine was far more widely reported than was Wilbur and Orville Wright's proof of it in 1903.

So forceful was Newcomb's reasoning and the reasoning of his fellow academics, and the skepticism of the average citizen, and the bone-deep suspicion of the simpler castes, that failed attempts with aeronautical devices were featured on page one, contributing a laugh to the start of the day and spreading some sort of "good news" that progress could only take us so far. Since the Wright brothers first got a power-driven plane to stay a course in the air only days after Samuel P. Langley suffered the prominent washout of his second attempt in the same line, most newspaper editors who printed stories on the events at Kitty Hawk relegated them to the "wildcat" page, with the UFO sightings and the hypnotism columns.

The secret of manflight, in short, was out, but virtually no one would believe it. Not till 1908, when the Wright Brothers returned to Kitty Hawk for further trials in the air and a newsman of some repute filed an eyewitness report did flight finally come into question as a real possibility, if grudgingly, and a batch of newsmen headed down to North Carolina to see for themselves. "Settle this nonsense for once and all" sums up the attitude of the nation's influential editors—but the Wright brothers refused to entertain any audience of their experiments, and the fourth estate pitched camp on the sly in hopes of spying out this wonder, if, in truth, it was such. On the third day of waiting, with nothing to show for their vigil, the reporters were debating whether to confront the Wrights and tell them off or just decamp and forget the whole thing when suddenly this nonsense was settled for once and all. As Byron Newton wrote in the *New York World,*

We saw the machine glide swiftly . . . across the white sand, saw men racing along by its side, heard their shouts, and then we saw the machine rise majestically into the air, its white wings flashing and glistening in the morning sun. On it sped at an altitude about fifty feet from the ground. I have never experienced another moment with like sensations. It was like standing in the presence of some overpowering calamity.

Many, many were to write in those years of their first view of a plane in full cry, and a fewer number were to speak of the ride itself. But by the mid-twenties, even those who, like the boy Lindbergh, could only take the measure of flight from the ground looking up, had begun to conceive of the possibilities. The height. The distance. The speed. After all, space flight is only these factors multiplied exponentially, and amidst the resistance there was—how could there not be—fascination. Just as with Babe Ruth's stamina, Gertrude Ederle's dip in the Channel, and even Valentino's froufrou materializations on his cinematic altar, flight was still something human, something that we ourselves had to do. Unlike baseball, swimming, or acting, it was something that very few of us knew how to do, and that made it all the more heroic.

And it was heroic, nothing else—bold, swift, and, especially, impulsive, for Lindbergh took off on the spur of the moment. You wouldn't expect that the first ride through the air from New York to Paris might be launched so lightly off the cuff (particularly after the detailed planning which Lindbergh had put himself through since the Orteig Prize had been renewed, getting his backers and his plane), but once he and *The Spirit of St. Louis* had arrived at Curtiss Field, Lindbergh and his competitors had nothing to do but wait out a spell of bad weather over the Atlantic. Lindbergh was the last pilot to set up camp at the aerodrome—Clarenc Chamberlin and Commander Byrd were already on the mark and set to charge the horizon, precedent, and chronicle—and the general feeling was that whoever took off first would probably do it.

Lindbergh took off first, in a sudden change of plan that interrupted a rainy visit to the musical comedy *Rio Rita*, a Western frolic that had recently inaugurated the new Ziegfeld Theatre on Sixth Avenue between Fifty-fourth and Fifty-fifth streets. Weather over the ocean had been continuing grim, but a phone call to the Weather Bureau revealed a shift in the storm pattern, and Lindbergh rushed out to Long Island, all thoughts of musical comedy, to whatever extent they could possibly have entered his mind, now out of it. It was the flight now, nothing but the flight. It had been nothing but the flight, anyway, for nearly a year, and if the sky over Long Island was wet and forbidding, so had the Midwestern sky been in many of Lindbergh's mail runs.

The first thing on Lindbergh's agenda was sleep, but he didn't get much in all the excitement and had to be at the hangar by 3:00 A.M. anyway if he was to leave, as he planned, at dawn. In a steady downpour, his craft was towed from Curtiss Field over to Roosevelt Field, much the better runway and technically rented out to Byrd but offered to Lindbergh by the commander himself. Policemen, reporters, photographers, and even a tiny crowd of rubberneckers followed the towing of the shrouded plane through the mud to the airstrip—"more like a funeral procession," Lindbergh thought, "than the beginning of a flight to Paris." Day broke. The wind shifted. The plane had been thoroughly checked, but because of the weather the engine sounded underpowered when they started it up. Everyone stood around watching. The experts, cocking an ear to the motor, either looked worried or tried not to, which is the same thing. Timing is everything, and time had already outraced the flight preparations. It was Friday. It was Long Island. It was just short of 8:00 A.M. on May 20. Go or stay? If you wait for perfect weather from here to there, you'll be racing Byrd and Chamberlin. Everyone watches. Lindbergh thinks. It's Friday. It's after dawn. It's raining. But it's clear sky over the ocean.

The press had already dubbed Lindbergh "The Flying Fool," also "Lindy" and "Lucky Lindy," though his nickname was Slim. The fact that he was tall, good-looking, Swedish-American, and only twenty-five had made him perfectly exploitable as far as the media were concerned, even admitting that all pilots, whether war heroes or near midgets, stalwarts or squareheads who could only have been heroes to their valets, were prime copy for romance. The attentions of reporter and cameraman were a sore nuisance to Lindbergh, but he

sure wasn't thinking of them; they and their games were uppermost in
their minds as they waited for him to fish or cut bait, for here, right
here, is where their plays were won or lost. They would do nicely
with Chamberlin if he made it, and they would go to town with Byrd,
who was already known for having flown over the North Pole the year
before. But Lindbergh, the so-adorable flying fool going it alone,
would be their Fort Knox.

He had already been something of a bonanza as it was in the last
few days. They were portraying him as part Middletown daredevil
and part cowboy knight, the boy next door if you lived on a ranch,
and the words they put in his mouth were calculated to bring him
alive in terms he neither understood nor respected. When he had
arrived on Long Island, Commander Byrd and Giuseppe Bellanca
showed up to shake his hand, which was fine—but it was less to his
liking that they did it several times over for photographers, falling into
place at their commands for profiles and smiles. The pressmen even
interfered with the major business of keeping the plane in condition,
such as planting themselves in his way one time when he was
landing, forcing him to bank too sharply to avoid them and effecting a
minor mishap with the tail skid as a result. This they interpreted as
his, not their, error:

> So terrific was his speed that in landing he slightly damaged the
> machine's tail skid. Undismayed by this accident, which he
> considered trivial, Lindbergh hopped out wearing a broad smile:
> "Boys, she's ready and rarin' to go!" he said.

Note the happy-go-lucky lummox of the quotation; Lindbergh never
talked that way in his life. They even harried Lindbergh's mother in
Detroit with questions that so aroused worry in her that she came east
to see him for what reporters assured her might well be a last farewell.
Unable to get mother and son to pose for the Kodaks in the manner
of the *Pietà,* they simply tossed off a composograph showing two
actors kissing each other with Lindbergh heads on them.

They were all pitched on the verge of glory, Lindbergh and the
hateful press caravan, deciding and watching the deciding in the rain.

This was the ultimate prelude for both sides, and oh! how they wanted him to go. What a story that would be. And if he made it, all the Bigger and Better. That was their reason for wanting him to get on with it. Lindbergh had a better one: he knew he could do it.

Well, the weather was crummy and the plane loaded with more fuel than it had ever carried, so the takeoff wasn't ideal. Dogged down the runway by a car containing an associate of the Wright Aeronautical Corporation (which had built Lindbergh's engine) and some policemen with fire extinguishers, the plane sagged back into the mud on its first lift but suddenly cracked aloft, just clearing some high-tension wires at the end of the airstrip. It was 7:54 A.M., Friday, and still raining. Something like thirty-five hours of voyage presumably awaited Lindbergh in the air.

"We" is how Lindbergh often referred to the pair who made that voyage, he and his plane—and it really was his; he practically *made* it by hand—and Our journey was crowded with event . . . cold, fatigue, a sleet storm, the darkness of night. Largely hugging the sea to save on fuel (the higher one soars, the more gasoline one consumes), Lindbergh held to a direct route, up the northeast coastline to Nova Scotia and then across to the edge of Ireland and on to Paris. Having jettisoned most standard equipment to save on weight, Lindbergh had only his instrument panel, his maps, a sextant, and a compass, and with the gas tank placed in front of him, he could only see ahead by leaning out to the side or using a simple periscope. But seeing was not crucial on the bulk of Lindbergh's trip over the ocean; he had to navigate with his charts and compass as if in a void, a speck chugging through the tossing infinite scientifically. There are few variables over the ocean, alone in a plane—certainly there were none of America's jazzy variables of the consumer machine. There is the true fact of getting there and, possibly, of coming back, a pure act motivated largely by itself. There is no way to debunk this.

This operation of austere intensity inspired in the landlubbers waiting at home an epic reception almost from the moment that Lindbergh departed. Not the Lindbergh that was, but the Lindbergh that must be, whoever he was, instantly took center stage in the theater of feats. He was alone—that was much of it. And he was

American—that, too. But there was more. A cartoon run by the *St.
Louis Post-Dispatch* the night before he left showed the wild,
boomeranging ocean below, the nasty heavens above, and, between
them, a fleabite of an airplane . . . and that sums it up for the nation,
however much it had been weaned on celebrity ghouls and their
shifty fame, as spurious as rotgut hooch. "A public," wrote the
shrewd Middle-American journalist Elmer Davis, "which had seemed
to find its highest ideal in Babe Ruth, Valentino, and Gertrude Ederle
(or, perhaps, in Peaches Browning and Ruth Snyder) suddenly went
wild beyond all precedent over this unknown young man."

So this was not a technological fact after all, but a lone-wolf act of
the doing, or risking the undoing. Lindbergh had confidence in
himself, and the spectators picked up on that, sharing it with him—
not the stupid rodeo confidence that the press had painted all over
him ("Boys, she's ready and rarin' to go!"), but the confidence that
sang out of the simple fact of his excursion. Somebody in that mass of
automobile buyers, moviegoers, and celebrity seers had ambition to
find something finer than normalcy, to see something clearer than
cinema, to say something stronger than hello to a sucker. Somebody
could connect the prose and the passion; it sure seemed that way to
everyone down below, waiting to hear that he had made it.
Storekeepers thrust his picture in their windows, newspapers dredged
up every item in his presumed dossier for recapitulation, fight fans at
Yankee Stadium were asked to take part in a moment of prayer for
the flier, a crowd surged in front of Mrs. Lindbergh's house in
Detroit, newspaper extras came out by the hour (with nothing to
express but hope, since without a radio Lindbergh was blanketed
from contact until he landed), fatidic experts rose up to speculate
favorably, and the Roxy Theatre in New York played and replayed a
newsreel of the takeoff to standing pandemonium.

It was pretty hectic out over the ocean, too, for with nothing in
sight to guide him until he reached the western jut of Ireland,
Lindbergh was busy charting and recharting his position, keeping his
eyes on compass points and dials as the hours went by. Sleep was his
worst threat, for *The Spirit of St. Louis* was more sensitive than most
craft to the nuances of steerage, and more headstrong when not being

fully steered. It was imperative that he drive the plane continuously, not just ride it, for otherwise it might easily have gone off course—and that, in the empty theater of night, could be a disaster. "To the pilot of an airplane without flares or landing lights," Lindbergh later wrote, "night has a meaning that no earthbound mortal can fully understand. Once he has left the lighted airways there are no wayside shelters open to a flyer of the night. He can't park his plane on a cloud bank to weather out a storm, or heave over a sea anchor like the sailor and drag along slowly downwind ... He has to keep his craft hurtling through air no matter how black the sky or blinding the storm."

Having promised himself to the night, Lindbergh plowed upward through fog to try to get a bearing from the stars and soon found himself, at 10,500 feet, in the embrace of an ice cloud. One of the most subtle and inveigling of air hazards, ice cripples planes like *The Spirit of St. Louis* by freezing its wings into inflexibility, meanwhile taking the entire ship in a loving, fatal velvet of water weight. Fighting his panic, Lindbergh weaved down through the clouds, slapping himself to stay awake, trying to concentrate on the easy equation that sleep, at this stage in his addition, meant death. He was into the seventeenth hour of his flight and he had been awake for something like two straight days and never, never in his life did his body so yearn for rest. Balancing his logbook on his lap, he made an entry, glancing up between phrases at his indicator panel.

Fatigue was the devil of that flight. It might not have been had Lindbergh not leaped on such short notice, but then one of the other two planes might have left in his stead. Drawing out of the storm at last, he could see the light of dawn brightening the sky to the east; he was two-thirds of the way there. This was a crossing of the bar, and a moment at which, had there been a radio to transmit from, he might have signaled his position to the anxious crowd back home. But there could be no such message and the suspense, just long enough to be unbearable without running out of crescendo, gripped the nation, eager for commotion. Surely there wasn't a single newspaper that didn't run an editorial that Saturday morning devoted to the *virtus*, or the command, or the meaning, of Charles Lindbergh. That in the *New York Sun*, "Lindbergh Flies Alone" stands as a classic of this

tiny era when miscellaneous hubbub gave way to a very specific
hubbub, and when for once, one grasped some idea of the scale of life
as measured by man's achievement. "Alone?" queried the *Sun*.

Is he alone at whose right side rides Courage, with Skill within
the cockpit and Faith upon the left? Does solitude surround the
brave when Adventure leads the way and Ambition reads the
dials?

So Lindbergh had company in the cockpit. Courage, skill, and faith
sat by him, and perhaps much of America in its mind's eye—babbitts,
highbrows, and celebrities—rode along. Rather than perish, the people
accepted the vision—whether of flight or exploit or symbolic reclama-
tion doesn't matter. Here, at length, was a hero. No other word will
do, and no other man of the age deserved it as well. Nothing
explodes the expatriate's assertion that America ran a "conspiracy
against the individual" more than America's exhilaration over Our
flight to Paris—for We was more than Lindbergh and his plane, more
even than his courage, skill, and faith. We was the whole crazy mob
that had been so busy going native that it had forgot what all those
skyscrapers and bridges really portended. The purely tectonic erup-
tion of achievement only moved the highbrows; it took personality to
inspire a response in the general public, the fact of man. Now, and
only now—but how briefly!—America took some note of a destiny,
and not one run by robots or materialism. Again, again, and thrice
again, democracy is strongest in its *demos* when its natural aristocrats
distill courage, skill, and faith, in some proportion or other, into
confidence and upgoing. Now, for this moment, we had got things
into some perspective.

After twenty-seven hours in the air, still drowsy, Lindbergh caught
sight of a boat a few miles to the southeast. Diving to within fifty feet
of the sea, he hailed a face that stuck out of a porthole and shouted,
"Which way is Ireland?" No answer. Pulling out of his dive,
Lindbergh climbed, turned about, and passed and asked again. Still
no answer; the man just gaped at him, didn't even point. Reassuring
himself that this was no mirage, that he was awake and probably near

land and had a rendezvous in Paris, Lindbergh flew on. Within an hour he achieved landfall—Ireland, from the look of it—so he was on course, ahead of schedule, and no doubt the most exhilarated and exhausted man in that part of the world as he sped on to Le Bourget. He had flown the course so unerringly that now he flirted with the idea of setting a new record before he set the old one by flying straight on to Rome.

This is the tense part now, home is the hunter and all, as Lindbergh sails over the Channel while afternoon cedes to twilight, takes his first bite of food in over thirty-five hours (one of the sandwiches that had been packed for him), and considers his options. He has no visa, no clothes other than his flying suit, a $500 bank check, and some letters of introduction. "We" were about to land. "Like a living creature," he was to write, "gliding along smoothly, happily, as though a successful flight means as much to it as to me ... *We* have made this flight across the ocean, not *I* or *it*."

We had been spotted at points along the route in Britain and France, and word had been sent on that they were going to make it after all. But Nungesser and Coli, too, had been spotted, as far west as Boston, so everyone tried not to be too confident about it, but everyone, on both sides of the ocean, was feeling this sort of scream rising up in him, and by the time We put down at Le Bourget that night, twenty-five thousand Frenchmen were gathered to greet them, proving that every nation has its seeing crowd.

And every crowd has its riot. Not unlike the New Yorkers who saw Valentino off with a street brawl, the hysterical French went tearing up to the plane to drag Lindbergh out and give him a hero's ave. The scream was ready—or, rather, the scream was out and deafening, unreasonable, a menace, not to be withstood. As the mikados of P.R. would rush Lindbergh on his return to the United States, so now did Jean and Jeanne D'Oe rush Us on the field. Lindbergh was pulled from his plane to the sound of ripping fabric and cracking wood; many differing versions of his first words on arrival tried to invent a suitable informality (Lindbergh himself recalled asking for a mechanic), but no one could have heard him, or wanted to, so satisfying was the release of the scream, and he was spread atop the heaving mob like an immobile and not very delicate idol. He feared he might fall beneath their feet and be too weak to save himself, but two French fliers grabbed his helmet and placed it on the head of someone who looked vaguely like him. In the darkness, the masquerade told, and thus Lindbergh was hustled to safety in a car and hidden in a nearby hangar.

Now, some thirty minutes after the flight proper had ended, the experience of the trip was over and the experience of the aftermath began; this will last for decades. Until his death in 1974 he (and still, sometimes, We) remained in a cloudy radiance, his fact undimmed by time but ruined for many by his refusal to accede to system. It must be difficult for Americans of today who were not around in 1927 to fathom the extent of the adoration, the profane piety of the Lindbergh religion, for his elitist nonconformity kept nostalgia from venerating him the way it does, say, Robert La Follette or Franklin Roosevelt or Douglas MacArthur. But in 1927 no one knew who Lindbergh was. One only knew what he had done. It was that simple. And it was tremendous.

Naturally, when Lindbergh got back to the United States, all the jazz came out to play. He had planned to return as We, flying east across Europe and Asia to cut home at Alaska, but the clamor for truth demanded that he materialize at once, in person, before the next murder trial or knockout prizefight threw him off the main stage. Such thinking underestimated the vision of the people, though, for they were about to invest Lucky Lindy with their most expensive and extortionate honor, staying power. Nothing—including his outspoken hatred of intrusion of his privacy, his removal to England in the 1930s, and his enemies' vicious attempt to wreck his political power by linking him with fascism and anti-Semitism—succeeded in defusing Lindbergh's long-range hold on the media. As the reporters had known on that rainy morning at Roosevelt Field when the pilot was deciding whether or not to chance it, Lindbergh was gold. He might be spattered with mud, but he just didn't ever wear out.

Confidence, that was his gift to the nation, his lesson, the Lindbergh idea—and not the confidence of the bull market and the big spender, not the confidence of the Village highbrow, a big spender in ideas, but the confidence of the winner. In a way, the image of Lindbergh suited Charles Ives's musical search for "the unity behind all diversity" in the folk panorama, for Lindbergh was taken to be the quintessential American—even if his background, former history, and character had got nothing from the rearing up of normalcy and the roaring of prosperity. How unlike anything in the twenties he was; thus he proved so palliative and at the same time so romantic an antidote. He looked and acted like what the twenties should have been all along. Oh, f'r a Moses: Moses had come.

The scream that almost strangled Lindbergh when he got to Le Bourget was sounded louder here, but then we had more of a stake in him. People went rushing from house to house up and down streets, spreading the news as if in some picture out of the Middle Ages. *The New York Times* gave the deed the most it can give, a banner headline with a touch of bravura in the wording: LINDBERGH DOES IT! TO PARIS IN 33½ HOURS: FLIES 1,000 MILES THROUGH SNOW AND SLEET: CHEERING FRENCH CARRY HIM OFF FIELD. Other, less judicious papers would have gone off the deep end in their jubilation had they not breached the point of hysteria for less imposing situations many times before. Then came the devotions, commenced with a spectacle of welcome in Washington, D.C. Lindbergh had come home with *The Spirit of St. Louis* but not in it; both rode back on the cruiser *Memphis* to be deposited on native turf with as much ceremony as the Navy could float in the water and the Army could fly in the air. Evangeline Lindbergh had again been summoned east from Detroit in the name of motherhood—this time by Coolidge—and that worthy did himself bestow the Distinguished Flying Cross upon the hero and even managed a reasonably long-winded speech in his honor.

If Coolidge had divined the extraordinary import that lay within, behind, and, mainly, ahead of Our flight, he didn't let on, and one Fitzhugh Green, a writer hired to cover Lindbergh's American tour, totally misread the situation in his depiction of the event: "Caesar was glum when he came back from Gaul; Napoleon grim; Paul Jones defiant; Peary blunt; Roosevelt abrupt; Dewey deferential; Wilson brooding; Pershing imposing. Lindbergh was none of these. He was a plain citizen dressed in the garments of an ordinary man." Wrong,

wrong, nothing possibly wronger. Lindbergh was dressed in a blue serge suit, true, but by no effort of semantic stretch could one term him a plain citizen. Plain is as plain does.

In fact, the surfacing of Lindbergh could only cast some dubious light on the nominal leaders of the nation, who in this age of resistance were personified by the nuncio of inaction, Calvin Coolidge. No one wanted to say it, for leftover normalcy—even in the face of Lindbergh's abnormal accomplishment—was strong in the heart, but if Coolidge was normalcy, normalcy was punk. And as for prosperity, *there* was the materialism denounced by the machine-hating highbrows; moreover, it was looking much less like the goods now that We had put the hero hustle into some relief. You never saw Lindbergh posing or prancing at the behest of the media for the elucidation of the medium; unlike Daddy Browning and Shipwreck Kelly, Lindbergh went out of his way to avoid, outwit, and offend the reporters and the crowd.

Of course, you didn't see our elected leaders exploiting themselves either, though Coolidge, for one, was not unversed in the uses of the newsreel. The national political scene incurs a certain minimum respect—if a cynical one—and the sarcastic jibes at Coolidge and his Puritan insensibility never quite rang with the smartass luxury of the Ford jokes. For all his millions, Ford was just a man (which is why the Ford for President movement took most of its energy from the anti-intellectual poor of the hinterland), while Coolidge was a rock of ages, and one whom the lapping waters of a million years would not diminish by so much as a molecule: if Coolidge had been Arizona, there would have been no Grand Canyon. Trying to get a White House luncheon off the ground one Sunday afternoon, Grace Coolidge dared to attempt to draw her husband out on the subject of the church service he had just been to.

"What did the minister preach his sermon on?" asked Mrs. Coolidge of Mr. Coolidge.

"Sin."

"Oh. And what did he have to say about it?"

"He was against it," Coolidge replied—or so the story goes.

There were many such Coolidge stories, all of a starchy exactness that would have spoiled a Ford joke. Clearly, the men at the helm were never confused with the men in the news, and if, say, both Mellon and Ford were businessmen, one was a statesman-financier, the other a screwball inventor. But the leaders and the personalities did meet, at least, on the front page—especially in 1928, when the stock market rediscovered the nosedive and prognosticative utterance from on high was in order. It was the late twenties, and prosperity was paramount, and while the Lindbergh fever had broken after the first tumultuous welcome home with ticker tape blizzards, speeches, and awards, Lindbergh was still the most famous man in the Western world. Had he wanted to go into politics himself and perhaps carry on the legislation of his father, he was nine-tenths of the way there.

He was likewise on the verge of movie contracts, uncountable endorsement offers, and a recording of his wit and wisdom on the flight, to a total of five million dollars worth of offers; all he had to do was say yes. Before he had taken off for France, he had signed agreements with a few companies, including Wright and Mobiloil, to recommend their products, since he did prefer them anyway, and eventually he was to sell his name for very limited use. But the bulk of the requests to rent him were declined, as was a bid of a million dollars from a group of businessmen, no strings attached, to "preserve his independence and keep him untainted by commercialism."

One cannot call Lindbergh perfectly untainted, but he did rigorously patrol the frontier that lay between fetishistic celebrity and the rights of a man of renown, taking his profit but only in such cases as suited his ethics. For example, he authorized Carlisle MacDonald to write a book about the flight, *We*, MacDonald doing his research viva voce aboard the *Memphis* on the way back to the United States from Europe. But when Lindbergh saw the proofs of the manuscript, written in the first person singular, he insisted on doing the job himself: how could a stranger properly write about Us?

The jazz Lindbergh found obnoxious, even more so now that he was eager to get on with a life that had earned about the most equal opportunity that ever an American has enjoyed. Lindbergh even won the Orteig Prize money, though technically he had not observed the full sixty days that were supposed to elapse between entering the contest and taking off. In a situation like this one, rules must be bent.

Many rules would bend for Lindbergh—rules of jazz, specifically, for after a few months of what he called "this hero guff," Lindbergh was ready to pack it in with fanfare. He had, literally, no privacy. Reporters followed him like Moroccan beggars, photographers lay in wait for him at windows, and he could never once eat a meal in public without being surrounded by a crowd. Even during the ticker tape parade in New York, that early in the game, he was disturbed by the essential bunk of it all. Upward of four million people—the biggest crowd in the city's history—turned out to see him at spots from the Battery to Central Park, yet photographs of the event show a clearly unimpressed hero bearing it, just barely. Imagine what must have been running through his mind during Mayor Jimmy Walker's oration at City Hall—the son of one of the era's most honest and courageous politicians having to stand and hear the jazz of one of the most corrupt.

At least Coolidge was no crook, and his speech in Washington didn't praise anything he didn't believe in himself—Walker believed in Walker and Tammany graft, in that order—but there, too, Lindbergh would not go the steps of the waltz. Accepting the Distinguished Flying Cross from the President, Lindbergh spoke 106 words—not exactly incorrect for the occasion, nor the shortest ever reply to a presidential statement, but evident all the same that the hero was going to live by his own lights (don't they all?), saying his piece and then standing aside. They couldn't have hoped for a more perfect hero in looks, origin, and ability. But they couldn't have got a more perfect hero in intractability. There would be no sentimental effluvia for quotation, no leap to Hollywood, no "shucks, fellows," no Bigger and Better. Recall, for comparison's sake, Daddy Browning rushing to the phone to inform the press when Peaches walked out on him. Recall Babe Ruth and his public gaffes. Recall Valentino and his exhibitions. And then realize that there is only one thing which jazz cannot contain, and that is dissent. Lindbergh subscribed to his own "communication," and he wasn't about to abet any other.

In other words, the God-sent leader would not lead the procession, nor even take part in it, and this was no Moses after all. Yet the public would have Lindbergh or no one. Chamberlin and Byrd both made it across the Atlantic later that year—the first to Berlin (or, more exactly, to a farm some seventy miles southwest of Berlin, where an enraged farmwife reportedly menaced the plane with a pitchfork), the second to Paris (after an emergency bailout into the Channel a few yards off the French shore)—but while both engaged the public and helped popularize a short spasm of pilot heroes, neither fulfilled the folk the way the lanky Swede had done. It is true that neither Chamberlin nor Byrd flew alone, and mishaps on both flights gave each a slightly ridiculous air, but these in themselves account for less than one percent of the gap between what they did and what Lindbergh had done—and would do, perhaps? The nation saw something of a kinship in Us, and only We would serve as the heraldic emblem of the day (insofar as such a day would order such an emblem). Thus the scream. Harold Stearns had called us "a democracy of mountebanks" with our "cranks, fanatics, mushroom religious enthusiasts, moral prigs, illiterate novelists," and such, and that is what we must have looked like to Lindbergh from his peculiar vantage away up at the top. How we looked to Coolidge was never made clear.

Hoover was more communicative. "That man," Coolidge said of his Secretary of Commerce in 1928, "has offered me unsolicited advice for six years, all of it bad!" (On the contrary: Hoover's advice was provoked by personal experience and a brilliant, farseeing mind. One of his advices no doubt related to stock speculation, the heedless expansion of which worried him, but Coolidge was determined to govern least—for the least was the best government—and Coolidge was one of America's "best" governors ever, perhaps the least of them all.) These were the leaders of the country, the chief executive and the heir apparent, as respectable as they come and, in Hoover's case, a very portrait of upward mobility, a former whiz kid and self-made millionaire who had proved an expert frustrater of starvation and chaos in Europe after the war. Now that the romance of aviation had arrived, after so much hesitation, for keeps, people great and small had some perspective in hand to apply to the enterprise of jazz, and could perhaps feel a little shame for their ready purchase of all that the "news" industry peddled. They had had some taste of action. Now it would not be so easy to categorize the fact of imbecile celebrities and that of the toplofty executive arena, for Lindbergh had thrown focus out of skew. If he, why not they? If some, why not all? Could there be only one such in all the land of all the era? Now let there be righteous leadership, finally now.

Would it come from Coolidge? Never. Yet they were prepared to landslide him in for a second elected term in 1928—Coolidge prosperity, you know. Even when they voted for Hoover, when Coolidge did not choose to run, they were opting not for action, but for more prosperity—as if the two do not, to a great extent, cohabit . . . as if one might sit still somewhere and prosper, making an omelet without breaking eggs. Not till Hoover failed to lead the nation out of the Depression did they vote for an "action" candidate in Franklin Roosevelt, but even so the seeds of action had been planted up and down the length of the decade in the persons of sports heroes, celebrities, and crazies, the People who Do Things. The only catch was that action was encouraged in them but discouraged in the real actors, the politicians, putting a funny color on the idea of leadership and then handing the word over to the wrong set. Machines happen fast; ideas change slowly. But here was an idea: to awaken from the sloth of inaction and move onward into the centuries—to take the world, as we had thought to do back in the imperialistic heyday of the 1890s. This was no tradition, admittedly, but tradition, like history, can sometimes be bunk.

So, with the scream for the reluctant hero ringing in our ears, let the newsreel carry us to the federal leader's encampment on summer holiday in the Black Hills of South Dakota, where Coolidge turns into the reluctant President. Whooping it up in the slobbering humidity of a bad July, Coolidge is vacationing, contrary to habit, in the West, where he holds office in a schoolhouse in Rapid City, some thirty miles from his residence at the thirty-room State Game Lodge. All is in order. All is normalcy with this sector of the world. Coolidge, neither beloved nor respected, but required, is a shoo-in for the Republican nomination next year, and the Presidency the following March. People fear that without Coolidge prosperity will dissolve and the occasional "crackpot" criticisms of the overplayed stock plunging will prove true. It is 1927, scarcely weeks after Lindbergh came home, his example a lustrous arraignment of what has been passing for leadership hereabouts since Progressivism died. No Republican has tendered even a mumbled bid for the presidential nomination. No Republican dares.

This is the time of the second international conference on naval disarmament, which opened in Geneva on June 20, and from its first politely dire moments, it is nothing like the one organized by Charles Evans Hughes. Either because Coolidge's Secretary of State Frank B. Kellogg and the American negotiator Hugh Gibson are no match for the foreigners, or because the goodwill fostered by Hughes has worn away, the conference is a shambles of slack cooperation. Italy and France refuse to take part. Those nations which are present are represented by second-rank delegates, with not a single prime officer of state at the table. The British send not diplomats but Navy men, who seek not limitation but expansion. Japan, now violently anti-American, will not discuss anything less than parity with the United States and England in the matter of warship tonnage. (Also, there are rumors that Japan has already advanced past the boundaries set by the Washington Treaty in shipbuilding, and is fortifying several Pacific islands.) Worst of all, the ancient Logan Act forbidding private citizens to engage in unofficial diplomacy is violated by one William B. Shearer, a loud "American, Christian, Protestant, and patriot" (he doesn't say in which order), who busies himself in Geneva doing a Bigger and Better number on behalf of American naval preparedness. The conference collapses, and some commentators credit Shearer's lobbying as being the final slap at global friendship and a much more effective weapon against peace than the Kellogg-Briand Pact of 1928 was for it. (In 1929 it came out that Shearer had been in the pay of a number of shipbuilding concerns and Bethlehem Steel. Said Samuel Wakeman, one of Bethlehem's vice-presidents, it was a "damn fool decision" to interfere with the conference. "I was just jazzed off my feet by Shearer." Oh, that word.)

But this all belongs to another newsreel. Ours, a popular issue, shows Coolidge at his sport in South Dakota, for Coolidge is an effective manipulator of jazz himself. Come see the Coolidge party arriving at the summer White House one bright morning; in fact, the Coolidges had pulled in the night before, but cameras cannot whir in the dark. Oh, and here's Coolidge the sportsman, holding up a trout as Grace Coolidge beams. And there's Coolidge at his fifty-fifth birthday party on July 4, modeling a flamboyant cowboy outfit, chaps, neckerchief, ten-gallon hat and all, presented to him by a local Boy Scout troup. There is even a minor controversy swirling around Coolidge this summer. Was it the matter of the Geneva Conference and some possible mishandling of it? No. It concerns the worms that Coolidge had used, *contra bonos mores*, to angle his trout.

Most people assumed that Coolidge had chosen South Dakota over Vermont for his vacation as a gesture to the agricultural America to which he had been so oblivious, especially in his veto of the McNary-Haugen Bill the previous February, farm relief to some, socialism to others. Not all the natives were thrilled by the visit, however. Carrying on in his father's style of tireless inquiry, Senator Robert La Follette, Jr., noted the million-dollar P.R. industry following Coolidge's every step and masquerading as news in a quiet summer, saying, "The President is attempting to make the farmer forget his veto of farm-relief legislation by wearing a ten-gallon hat and catching trout with milk-fed worms. The President will have to find better bait than this to catch votes in the west and northwest." But there was no chance that Coolidge would not win the next election, as everyone, including La Follette, knew. "If a blacksmith with a can-opener would climb Bartholdi's statue," wrote William Allen White, "he would find if he cut into the Goddess of Liberty these words graven into her heart: 'Let's get the car paid for.' Coolidge has poured into himself the incarnation of this sentiment. And that's why you can't beat Calvin Coolidge."

The alleged materialism of the machine age was as nothing compared to the remorseless hunger of prosperity, it appears, and many were the Americans determined on another four years of Coolidge luck. Republican party leaders, of course, had even more of a stake in Coolidge's reinstatement than the booboisie, and they were quick to debate the suggestion that eight years plus the year and a half of his assumption of Harding's term, which would be the Coolidge total if he served a full second term, were too much of a good king. Theodore Roosevelt, it was pointed out, stepped down after only one elected term because he had inherited most of McKinley's second four years. But Roosevelt, came the answer, had run again four years later.

To all this, to the questions of reporters and the entreaties of his fellow Republicans, the President said nothing, which, as we know, he said very well. But suddenly, on August 2, the fourth anniversary of Harding's death and Coolidge's famous after-midnight oath of office, Coolidge gave the press a statement at his office in the Rapid City schoolhouse: "I do not choose to run for President in nineteen twenty-eight." That was all he would say.

That was enough. If Lindbergh had given America the great adventure of 1927, Coolidge gave it the great ambiguity. What did he mean by those twelve words? Depending on how one read them, they amounted to yes, no, maybe, and all of the above. Was it: I do not *choose* to run (but will if pressed)? Or: I do not choose to *run* (but wouldn't mind being elected)? Or, possibly: *I* do not choose to run (but others may choose to run me anyway)? In any case, the dam that had been blocking Republican hopefuls was now busted, and the many could make their move, though the right of first refusal clearly went to Herbert Hoover.

Discussion among Americans was acute, amused, flustered, bored, short-winded, and suspicious of bunk, as discussions had been ever since the decade took off and became the twenties. One can imagine the new Ford jokes that would be trotted out to go with Coolidge's bombshell:

What did the Tin Lizzie say to Calvin Coolidge?
Me, too.

He did not choose to run. In New England, whence Coolidge came, when a man says something, he means the words he says. Coolidge was out of the running, definitively, and no interpretation need be made of his message—though it is said that he threw himself across his bed in despair when the 1928 Republican Convention, in Kansas City, nominated Herbert Hoover on the first ballot.

It is fitting that Hoover enter the presidential arena at this point, post-Lindbergh, for of the three Republican executives of the decade, he alone was fit to hold office. Had his advices and queries to Coolidge about uncurbed stock speculation not been faced down with a look, Hoover might have governed an era of true prosperity and been remembered for the uncountable Hooverstrasse of postwar Europe, not the Hoovervilles of the American Depression.

Orphaned at the age of eight, Hoover had been flung from the security of his Twainlike Iowa boyhood into early independence. He was one self-made man such as he described in *American Individualism,* a welfare capitalist more sensitive to ideas than to goods; to the pious money-grubbing of the Bruce Barton businessman image, Hoover brought a moral armament, a foundation on which not to hoard but to build. From his days as a mining engineer in such scattered territory as China, Western Australia, Egypt, and Mandalay, Hoover rose to take the most emergent position in modern America, as Lord of Commerce in the 1920s. Nobody, nobody in the world had more fact than he—but, paradoxically, he had more than a touch of resistance as well, and no informality whatsoever. There would be no photographs of Hoover in cowboy outfits. He was an adventurer, no doubt, but by the time he became prominent he looked like just another contented millionaire. He, at last, was a leader.

Lindbergh had the myth—still has it today—while Hoover had been merged into the frieze of marmoreal business-politics along with Mellon, Morgan, and that crowd. Unlike Ford and Coolidge, Hoover was not an item for joking familiarity; shrugging, they let him be famous. When he was nominated by his party, they accorded him the expected landslide. But they were as quick to turn on him when he failed to protect their misapprehension of how prosperity works as they were to turn on Lindbergh when he refused to live up to his fact on their terms.

By 1928, when Hoover faced Al Smith for the Presidency, Lindbergh had proved beyond any doubt that he had the potential for staying power such as few men were ever born to, attained, or had thrust upon them. His career cuts briefly into Hoover's at this point, in a telegram that Lindbergh sent to the candidate endorsing him for President: "Your qualities as a man and what you stand for, regardless of party, make me feel that the problems which will come before the country during the next four years will best be solved by your leadership." For himself, Lindbergh discovered that his qualities and what he stood for were arrogated by the press as public property, though he was not to follow the fabulous flight with anything like an encore.

Lindbergh not only retained his symbolic fascination, but confirmed it repeatedly in a tragic decade that alienated much of his support without putting a lid on his copy value. The more Lindbergh said or did as an actor or experienced as a prey, the greater his draw on the spectator. We have to step out of the twenties for a moment to see what became of this chivalric avatar, for Lindbergh's "downfall" as a universal hero is the key to the price which the American consciousness paid while getting raised by focus. We've seen the fast ordination and defrocking of numerous personalities so far; with Lindbergh, it was different. When in 1929 he married the daughter of Dwight Morrow, the American ambassador to Mexico, the nation cooed (though the engagement and wedding had been kept secret until the couple had left for their honeymoon). When the Lindberghs' firstborn child, Charles Augustus, Jr., was kidnapped and murdered in 1932, the nation was aghast and outraged. When Lindbergh clashed with the Roosevelt Administration over the logistics of airmail management and Lindbergh's personal stake in the aviation industry, the nation grew perplexed. And when Lindbergh swallowed his revulsion of public exhibit to throw his weight behind the isolationist America First movement to keep the United States out of the latest European war, some fraction of the nation denounced him and some other fraction cheered. Unfortunately, Lindbergh's antiwar stand coincided with what appeared to be pro-German sympathies and a curious lack of disgust for fascism; according to the diaries of Truman Smith, the American military attaché to the Reich, Lindbergh was in fact engaged in some delicate surveillance of Nazi air power and, on one visit, on a mission aimed at arranging with Goering for emigration for Germany's Jewish population. But all this was unknown at the time (Smith's memoirs are still unpublished), and as Lindbergh disdained justifying himself, his reputation suffered. By the late 1930s, the hero was despised by many for continuing to be what they had adored him for being in 1927. One recalls Kay Boyle's broadside mailed home from Paris back in the days of gleeful expatriation, about America's "conspiracy against the individual." For what, Trudy? For universal admiration, provided one's moral scruples are those of the majority? But what had happened to courage, skill, and faith—especially the faith of the audience?

It seems that heroes in life were expected to correspond to heroes in the popular arts, with all the pasteboard range and reinforcement of majority values of the Zane Grey cowboy. The rubbernecking of the crowd that sees never stopped looking for glimpses of Lindbergh, but his latter days were no fit denouement for so celebrated an entrance. Lindbergh hadn't changed; he had simply emerged through the false focus. An unceasing enemy of press intrusion, he refused to play by their rules, refused to polish his fact for them. He was the essence of a thing, that thing being unconditional individualism, useless for purposes of focus for its self-determination. Lindbergh might have said, reversing the terms of Napoleon, "I am not an event, but a man."

The reputation of Hoover, too, was defaced by the crowd's unwillingness to look an idea, rather than a photo, in the face, once it became clear that nothing that Hoover could do was going to ease off the Depression that steadily deepened during his tenure. The idea, again, was individualism, less bespangled on Hoover than on Lindbergh, but even more outgoingly stated, for Hoover had not the one but many facts in his dossier, and his book, *American Individualism*, tackled the concept of self-determination more rigorously than did Lindbergh's *We*. Both men were doers, but Hoover, furthermore, was a doer on the grand scale, an organizer, paternalistic with the downtrodden victims of devastated Europe and respectful of the laissez-faire with the American business community when he ruled the Commerce Department.

That in itself was Hoover's tragedy, for his Depression demanded not laissez-faire but paternalism in its medicine. He had been willing to reorganize the corrupt wasteland of Europe, but not the undefiled freedom of the United States—at least not until the final year of his regime, whose bashful but active federal interventions are largely forgotten today. It was Doctor Roosevelt who fully healed the patient with socialism and war production—*after* he learned from Hoover's example that tried economic cures were bootless. It was a lesson that the whole country learned, the hard way. But Hoover learned hardest of all, for no matter how he applied the tactics of tradition and the "rugged individualism" by which he had raised himself, the Depression just lay there and moaned. He was seeing everything that he looked for in America falling in on itself, and all of America blaming him for the failure. A Washington joke of the day had Hoover asking Andrew Mellon for a nickel so he could call a friend. "Here's a dime," says Mellon. "Call them both."

Almost no one had an inkling of what was to come when the twenties prepared to choose its third President, of course. To the electorate of 1928, Hoover was a substitute for Coolidge, rushed onto the field to make touchdowns for continued prosperity. Yet Hoover had already made it plain what he stood for. As with any Quaker, success in business was to be wished for, but not devoutly, not with the hypocritical identity manipulation of the Bruce Barton school. Belief in self, in others—in the inner light of wisdom, human but transcended by the ethic of God—was only the core of one's success, not the success itself. No one was better placed to debunk the "materialism" of the machine, for Hoover was a humanist as well as an engineer. And no one was likewise in a better position to fix the difference between individualism in its European and American guises. Hoover had crossed the Atlantic in 1918 with the memory of painting, architecture, and literature lighting his way, but his memoirs reveal a dispiriting confrontation between the Europe of art and the Europe of politics, with imperialism, vindictiveness, xenophobia, larceny, and duplicity not defeated by cataclysm but actually encouraged.

This was the basis for *American Individualism,* Hoover's credo. Europe's antidemocratic systems made for "individualism run riot," whether under monarchies or socialism; any new egalitarianism in Russia was as putrid as that old version devised for the French Revolution. Like many other Americans before him, Hoover pointed to the tumultuous mob as the variable of chaos in stable societies. "The crowd is credulous," Hoover wrote. "It destroys, it consumes, it hates, and it dreams—but it never builds."

Man it is who builds, in solo flight: this was the Lindbergh idea, anticipated by Hoover in his book five years earlier. But none of this was of moment to the voters when they chose between Hoover and Al Smith in 1928. So little had been happening in the land of change and resistance that the only two campaign issues were Prohibition and Catholicism, specifically in that Smith wanted to repeal the former and happened to adhere, at least nominally, to the latter. Neither party even remembered to suggest, as earlier, a U.S. participation in the World Court; it was a tidy campaign, very domestic.

Smith, too, had been nominated on the first ballot when the Democrats met in Houston. As it was worked out, the party platform included a plank for enforcement of Prohibition, and Smith duly pledged himself to enforce any law on the books, but he had made no secret of his distaste for this law. With the two major candidates named, the drys massed up for battle, linking "Rum and Romanism" in their by-campaign, while the Republicans emphasized prosperity. "Republican *efficiency* has filled the workingman's dinner pail—and his gas tank *besides*," stated a party advertisement in an orgy of out-of-sync italics, "made the telephone, radio, and sanitary plumbing *standard* household equipment. And placed a whole nation in the *silk stocking* class." For his part, Hoover stood behind Prohibition, calling it "a great social and economic experiment, noble in motive and far-reaching in purpose." There Hoover disappoints, for the evidence to the contrary stood at right angles to sense and order, lit by neon for all to see.

The election of 1928 was a filthy contest. Before it was over, the mud slung at Smith for his religion, his wetness, and his city strut covered him from his toes to the tip of his famous brown derby. Not only Republicans, but even some Democrats excoriated the ghetto slicker; this being a day when people weren't afraid to name their enemies, the prominent Democrat and bishop, James Cannon, Jr., fought his party's candidate as a deputy of "the foreign-populated city called New York."

1928 was a strange contest, too, very much of its time in its Wall Street orientation. The stock ticker had already begun to register the year and a half of irregular behavior that would culminate in The Crash, but even so not only the Republicans, but the Democrats tried to ally themselves with "the chicken in every pot." After the debacle of 1924 in Madison Square Garden, the Democrats had shaped up remarkably, culling drys and wets, rurals and urbans into a restive hammock cradled by the new party chairman, John J. Raskob, a bigwig of the General Motors Corporation, the Bankers Trust Company, and the Du Ponts and until his appointment a Republican. New to politics but old to business, Raskob turned Democrat with ease, making the point that whilom party alignments would not do for the new times. Everyone, now, was for Wall Street. As the old joke goes, if Bryan had been alive to see it, this would have killed him.

So, on the face of it, the 1928 election was a battle between Coolidgeism and Coolidgeism, all for prosperity and prosperity for all (normalcy was officially over)—or so the two parties would have had one believe. In fact, while Hoover swore to continue with Coolidge's policies—what on earth could he have meant by that, given that Coolidge had none?—he was too progressive an officer not to take his office in active charge, and Smith had the highly un-Coolidgelike idea of enacting some relief legislation for the farmer, if not precisely the price-fixing McNary-Haugen Bill. But back of it all, in the public's mind, was that blunt, taciturn, honest, cool, cool nobody Calvin Coolidge. The battle was waged in his honor, the winner to be whoever seemed most capable of creating a "whole idea" charade of the businessman-Christ. Taking in the Republican Convention, Will Rogers reported that his mind wandered during a speech, and when he pricked up his ears again he gathered that the speaker was singing the Lord's praises. He was. The subject of the discourse was Calvin Coolidge.

Election Day belonged to Hoover; 21,391,000 voters picked him to 15,016,000 for Smith. (Norman Thomas, the Socialists' choice, didn't clear 300,000.) In the Electoral College, the Democrats could not even take the so-called Solid South, but with Catholicism and liquor in his way, it is perhaps surprising that Smith carried any states south of New York. As it was, he won only eight—Arkansas, Louisiana, Mississippi, Alabama, Georgia, South Carolina, and in the north, Rhode Island and Massachusetts. Even Smith's home state, New York, went for Hoover (though it elected a Democratic governor, Franklin Roosevelt). Will Rogers framed an imaginary wire to the Pope: "Unpack!" and the bulls on Wall Street chuckled, "Four more years of prosperity!" Indeed, market prices promptly rose to record levels, with Radio Corporation of America, always an exemplary stock, at 400, and that November of '28 brought the volume of trading to an incredible high, with some days exceeding the six-million share level.

Prices would soon fall, however, and rise again, and fall again, for another eleven months; that's the way it works, one was told, should one have been foolish enough to ask. Wall Street wanted it the way it was—no interference—and so, it appears, did a majority of the people . . . or did they? Who knows how many of Hoover's constituents were hoping for another Coolidge and how many were hoping for Hoover himself, the "Great Engineer"? They had had the chance to see what initiative can achieve; they had seen, graphically, the difference between achievement and just being there. "Our place must be great among the nations," Theodore Roosevelt had told them. It could be, and now was the time. Even today, having bungled several chances to ensure republican reason in the global community, ours remains the only "more perfect union" on the globe, and the last defense against what the prescient De Tocqueville could not foresee— the great and imposing mass of a species at large, the world mob. Here was the cusp of responsibility, the twenties—responsibility to ourselves, and to the will and ideals of the West.

Did anyone know? (How many know today?) Did the American voters of '28 think or merely react? Did they see in Hoover what they saw in Lindbergh? Lindbergh they had *seen*, not clearly—for that came after, and then they changed their minds about him—but, dimly, they must have sensed the concept in 1927, for nothing was more relevant that year than Lindbergh and his flight: the right time (an age of jazz), the right place (Romance City), the right man (We). True, no one sensed anything who called Lindbergh "Lucky Lindy"—that was planning and proficiency, not luck. Nor did it show any grasp of the event to dub him "the Lone Eagle," as if no one had ever flown solo before. But whether they got it or not, they knew what they wanted— a national biotype, something in the way of self-expression that could be met halfway. Elmer Davis, charting the Lindbergh binge, asked, "What conceivable impulse could have stirred up a nation impatient of exactitude and devoted to ballyhoo to fling itself . . . at the feet of a man who is everything that the average American is not? It suggests some dissatisfaction with the way we are going, a feeling that the things we are doing are not the things that ought to be done, or that our way is not the right way to do them; it suggests a pervasive insecurity, a loss of confidence."

Just so—but was this confidence to be won from any of our titular leaders? Hoover, for all his visibility, was a phlegmatic and cere- monial figure, unable to dramatize himself, not to be seen. Lindbergh, too, refused to dramatize himself, but in his case action was enough. Action is fact. Hoover's action, by 1928, was a thing of the past, something for books. The hero must make himself known to all with the national entente of success; that is his secret.

Not that it matters. Either way they're going to get you if you frustrate their focus. Both Hoover and Lindbergh were stars in the twenties who came to grief in the following decade, for different reasons, but for the while they have lit up the heavens after years of dark malaise. They feel climactic, though there is a lesson to be learned yet in Lower Manhattan, and the tale is not over. Still, this is the brightest moment in the play of events, when "For what, Trudy?" at last gets its answer. For what: because it's there. Because we are. Because not to is to decline. Because the machine is power but man, American man, drives the machine. Lindbergh, one such man and Hoover, another such, expressed something coherent in that collage called, variously, the postwar recovery, normalcy/prosperity, the Jazz Age, and—the only correct term—the twenties. One is about to get married, the other to be President. And the nation that cried for Coolidge is in for a surprise.

ELEVEN

They

Such a decade as this one, festooned with gaud both human and theoretical, must go out with a bang. Lindbergh's destiny is discharged in ensuing years (with growing resentment from the press and a discovery by liberals that winners mostly see no fascination in losers), and even Hoover's brief trial in the unloving limelight drops three of its four years in the thirties, past our border. Something happened, however, with which to close this book on an uproarious note—and beautifully timed, too, in the last months of 1929.

The mad-scene finale is not the stock-market crash per se (though this yields bang enough as the big bull market heaves to and hits the earth with a noise), but rather a crisis of leadership. The Wall Street disaster was symptomatic of a condition that had plagued the land since the war had ended, leadershipitis, virulent in both its somnolent and aggravated stages. Ever since the repudiation of Wilson, we had been having trouble in coming to terms with the idea of guidance, in setting out exactly what we required of a captain and in finding captains to fit the bill. First came the false normalcy, then the false (as will be seen) prosperity, both of them all-pervasive, enthralling, and, finally, debunked. Teapot Dome, the depression of 1921-22, and the realization that the United States had never felt less normal all tore the mask off normalcy, and the stock-market crash will shortly finish off prosperity. By early 1930, peering around the corner, we note that Harding and Coolidge, gods for a day, are in twilight, along with Hoover, innocent of crime but guilty of being in charge of the bank when the ink ran red.

The example for leadership, obviously, was Lindbergh, but he had no interest in holding office; he had logged his public service, of its sort, in the thirty-three and a half hours of the flight. In their capacity for achievement, Lindbergh and Hoover—but Lindbergh most particularly for the glamour in his fact—proved that Bigger and Better was there in human as well as technical terms. What America en masse proved, however, was that the concept which lay behind Bigger and Better, the absolute of individuality, was too slow for this dynamic age. The folk could not get the concept, would only see the men, not the Things. While Lindbergh's flight was just what the nation might have ordered—Bigger than dying in a mine cave-in and Better than flagpole sitting—Lindbergh was and was not. Was, for his broad appeal as a person; was not, because he figured that persons belong to themselves.

The people didn't see it that way, and thus ended the national love affair with Lindbergh. MEN ARE WHAT THEY DO should stand as a kind of synoptic headline for this whole decade of headlines; it explains why there was so little understanding of time and place by those who were there then, and why the era is recalled more as a madcap fete of vo-dee-o-do than as a time of great change in American mores. How can we of today expect to see the age properly when they themselves, living it, saw so little, though seeing was all that they did? Events, not achievements, were the trade of the twenties, and celebrities, not ideas, provided the ware. Implicit in Lindbergh's reaction to the national shivaree was a suggestion that America attempt to separate the "fact" from the facts, to apprehend a concept, not a personality.

No chance. The machinery was too well set up to admit of perspective. Fitting the difficult Lindbergh in as best it could, and limply reviving as much of the "humanitarian-engineer" in Hoover's legend as seemed appropriate for a President-elect, the media greeted 1929 with joy. This year would be the cats (voguish short form for the old-hat "cat's pajamas"), no doubt, as much fun and profit as before, only more so. There would be the thrills, chills, and spills of fame made, unmade, or confirmed, and there would be jazz. Even Mickey Mouse bowed to the prevailing hooey, "doing" Jolson in a cartoon, *"The Jazz Fool"*; and on Broadway in *Follow Thru*, a "musical slice of country club life," Zelma O'Neal opened the year with the apt anthem, "I Want to Be Bad." Around about it all, that crowd would stand there and take it in.

The awareness of the national will to attainment, the *self*-awareness as reinspired by We, was more or less retired by 1929, along with the silent film stars who couldn't match their voices to their personae. Not that Lindbergh's flight had been forgotten; on the contrary, in some ways its effects were still being felt. But as the capstone of its time, it was hard to live up to. They had tried to paint Lindbergh as the average American, but he wasn't and everyone knew it. We, in the end, was They, not We—it was Lindbergh and *The Spirit of St. Louis*. We could share in such a deed up to a point, just as we shared Hoover's vision from the outside, liking and believing it without bothering to grasp it. It was too grand a commotion. It lacked that reassuring informality.

How much easier it was to respond to Roy Riegel's tremendous sixty-yard run in the Rose Bowl Game in Pasadena on New Year's Day of '29. Football was scrutable and college was amusing, so this meeting of the University of California and Georgia Tech was a dandy way to take one's heroism. Throughout the decade, football had become something of a minor industry, with charges of "professionalism" being leveled at schools with an active recruiting system (the University of Iowa was suspended from the Big Ten Conference, briefly, for its lack of academic procedure in sorting out a team), but professionalism made for exciting football and the game was catching on with the masses. The California-Georgia Rose Bowl in particular demonstrated the human—informal—character of sports in Riegel's wild race to the end zone, the talk of the season. In the second quarter of the game, Georgia fumbled the ball and Riegel, California's center, grabbed it up, eluding the enemy on all sides. Twisting and tacking to a clear path, he somehow lost his bearings, and when he had broken free he was facing the wrong direction, speeding like a demon for the wrong goal line. With a roar, California fans leaped to their feet, screaming, pointing, cursing . . . but who listens to advice from the stands when en route to a touchdown? A California halfback managed to intercept Riegel at the three-yard line and turn him around, but just then a pack of Rambling Wrecks fell on the center and a groan rose up in Pasadena. Georgia won the game, 8-7.

It was just the sort of inauguration a wild and wonderful year ought to have, and only added to the impression that all of America was dancing the Charleston on a diamond as big as the Ritz. For those who had never subscribed to resistance, or who had succumbed to the thrill of the change, it was like being the prime depositor in a bank of lore, every man and woman his own sheik and flapper with It and pep, all of them suckers and loving it. Even if the market took an occasional dive, prosperity reigned. Everything was jake. On the other hand, maybe the profile of 1929 is better filled out by the St. Valentine's Day Massacre than by "Wrong Way" Riegel—wild more than wonderful, diamond-hard and Charleston-quick and, as gangland killings go, altogether Bigger and Better.

Prohibition was still there, and if anything its abuses of liberty were more advanced than before. In January of '29, Michigan law handed the prescribed penalty of life imprisonment to the mother of ten children for her fourth offense of the Volstead Act—selling two pints of liquor. Asked for a comment, that upright man and spokesman for "temperance," Clarence True Wilson, nodded his assent: "When one has violated the Constitution four times, he or she should be segregated from society to prevent the production of subnormal offspring." In truth, the rank violation of the Constitution had been committed by this Wilson and his vindictive fellows with their repressive amendment. You could tell by the blood on their hands.

Much of it was the blood of criminals, but only much—by no means all. Bystanders and innocent suspects were shot down all over the land—more by federal agents than by gangsters—heedless drinkers were poisoned, lamed, or blinded, twenty million dollars was thrown away yearly on police busts, and the very image of order was contaminated by the attempted Constitutional amortization of organized crime and police corruption. It was in Chicago, naturally, on a snowy February 14, that the most brazen of Prohibition's coin was minted, in a garage at 2122 North Clark Street.

The St. Valentine's Day Massacre marked the high tide of a feud that had been brewing between the Bugs Moran gang and the Capone mob for months. Moran's crew, passed to him through the consecutive ... retirements ... of Dion O'Banion, Hymie Weiss, and "Schemer" Drucci, were the victims; Capone's, the malefactors. Neither of the two leaders was present: Capone was vacationing in Florida at the time, and Moran, who *was* to have been there, arrived at the scene a few minutes late, and so missed out on his own murder.

Yeah, see, what starts it all is this deal that Capone makes with the Detroit Purple gang, who are the purveyors of Old Log Cabin whiskey, a drinkable but overpriced blend. Old Log Cabin is the brand which King Capone assigns to Moran's turf, and Moran balks, which is a most unfortunate way for Moran to be behaving to Capone, since Capone is not a man to be joyful when his business associates are feeling mutinous. Moran makes an alternative arrangement for a cheaper Canadian brand, but his clients turn out to suffer a nostalgic preference for Old Log Cabin, which causes Moran to feel very sore and unloved. Seething, Moran goes back to Capone. "I'll take the old arrangement," says he. "No deal," says Capone.

So Moran takes time out to ponder the set-up, and soon he is coming to the conclusion that if he is to stay in business—not to mention retain his self-respect as the captain of his territory—he is going to have to borrow some Old Log Cabin, a project for which his gang has a noted talent. Time passes, and Capone gets to noticing that shipments of a certain brand of whiskey are beginning to disappear. He is suspecting foul play, and he has an idea whom to suspect. After a gigantic cargo of Old Log Cabin comes to be borrowed on its way from Detroit to Chicago, Capone decides he has been patient to the far side of generosity, and suggests to his cohort that it is better for all concerned if certain drafts made on his Old Log Cabin account are to be refused in future. Whereupon, a Capone spy infiltrates the Moran sector, wins Moran's confidence by slipping him some shipments of Old Log Cabin, and sets him up in the following manner. "Got a truckload for you," says he to Moran, "right off the river, cool and clean, fifty-seven dollars the case." Says Moran in reply, "Yes."

Moran and Capone's agent agreed that the whiskey would be dropped off at Moran's North Clark Street garage at 10:30 A.M. on St. Valentine's Day. A bitterly cold winter morning such as Chicago specializes in, the time was ideal for a hit. "Another bootlegger raid," murmured Alphonsine Morin, the proprietor of a boardinghouse across the street, when she saw a police van pull up at the Moran place to disgorge three policemen and two plainclothesmen at about 10:50. A few people in the vicinity heard a sustained mechanical chattering and two smallish explosions—a truck backfiring in the garage, probably—and four curious pairs of eyes, attracted by the noise, watched the five men come out again. Only this time the two plainclothesmen marched in front of the three policemen, their hands in the air and guns leveled at them. They all got in the van and rode off. Strange, no?

Very strange—so much so that neighbor Jeanette Landesman came out to take a look. With the help of a man in her building, she got the jammed door of the garage open, and the man went inside to see what was up, giving way to an impetuosity unusual in Chicagoans of the twenties, who if anything were likely to mistake the noise of a truck backfiring for machine-gun fire, not the reverse. The man came running out saying that the place was "full of dead men," and Mrs. Landesman called the police.

The story of the St. Valentine's Day Massacre, as reconstructed by the police, was overreported and overdramatized, and has been overemphasized ever since—including here—except in that something that won so much emphasis in its time, however louche, deserves some presentation in the annals. No one, of course, was ever arrested for the crime (though some retaliation from Moran gang survivors attempted to even the score), and this latest evidence of the fungus on the nether face of the big diamond of prosperity was something for the nation to consider. It was one of the more smartly planned maneuvers in the history of the gang war, for disguising Capone's

three front men as officers of the law led the seven Moran boys to
think it just another police roundup, and they dutifully obeyed orders
to turn and face the wall without going for their guns. It was then
that the other two Capone stooges, hidden before, came forward, one
with a Thompson submachine gun and the other with a twelve-gauge
shotgun. Before the Morans knew what was happening, they were
sprayed with machine-gun fire, row upon row of bullets back and
forth between ears and thighs—so thoroughly that some of them came
intricately apart as they fell. The shotgun, on hand to dispose of any
diehard twitching, was applied in two cases. Then the two gunmen
handed their arms to the three "policemen" and stoutly marched
themselves away.

Smoothly directed, smoothly acquitted, the massacre failed in only
one respect: that Moran was late and thus missed the party. It was
generally known that Capone was behind the whole thing, but with
his gift for overkill, the king of Chicago was not only in Florida that
morning, but actually managed to be in conference with the district
attorney of Miami. Incredibly, one of the seven Morans, Frank
Gusenberg, survived the shooting, though he died moments later in
the hospital. "They never gave you a chance, Frank," said police
sergeant Clarence Sweeney. "Who shot you?"

"Nobody shot me," Gusenberg replied, true to his code.

(For a while, some thought that the murders had been pulled off by
crooked cops; so corrupt had the world of booze and jazz become that
this was widely believed until some bit of evidence threw it out of
possibility.)

All prosperity is not to be summed up by this mobsters' picnic.
But much of the rudderless spiral of the late twenties, the years of the
"endless" boom (right; it was also known at one time that the earth
was flat and rode through the sky on the back of a giant turtle) is not
unlike the round of life in Prohibitive Chicago in its easy pickin's
morale and distrust of/belief in the powers that promoted it. It was a
cynical subscription, but it sold. This is not to say that Andrew
Mellon or J. P. Morgan are comparable to Al Capone, even if some of
the most admired millionaires of the time, such as Samuel Insull, were
shortly to be revealed as having gotten their gains by what might

leniently be called legal stealth—and Insull, too, was of Chicago. But prosperity was in one sense rotten underneath, because its rationale was founded on several grand hoaxes—one, that the country *as a whole* was prospering; two, that since one couldn't beat jazz, one might as well join it; three, that American leadership conduced to whoever had last been voted into office; and four, that all of the above could continue indefinitely.

Oh, it was, no question, a snazzy time, much more fragile than it admitted to being, and indeed a lot of the snazz now reads, sounds, or looks like a protesting too much. At the end of the twenties the Ku Klux Klan was on the outs, the old Tin Lizzie had raised cudgels in the marketplace with the spiffy cars of choice, William Jennings Bryan and all that he had represented was gone, either regrouped or repented or just gone, the dialect of *Amos 'n' Andy* was heard in the land, and expatriates were hurrying home to be in on the fun. It was the high twenties: wine ran in the streets. As F. Scott Fitzgerald wrote, "Even when you were broke, you didn't worry about money because it was in such profusion around you." Festal days, from the look of things—wrong-way yardage at the Rose Bowl and just desserts in red-hot Chicago. This is the twenties as we most want to recall them—the Jazz Age, might as well admit it—when the snazz decided to see just how far it could go . . . and then fell right off the flat edge of the earth.

If one looks hard enough, one can find examples of antisnazz in 1929, but then there are always exceptions—just because William Faulkner wrote *Sartoris* and *The Sound and the Fury* doesn't mean that all that many people were going to read them. In the world of the theater, for example, as the new year rolled in on Broadway, the solipsistic Chicagoan spunk of *The Front Page* (just ending its run) was mitigated by the gentle *White Lilacs,* an operetta with music pinched from Chopin and plot remotely modeled on his life. Not only Chopin and—by way of romantic gala—George Sand, but Heinrich Heine, Giacomo Meyerbeer, Franz Liszt, Marie d'Agoult, and Honoré de Balzac flitted in and out of the script, lifting their voices in song set to one or another of the etudes or nocturnes. What could be less snazzy? But then *White Lilacs* was rather overshadowed by *Animal*

Crackers, a more naturalistic endeavor in which the proletarian Groucho, Harpo, Chico, and Zeppo Marx broke up Margaret Dumont's posh Long Island house party. Later on, the fall of '29, James Thurber and E. B. White produced their spoof of Freudian investigation, *Is Sex Necessary?*, a reply to the psychoanalytic craze in the form of a manual on American amour, as in this caption showing woman busy with saucepans while man, seated nearby, fumes: "The female, equipped with a Defense far superior in polymorphous ingenuities to the rather simple Attack of the male, developed, and perfected, the Diversion Subterfuge. The first manifestation of this remarkable phenomenon was fudge-making."

Clearly, the debunkers were in their element in '29—but where were the proponents of any positive moral structure? Normalcy, while a reaction *against,* was at least predicated on spiritual imperatives, and was in search of something *for.* Prosperity, however, was Godless. The Chrysler and Empire State buildings were going up, engaged in a height contest, literalistic images for this age of winners. What did the winners believe? They believed this: winner take all.

It's time to dissect this prosperity, now in its last of what Frederick Lewis Allen pointed out were the seven fat years (need one be reminded as to what came after them in Joseph's Egypt?). On the skin of it, much is to be admired. The total national income, for example, had climbed from sixty-five billion dollars in 1922 to nearly ninety billion in 1928. President Hoover, in 1929, even managed to get his version of farm relief passed only three months into his reign, the Agricultural Marketing Act, a measure without the socialistic federal subsidy scheme of the McNary-Haugen Bill. Thus late prosperity attempted to do what Coolidgeism couldn't—renegotiate the fading situation of the farmer. Still, only twenty-two percent of the population was either wealthy or comfortable. The other seventy-eight percent consisted of families subsisting on incomes of less than $3000 or individuals on less than $1500. Farming production had saturated the agricultural market, debilitating the already weakened income base of the farmer. The price of coal had dropped with the adaptation of new energy sources. Mass absorption of "soft" (i.e., consumer) markets, despite appearances, was falling behind production in most industries. If credit for the small business and the farm was hard to swing, credit for the stock speculator and the foreign gamble was all too available, even in the unstable and disorganized American banking system. Pace prosperity, something like 8 percent of the nation's banks, mostly small Middletown operations, closed up shop between 1926 and 1928, the high water of Coolidgeism.

Proponents and beneficiaries of prosperity were, in the main, unrealistic and shortsighted, whether academicians, Wall Street lords, or men in the street, but then the study of economics, always a fractured and quarrelsome discipline, had not caught up with the postwar situation. The few critics who looked askance at the throes of the bull market were looked upon in turn as crackpots. The delicate distension of the investment structure of the twenties seems so clear to us now, with foreign ventures overextended and quasi-paper speculation at home so rife, with the inscrutable pyramids of the holding companies so vulnerable to failure from below, and with the tricky stock pool taking thousands of gamblers in a roller coaster ride gradually up and hurtling down . . . why did it seem so okay to them then? Why, at least, didn't the insiders know?—for when the tornado hit, everyone blew away together.

It has been said that one learns from a bust, not from a boom, but most people don't learn anything either way. Only new buyers can get the motion toward high-paying prices off the ground, and new buyers there were aplenty in the late twenties. Yet they had a perfectly reasonable bust to learn from as recently as 1926, when the great Florida land boom got eighty-sixed on overextension, fraud, and two acts of God.

If California, why not Florida? the hypothesis ran—and Florida was even closer to where more of the money was. Move! Retire! Commute! Or just: Invest! By 1925, whole cities had sprung up on the east coast of the state, the west coast was opening up just as speedily, and the future seemed to hold no limit on what was to come (which is the very pith of what the word "boom" means to its clients; they assume the infinite). It was a chance to settle a frontier with machine-age proficiency. The Ford idea processed these covered wagons; anonymous speculator pools led the lot auctions; and of course P.R. created the promotion: "Go to Florida . . . where you sit and watch at twilight the fronds of the graceful palm, latticed against the fading gold of the sun-kissed sky."

People were wild to buy, many for purposes of owning the land, but most simply to hold and resell it at fabulous profit. Buy at $10 an acre—sell at $20! $45! $60! Why, Miami seemed at times to be inhabited exclusively by real-estate agents; so thick was the bargaining back and forth that the authorities were forced to pass a law forbidding the sale of property—even the handling of a map—in the street to relieve the congestion. Tractors, dredges, pipes, steam shovels, and land-fill equipment were in such evidence as to be worthy of a special census solely for machines, and Miami, one of the fastest-growing towns in the history of the West, was hard put just to keep up a minimum of public utilities to service its escalating population. From thirty thousand in 1920 it bulged up to seventy-five thousand just five years later—counting residents only, this, not transients—and S. Davis Warfield, president of the Seaboard Air Line Railway, gave it another ten years in which to clear a million.

Such was the captivation of prosperity that people saw it as a perpetual motion of ever-increasing circles, a welfare capitalism doing good for all as it did well for a few in a Bigger and Better world without end, amen. Those who could afford only a small patch of land bought with the confidence that within a few years they could erect a house on it; more than a few were bilked by a lying prospectus or a cagey sales pitch ("lush Venetian environment" meant swampland, not gondolas) and ended up with property in a "city" that the developers hadn't bothered to build. Far more got themselves entangled as amateur real-estaters in the trap of binders, options, assessments, and defaults and found that land values could go down as well as up. By mid-1926, an overbought market had slowed the boom, and in September a pair of hurricanes murdered what was left of it—the second one, with special ferocity, right at the heart of the action in Miami.

The ghastly destruction by wind and rain didn't cause the great Florida land bust, which was already on its way, but it dramatized it with an elegant sense of timing. By 1927, whole sections of the state were approximately bankrupt if not leveled; the banks themselves were failing like dollar watches. Just as other parts of the nation were moving into the big-time of prosperity, Florida sank, economically halving itself by the year.

Easy money. Or, rather, easy come, easy go, while we're quoting homilies. As Fitzgerald said, it was in such profusion about you, you felt certain that the right tip and a small capital investment would take you, in a limousine, to a mansion on the Street of Winners. After all, this was one of the nation's traditional promises: anyone can make it. The only problem was that the nation had made its promises before the machine, before robber baron industry and Wall Street skyrocketing. Yes, there was speculation in 1800, too—but that was also a time when farmers were gentlemen and doing rather better than subsistence. We had traveled some space since a gentleman-farmer turned President, named Thomas Jefferson, could project commerce as "the handmaid of agriculture": the language of making it had changed. So, perhaps, had the value.

Not that there is anything wrong with material gain, but to make it overnight on a fluke is to misconstrue what making it is made of. There is a moral substructure implied in the system of success and failure—an achievementness, as it were. As the Florida land disaster proved (and on a scale too grand for anyone to miss, whether or not he had been in on it to learn at first hand from the mistake), there is no get-rick-quick to be erected on marshland; there is little get-rich-quick to be found anywhere. Anyone at all can buy a winning sweepstakes ticket, but anyone at all is not necessarily a winner, and there are just so many winning tickets to be had. We've seen a parade of winners in these pages so far, of every stripe—Ford, Mellon, Capone, Guinan, Tunney, McPherson, Walker, Barton. If one hadn't yet been willing to admit that the twenties put America in touch with a new sense of itself, surely that lineup would convince one at last. *Never* before that 1920 census and its city majority did the nation sport this startling profile. We have never lacked for blackguards, scarlet women, and mountebanks filling up gaps between the inventors and presiders—but never were they so dense of kind, so deeply in fashion. Never before were things made so much of so quickly, what with the immediacy of the microphone and the wire and the sudden satrapy of media impact. Compared to the twenties—light-fingered if heavy-handed, quick to touch and take, looking all around and thinking, Let's see, what shall we start next?—the America that preceded it looks like something old and bulky and slow. A hippo. A bireme. A thirty years' war.

That was another America, of smashed precedents, of a value system worth fighting for that now had to be fought for. As the Ku Klux Klan, as Willa Cather's novels, as the case for the prosecution in the Scopes Trial, or as normalcy, resistance dug its heels in on change, but what can you do?: prosperity just shoved it all aside, along with the farming community and organized labor, two polities whose difficulties put the lie to this golden age. Once there was Jefferson, Randolph, Clay, Calhoun; there was even Bryan, once—all country folk. But these days history was being recorded in the cities, by Mellon of Pittsburgh, Capone of Chicago, Guinan and Walker of New York, and those left out on the land were turning into virtual outlanders. Certainly, there was no lure of get-rick-quick out in the corn belt, nor in the small Middletowns of the industrial Midwest, and the boondocks of Florida had to take on the hustle of Urbantown while the acres changed hands. City people were setting the tone.

Yep. The national profile was undergoing definitive revision, and the Czolgoszes were beginning to find themselves in statu quo with the Coopers and Johnsons. Not only in city politics, but in the culture as well, non-WASPS were invigorating the mainstream with alternative folkore; just to pick one example, Irving Berlin's city ragtime and very slightly blues-shaded melodies were being hailed as *the* all-American construction for popular song, though—as already noted—Berlin was raised in the cosmopolitan Lower East Side of New York among barely naturalized foreigners. Berlin naturalized himself fast, but, really, how natural was it? It was natural for New York, all right, but New York is not your common or garden-variety American city.

"Foreign-populated," Bishop Cannon had called it when Al Smith was proposed for President; sometimes it seemed so. In Chicago, the gangsters stood out for, among other things, their foreign (mainly

Italian) names, especially when compared with the city administrative and police personnel who supposedly opposed them, the Thompsons and the McSwiggins. But New York bore the savor of a vast Irish, German, and Jewish descent, and even the "pure"-sounding "Al Smith" belonged to a Roman Catholic. Very ethnic, New York. It was easy to believe Smith's no doubt fictitious tale of a stunt that he pulled as president of the New York Board of Aldermen, when that largely Irish aggregation was about to vote on an ordinance dangerous to Smith's plans. Determined that the voting be postponed, Smith had a page burst in on the meeting and shout, "Alderman, your saloon is on fire!" The room emptied in seconds.

The white Protestant actuation of American habit still dominated the era nationally, however. If Hollywood was regarded with suspicion as the citadel of Jewish producers, if the black emergence in entertainment deliberately emphasized the exotica of Afro-Americana, its "low down" and "diga-diga-doo," the arenas of banking, the law, and national politics—the real leadership—were still the preserve of long-established America. It was for this reason that Lindbergh's action of and Hoover's expression of American valor had to count heavily, as much for what they represented of the nation's manhood as what they did as men. Winners they were, too, as leaders must be, and living bars to any possibility of a counterculture in the overflow of prosperity. No wonder Congress, when planning the Immigration Act of 1924, wanted to set its quotas for foreign ingress, as apportioned by nationality, according to the census of 1890 (in 1929 it was moved up to the 1920 census), thus preferring the more assimilable newcomers of northeastern Europe and limiting even them to 150,000 a year. The very heart of normalcy beat for a ban on Europeanism, and Coolidge, inheriting normalcy as it blew up into prosperity, held the line. "Those who do not want to be partakers of the American spirit ought not to settle in America," he explained, for the benefit of the radical legions. "America must be kept American."

The tempo was change, and the hit-or-miss ballyhoo of jazz brought out the mob in people. As if to prove De Tocqueville right, it substituted weekend "winners" for achievers. Fame replaced action in this amoral climate, for the "fact" underlined the one and obscured the other. What was Daddy Browning's achievement? What Kelly's? What Guinan's? What Dempsey's? We had so succumbed to celebrity sell that we expected the real winners to behave like the pseudowinners—that is what focus does; it equalizes variables. Inadvertently mocking the very idea of individual accomplishment, it leaped to the imbecile conclusion that anyone could win, that everyone should win, Bigger and Better for all with no investment in growth or self-realization and no perception of what greatness entailed. Every man was to be his own pocket celebrity, and get-rich-quick was a good way to start.

The New Era, they called it. It may sound like a movement—something to be founded and maintained—but it was just a synonym for Coolidgeism, which was there, anyway. There was some earnest discussion of the higher intentions of the New Era, especially as regards the beneficent utility of welfare capitalism, and it is true that in an industrial nation such as this, a healthy economy is impossible without a free and thriving business plant. But business had been thriving long before the application of the term, "New Era." This rationale for what was necessary was a self-congratulatory afterthought typical of this businessman's age; one half expects to learn that Bruce Barton came up with it at a conference of advertising men at the express requisition of Calvin Coolidge.

Calling the twenties the New Era sounds particularly hollow when one considers that the phrase was most frequently invoked later on by stock-market speculators, for most of the million or so Wall Street touts weren't even legitimately connected with the world of business to begin with. What a vague word, "business"—does it mean the making and selling of commodities (i.e., industry) or the extracurricular discount gambling on commodities via stock certificates? To the indiscriminately big spenders of the bull market, business was both, and business was all—and business was just fine because business leaders were sweepingly optimistic about the endless cycle of the New Era, especially as buoyed up by the untamed riot of stock speculation.

On all sides, from Wall Street to the universities, theorists arose to justify the economic honeymoon. "They defended speculation," wrote Frederick Lewis Allen, "on the ground that the great men of all time had been adventurers, that Columbus, the American Revolutionists, and the pioneers of the West had been in heavy bondage to speculative fortune, and even that 'Christ himself took a chance.'" (There's the Savior again, sitting in at boardroom summit meetings with the money bosses.) The citation of the above achievers as antecedents of the fanatic riders of the ticker tape is as outrageous a swindle as could be made of a juxtaposition of the past and the present; what fools these heroes be, these stock plungers in heavy bondage to fortune. The confidence they showed, like that of the Florida land investors, reminds one more of a fool rushing in than of any great adventure. An American confidence in self-determinism had been reduced, from its free-speaking heyday in the Old West, to simple greed, and even after Teapot Dome, belief in the leaders of the business community was widespread. If they said a thing is so, then so it was, and what they were saying was "Business is sound"— whatever that means.

Trusting the godly powers of Wall Street, the stock speculators hitched their wagons to slogans of Individualism and Achievement without connecting with the concepts. Just as the news media, the movies, and radio fabricated cultural symbols out of clay, borrowing the shape of moral imperatives but not the substance, so did the New Era mythologize ancient and nonnational trade into something peculiarly modern and American: Come, pioneers, to the last frontier— Wall Street! While the new or reconstructed media had been assimilated into the cultural bloodstream, old Wall Street stood out—a whole idea in itself, tremendous, the crowning glory of the age of prosperity and, when it broke, a climacteric for the postwar era, 1919–29, *ipso facto* ... from disorientation to Communications. To false communication and to false achievements. To the Crash.

Only a tiny fraction of the population actively engaged in the stock lottery, but since those involved were drawn mainly from the leadership classes, highbrows and Babbitts alike, the national concern with the phenomenon of the Wall Street headline was acute. By 1927, some two years after the market was unmistakably on the rise, the financial lead item was a daily affair in the press. Everyone wanted to know how things were going; everyone wanted to read the latest manifesto of commerce. Whether or not one was in on it himself—even if one not only never owned a share of stock in his life but wouldn't have known where to go to buy one—one took a proprietary interest in the market because the market was national business in microcosm, and the national business was, likewise, the nation. Lucky that there are real smart people up there in charge of it all, everyone said—millionaires and such. Everyone rich is smart.

And so, everyone took note of the sensitive ticker as it translated words of praise or blame into the money code. There was always a throng in the visitors' gallery of the New York Stock Exchange, and a much larger throng scattered across the land pricked up its ears when a rich man spoke. Thus encouraged, the many bought and sold. Let John J. Raskob wax fervent on the golden future of General Motors, one of his several employers, and General Motors stock would rise some ten or twelve points in two days, with tasty side effects for other automotive issue; let the New York Stock Exchange but suggest a possible investigation of Radio Corporation of America and its stock would drop twenty points that afternoon. Opening quotations, closing quotations, regrading, scaling, forestalling, watering, siphoning, revaluation, equity capital, terms, terms, terms ... most of the speculators hadn't the vaguest idea what it was all about. But they had confidence in the "captains of industry." And why should they not? Had any ship ever before filled its sails so fully with such wind?

The captains, too, had confidence in themselves. So laudable were they now in the public mind, so strategic their joust in the heroic tournament of the New Era, that they had come to believe their own P.R., though they were well aware that a few of the most highly placed of their kind couldn't have been less scrupulous. Acting upon the same dictates that moved the highly questionable Samuel Insull (whose warts and all were to be unmasked in the early thirties), many of these highly respectable captains salted away piles of profit at the expense of a gullible public in the swindle known as the stock pool— known at the time, however, as no swindle at all.

The pool was a matter of simple manipulation through the agency of the ticker tape, which, as everyone knew, "never lies." Quoting all stock transactions as they occurred, the tape registered only the price and volume of each particular commodity, and yes, the tape never did lie—but a shifty operator *could* get it to gossip. Those who planned to work a pool gambit were banking—almost literally—on the outsiders' belief in the first law of the bull market, which may be stated as "what goes up can possibly never come down."

Hiring the services of an experienced manager, the backers of a pool began by letting him operate the selected stock in transactions involving them all. Buying and selling shares arbitrarily, simulating chance, the manager would thus energize the stock in what appeared on the tape to be a flutter of profit activity. The public would note the revelation of the stock and deal itself in, thereby weighting the manipulated activity with a genuine, innocent activity of its own. Then the bidding would grow hectic as the manager would continue his delicate finagling, now creating diversionary ruses of selling, now firing the fever with buying. The latter had to be timed just so; if handled right, it would convince as to inspire an orgy of collaboration from the public, forcing the price quotation way high and replacing the manager's fastidious venture with the promiscuous buying panic of the outsider. Then came the rout as the manager dropped the pool's shares of the stock bit by bit into the market. The price would fall back to its old niche in the commodity pecking order and the pool would retire with its winnings from a high selling price. The public, stuck with the low before it knew what had happened to it, would foot the bill.

Was there anything crooked in this? Not from where Wall Street stood; such were the rules of sport. As the journalist John T. Flynn saw it, "The game of speculation is one played by some three or four insiders and some half a million outsiders on terms of complete inequality." It was the business era, and business leaders had to be right. This was the key to the colossal mistake made both by tyros and by initiates in the matter of the bull market, the tragic flaw that brought down a million would-be heroes along with most of their countrymen. They thought they had understood about Lindbergh and Hoover, about achievement, about individualism. They hadn't. All they had gotten from the hero, after all, was self-confidence.

They all had it. Richard Whitney, whose personal fortune was as badly balanced as speculation itself—whose fortune, in fact, *was* speculation—believed his own defense of Wall Street practice when under the fire of the Senate Committee on Banking and Currency in 1932 (though his own practice was to send him to prison later on in the decade). Of course he believed. Was he not Richard Whitney, the pride of The Street, descendant of passengers on the *Arbella* (second only to the *Mayflower* in rank of immigrant priority), Groton prefect and team captain, Harvard Porcellian Club, brother of a top-okay junior partner of J. P. Morgan and Company, acting president of the Stock Exchange during the coming tumult of October 1929, a high-and-mighty package of arrant WASP serenity? Wall Street did no wrong; not only Whitney but much of nonagrarian America believed this. Among those who did not concur was Senator Smith Brookhart of Iowa, on that investigating committee that called Whitney to account, and no tyro in matters economic. From the table, Brookhart fumed at Whitney like William Jennings Bryan come back to life as a volcano, saying, "You brought this country to its greatest panic in history." Coolly, Whitney retorted, "We have brought this country, sir, to its standing in the world through speculation."

Imagine holding that America's eminence could be built of banking, whether respectable or not. Many held it so, and that's the New Era for you. Date its period of flower from Lindbergh's flight for purposes of irony, for while both We and The Crash stand high on the list of symbolic motions of the day, solo flight is an exception and get-rich-quick proves the rule. Nobody but Lindbergh did what Lindbergh had done, but "everybody" did what everybody else was doing. Buying on margin made it easy to do, because margin credit was easy to get—the banks saw to that. One took full title to purchased shares, bought on a bank loan, by parking the securities with one's broker as collateral on their own purchase; the catch was that if the securities fell below their price of purchase, the broker would demand more money from the owner to cover the depreciation of said collateral. Otherwise, he would have to dump the shares back on the market to make up the loss. And that made for a shaky market. The possibility of many brokers doing that at once had already occurred to a few critics of the speculative system; moreover, it was starting to happen. There were several minor crashes en route to the big one of October, '29, in June and December of '28 and again in March of '29.

But nobody learns from a boom, and the boom, despite these regular setbacks, bulged apace. These small crashes were even counted as something of a blessing in their "purifying" the market of the flimsier investors. Those who had gone down stole away to lick their wounds, but others came in to take their place. By the start of 1929, the volume of brokers' loans outstanding was nearing the record level of six billion dollars, and even so the peak had not yet been reached. Why? —with all the risk involved? Because while stock dividends—i.e., the working value of the commodity represented by the share—were far lower than the interest on a broker's loan paid out to swing the investment in the first place, the market value of ownership in the commodity was rising as nothing had risen before, possibly excepting the Tower of Babel. *The New York Times* index of the average price level of twenty-five standard industrial quotations stood at 110 in early 1924, 135 in early 1925, and 338.35 in January of 1929. And canny plunging could earn even more striking rewards: common stock in Radio Corporation of America, which stood at $85 a share in early 1928, was quoted at $505 a share in September of 1929. Of course, not all stock issues succeeded even during the boom, and more than a few crawled through the high tide from the flat depth of the market sea. This was considered no deterrent to the hopefuls crowding the lists. One simply took care to choose the promising titles—that was what the boom was all about.

"I am firm in my belief that anyone not only can be rich, but ought to be rich," stated John J. Raskob in an interview written up by Samuel Crowther and published in the *Ladies' Home Journal* in August 1929, during the most exciting summer in Wall Street's history (summer, this is, when financiers were usually off on vacation—but not this wonderful year). Fifteen dollars a month wisely invested in common stock, Raskob announced, would in twenty years yield a nest egg of $80,000 and an income of $400 a month. Such articles were filling the magazines, as they do today, and most of them were careful to point out that sound investment is unlike gambling in that nobody has to lose for someone to win. Buy Radio at 85, sell at 505. To whom? What difference? It was one of the sweet mysteries of market life that there is a buyer for every seller. And whoever buys at 505 can sell at 600. That share prices had far exceeded the value of the business represented by the certificate was of little moment; that said businesses were being "owned" by a wide-flung and liquid mass of creditors was likewise put by. Anyone ought to be rich, and the market was like a chain letter: send five quarters to the following five people, get back ten thousand quarters in three weeks. But somewhere, somebody is going to have to fork over $2500.

Indeed, folklore of the day told of anyone actually getting rich. Ribbon clerks, chauffeurs, plumbers and such reportedly became millionaires or were wiped out in a matter of weeks. Andy Gump of Sidney Smith's repulsive and unfunny but enormously popular comic strip of domestic life, *The Gumps,* was cleaning up like any lord; Bernarr Macfadden brought out a Wall Street newspaper for laymen. The perspective, in Urbantown, was general: everybody ought to be rich.

It wasn't a true perspective, of course. For that we apply to the critics of speculation, whose number grew despite the anger with which Wall Street/business greeted any headshaking on its behalf. In August of 1928, Sinclair Lewis surveyed midtown Manhattan from the office of his publisher Harcourt, Brace and predicted a "terrible financial panic," giving it a year (close enough—only two months off). "I can see people jumping out of windows on this very street," he said. But this was a poet's idyll. Censure of some foundation came from more expert economists, from Alexander Dana Noyes of *The York Times,* and from the *Commercial and Financial Chronicle,* which in January of the following year called the spiral of margin buying a "menace to the entire community." Shortly thereafter, Paul M. Warburg warned that if some halter were not roped around the speculative urge, the ensuing collapse would "bring about a general depression involving the entire country."

Whose job was it to regulate the ins and outs of economic flux? Not Wall Street's, certainly, nor any Senate committee's, nor yet the President's—so William Z. Ripley had told Coolidge. The onus for leadership in this concern lay with the Federal Reserve Board, supremely independent of all branches of government and empowered to tighten credit by raising its master interest rate to reduce lending reserves in Federal Reserve Banks. But the board had contributed to the credit tide, not stemmed it, by *lowering* the credit discount rate in 1927, a move that caused consternation in Reserve Banks across the country, and one not unlike inviting a diabetics' convention to Hershey, Pennsylvania. After the crash of June 1928, the board altered its policy and pushed up the interest points to 5 percent, but it was too late by then. Paper speculation had expanded too well to die; if anything, all that the board could do was cut off the inflow of business capital and create not deflation but a recession, which is exactly what started to happen.

By delaying action, the Federal Reserve Board had put itself in the position of damaging the health of the economy and encouraging the germs at the same time. The board's next play, in February of 1929, was to divert Reserve funds from the channel of speculation by forbidding Reserve banks any further traffic with brokers' loans on stock securities. This precipitated a market crash in late March, for "scare" selling shot prices down, necessitating calls for more margin (more collateral on the devalued stock), which in turn shot prices down further when more margin could not be scraped up. Hopes were dashed aplenty that March: people didn't just lose, but were sold out of all they owned. To defeat further panic, Wall Street saved Wall Street when Charles E. Mitchell, the president of National City Bank, earmarked twenty million dollars for continued brokerage loans with an arrogant public flourish.

Speculation simply was not to be stopped—not by the methods advocated by the Federal Reserve Board (which body was further to bungle its trust during the bank panics of the early thirties). With Coolidge retired to his Northampton, Massachusetts, homestead to taste of prosperity as a citizen and Hoover technically powerless to do more than pray, the market spoke up in June of '29 more prosperously than ever before, and all bets were on. But state and private construction, the steel, coal, and automotive industries, and small-class business projects were curtailed, and by the time of the savage

upward explosion of the summer of '29—the biggest, most bull
market ever—American capital *goods* were overproducing yet limited
of expansion (because of anomalies in the credit system) while capital
investment was increasingly volatile yet oversubscribed, particular in
regard to iffy foreign deals. The American economy was ready to
crumble.

Well, now. We've come some distance and we're almost home.
From the Red scare of 1919 and the mandate for escape that settled
the Republicans in office for twelve years, we have spiraled up and
outward to arrive at that famous Black Thursday of bodies plummet-
ing to the street from on high, of glazed looks about the eyes and
degraded authority, and of financier Thomas W. Lamont's beautifully
turned understatement, "There has been a little distress selling on the
Stock Exchange." We have also reached a crisis of confidence, and
about time, too—for much confidence has been misplaced herein. Too
ready to "see," the people materialized moral precepts into rationales
of instant acquisition; and they saw the men as well, trusting the
advance guard of the business community without comprehending
where American leadership was meant to take.

And when the walls came tumbling down, the world went with
them. The worst of The Crash, the big one of late October, was that
it wasn't just one crash: it kept crashing in a series of Bigger and
Better crashes, and each time, after it felt as though things had
reached a low, suddenly the bottom dropped out and down it all
went again, lower still. No wonder a splurge of suicides circa October
of '29 has won the confirmation of legend, for what worse despair is
there than to see no end to catastrophe? But there was no splurge,
and more suicides were reported in New York in the peak summer
months of the year than in October and November, when fortune was
at its meanest ebb. Actually, the national suicide rate had been
steadily rising right through the twenties and continued to rise—
steadily, with no jump in 1929 or 1930—until it tapered off
somewhat in 1933 and 1934, the dead center of the Depression.

Perhaps the nightmarish relentlessness of it all numbed the ruined
beyond thoughts of anything so active as self-destruction, though

there was nothing numb about the scene on the Stock Exchange on those first days of the last of prosperity's bad breaks, the neither only-begotten nor once-and-future break, but The Big One for sure. It was quiet (but populous) in the New Era's parish chapel, Trinity Church; everywhere else in the area communicated the great noise of a highly democratic doom, knowing no names. The great, the near great, the just arrived, and the all unknown massed up in one of New York's few genuinely heterogeneous crowds for the death, wake, and funeral of the decade's most fabulous celebrity, the bull market. This is Monday October 21, 1929, following a poor Friday and a foul half-day session on Saturday—following, more broadly, a touchy September that opened with record highs for the stronger stocks but weak placement for many others that had previously made respectable showings. In an atmosphere of skittish instability, the sedative affirmations of Wall Street's bullish spokesmen were beginning to fall flat while the prophets of disaster were coming to be harkened to, grudgingly and on the quiet, but with an upheaval of fear reflected in market prices. Two days after the highest-yet high of September 3, a little-known financial adviser named Roger W. Babson repeated a prediction he had been making of late that "sooner or later a crack is coming"; Babson's line was quoted on the Dow-Jones news ticker that afternoon, and prices fell as fast as it takes to call one's broker—Steel, for example, dropped nine points in the last hour of trading. Clearly, the "big surprise" that was coming should have been no surprise at all.

By October 21, the general shakiness was expressing itself more distinctly than before. People were selling at the drop of a . . . hat. Here it is again: selling meant a decline in prices, which meant that brokers had to call for more margin security from speculators, which meant that since in most cases speculators could or would not ante up further collateral, their holdings had to be sold to make up the difference, which meant a decline in prices, and so on spiraling downward, descending on the far side of the boom. The sales volume for this day totaled 6,091,870, the third highest in memory; as on certain other busy days, the ticker could not keep up with developments and lagged behind. In the past, this was looked upon as part of the fun, for when the final account was made, one turned out to have done even better than one thought. But the indexes were pointed in the opposite direction on October 21, and what had been fun now read as horror: no one could tell from looking at the ticker just how low one's fortunes had *already* sunk.

Still, Monday was at worst only a retreat, and Tuesday saw something of a recovery. Wednesday, however, was evil. After a quiet morning, the tempo shook and strained and then selling volume threw off the reins for a wild gallop into the chasm. The last frantic hour sent *The New York Times* industrial index down to 384 (from a morning level of 415—remember, it was 110 in early 1924), for the tape again could not keep up with the trading, and fear of having lost even more than one could ascertain at any given moment convinced many to quit while they were behind but not totally out. Brokers spent all night on the phone lines demanding more margin payments, optimistic panaceas staled in the mouths of the bulls . . . and Thursday, October 24, dawned, the hulking, hideous Black Thursday of the altogether exact certain situation of true crash, like the morning of a final battle in a war already lost. There would be no survivors.

It didn't take all day to get the terror going: by eleven o'clock the Stock Exchange was a shambles of selling. Sheared lambs and crippled wolves lost their cool, giggling, moaning, weeping, doing strange things with themselves; Trinity Church took on the flair of a wailing wall; the visitors' gallery of the Exchange was closed in the name of decency; and outside in the street a mob mistook a laborer engaged in some high-altitude repairs for an incipient suicide and waited to see the jump. Rumor had it that money boss George F. Baker rose from a sickbed, thrust a protesting doctor from his path, and staggered off to Wall Street, saying, "I have made money in every panic in the last sixty years and I don't intend to miss this one."

Across the nation, checking the tape, people couldn't believe what they were seeing—newcomers who weren't aware that the price ladder had a bottom at all suddenly got the chance to learn from a bust. This was when Thomas Lamont stepped in with his statement about "a little distress selling on the Stock Exchange," for he and some other banking overlords had met a little after noon in the offices of

J. P. Morgan and Company at 23 Wall, and a statement was indicated. Wall Street and business had, till the moment, been one; now Lamont separated them for reporters. Business was solid; the present motion was just "a technical condition of the market," one "susceptible to betterment."

The last hope was that Lamont and his colleagues could bolster the sagging market with "organized support," and when Richard Whitney strode onto the floor of the Exchange at 1:30, hell-bent for business, hope surged anew. Heading to the post where U.S. Steel was traded, Whitney put in a spectacular bid—10,000 shares at 205, some points higher than the rate of the moment, an impressive largesse. Then he rounded the floor from post to post with comparable bounty, leaving an apparent rally in his wake, and he was hailed in the press as the "white knight." Obviously acting for the pool of bankers—organized support!—Whitney had dropped between twenty and thirty million dollars' worth of reinforcement, and at first it seemed to work. Steel even closed the day with a two-point gain over Wednesday, and many other of the surer securities didn't lose as much as they might have done.

But that was some day in all. The ticker did not register the last sale of the day until four hours after closing, at 7:08 P.M., and erstwhile frissons of delight in the five- and six-million-share days of the boom had not prepared anyone for the behemoth of a thirteen-million-share day in a bust. "S-T-E-A-D-Y Everybody! Calm thinking is in order," was the message of a Boston investment firm in an advertisement in *The Wall Street Journal,* rather posthumous advice in all. Nevertheless, out came the incantations from the mikados of prosperity, juggling the two words considered obligatory by connoisseurs of economic jazz, "fundamental" and "sound." Thus: "The business situation is fundamentally sound." "The fundamental situation is sound." "Sound fundamentals will promote stability." "Stability will promote a fundamental soundness." Sounds are fundamental.

President Hoover put in his oar, forced by his position and external circumstances to rescue a condition he had wanted to head off years before. "The fundamental business of the country, that is, the production and distribution of commodities," he said, "is on a sound and prosperous basis." As we now know, it wasn't and while the collapse of the market didn't create the Depression by itself, it made such Depression as was coming a lot more thorough than it would otherwise have had to be. Again, and again, and again, the worst appeared not to be over. Friday and Saturday tried to hang in there while Wall Streeters reminded everyone who wasn't yet sold out that with prices where they were, an entire portfolio could be acquired for a song. But then came Monday—which is to say, vengeance is mine, saith the Lord.

The drop in prices on Monday, October 28, was the stiffest so far, with Steel down 17½ points, Allied Chemical down 36, and General Electric down 47½. Fewer shares traded hands, but volume was as nothing compared with decline, and after Monday came Tuesday, October 29, the worst of them all. This was the locus classicus of panic. No sooner did the gong signal the commencement of activity than all present proceeded to liquidate the paper valuation of the American economy. For once, buyers to match the sellers were lacking, and there appeared "air holes" (gaps left by stock offered for the taking on no bid in particular, a kind of running-ostrich sale), infuriating the higher-ups, who liked a methodical market that accorded to equations even in collapse. With the help of John J. Raskob, John D. Rockefeller and his son, and a few others, the bankers plugged up the air holes as best they could.

Still, the dike had been blown away and the ocean of despair roared in. October 29, the last of the crashes, is a final date for our purposes, as it marks the end of The Twenties and the start of The Great Depression. The panic had by no means ended, but thereafter disaster was managed in a more orderly fashion, the color seeping out of the market madness like a technicolor print fading into a daguerreotype. What follows now, truckling and arranging and cleaning up, we leave for others to cover. It dwindles away as an image as the New Era dwindled in the last two months of the decade; our camera and microphone pull back now. Let there be no excitement, for if there is an apocalypse to be found in the passing of the age, it is not in The Crash—or, rather, in the crashes—but in the blasting of the optimism of the time, the sullen self-possession. It had been an insufficiently moral time, an Era of New Prerogatives but not of New Responsibilities nor of many New Achievements, not only on the field of state but in virtually every arena except that of the arts. It was that worst of times, one without purpose.

So long, sucker, and good-bye to all that. The economists can learn from the bust; we, one hopes, have learned from the boom, the boom of resistance and change and the final days of the old America of the man-to-man measure. What was it all for, and what were we to do with it? It was to determine what we were wont to be, and to accomplish its being—a superb and terrifying prospect. With such power to command, those secret names at our disposal to invoke and make one's demands of, the force to ride on and the imagination to lift up with, we caught glimpses of us every so often, most of them misleading. If only we could have seen past the hurly-burly and got the concepts along with the pictures; one scrapes the skies with the essences of Things—with ideas—too.

But that jazz ... how were we to determine anything when all around is a bill of goods and leadership is any name in the news, when those to the fore shout forward! and those to the rear cry back! and in the middle, highbrows argue and scientists are unintelligible and the bourgeoisie is misrepresented and the worker and farmer obscured? Whoever needed the cheery conformity of the focus?—liars called its codes. Only with the emergence of We did America have the chance to look into the mirror of truth, for in Lindbergh the present had a face. That flight, which we still speak of as one of the great American Things, sang, for once, some moral content over the jazz—yet it was very much of the twenties, in its revelation of the limited covenant of the hero, the "they" we found in Lindbergh's We, the self-interest without which there can be neither initiative nor success nor prosperity. Lindbergh was better than what we were used to in the way of heroes, but he was not unlike some others of his day in his sense of going forward while holding on to values. He was the change of courage, skill, and faith, but he was the resistance of reason, like Hoover, like Hughes, like Addams. There's always something that needs doing that hasn't been done before, but working without an ethic and a national tradition is writing in mud.

It is too pat to see the Depression as a punishment for the recklessness of prosperity—as some would like to—for prosperity was as much a pragmatic accommodation to the metamorphosis of modern life as it was an amoral vacation from responsibility. Mad, bad, and glad times in the folklore, the twenties were no such thing. It was an epoch of assimilation and speeding ahead; but we sped too far without properly assimilating the imperatives of movement. Well, that's easy for us to say. Everything that was, had to be, say some; others point to accidents and misjudgments, here and there, such and so. But no bad times ever claimed a Lindbergh. No mad times felt so secure in the capacity to build an economy. No glad times deserved Prohibition. Cheap slogans, like those of P.R., raunch the investigation; one would see past the bunk and debunk but for bunk's inordinate staying power, for jazz is still too much with us and the media are five decades more adept at imposing their dank light, their fun-house mirror, upon us.

And history is bunk, and people perish without a vision, and everybody step, and the crowd still sees, and Communications blare, and whatever became of We? Most immediately—by way of What Happened Then—We enrolled in poverty, in sociopolitical polemic, in breadlines, in social art, in knock-knock jokes . . . in the thirties. Ah, why did so few see the punch line coming? Misery, not Texas Guinan, told this one:

"Knock-knock. I'm here."

"I'm? . . . No, first I say who's there and then—"

"Not a joke, friend."

For Further Reading

There is no scarcity of books on the 1920s that tack to the "mad times! glad times!" approach; perhaps it would be helpful to list instead a few works on the serious side, those that can serve the reader in a specific field or with an alternative understanding to that of the present volume.

Of books on the decade in general, the classic is Frederick Lewis Allen's *Only Yesterday* (New York: Harper and Brothers, 1931), still fresh and discerning nearly fifty years later and of interest for its contemporary immediacy. Similarly, Mark Sullivan's *Our Times*, vol. VI (New York: Scribner's, 1935), which covers 1919 to 1925, has the fascinating nonchalance of the eyewitness. Sullivan was a newspaperman, and his work is thronged with documentary witness—photos, cartoons, anecdotes, and a naive but intriguing analysis of popular song, complete with musical examples.

Of more recent work, J. C. Furnas's huge "informal social history" *Great Times* (New York: Putnam's, 1974) is highly recommended. In this sequel to his even huger *The Americans* (New York: Putnam's, 1969), Furnas ranges from 1914 to The Crash, dealing with cultural rather than political life with the writer's sharp wit and the historian's appreciation of the extraordinary. John D. Hicks's *Republican Ascen-*

dancy (New York: Harper and Row, 1960) hews to the political and economic area with the probity of academe, and Paul A. Carter's short but lively *Another Part of the Twenties* (New York: Columbia University Press, 1977) proffers a complementary perspective to balance the more traditional "roaring," and should prove just the thing for the reader who has had all he can take of jazz as metaphor.

In the matter of biography, the possibilities are, as the phrase-makers make it, endless; let us be brief. For a look at Wilson in his prime—for the man is not at his best in these pages—try Arthur Walworth's *Woodrow Wilson*, rev. ed. (Boston: Houghton Mifflin, 1968). Francis Russell's *The Shadow of Blooming Grove: Warren G. Harding in His Times* (New York: McGraw-Hill, 1968) is far and away the most complete work on Harding, even though Russell was legally blocked from quoting from the President's love letters to one Carrie Phillips, the wife of a friend of his in Marion (letters which Russell thought important enough to invoke via blank gaps in his text). Coolidge needs someone as thorough as Russell; meanwhile, there are William Allen White's *A Puritan in Babylon: The Story of Calvin Coolidge* (New York: Macmillan, 1938) and Donald R. McCoy's *Calvin Coolidge: The Quiet President* (New York: Macmillan, 1967). White, who detested Coolidge, is the more entertaining, McCoy the more reliable.

No Hoover biography quite supersedes his three-volume memoirs (New York: Macmillan, 1951-52); on the other hand, Charles Lindbergh at his most eloquent (in *We, The Spirit of St. Louis,* his journals, and his very recent and posthumous *Autobiography of Values,* edited from drafts, sketches, and fair copies by William Jovanovich and Judith A. Schiff) reveals less than his several undistinguished biographers. Leonard Mosley's *Lindbergh* (New York: Doubleday, 1976) is the best so far, though Brendan Gill's *Lindbergh Alone* (New York: Harcourt Brace Jovanovich, 1977) has the advantage of imposing art direction and photography. To seek out other emblematic men of the era, consider *Robert M. La Follette* (New York: Macmillan, 1953) by Belle C. and Fola La Follette, who ought to know; Lawrence Levine's *Defender of the Faith: William Jennings Bryan: The Last Decade* (New York: Oxford University Press, 1965);

Matthew and Hanna Josephson's *Al Smith: Hero of the Cities* (Boston: Houghton Mifflin, 1969); Allan Nevins and Frank Ernest Hill's *Ford: The Times, The Man, the Company,* 2 vols. (New York: Scribner's, 1954; 1957); William Manchester's *Disturber of the Peace: The Life of H. L. Mencken* (New York: Harper and Brothers, 1951); Mark Schorer's *Sinclair Lewis: An American Life* (New York: McGraw-Hill, 1961); Arthur Mizener's *The Far Side of Paradise: A Biography of F. Scott Fitzgerald* (Boston: Houghton Mifflin, 1951); and, of course—since Our Lord figures so largely in the incantatory rationalizing of the New Era—Bruce Barton's *The Man Nobody Knows* (New York: Grosset and Dunlap, 1925).

A veritable library of books awaits on miscellaneous doings of the 1920s. Fundamentalists and Darwinians alike may get together on L. Sprague DeCamp's good-humored *The Great Monkey Trial* (New York: Doubleday, 1968), if not on David M. Chalmers's sober *Hooded Americanism: The First Century of the Ku Klux Klan* (New York: Doubleday, 1965). Don S. Kirschner's *City and Country: Rural Responses to Urbanization in the 1920s* (Westport, Conn.: Greenwood, 1970) closes in on the focal question of topographical life-styles, and the other side of prosperity is addressed in Irving Bernstein's *The Lean Years: A History of the American Worker, 1920-1933* (Boston: Houghton Mifflin, 1960). Too, the younger generation takes its place in chronicle in Paula S. Fass's *The Damned and the Beautiful* (New York: Oxford University Press, 1977)—to judge from the currency of some of these titles, it is clear that not all of the social and political evidence on the Jazz Age is yet in.

As for the Sacco-Vanzetti case, the standard work is Francis Russell's *Tragedy in Dedham* (New York: McGraw-Hill, 1962), an impartial and exhaustively sleuthed account. Connoisseurs of the controversy will want to check out Herbert Ehrmann's *The Untried Case,* rev. ed. (New York: Vanguard, 1960), which almost manages to convince that the culprits were in fact the Morelli gang of Providence. Speaking of crime, one should not miss Kenneth Allsop's *The Bootleggers,* rev. ed. (New Rochelle, N.Y.: Arlington House, 1968), a highly readable look at gangsterism in Prohibition-era Chicago. For a report on Prohibition in general, numerous books suggest themselves;

try John Kobler's *Ardent Spirits: The Rise and Fall of Prohibition* (New York: Putnam's, 1973), which features a series of reminiscences by thugs, alcoholics, lawyers, Feds, saloonkeepers, and various wets and drys of the day.

On the political scene, Betty Glad's *Charles Evans Hughes and the Illusion of Innocence* (Urbana, Ill.: University of Illinois Press, 1966) subscribes to the prevailing view of Hughes as a lone Progressive in a time of sullen stasis. Wesley M. Bagby's *The Road to Normalcy*, rev. ed. (Baltimore: Johns Hopkins University Press, 1968), on the 1920 election, and Robert K. Murray's *The 103rd Ballot* (New York: Harper and Row, 1976), on the Democratic Convention of 1924, recall the old forms of democracy to reassure anyone who thinks they have changed in the interim; Murray's *Red Scare: A Study in National Hysteria, 1919–1920* (Minneapolis: University of Minnesota Press, 1955) is also helpful—though in this case the forms (of antiradicalism) *have* changed, and a book on the present America's reaction to the threat of Communism might well be called *Red Welcome.*

In the economic arena, Frederick Lewis Allen matches the literate candor of *Only Yesterday* in *The Lords of Creation* (New York: Harper and Brothers, 1935), the lords, of course, being the money bosses before, during, and after the New Era. John Kenneth Galbraith's urbanely scathing *The Great Crash, 1929* (New York: Houghton Mifflin, 1961) is a popular entry, though of course conceived through the bias of Galbraith's low-Keynesian mumbo jumbo. Those who like to sample both sides of questions might want to make a double bill of *Taxation: The People's Business* (New York: Macmillan, 1924) by the champion plutocrat, Andrew Mellon, and *The Great Steel Strike and Its Lessons* (New York: B. W. Huebsch, 1920) by William Z. Foster, the Communist (actually Workers') Party candidate for President in 1924.

Secondary sources do not cover the art world well except in literature. At least there are Frederick J. Hoffman's expansive *The 20's*, rev. ed. (New York: The Free Press, 1962) and Malcolm Cowley's more intimate *Exile's Return* (New York: Viking, 1951), two classics on the literary scene. An arresting sampler of points of view called *The Culture of the Twenties* (New York: Bobbs-Merrill,

1970) offers excerpts from such as John Dos Passos, H. L. Mencken ("Was Bryan Sincere?"), and Walter Lippmann without coming to terms much with the art component in culture. True, there is the excitement of discovering LP transcriptions of Bessie Smith (the complete recorded legacy of 160 songs in five volumes: Columbia CG 33, 30126, 30450, 30818, 31093) for oneself—but where is the book on our popular music of the 1920s? Its public dialogue generally underrated by historians, pop music is a primal energy in the culture, a strategy in the deciphering of attitude and style. Why, surely, someone fifty years hence will give us a social history of the 1970s entitled *That Rock!*

Index